THE INCENTIVE

THE INCENTIVE

By

Carla Gibson

ISBN: 1-58961-341-4

Authors website: www.carlagibson.com

Published by PageFree Publishing, Inc.
109 South Farmer Street
Otsego, MI 49078
(269) 692-3926
www.pagefreepublishing.com

Dedication:

Mom, I love you.
Dad, I miss you.

...and Sis, thanks for your unwavering support.

CHAPTER 1

ROBERT thought it might just be a muscle pull until the chest pain started worsening. He stumbled into the garage and set down the cement patio blocks that he had been carrying. They were extremely heavy and he knew he should have used the wheelbarrow to move the last five of them, but thought it would be too much trouble. The lightheadedness and nausea he felt, he simply attributed to the physical labor of working in the hot summer sun. He should get in the house and cool off in the air conditioner, he thought. It would make him feel better and the chest pain would probably go away. Lifting the Detroit Red Wings hat off his head, he ran his hand over the wet hair underneath and peeked around the corner of the garage to the backyard, where his wife Helen was pulling weeds.

"Helen, I'm going in the house for a few minutes. I'll be back," he hollered, not wanting to worry her.

"Okay, Robert," she called back without looking up. She stooped down to pull another weed and threw it in the pile next to her.

Feeling like he was walking in slow motion, Robert made it to the door inside the garage and eased himself up the two steps into the kitchen. The pain was spreading to his shoulders, his neck, his arms. It seemed like a heavy weight sitting on his chest, making it difficult to breathe. He drudged to the sink and splashed cold water over his face, letting it run down his neck and drench his shirt. Hardly able to walk, he eased himself along the countertop for support until he made it to the kitchen table and sat down.

"Am I having a heart attack?" he muttered aloud, trying to stay lucid.

The doorwall to the patio was right next to the kitchen table where he sat. He forced himself to get up and tried to pull the heavy door open to call Helen, but he was too weak. Falling back into the kitchen chair, he looked outside as the sun peeked through the purple smoketrees lining the deck. A feeling of impending doom washed over him.

"Helen, honey, don't you be the one to find me," he whispered as he started to slip down a dark hallway.

Mercury Memorial Hospital was a modest, two-hundred-bed facility located in an area once vibrant with families and businesses, but now decaying from neglect and age. A beacon for the community, it dispensed quality health care in a cost-effective manner during its peak in the 60s and 70s until urban sprawl took over and a place called Southeast Regional Medical Center was built. Mercury was left quivering in the wake of the best healthcare that money could buy—and it couldn't compete. Not enough funds to add on a large cancer center with the most up-to-date procedures and equipment or a residential treatment facility for alcoholism and drug abuse. But the dignity was evident in the people who worked there, those who still believed in delivering quality healthcare to whoever needed it. The north side of the hospital had Mercury's name proudly written in cement with the date "established 1945" underneath it, which you could barely see amid the vines. The brown brick three-story building looked dirty and worn, but it had character—character and Dr. Michelle Campbell.

Michelle hurried through the emergency room doors, pulling off her green mint cotton canvas blazer and tossing it on an available chair behind the desk. She combed her straight black hair briefly with her fingers, then checked to make sure her favorite Louis Vuitton purse was secure and placed it firmly underneath her blazer. "Where's my new patient?" she asked the emergency room ward clerk who was busily putting papers together to make up a patient chart.

The clerk looked up and started to open her mouth, but before she could answer a voice boomed, "Michelle, he's in ER#2."

Michelle quickly turned to smile at Dr. Paul Roth, who was walking over to her. "Paul, haven't seen you for awhile. What's going on?" She held out her hand toward him.

Tall and athletic, Paul was a man who thoroughly enjoyed his job as an emergency room physician at Mercury Memorial. "Feast or famine" was what was always said about the ER. Today was a feast. "Classic symptoms of myocardial infarction after strenuous physical labor. 12-lead electrocardiogram shows ST elevation and we have elevated cardiac troponin levels." He handed the chart to her. "Sixty-year-old male. Robert Gray. On oxygen, IV fluids, cardiac monitor. He's all yours, Michelle. I'm needed in ER#5."

"Thanks, Paul." She smiled again at him as he left. Glancing through the chart as she stood at the desk, she addressed the clerk awaiting her orders. "Call the cardiac cath lab and have them open the room. I'll talk to the patient and his wife."

The clerk nodded as she picked up the phone.

Michelle grabbed a consent form from the desk and started filling it out as she marched toward ER#2. At 38 years old, she was full swing into cardiology and working as much as possible for one reason only. It didn't matter what the cardiac cath showed. Unfortunately for Robert Gray, he would be getting a coronary bypass tonight, whether he needed it or not. Reaching ER#2, she pulled open the curtain.

A thin man in a hospital-issued white gown with blue polka dots was propped up with pillows on the stretcher. Although hooked up to nasal oxygen, he was painstakingly taking each breath through his mouth. His fear of the unknown was apparent. His eyes were opened wide and he was perspiring. His wife was sitting at his bedside, doing a poor job of trying not to look terrified.

"Mr. and Mrs. Gray, I'm Dr. Campbell," Michelle stated. "I have reviewed your chart and discussed your case with the emergency room physician. You've had a heart attack and need to have a cardiac catheterization done as soon as possible. It will tell us how much damage your heart has suffered and what we need to do about it."

Robert stared straight ahead, not looking at Michelle, while Helen watched her every move.

Michelle continued. "Let me just go over a few things with you. I'll be taking x-ray pictures of your heart. A groin needle insertion site will be used for your cath and a local anesthetic will be injected at that site. A special needle will be put in the artery at the injection site through which a flexible wire is inserted. That needle will be removed and a catheter sheath fitted over the wire and into the artery. A dye will be infused into your coronary arteries to obtain the needed pictures. I will get a preliminary idea of your problem and will make a final determination after I review your films. A stitch will be put in the artery I use in your leg, and you will only have to lay flat for a short period of time." She looked at each of them to try to ascertain their understanding.

"Your consent will be signed for emergency coronary angioplasty, stent placement, or coronary bypass—if needed. If an emergency develops, you will be taken by ambulance to Southeast Regional Medical Center. The surgeon and equipment needed for bypass is there." She turned to Helen. "I'll come to the waiting room to talk with you after the cath. Any other questions?"

They shook their heads "no" as Robert signed the consent with a shaky hand.

Michelle did her cardiac catheterizations at Mercury, but if patients needed further surgery, they had to go over to Southeast. Mercury only had a small ICU of five beds. The equipment and suites needed for the bigger surgeries weren't at Mercury, and they couldn't afford them anyway. The cardiac cath unit was all it had, and it was needed to be kept viable as it helped the old hospital pay bills. Any day of the week could now be a procedure day for Michelle, and she planned on keeping that pace as long as necessary. Her partner, Phil Richards, hadn't minded that she do most of the procedures for their practice. She wanted to be as busy as possible, and he wanted to slow down a little as he eased into retirement.

Helen bent down to kiss her husband on the cheek, then picked up her purse and left, just as the cardiac cath nurse arrived to help Michelle.

"Let's do it," directed Michelle as she slid the chart into the side of the stretcher, unlocked the brakes, and started to wheel him over to the cath lab.

Heart catheterization proceeded without difficulty, as Michelle was very adept at her craft. After the cath, Robert was wheeled into the recovery room, awaiting his fate. Michelle pulled the surgical hat off her head and untied her mask as she went out to talk to Helen in the waiting room.

Helen stood up immediately at seeing Michelle. "How is he?" she asked with frightened eyes.

"Please sit down," Michelle murmured. "He's going to need further treatment, as he has high degree blockages in three different arteries. I'm going to give the surgeon at Southeast a call, Mrs. Gray. Your husband needs to go over there as soon as possible for a coronary bypass."

Helen began wringing her hands and looked as if she was going to cry.

"These are done all the time," Michelle added, trying to reassure her. "The hospital will let you know when the ambulance arrives, then he will be taken over there." Making an effort to smile once more, she turned and left. The smile left as soon as Michelle did. She walked just a little ways down the hall to a door that said "Jeff Elliott, Radiologist" on it. Turning the knob, she entered without authorization.

"Hi, Michelle," Jeff said, lifting his head up from the report he was reading. He moved his wavy, brown hair out of his eyes and pushed his glasses up higher on his nose.

"Jeff, I have another one for you to look at. I need some adjustments made."

"Not a problem," he said confidently.

"My results will be ready for you to look at shortly, but I need everything back ASAP."

"I'm a little bogged down right now with all the x-rays done yesterday, but you know what my priority will be," he said, looking at his watch.

"Thanks, Jeff." She closed the door and walked briskly down the hall to her office to make a few notes in her Palm Pilot. Things had been going very well and she knew she was on a roll. It wouldn't be much longer until she had all the freedom she had dreamed of. Smiling, she picked up the phone.

Erin looked out of the Boeing 777 as it approached the Detroit Metropolitan Airport runway. The flight had been long and tiring from California, and she badly needed a change of clothes and a walk to stretch the legs that hadn't moved in hours. A nap that involved laying flat on anything would also be very welcome. She could see the squares of greenery and fields of dirt, and now the cars moving east and west as the plane passed over the I-94 expressway, ready to touch down in moments. Home again. It would be nice to see the end of summer in Michigan, and even snow was something she might not mind this year if she stuck around long enough for winter to hit.

She was coming back for her only sibling, Lisa's, wedding. Lisa was marrying someone Erin had never met, but had seen perform years ago when she was still doing her undergraduate work at Michigan State University. He was the guitarist in an English rock band called "Odyssey" that had been around for 15 or so years and still going strong. Odyssey was in the United States on tour, promoting their new album, with the wedding strategically planned right in the middle of the tour. Jimmy was flying back to Michigan to be with Lisa every few days when there was a break in the action.

The other reason she had returned was that she was running away from her life in California. Her breakup with Chris had been very rough and she thought it best to leave everything: her job, her condo, even the state. Erin was a physician and was going to work at the health insurance company her father worked at until she decided what she wanted to do next.

The plane hit the runway smoothly and slowed down as it moved to the gate. Erin took out her compact to powder her nose and apply lipstick as the captain expressed appreciation for flying with his airline. As she brushed her shoulder length blonde hair briefly, she was aware that the man across the aisle was watching her again. She self-consciously put her things away and ignored him, as he had been stealing glances at her the entire trip. Grabbing her bag from under the seat, she stood up the best she could, getting into the aisle with the other passengers as they inched toward the terminal. When she reached it and could breathe again, she saw her dad with his hand up in the air, trying to get her attention. She grinned. What a healthy looking man he was, in his early sixties with salt and pepper hair and a big smile. How wonderful to see him again. After wiggling her way through the other passengers, she threw her arms around him.

"Dad, it's great to see you! I can't believe it's been almost a year."

"Erin, I'm glad you're here. I'm telling you right now that I hated it when you moved to California. I don't know if I ever told you, but I never liked Chris anyway."

She decided not to dwell on the Chris comment. "What did you think about Lisa living in London?"

"I didn't like that either, but at least she'll be living out East for a while now. Your mother and I are just glad that both of you are home, and we'll enjoy being with you for as long as it lasts."

"How's Mom doing?"

"Fine. She's always busy, it seems. Of course it's really been an advantage that she has a party-planning business—with your sister's wedding and all. Arlene knows what to order, and she and Lisa have planned every detail."

They walked a long hallway, then down the escalator to the baggage claim area. The conveyer belt began to turn just as the luggage from Erin's plane was unloaded onto it. It seemed forever until she saw her two enormous navy blue suitcases coming around the corner of the carousel, and they went over to grab them.

"I'll get them," said Rich as he lifted the heavy luggage off the conveyer belt.

"I'm having my other things shipped. I hope there's room at the house."

"We'll make room. The truck is parked in the garage across the street on the fourth floor," he said as he motioned to an elevator about 500 feet away.

As they reached the Yukon, Rich put the luggage in the back and the two climbed in. In a few minutes they were on their way home.

"We do have an additional guest at the house when Jimmy is in town. He's the singer from the band; his name is Steve. Quite a nice young man. I like him a lot."

Erin just nodded and tried to remember what Steve looked like.

"He's the best man in the wedding and is looking forward to meeting you."

As they got off the freeway, Erin looked around at the small town they lived in. Even though it was only a couple of blocks long, it had upscale restaurants and specialty stores in a beautiful downtown area. People had always been friendly here, and peering out the car window Erin saw two people waving to each other from across the street.

Rich and Arlene's home was a few miles away from town out in the country, in one of the more elegant subdivisions full of hills and winding driveways. Each estate was on about an acre of land with the houses all custom-built and different in architecture. The Tyler home was a two-story red brick, with huge windows extending from the first to second floor in the foyer, and a chandelier that could be seen from the road. The back of the house had a spacious wooden deck with a large green backyard, sloping down to an all-sports lake where their pontoon boat was docked.

They pulled into the driveway and parked in the circular drive. Erin and Rich collected the luggage and walked to the front door. As she lifted her right hand to turn the doorknob, it opened before her. A tall, handsome man with blonde layered hair that touched his collar, and deep-set green eyes stood in front of her. He smiled as his eyes first looked at her face, then quickly ran over the curves of her body. Picking up her hand, he kissed it, leaving his lips there longer than necessary.

"Erin, this is Steve," said Rich, setting down Erin's luggage.

"Hello, Erin," he said in an English accent as he studied her face. "I have been wanting to meet you for a very long time."

Erin could feel her heart beating. "Hi," she said, recognizing him.

Steve's eyes stared directly into hers. She broke the stare and glimpsed around the large foyer, looking anywhere except those eyes. She heard a commotion down the hall toward the kitchen. Erin turned around and saw Lisa running to greet her.

"Erin!" she cried out. Lisa had chin-length auburn hair and always seemed happy. As usual, she was dressed in matching everything. She hugged Erin and they grinned joyfully at each other.

A spike-haired man with a gold hoop in each ear appeared at Lisa's side.

"This is Jimmy," Lisa gushed as she grabbed his hand and squeezed it.

"Hello, Erin," smiled Jimmy, also with an English accent. "It's fabulous to finally meet you after talking on the phone so many times."

"Welcome to the family." Erin grinned as she leaned toward Jimmy to give him a hug. He seemed very personable, with warm eyes and a cute smile.

"You didn't greet the best man that way," Steve quipped as he turned to Erin with his arms out. "I'm a bit in need of a hug myself."

Erin ignored him and turned to her sister. "How are the wedding plans?"

"Everything is almost done with the planning, but your dress needs to be altered. We're down to three weeks until the wedding, you know," she said. "Look at my ring." She held out her left hand for Erin to see the 3-carat round diamond with a sapphire on each side of it.

"It's gorgeous!" A noise behind Erin made her turn and she saw her mother come down the hallway and walk up to them.

"Erin, how long has it been?" She put her arms around Erin and kissed her firmly on the cheek. Arlene was an attractive woman in her early 60s, with a full head of strawberry blonde hair and a face that could pass for someone much younger.

"Almost a year, Mom."

Arlene shook her head. "Too long. I know you have to be tired from your long plane ride. Maybe you should go upstairs and rest a while."

"No, she can't," broke in Lisa. "We've been waiting for Erin to get here so we could go out on the pontoon boat. The guys have never been on one before."

"I need a nap," said Erin, yawning. "Can't we go out on it tomorrow?"

Lisa shook her head "no." "You can take a nap on the boat. I'm sure you slept on the plane, too. Don't waste your whole day sleeping. Summer will be over in a couple of weeks."

"Steve has courteously offered to carry your luggage up to your room. He is such a dear," said Arlene, smiling at Steve and patting him on the cheek.

Steve looked up to the heavens as if he were an angel.

Erin wasn't so sure, as she peeked back at him. "All right. Give me about half an hour and I'll be back down."

Steve picked up the heavy luggage. "After you," he said, while raising his eyebrows at her.

As she walked up the stairway, she felt as though he was watching every inch of her.

"You're in the room next to mine," he said, opening the door to her room and setting down her luggage. "All right, then. If you need anything, just knock on the wall and I'll come running."

"This is my house. There shouldn't be anything I need that I can't handle on my own."

"Then I best be going. Don't keep us waiting too long." He backed out of her room, then closed the door and left.

Erin breathed a sigh and threw herself on the bed, exhausted.

Southeast Regional Medical Center was a five-hundred and seventy-three-bed hospital, located in a park-like setting on forty acres. The hospital was associated with superior performance, and they were known throughout the Midwest. Their surgery volume was high, and with mortality and surgical complications low, they were the place to go to have a coronary bypass—or any other major surgery done. The third floor housed the modern cardiovascular and thoracic surgery department where all operations on the heart and lungs were done. It also had a surgical intensive care unit and step-down unit so the patients could be kept on the same floor throughout their hospital stay.

The hospital spent millions of dollars focusing on the safety of its patients. Computers were based throughout the hospital that kept the paper trail to a minimum. Physicians were required to enter their pharmacy orders and progress notes in the patients' electronic chart themselves, therefore cutting down on the human error that's associated with prescribing and interpreting someone else's handwriting. Medical personnel flocked to work at this paragon of 21st-century excellence.

Dr. David Keller sat at the step-down unit on the third floor, charting on one of his hospitalized patients. It had been a busy day and he had spent the last four hours in the operating room doing a coronary bypass. Having already been to see his patients in the surgical ICU, the rest of the day should be fairly calm back at his office seeing patients for the last few hours of the afternoon. He might even finish early enough to run downtown for a few hands of poker at Greektown Casino, where he was well-known as a big spender. Looking over Delores Nesbitt's electronic chart, he thought she was doing well since her bypass a few days before. Her latest lab work reported that things were good, and David contemplated sending her home tomorrow.

The phone rang at the step-down unit desk where the clerk, Wanda, was busy working on the hospital computer. Stopping what she was doing, she rolled her chair down a few feet to pick up the phone. She stuck the handset between her chin and shoulder and stretched the cord to its limit as she rolled back down to the computer to start typing again.

"Surgical ICU step-down," she said. "Dr. Keller? Yes, he's right here."

She again stopped what she was doing, rolled her chair down to David and handed him the phone.

He took it from her and placed it up to his ear. "Dr. Keller," he responded.

"Dr. Keller, this is Dr. Michelle Campbell over at Mercury Memorial Hospital," the voice said. "We met last week. Remember? You had dinner with Dr. Charles Patton and me. I told you it wouldn't be long before we needed you."

David began to perspire and he cleared his throat. Touching his forehead, his short, white hair was plastered against it. He hoped that none of his colleagues came around the corner, because he knew he didn't look very well. Trying to sound upbeat, but barely able to force a voice, he said, "Dr. Campbell. Of course I remember. How are you?"

"I'm fine, thank you," she replied in a business manner. "I have a sixty-year-old male positive for myocardial infarction. He was doing strenuous physical labor outside and started having all the classic symptoms."

"Yes," David said, his own heart pounding.

"Luckily his wife found him. She called EMS and they brought him here. He was started on standard protocol while in the emergency room. I was called in to evaluate him and I decided to do a cardiac cath."

"Go on." He felt nauseated.

"He is showing coronary artery triple vessel disease. His blockages aren't as high as we would like, but we can take care of that for the health insurance purposes. I talked to him and his wife about a coronary bypass needing to be done as soon as possible. They agree that it sounds like the proper course to follow."

David wasn't happy with the situation. Putting his fingers on his white goatee, he stroked it as he listened to her. The physician in him took over, but he chose his words carefully. "Michelle, I really prefer to have my patients a little more stable before I do surgery on them. It is still controversial to do coronary bypass surgery immediately after an acute myocardial infarction, and I am from that school of thought," he said, immediately regretting his words.

Michelle growled on the receiver. "David, you agreed to the rules. The conditions are right for this and the decision has already been made. Your patient will be over in a little while for you to see. I trust you won't let us down."

He could picture her frowning face and narrowed eyes. David hesitated, but then conceded. "All right." He knew there was no use arguing with her.

"I'm having the cath report and cardiac films finalized to our expectations and will have them sent with the patient. His name is Robert Gray and I hope you can do his surgery tonight," Michelle said, hardly taking a breath as she spat out all the data. "You have my beeper if you need me. Goodbye, Dr. Keller."

David felt sick as he placed the receiver back into its cradle. Leaning over so his arms rested on his knees, he placed the fingertips of each hand over his temples to rub them. He closed his eyes and shook his head.

Wanda stopped what she was doing and stared over her glasses at David. "Dr. Keller," she said, "is there anything wrong? Anything I can do?"

"No, Wanda, everything is fine. I'm just tired." He tried to smile at her as he straightened up in his chair. "There's a new patient coming over from Mercury Memorial. Have whoever is on beep me and I'll come see him."

"Of course, Dr. Keller." Wanda made a note, pushed her glasses up, and turned back to her computer screen to start working again.

David walked away from the desk, hardly able to lift his feet. He was a competent and confident cardiovascular surgeon, but sometimes he could be impulsive. This impulsiveness was apparent when he had agreed to get involved with Michelle and Charlie at the nice little dinner they had together. Turning down the hall toward the elevator, he didn't even acknowledge two colleagues who greeted him. He had to get on that elevator and out of this hospital before he vomited.

CHAPTER 2

ERIN really didn't feel like going out on the boat and socializing, but she had no choice. Getting up from the bed after resting her eyes for a few minutes, she opened her suitcase, rummaging through it until she found her pale yellow bikini. She took it out and closed her suitcase. Looking in the dresser mirror at the dark circles under her eyes, she brushed her hair and sighed as she put on her bathing suit. This was as ready as she was going to get today. Walking downstairs, she went through the hall into the kitchen and saw everyone outside in the backyard. She went out on the deck and looked around. This was such a pretty place, with the well-manicured yard sloping down to the lake. The lake was glistening today from the sunshine and she could see and hear many boats out on the water.

"Erin, come on," hollered Lisa. "The guys have the cooler. I have our towels."

Erin walked over to Lisa as she saw Jimmy and Steve putting the cooler on the boat. "What's in the cooler?"

"Wine for us, Guinness for them. That's their favorite drink," she said, laughing. "We have cheese, crackers, and a bowl of grapes. I also brought chips and dip."

"Are there any water bottles in the cooler? I think I'm dehydrated from the plane ride." Erin yawned.

"We have water, too. Let's go," said Lisa, turning toward the boat.

They walked down the wooden dock and stepped onto the front deck of the pontoon boat. Opening a small gate, they took the few steps to the long, blue vinyl bench seats on each side and Lisa set down the towels on one of them. Jimmy was sitting on another bench seat at the back of the boat that had a small table in front of it. The captain's chair and steering wheel were directly in front of the back bench seat and Steve was looking at them. A blue and white striped canopy hung over the back half of the boat to provide shade.

"Erin, check for the life vests," said Lisa.

Erin pulled forward on one of the bench seats and opened it up. She looked through the life vests and counted. "We have plenty." She closed the seat back up and spread out a towel with a tropical scene on it.

"I'm driving," Lisa said to Steve, gently pushing him out of the way. "Why don't you go sit in front?"

Steve went and sat down on the other front bench seat, across from where Erin was sitting. Studying her, he thought she looked brilliant in her yellow bathing suit.

Erin got up and walked to the front of the boat. Freeing the boat from the dock, she untied the ropes and threw them to the side. Lisa started the engine and put the boat into gear. They were on their way.

"Look, Steve," said Jimmy smiling, "these girls can do everything. All we have to do is sit back and drink our beer."

Steve agreed as he watched Erin. Her bikini top was cut very low and barely covered her breasts. "They can drive me around all day."

Erin sat down opposite Steve on the other bench seat.

"Would you like a bit of the drop?" he asked.

"What?" she questioned, not understanding him.

"Can I get you a glass of wine?" he asked, smiling at her.

Erin knew she should have water, but felt like she needed the wine. She nodded.

"Very well," he said, getting up and opening the cooler. He took out the chilled bottle of Pinot Grigio, removed the loosened cork, and poured the wine to the top of a plastic tumbler. Replacing the wine bottle in the cooler, he handed it to Erin.

"Thank you," she said as she looked out at the lake. It was a hot day and the warm breeze felt good as the boat got underway. A beach volleyball game was in progress onshore and Erin watched it as they cruised by. A ball was served and a tall girl with brown hair dove for it and appeared to do a flip in the sand. Erin strained to see what was going on because the girl was just sitting in the sand looking at her arm and everyone was running over to her.

Steve pulled off his gray tee shirt and threw it down on the seat. He picked up his beer from the cup holder and took a long drink.

Erin looked at him out of the corner of her eye, forgetting all about the girl sitting in the sand. Steve only had black and white checkered bathing trunks on as he sat back on the seat and looked at the scenery as it passed by. No tattoos and muscular arms…

"Can I drive?" Steve asked, looking back at Lisa.

"I don't know if the lake is big enough to let you drive on it. You know driving isn't one of your strong points. Besides, it's a little busy today because of the weekend."

"Right then," said Steve, looking back out at the lake. "I'll just look at the landscape."

Lisa drove around the lake at a slow pace. Erin relaxed as she watched people onshore barbecuing and children swimming. She knew the wine was helping, too.

"I think I'll park over at the sandbar now," Lisa said as she aimed that way. "We're going to the less-populated one over at the corner of the lake."

"Good," said Erin. "I need a nap."

Lisa drove over to the sandbar and cut the engine. Erin went up to the front of the boat as it stopped. She picked up the anchor and threw it off the side of the boat and then jumped into the waist-deep water. Pulling the boat over a little, to the middle of the sand bar, she adjusted the anchor and climbed back into the boat.

Steve stood up as she walked down the aisle. "You're amazing. You moved the boat."

"The boat is easy to move in the water." She dried her hands off with a towel.

"Tell me about the sandbar."

"All right. Come here." She picked up her wine and walked with him over to the side of the boat so he could see into the water. "You can see the sandy bottom through the water and it's only waist deep here. It is actually a bar of sand that has deep water on the other sides of it and this sandbar is one of the smaller ones on the lake, so just be careful when you're out there."

He turned his eyes back to her and smiled. "If I fell off the edge of the sandbar, would you save me?"

She paused a moment before she answered. "Just don't try it."

Lisa got up from the captain's chair and went over to the back bench seat with Jimmy and sat down as they started talking together. The boat was gently rocking, with the waves lapping against the pontoons.

Erin finished her wine, then picked up her towel and suntan lotion. She went to the front deck of the boat and lay down on her stomach as she started rubbing suntan lotion on what she could reach of her back.

"Let me do that for you," Steve said, coming up front with his beer and sitting down by her. "You seem to be having a bit of trouble."

She looked at him suspiciously.

"Come on then," he said holding out his hand. "Let me have your suntan lotion."

Reluctantly, she gave it to him and lay all the way back down.

He started rubbing the suntan lotion on her upper back, taking his time when it could have been done much quicker. Drinking his beer and humming, he moved onto her lower back, thinking about what a cute bum she had as he looked at it. Squirting some more lotion onto his hands, he proceeded down to her legs.

"That's enough," she said, resisting, because he seemed to be having too much fun. "Are you making a day of it? I can put it on my legs."

"But I'm already here," he said, trying to convince her. "Just lie back down."

She was much too tired to argue and let out a sigh. "All right. Hurry up." She closed her eyes and tried to relax.

After he was done putting the lotion on, he sat back and alternated between the view of the lake and the view of her.

She lifted up her head in what seemed like moments to her. "Have I been sleeping?"

"About thirty minutes, I believe."

As she sat up and crossed her legs, she felt pain on her shoulders where her straps went across. "I feel a little burned. Could you tell my back was burning?" she asked.

"I didn't notice. Your back wasn't what I've been looking at."

She tried to ignore that comment as she stood up, taking her empty glass with her to the cooler. Opening the wine again, she filled her glass. Lisa and Jimmy had their arms draped around one another as they appeared to be taking a nap on the bench seat across the back of the boat.

"Have they been there the whole time I was asleep?" she asked.

He nodded. "They haven't seen each other for three days, so don't expect them to talk to us much. It's just me and you, Erin."

Erin would have words with Lisa later for leaving her alone with Steve. "Did you go swimming?"

"No. I was afraid I would drop off the sandbar. You were sleeping and wouldn't be able to save me if I fell off."

She couldn't be sure if he was serious or not as she sat down on the front bench seat again and tried to wake up. Drinking her wine down fast because she was thirsty, it was gone in moments.

Steve got up from the front deck, went back to the cooler and got out another beer.

Erin looked at him more closely. He really had quite a nice looking chest, solid and slightly hairy. And he was cute, with his blonde hair and green eyes, but maybe the wine was starting to influence her too much. She was starting to feel a little drunk. Not remembering the last time she had eaten any food, she knew she needed to eat.

Steve brought the bottle of wine over to her. "You're looking a bit brighter."

Erin nodded and noticed that he had very large hands as he refilled her glass. She was having difficulty focusing, and closed her right eye for a moment as she looked at them.

Lisa and Jimmy started to awaken and sat up on the back seat, yawning and stretching their arms.

"Steve, can you give me the bowl of grapes while you're digging in the cooler?" asked Lisa.

"Sure," said Steve, getting out the bowl and handing it to her. He walked back over to Erin's side of the boat and sat down near her, drinking his beer and watching a skier dart by.

Erin looked at his green eyes as she took another sip of her wine. You could call them emerald eyes. That's what he had. Sparkling emerald eyes. And actually, he was very cute. Looking back at her sister, she saw Lisa was lying on her back with her head in Jimmy's lap as he fed her the grapes.

Steve saw Erin looking at them. "I can feed you grapes for a bit, if you like," he said, raising his eyebrows.

"No," she said, shaking her head.

"Come on," he said, looking her over.

"No, and you can stop staring at me like that."

"I can't help it. You're beautiful. Just one grape?"

"No," she said, laughing. "Are you always so annoying?"

"I'm only asking for one grape."

She relented, hoping he would shut up if she let him do it. "Okay. Just one."

He jumped up and went to the back of the boat to get a grape from Lisa.

Erin had been in Michigan for less than three hours and had been out in the hot sun for over half of that time, drinking wine. Looking down at herself, she noticed she was dressed in one of her skimpiest bikinis. No wonder he kept looking at her. Here she was—jet-lagged, drunk, sunburned, and almost naked—and she had just agreed to let this English guy she didn't know put a piece of fruit in her mouth.

"Are you ready?" he asked as he returned to her side and sat down next to her.

Feeling her heart beating, she didn't know why she seemed to be getting excited. She took in little breaths through her mouth, trying to calm herself, and nodded her head, hoping to get this over with quickly.

He enjoyed watching her breathe for a moment, then leaned over and put his arm around her bare shoulders. "Open your mouth a little bit."

She parted her lips and looked at him.

He got close enough to her to get the scent of the suntan lotion mixed with her sweat. Breathing it in, he focused on her mouth. He put the grape in her mouth and very softly touched her lips with his fingers.

Although it was a blazing eighty-eight degrees, Erin's entire body shivered.

Triangle Health Plan was considered a medium-size health insurance company that serviced the lower half of the state. It boasted over 200,000 members, and numbers continued in the upward direction at each open enrollment period, thanks to an aggressive marketing department. The offices for Triangle were on the fourth and fifth floors of a sizable office building of fifteen floors in an affluent area of town.

Dr. Charles Patton was chief medical officer of Triangle and was generally regarded as a pain in the ass to everyone he had direct contact with. His office was on the fourth floor, in the northwest corner of the building where it had windows with floor-length beige vertical blinds on two walls. This made it a little more special than the other offices, which only had windows on one wall. It held a massive mahogany laminate-finish desk with gold-plated handles, matching bookcases and a conference table. He had maroon felt-lined drawers and a high-back black leather chair that swiveled or rocked, according to his command. Beige walls and carpet and a single palm tree over in the corner completed the ensemble. Charlie always made sure his office door was closed when he put in the floppy disc for his own little private business that he called CAP. Being a devious son-of-a-bitch and an egotistical monster, he really didn't worry about getting caught, but there was nothing wrong with being careful.

Putting the CAP disc in his computer, he reviewed the columns. CAP had been in business since January and had made steady increases every month. Adding in July's numbers, he smiled. Things were going really well, mostly due to Michelle. She could throw a surgical instrument around all day like nobody's business and still have the energy to exhaust him in the evening. Looking up, he saw Rich Tyler coming toward his office with a young woman. This must be the daughter who was going to be a temporary medical consultant for a few weeks until she got into a practice. Saving his work, he removed the disc from the hard drive and placed it in his briefcase. He took a comb out of his desk and quickly attended to his thinning hair, combing it straight back. Straightening his tie and his jacket, he smiled.

"Good morning, Charlie," said Rich, walking into the office. "I want you to meet Dr. Erin Tyler, my daughter."

Erin gave Charlie a cordial smile and shook his hand firmly. "Dr. Patton, my father has told me so much about you."

"Now that really worries me!" he exclaimed, laughing heartily. "Rich, you're not supposed to ruin her the first day." He gave a little bow. "Charles Patton, chief medical officer here at Triangle Health Plan." He viewed the pretty blonde woman for a moment but blocked the perverted thoughts that filled his mind.

"I was going talk to Susan about letting Erin have Dr. Kramer's old cubicle. Would that be okay with you, Charlie?" Rich asked.

"Oh, sure. Wherever there is an available spot," Charlie said nonchalantly. "Sorry we don't have an office for you at the present time." Charlie picked up her hand and covered it with both of his. "Let me take you to lunch and we can get to know each other better, Erin."

"I would be happy to. Dad, will you be joining us?"

"I can't. I have an Ethics Committee meeting at noon," Rich said, looking at his watch. "Charlie, aren't you going to that meeting?"

"I've already made other plans, as you can see. But Rich, you have my permission to run the meeting." said Charlie, still holding Erin's hand. "Send them my regrets."

"Go ahead, Erin, and get to know Charlie. I'll catch up with you later." He left Charlie's office, thinking he should have warned Erin about Charlie's demeanor, but he was sure Erin would catch on.

Charlie led Erin out of his office. They started walking, stopping first at his administrative assistant's desk located just outside the office.

"Dr. Erin Tyler, this is Susan," Charlie said as the two women shook hands. Charlie could see Susan's breasts straining against her tight pink sweater as she stood up. He had to make his mind focus back on business and take his eyes from the sweater. "Dr. Tyler will be sitting in Dr. Kramer's old spot. Let her order any desk supplies she needs."

"Welcome to Triangle, Dr. Tyler." Susan smiled at Erin but glared at Charlie. "Let me know if you need anything. I'm here every day." She turned and sat back down, returning to her keyboard.

"She's a great gal," Charlie said, sighing. "I couldn't keep up with everything if she wasn't here to keep me on the ball." He frowned as he turned away from Erin, wondering why Susan was glaring at him.

He took her around the floor, introducing her to a few people she might have to deal with, then directed her over to a row of cluster workstations with low partitions and cushioned cranberry swivel chairs.

"We have been moving departments around again, so right now only you and another woman are on this row," he said. "There should be some supplies here, as another physician sat here before you."

Erin looked around at the U-shaped gray desk, with two drawer files and upper cabinets on one side, that would become her home during the day. *This is probably going to be a boring job*, she thought. Glancing down her row, she saw another woman sitting in a workstation farther down.

"It's noon," Charlie said, looking at his watch. "Want to go out for a bite?"

"Sure," replied Erin.

Charlie smiled.

They walked out into the foyer that separated the rest of the floor from the elevator and went down to the first floor. Charlie led Erin out to the parking lot and they walked to the parking space labeled "Chief Medical Officer."

"I like your car, Dr. Patton," Erin remarked, looking at the shiny green auto.

"It's a Jaguar XJR 4 door sedan," said Charlie as he surveyed his car, patting it on the hood. "Elegant and powerful. Hop in." Charlie put the stereo on low as they drove just a few miles down the road. "Where did you live in California?" he asked.

"Just outside of San Jose."

He nodded. "What kind of job did you have?"

"I worked for an internal medicine clinic in the city."

"Low pay, poor working conditions?"

She nodded. "I miss it already."

Charlie rolled his eyes, but didn't let Erin see him.

They arrived at a fashionable restaurant on a corner in Royal Oak where Charlie seemed quite at home. From the valet, to the hostess, to the bartender, everyone knew him. The place was dark and quiet and the candles at the tables were lit, even at lunchtime. Erin followed Charlie as he sat down in a wooden booth at the back. The waitress brought his drink at the same time as the menus.

"Hello, Laura," Charlie said smiling. "How are we today?"

"Hello, Dr. Patton," she beamed as she set down his drink. He always tipped her well. Turning to Erin, she asked, "Something to drink?"

"An ice tea, please," Erin said.

The waitress turned away and walked over to the bar.

"Erin, I know that you probably won't be working for us that long. Your father said that you may want to get into a group practice," Charlie said as he sipped his drink.

"That's one option. I'm really not sure if I will even be staying in Michigan," Erin said thoughtfully.

"Excuse me, I have to go to the little boy's room." Charlie got up, looking around the dark restaurant, and walked to the restroom.

As soon as he left, his cell phone started ringing. Erin glanced over at the caller ID and it said "Michelle." The phone started beeping every minute after that, indicating that the caller had left a message. Charlie came back to the table at the same time the waitress brought Erin's ice tea.

As he sat down, Charlie said, "I'll have the corned beef and cabbage. What would you like, Erin?"

"Club sandwich."

As the waitress left, Charlie made it very obvious that he was watching her. "Nice little caboose," he said almost inaudibly.

Erin was surprised at his comment. A chief medical officer should be more respectful while he was out on a business lunch with his new employee. She was not very impressed with Charlie so far. Just then his phone beeped again. He picked it up and listened to the message.

"Excuse me, I have to make a quick business call. A chief medical officer's world is very busy." He hit the #2 and the display showed the number to be called and dialed it. "Michelle, baby, what's going on?"

Erin could hear someone talking, but couldn't tell what she was saying. She began stirring her ice tea, feeling a little uncomfortable. Charlie started smiling and seemed happy.

"Great, doll, just great. He's getting his feet wet. That's just fine. You did go over the quota system with him? Oh really?" he said raising his eyebrows. "Well, we didn't anticipate any objections. He's got a lot of nerve, after everything we're doing for him. Will I see you later?" asked Charlie, listening to her speak. "Great. See you tonight." He ended the call and set the phone on the table.

Erin didn't say anything. She stirred her tea again, waiting for him to speak.

"My friend and colleague," he said. "She has a new employee that's giving her some grief. Speaking of new employees, I have your first assignment."

Erin waited.

He was interrupted by the waitress with their meal, which she set down in front of them. "Thanks, babe." He winked at Laura as she left. "Pharmacy costs are driving us batty. Did you know that pharmacy is the largest component of payment out?"

Erin shook her head and began to eat.

"Pharmacy costs are more than hospital and physician expenditures combined. Some of the most prescribed drugs are the most expensive. The cholesterol-lowering drugs, narcotics, and you can't forget the anti-depressants, because everyone is depressed these days. Every managed care organization needs to get control of their pharmacy. Too bad we can't micromanage it, because we'd probably save a ton of money. We just have to get the physicians to start prescribing more generic and not to write prescriptions for drugs the patients don't really need. You wouldn't believe the amount of narcotics that are getting prescribed." Charlie shook his head as he took a few bites of his meal.

"What do you want me to do?" Erin asked as she ate.

"You have all of the Data department available to you to extract prescribing patterns for our physicians. I want you to look into which physicians are ordering most of the big money drugs and perhaps go out to their offices and talk to them. Any questions that come up, discuss with me. Our chief executive officer, Bruce Washington, wants a report in one month. Have you met him yet?"

"No," said Erin as she finished up her lunch. "My father was going to take me up to his floor another day." She looked at Charlie's plate and noticed that he had hardly eaten anything—not even half of his meal. "Don't you like your food?"

"I'm just watching my figure. Got to pay attention to those calories." He sucked in his abdominal muscles and laughed, then picked up his drink and drained it. "Time to get back." He threw some money on the table and stood up, waiting for Erin.

They had hardly been there a half-hour, but Erin got up to go. She had been shocked at his behavior ever since she had met him, not understanding how Charlie had gotten into such a powerful position. Why would a health plan keep such a dreadful man? First impressions were important, and he was definitely just being himself and not putting on any pretensions for Erin. Already hoping that she wouldn't have to spend a lot of time with him, she stood up and tried to smile. "Thanks, Dr. Patton, it was nice getting to know you better."

"Sure," he said as he blew a kiss to Laura when they exited the bar. "I also want you to help your father out with some of his excess work. He reviews charts for Utilization Management, which he can explain to you. It seems like I've needed him lately to help me with my work, but he's getting too bogged down. Go figure."

Erin nodded.

The ride back was quiet, but Charlie seemed a little edgy with the traffic. He weaved in and out of it, cursing at other drivers and ran a red light. Pulling into Triangle, going a little faster than he should, he parked in his spot.

Erin let out her breath, relieved to get out of the car. He had more than frightened her.

"You need a code if you'll be entering the building after hours," he said as they walked inside. "Sometimes we have night meetings, so there are a few of us who have it."

They went up the elevator to the fourth floor.

"I'm going back to my office. If you need anything, ask Susan. She can usually help you." He smiled at Erin as he turned toward his office.

Erin walked over to her row and sat down at her desk, going through it to see what she might need. She opened one of the drawers and found an old yellow sticky note with something written in pencil. It was smudged and she could barely read it, but she thought it had "save" written at the top and said "Dr. Carroll" and "Dr. Fab". There were a couple more letters written after "Fab" but they were illegible. She shrugged her shoulders and threw the note back in the drawer.

Charlie went into his office and closed the door. Sitting down at his desk, he put his feet up and leaned back on the soft black leather chair, admiring the gold-plated frames hanging on the wall with his credentials in them. He knew that being the chief medical officer for a growing health insurance company was a nice position to be in. Big salary, big office. Having just turned 58 years old last month, he felt very vibrant and alive. He enjoyed his job, but there were going to be changes. Many changes. He brazenly took a small, brown glass vial and tiny silver spoon out from his jacket, just barely looking through his blinds to see if anyone was watching. Opening the vial, he stuck the tiny spoon inside and took out a heaping spoonful of white powder. He put it up to one nostril and inhaled deeply. Doing the same to the other nostril, he screwed the lid back on the bottle and placed it in his pocket. He felt great! He grinned like a Cheshire cat and patted the vial that was now secure in his pocket; he knew that his life was good and it was only going to get better.

CHAPTER 3

RICH looked up from his desk as Charlie sauntered by, whistling. Charlie acted as though he didn't have a care in the world. Always giving the impression of one of those guys that just skates through life, he did the bare minimum to get by, but somehow always did things right. Rich was shocked when Charlie had gotten the chief medical officer job for Triangle. He and Charlie had been there just about the same length of time, but Charlie was a better ass kisser than Rich and had been able to convince Bruce that he was the man for the job. Not letting it bother him, Rich got up to stretch and saw Erin down the hallway at Susan's desk. He went out of his office and walked down to the women.

They looked up as Rich came over to them.

"Good afternoon, you two. How was lunch with Charlie?" he asked Erin.

"As well as could be expected." Erin smiled at him.

"I see you're getting to know him," Rich said and chuckled.

"Dr. Tyler, look how big Trevor is getting," said Susan. She showed Rich her baby's latest picture, which featured a laughing, chubby baby boy splashing in a kiddie pool.

"He's a handsome young man," Rich said as he handed the picture back to Susan, thinking that the baby looked more like Charlie every day.

"Trevor is adorable," smiled Erin.

"Erin, did you get a chance to start on the pharmacy project Charlie was going to give you?" asked Rich.

"I just put in a request for narcotics, cholesterol lowering agents, and antidepressants written over a month timespan," she said. "If I requested longer than a month, the information would be too much to start with. The Data department said it would take two days to get the information to me."

"How do you plan to proceed with your investigation?"

"Dr. Patton said I could do it any way I wanted," she explained. "I think I'll just look at the basics of who has prescribed, how frequently, and the quantity first to see what it looks like and go from there."

"Sounds like a good start. By the way, Lisa wants you to call her. She wants you to go out with her and the boys to discuss the wedding."

"Dad, I don't know," Erin said, feeling wary. "I was just out on the boat with all of them."

"You might have fun." Rich understood Erin being hesitant, but really thought she needed to socialize more, and the sooner the better.

"I'll call her when I get back to my desk," Erin said with a half-smile. "Dr. Patton also wanted you to explain to me about what to look for with the Utilization Management charts. Do you think you'll have time today?"

"Why don't you come by my office later this afternoon?"

"All right. I'd better go call Lisa. I'll see you later." Erin smiled at both of them and walked over to her own desk.

"Susan, do you know when Charlie is getting back in?" Rich looked toward Charlie's office, but it was dark.

"He just left a few minutes ago. Dr. Patton is meeting with another doctor and will be back around 3 p.m. Would you like me to page him?" She picked up the phone and looked at Rich, waiting for his reply.

"Oh no," Rich said shaking his head. "That's all right. I'll talk to him later." He smiled at Susan and walked away.

Erin reached her desk and saw the light on her phone, indicating a voice mail. She picked up the phone, listened to the message, and frowned, because Lisa was pushing her to go out tomorrow. Erin picked up the phone and dialed.

Lisa answered on the second ring. "Erin, I'm so glad you called me back. The guys are coming back from Indianapolis tomorrow. I want all of us to go out so we can discuss the wedding."

Erin didn't want to go. "I told you already that I'm embarrassed about what happened on the boat."

"Oh, Erin, the guys were very understanding. You hadn't eaten and you had been on a long flight. The wine just got to you in a hurry, and being out in the hot sun didn't help. Why do you worry so much about everything? Nothing's changed with you. Always the worry wart."

"Sure."

"In fact, Steve said he had a great time and is looking forward to seeing you again. He was sorry that you fell asleep for the entire evening after we ate all the food in the cooler. He was hoping to get to know you better."

"I bet he was."

"Why are you saying it like that?"

"Lisa, I think he took advantage of my having too much wine. I can't believe I let him put suntan lotion on me and feed me a grape."

"But you agreed to it, right?"

"I only agreed because I was drunk. Good thing you know I fell asleep, because I don't remember a thing after the grape."

"Don't worry, drunk or not, I'm sure he didn't mean anything by it. He's a nice guy. Anyway, I thought we could go over to this little place on Maple Road. They don't have much to eat, but it's fun. Will you go?"

"That'll be fine." Erin hung up the phone and made an unhappy face.

Charlie was humming to himself as he turned down Balsam Boulevard. He saw Dr. Edward Carroll's office just a little ways up the road on the right and turned into the gray brick building parking lot. Parking in the front row next to Ed's Pacifica and a brown van of some sort, Charlie got out of his car and looked around. Today the office was only open for patients in the morning. Ed's staff had already left, but he was there with a potential new recruit. Charlie walked up to the glass door and tried to open it, but it was locked. He placed a call to Ed's cell phone and Ed picked up.

"You here, Charlie?" Ed asked.

"Yep. This outside door is locked," said Charlie as he pulled on it and looked behind him.

"I'm coming, I'm coming," Ed replied and hung up.

Ed came slowly into view through the double glass doors. He pulled open the first door that was already unlocked, then took a set of keys from his right pants pocket and turned them in the lock to open the outside door for Charlie. He was still limping from his recent knee surgery.

"Still having trouble, I see," Charlie said, looking down at Ed's knee as he entered the building.

"It's a pain in the ass, but it's getting better," Ed said, locking the door again. "Still have to ice it down almost every night. Judy is in my office. I've gone over a few things with her already and I think she'll be fine. We've been trying to recruit her for a couple of months and she finally got back to me this week."

"Well, my friend, just watch the master at work." Charlie raised his eyebrows.

They walked down the hall to Ed's office where a woman in a forest green suit was seated alone at a round table surrounded by upholstered chairs. She stood up when they entered.

"Hello, Dr. Patton," she said as she shook Charlie's hand. "I'm Dr. Judith Saunders—Judy. I've been with Triangle for about a year, but I don't believe we ever met."

"Nice meeting you, Judy. Please sit down." Pacing back and forth in the small office for a few moments, Charlie appeared to be collecting his thoughts. He then started his spiel as Judy and Ed listened. "As I'm sure you know, Judy, there is not much of a demand for primary care physicians anymore. This would include internal medicine, family practice, and pediatricians."

"I have many days when my office is not booked and sometimes I have no one in the hospital," Judy said.

"It's all about being a specialist these days. That's where the money is. The salaries for the primary care physicians have leveled off and the need is just not there any more."

"Some months I'm barely solvent," Judy remarked quietly. "I have a house for sale over on Arrow Lake, if you're interested."

Charlie talked as he continued to pace back and forth in the room. "Believe me, I know the dissatisfaction you're feeling with the profession. You're subjected not just to Triangle's rules, but every other health insurance you deal with. You have utilization review issues for hospitalization and preapproval requirements for surgeries and treatments that differ with each health plan. How can you or your staff function in a constantly changing environment like that? And the reimbursement issues! The insurance company tells you what they'll pay you. Unbelievable. It's never ending. And don't forget how the patients never stop asking questions. I read this on the Internet. I read that on the Internet. They're told to question everything you do. What a pain. You've lost your autonomy completely. In this day and age, it makes you wonder why you ever became a physician."

Judy was listening, and nodding her head.

He stopped pacing and sat down with them. Placing both hands, palms down, on the table, he continued. "Let's get down to brass tacks. If you would have been in CAP, which is our acronym for Cash And Physicians, last month you would have made an additional $5520 for doing almost nothing but talking to a few patients. And that amount is going up every month. I have it on hard copy, if you want to see it. Being the internist, you have the least risk of anyone, and accordingly, would make the least amount of cash. However, that money is tax free and deposited in an offshore account for you in the form of credit for your Internet, phone, fax, mail transactions and debit for your in-person transactions. Most importantly, that account cannot be tracked by the government."

"Ed told me what I would need to do to get in CAP. I have been grappling with the idea." She paused for a moment. "I have two children in college out East, an office staff, and rent on my building."

"Do you know if any of your partners would be interested?" Ed asked, looking at her intently.

"No, I don't think I want to divulge any of this yet. Let's see how it works for a while first."

"Remember, Judy, there is really no risk to you," Charlie said slowly. "All the risk belongs to the cardiologist and cardiovascular surgeon."

Judy let out a heavy sigh. "So it finally does come down to money," she said.

"As the saying goes, money is everything. I'll send you a statement online each month of your accounts. We are very cautious and this won't go on forever," Charlie said. "This is only a temporary thing, so the risk is even less."

"What if I decide I want out?" Judy asked.

"If you request to leave before I end CAP, then you will have no money in your account. Everything will disappear and there will be no trace of anything. We can't take any chances, you know." Charlie said, observing a stoic Judy. "If you need a few more days, Ed can give you a call this weekend." Charlie glanced at Ed, who was rolling his eyes. Ed thought Judy had already made up her mind before she came to the office.

"No, no, I've had plenty of time to think about it," she said, pausing momentarily. "I'm in."

"Great!" Charlie stood up and shook her hand. "We'll be in contact with you soon. Anything sent to you must be deleted as soon as you read it. Make your hard copies any way you please, but they are for your eyes only." He turned to Ed. "Okay, we're good. I have to get back to the office. I'll talk to each of you soon." He shook both their hands.

"I'll let you out," Ed said. Turning to Judy, he asked, "Are you ready?"

"Yes, I have to get to my office, too."

Ed let them both out and locked the door again. Judy got into the van that was parked in front and drove away. Charlie lingered a bit as he took his time walking around to the passenger side of his Jaguar and threw his jacket down on the seat. He wasn't in any rush to get back to the office. As the jacket landed, his glass vial of cocaine fell out and broke when it hit the ground.

"Damn!" he grumbled. He opened his glove box and took out a napkin. Wrapping the broken vial up, he put it in the small garbage can in his car. There was always more where that came from. Having no worries, he got into his beautiful Jaguar and drove off.

"Isn't this strange?" asked Rich as he and Erin walked up the driveway together. "You and I getting home from the same office at the same time?"

"Yes."

"Erin, I've decided to let you use my Mustang for work. I only drive it on the weekends anyway. Lisa doesn't need it as she's been using your mother's car most of the time. I know you like it, and I want you to feel like you have some freedom. Besides, you'll need a car to go visit the physicians you need to see."

"Thanks, Dad. That would be great!" She smiled and rubbed his shoulder as they entered the house.

Arlene and Lisa had made a wonderful dinner of grilled salmon and vegetables that was just being taken off the grill as they arrived. Erin helped her mother get out the plates and silverware, taking them out to the back deck. Since it was such a warm, clear day, the family decided to eat outside.

"Well, girls, this seems like the old days," said Rich as he picked up his fork and started eating. "I remember when you two were little and we'd sit out here discussing your days at school. Things have really changed over the years. It's hard to believe that both of you are grown up now and here with your mother and me. And things are getting ready to change again," he said matter-of-factly.

The sober thoughtfulness that came with the moment only lasted a few seconds. They all truly appreciated their time together.

"Your father and I are so glad you're both home again for a while," said Arlene, as she squeezed both girls' hands, and the family continued eating.

Rich turned to Erin. "So what do you think about Jimmy and Steve?"

"Jimmy seems fun and really sweet," Erin said looking at Lisa. "I can see how you fell for him."

"He's so special to me," said Lisa smiling. "Jimmy loves people and is always happy and he makes me laugh. You have to hear him play guitar. He is awesome! His family is wonderful and they've accepted me without any problem. And England! What can I tell you about England? You've got to go there, Erin," Lisa said, her eyes lighting up.

Erin smiled. There was Lisa being happy again. "England has always been on my list."

"And Steve is great, too" said Lisa, continuing. "Handsome, articulate. You have to get to know him. He's never been married, Erin. When you keep making new music and touring like the guys do, it's hard to find a girl willing to put up with that lifestyle."

Rich and Arlene took that as their cue to get up and clear the dishes. The girls wanted to talk.

"So you're sure Jimmy is ready to get married?"

"I do. He's told me many times."

"So you've known him about two years now?" asked Erin, thinking about the time she'd first heard of Jimmy.

"I got backstage after a show and there were sparks," said Lisa, smiling. "What can I say? I've been living with him in England for almost a year while they worked on their new album. Then he asked me to marry him. It was totally unexpected, and I was shocked. But after thinking about it for awhile—maybe five minutes," she said, laughing, "I said yes."

Erin and Lisa turned their heads toward the house as the phone rang.

Rich called from the house. "Lisa, it's Jimmy. Do you want it out there or are you coming in?"

"I'm coming in," she yelled at Rich, then turned to Erin, grinning. "We have to whisper sweet nothings to each other. Better I do it alone upstairs."

"Go for it," Erin replied.

"Bye," said Lisa, jumping up. She ran like a teenager to the kitchen.

Erin sat at the table, pondering what Lisa had told her, as Rich came outside and pulled dead leaves off a flowering basket hanging on the deck. They both looked up as a boat went by, carrying a skier, making large ripples that fanned out for many yards over the lake. Many other boats could be seen in the distance. It was a typical scene repeated many times on a Michigan lake in August.

"Do you feel like a little work-related conversation now? I'm used to Lisa talking to Jimmy for quite a while."

"Sure, Dad."

Erin got up and they went in the house through the kitchen. Arlene was rinsing the dishes and loading the dishwasher.

"Where are you two going?" she asked.

"I thought this was a good time to tell Erin about Triangle," said Rich.

"Try not to bore her too much, Rich," said Arlene. "You know how much you enjoy talking about your job."

Rich smiled.

They walked into the spacious living room and sat down on the brown leather couch. Erin leaned back on the couch and put her feet up on the large ottoman. Rich looked deep in thought, then put his hands together and began.

"I just thought you might want to know a little bit about managed care organizations, which is what Triangle is," he said. "Triangle Health Plan was named for the physician, member, and health plan working together as a unit, like a triangle. You know every member of the plan has a primary care physician that they have picked. The primary care doctor directs the member's care, and all specialized care must be approved by that doctor."

Erin nodded her head in understanding.

"The plus for the member is that they have less out-of-pocket expense, but the down side is that they have less control over what specialist they see, where they can go for testing, et cetera. If they go out of the plan's network for care, they usually will not be reimbursed for the care received."

"I understand."

"Managed care organizations like Triangle can make a large contribution to health care. We are trying to help prevent, control, and treat the diseases that plague our nation."

Erin nodded.

"Triangle has capitation, which means that primary care physicians get a payment for each of their members every month. The amount can vary, according to the member's age and sex. We also have something called "an incentive." Our physicians get a bonus every six months for doing a good job. The bonus is dependent on a variety of factors and includes a patient satisfaction component, how they did on chronic disease management, what kind of medication-prescribing patterns they have, to name a few."

"Is that why Charlie gave me the pharmacy assignment?" interrupted Erin.

"Yes. As I'm sure Charlie told you, medication costs are our biggest pay out and our biggest headache. We are trying to motivate physicians to provide quality care and that is the fundamental aspect of giving an incentive."

Arlene came into the living room but stood at the doorway with arms crossed. "Enough work talk, you two. The four of us won't be together much longer, and I want us to spend quality time together."

Lisa suddenly appeared next to Arlene. "Erin, the boys will be back tomorrow night and agreed to go out. They are both looking forward to getting to know you better."

"Wonderful," Erin said with secret dread.

"How about if we do something fun?" Arlene asked. "We used to all enjoy going out and playing miniature golf. How about it?"

Everyone agreed.

"Let me run upstairs and change clothes first. It will only take me a minute," said Erin.

"All right," said Rich. "I'm going to change out of my suit, too. Everyone meet me outside in five minutes." He looked at his watch.

"Let's start locking up the house," Arlene said to Lisa.

The family scattered in four directions, each one hurrying to be outside in five minutes. They laughed together as they all arrived at almost the same instant. Everyone piled into Rich's Yukon like in their younger days and they were off toward the greens.

Erin was eager to look out the windows at all the changes in the community. It was really building up. As they got closer to the miniature golf course, they started passing some rundown areas that had seen better days. New strip malls had taken the place of older ones. New multi-pump gas stations with fast food restaurants inside had replaced the older, more personal gas stations with full-service pumps and a mechanic inside. Erin fixed her eyes on one of those old gas stations on a side street that they were passing. The name could still be seen in fading paint over the front door. It was closed long ago and had boarded-up windows, but the front door was open. On the side of the gas station was a beautiful green Jaguar that was pulled up as far as it could go to the back fence. The car looked familiar and it appeared that someone was inside. Just then an older, noisy car pulled up to the Jaguar and it's two occupants got out. They had hooded sweatshirts on and appeared to be turning their heads in all directions, looking around. They walked up to the Jaguar as its driver got out. As Rich pulled farther away from the scene, Erin strained to see the person in the Jaguar. He briefly turned towards her. It was Charlie.

CHAPTER 4

ROBERT sat up in his hospital bed, stuffing pillows behind his back for comfort as he turned on the television to relax. He had just been up walking down the hall in cardiac rehab and wasn't the least bit short of breath. Suddenly he felt a twinge of pain as his gown caught on the staples that ran down the front of his chest. Thank goodness it wasn't the chest pain coming back. He lifted the gown off of his staples and looked at the long, ugly incision that had saved his life.

Hearing a noise outside his door, he looked up as his wife Helen came around the corner. He knew she tried to be cheery everytime she came to the hospital. It hadn't been easy, especially when she was worried that he was going to die. She had learned to fake happiness instead of worry.

"Hi, honey," she said, bending over to kiss him. She smiled.

"Guess what?"

"What?"

"I get to go home tomorrow."

"Did Dr. Keller come in already?" she asked, quite excited.

"No, but my nurse said I was doing good enough that tomorrow will be the big day."

"It seems awful quick, don't you think?"

"If you're doing well, the doctor lets you go home in a few days now."

"Oh, really?" she said, trying to think if she had ever heard that before.

"Yeah. I'll have to go to cardiac rehab for a while and keep up my medications, but they say I should be fine."

"I'm so relieved. Maybe I should start taking some stuff home today."

She looked in the closet and opened the hospital bag that held the clothes he came in with. It sent shivers down her spine, remembering that awful day when she came in the house and found him slumped over the table. Robert had been ashen and barely conscious. Hardly able to think, she had forced herself to pick up the phone and call 911. She sat with him in the ambulance and it seemed only minutes until they got to Mercury Memorial Hospital, where treatment began. The diagnosis was acute myocardial infarction. Their primary care doctor, Dr. Jane Marshall, wanted the cardiologist, Dr. Michelle Campbell, to see Robert immediately. Dr. Campbell seemed very knowledgeable and did his cardiac catheterization right away. Being transferred from Mercury to Southeast, his bypass was done by Dr. David Keller, and it went very well. Helen packed some of the things in Robert's room. She had better bring him some clean clothes tomorrow if he was going home.

There was a knock at the door and they both turned toward it as David entered.

"Good morning," said David, nodding to both of them as he rolled in an elevated cart with a wireless black laptop on it. "How are you feeling today, Robert?"

Robert picked up the remote control that was lying on the bed and turned down the television. He sat up straight, trying to look like someone who didn't need to be in the hospital any longer. "Dr. Keller, I'm feeling great. Ready to play golf."

David smiled. "You need to increase your activities slowly. I don't think golf will be on the agenda for a while." He accessed Robert's electronic chart and looked at Robert's recent vital signs for a moment. No fever, blood pressure 124/72, pulse 82 per minute. "Let me listen to you," he said as he took a black stethoscope from the pocket of his white lab coat.

"Sure, Doc."

David walked over from the cart and listened to Robert's heart and lungs with his stethoscope—first from the front, then from the back. He lowered the bed so Robert could lie down and David felt his abdomen, looked at his leg incision, then his ankles. He sat down in the brown vinyl chair next to the bed. "Everything is good. Your lungs are clear, heart sounds good, sternum and leg incision healing, and no swelling in your ankles. I'm going to let you go home tomorrow, with limited activity. You're going to continue on the aspirin and Tenormin and I want you to start outpatient cardiac rehab next week."

"Sounds good." Robert nodded, finding it hard to contain his excitement.

"The nurses on the unit will give you two books to take home. One is an open-heart surgery recovery manual and the other a heart-healthy cookbook. Southeast also offers classes on a variety of health topics that may be of benefit to you and your wife. Diet, exercise, and keeping your cholesterol down will continue to be of the utmost importance for you, even when you stop seeing me. There needs to be a complete lifestyle change for you now, Robert, and working closely with your internist will be in your best interest. Any questions?" David looked back and forth from Robert to Helen.

"I'm at a loss for questions right now," said Helen, shrugging her shoulders as she smiled. "We're just so happy that the surgery went well. Will we see you in the morning before we go home?"

"I have surgery in the morning and won't be finished before you're discharged. Call my office later today and speak with my nurse. She should be able to answer any questions that may come up today. She will make an appointment for you to see me in three weeks."

"Thanks, Doc," said Robert.

"Thank you so much, Dr. Keller," said Helen. "For everything." She went over to Robert and hugged his shoulders as David left the room.

David pushed the rolling cart down to the nurse's station to finish up his charting. Since there were sometimes problems with patients being discharged while they were still medically unstable, Southeast now required their physicians to go through a one-page computer program to see if the patient met criteria for discharge. The physicians had resented this at first as an affront to their judgment, but now they just accepted it. David knew that Robert met the requirements as he checked them off in the computer one at a time. No fever, stable vital signs, lungs were clear, incisions healing, no leg swelling. The computer agreed that it was safe to discharge Robert and that page was added into the patient's electronic record.

He tried not to think of the overwhelming guilt that came with doing surgery on someone who didn't need it. If he continued to dwell on it, he knew he would make himself physically sick. He just had to put it out of his mind and be strong. After all, he did have an ego the size of Lake Superior, and it shouldn't really be hard to put himself first again. With that thought, he finished typing in his orders and made sure to smile at all the nurses as he left the unit.

Charlie sat in his office, reviewing numbers from each of his doctors in CAP. He glanced at his gold Rolex: one hour until the next meeting. He hoped that no one would be a pain in the ass today and talk too long or ask too many questions. Being the CMO required at least one daily meeting, it seemed, and what a waste of time most of them were. Besides, Charlie wasn't feeling so well this morning. Staying up way too late last night, he had a cocaine hangover today that could knock over a horse. He just had to stop doing drugs on work nights, because he wasn't so young anymore. Sleep was really important to his job-functioning the next day, but he was unable to help himself when he had a brand new stash, and he always overdid it. Charlie looked up and saw Rich walking outside his office. *Go away*, he thought. Rich was really getting on his nerves lately. Always coming over. Always asking questions. Charlie wished he would just stay in his own office. By his own admission, Rich was overloaded with Utilization Management charts and that was why Erin was going to help him. Charlie let out a breath and relaxed a little when Rich walked by without stopping. Now he could get back to his CAP doctors.

Ed Carroll was really doing the best. He sent many people to Michelle, had an eye for business, and liked the perks of additional money he could hide from his wife. Maybe Charlie should let him know what was going on before CAP abruptly ended. Ed might like to carry on as the boss and get things started again. Charlie made himself a note in the computer.

Mike Fabian. A somewhat straight arrow. Not doing all that he could do. Still paying off school loans. Probably a little afraid. Very poor performance. He must be talked to. Charlie made himself another note.

Jane Marshall. Quite a piece of work in more ways than one. Encouraged her patients, listened to them, then the guillotine blade descended before they even knew it.

Dean Peach. Becoming somewhat lazy and Charlie didn't know why. He tapped a finger on his cheek. Dean wasn't doing as good in June and July as he did in February and March. Charlie would have to look into that more.

Finally, the new recruit: Judy Saunders. She had gone back to her office yesterday after their meeting and referred a patient to Michelle. Charlie nodded as he swelled with pride. *Now that's a healthy start.*

His phone rang and he picked it up on the second ring.

"Dr. Patton," he announced.

"Good morning, Dr. Patton. It's Erin Tyler. How are you today?"

"Erin, I'm great. I trust you've settled in. Susan helping you out?" He frowned as he wondered if Susan would talk to him today.

"She has been very helpful."

"Wonderful. How are the July numbers?" asked Charlie, still reviewing his CAP disc.

"Looks like a lot of prescriptions of OxyContin for the narcotics. Many of the most expensive trade names for some of the other drug classes. I'm working on specific doctor names now. Do you want me to just call the physicians, or go out to see them?"

"Go out. Tell them you're acting on my instructions."

"What specifically do you want me to tell them?"

"That pharmacy is killing us, that they need to prescribe more generic, that if the patient doesn't really need it, not to prescribe it."

"All right, Dr. Patton."

"Erin, you only need to report to me once a week. How about every Friday?"

"Friday is fine. Thank you." Erin hung up the phone.

Charlie looked at his watch. Damn! Time for the meeting. He saved the new information he had added on his disc and took it out of his computer.

Ed Carroll scanned his office for the improvements he could make in the next few months. Money was starting to really roll in and some changes were imminent. He needed to have the office painted and wanted new carpeting and furniture throughout. New pictures in the waiting room would work, too, as he was tired of looking at the same pictures he'd seen every day since he opened his practice ten years ago. "Trains!" he snorted. What made him pick trains? How many pictures can you look at of a train anyway? Speeding out of a tunnel, going into a tunnel, rushing over a bridge, stopping at a rail station. Yes, he was definitely over trains. He nodded to himself as he thought, *Maybe some nice beach or mountain scenes would be relaxing for his patients and would be an incentive for him to be where those pictures were from.*

He picked up the list of patients for the afternoon that was lying on the receptionist's desk and perused it. Mr. Khalifa was coming in for a physical, Mrs. Summers was in for follow-up on her diabetes, and Mr. Kaczynski needed his blood pressure checked and prescription renewal done. Farther down on the list he saw that Mrs. Jones was complaining of either acid indigestion or chest pain—she wasn't sure which one it was. He stopped and thought. That would probably be the referral for today. His part was done after the referral was made and he always went to see his patients in the hospital after they had their surgery to show his concern. Picking out Sandra Jones' chart from the heap, he put it under his arm.

"Chrissy," he said to his receptionist who was just returning from lunch, "will you try to get Dr. Campbell on the phone?" He turned and started for the medication room, knowing she would call him when Michelle was available.

"Yes, Dr. Carroll," Chrissy said. She knew the number by heart now, as she had called it so much, and she started dialing even as she put her purse in the bottom drawer of her desk.

The phone rang at Dr. Campbell's office and a girl answered.

"Mercury Cardiac Care. How may I direct your call?"

"Stephanie, is that you?" asked Chrissy as she held the phone with one hand and opened a soda with the other.

"Yes, who's this?"

"Hi, it's Chrissy from Dr. Carroll's office. It seems like we've been talking a lot lately."

"I guess there are a lot of sick people out there."

"Looks that way. Dr. Carroll wants to know if Dr. Campbell is in today."

"She's here, but she's with a patient. Do you want to hold?"

"Yes, I'll go get Dr. Carroll. Thanks, Stephanie." Chrissy put the phone on hold and got up to look for Dr. Carroll. She found him in the medication room looking through the pharmaceutical samples that were given to him by the drug companies. The shelves were stacked to capacity.

He looked over at her. "Chrissy, some of these samples have expired. Can you and Tonya go through these and throw the expired ones away? I don't want to make the mistake of handing these out to my patients."

"Sure, Dr. Carroll. We can do it this afternoon. Dr. Campbell will be on line two in a few minutes."

"Thank you." He went to his office and closed the door. Picking up the phone, he realized Michelle wasn't on yet, so he turned his office chair around to look out the window. What a beautiful day. Sunny and not a cloud in the sky. He heard a click on the phone and Michelle answered.

"Ed, how are you? Keeping busy?"

"Not as busy as you," he replied, turning back around and putting his bad leg up on his desk. "I bet you haven't had much free time since January. Do you ever get a night off?"

"Not usually. I do my surgeries in the morning, office hours in the afternoon, and back to the hospital for rounds in the evening. I'm a workaholic."

"I don't know if I could keep up that kind of schedule."

"It should level off soon and I'll be used to the pace. Do you have a new patient for me?"

"Yes, I do." He opened up the chart, going through a few pages. "Her name is Sandra Jones. She is 55 years old and is coming in today for either a stomach problem or chest pain; she doesn't know which. I was going to check her out here and send her over to you as a referral."

"Sounds great, Ed. You go ahead and do her workup. When I see her, I'll probably start off with an exercise treadmill."

Ed laughed. "You must be making a lot of dough with the cardiac testing section of your office, too. Enough to keep you in Cristal any day of the week?"

Michelle didn't laugh and her voice wasn't friendly anymore. He realized his error.

"I only drink Cristal Champagne on Saturday night," she said coldly.

He knew he had better get off the phone before she got even angrier with him. "My other line is ringing, Michelle, gotta go. You take care."

The phone clicked before he finished his words.

He hung up the phone and stood, but felt a twinge of pain in his knee as he put his weight on it. Doing too much again. He'd need to ice it down tonight. He hobbled out of his office and went to the first examination room that held a patient. Picking up Mr. Khalifa's chart from the rack outside the door, he looked at it briefly, then knocking on the door, he turned the knob and went in.

Erin looked around the guestroom where she had been living for the last few days. It was her mother's country-themed room, filled with antiques and family heirlooms. Her mother had rug beaters hanging on the wall, blue Depression glass sitting on the dresser, and old black and white pictures of the family in frames scattered about the room. She opened the door to the closet and searched through her clothes, moving the hangers one after another, not knowing what to wear this evening. Settling on a pair of low rise jeans, brown belt and shoes, and a powder blue tee shirt that complemented her blue eyes, she dressed quickly. This was her first night out in a long time and the first time she would see Steve since the day on the boat. She still felt self-conscious about all that had happened on the boat, even if Lisa had dismissed her embarrassment, telling her that Steve didn't do anything wrong. Erin believed he had taken advantage of her in her precarious state and vowed that she would be more careful tonight.

Steve and Jimmy were sitting on the couch, watching television with her father when she went downstairs. They were watching one of the travel channels and discussing Wales.

"We've been to Wales many times," said Jimmy. "You should see the Millennium Stadium in Cardiff. It's fabulous."

"It's the most spectacular stadium in the UK," said Steve.

"Soccer is a sport I just haven't seen enough of to understand," Rich said, shaking his head from side to side.

"You mean football. Soccer is a word almost never used in England or any other footballing country in the world. We just say football," said Jimmy.

"So 'soccer' is an Americanism?" asked Rich.

Jimmy nodded his head "yes."

Rich shook his head. "Hockey is my favorite sport and the only one that I watch regularly. Have you ever heard that Detroit is called Hockeytown?"

They shook their heads "no."

Rich glanced up as Erin came down the stairs into the living room.

Steve looked at her and smiled. "Hello again."

"Anyone know where Lisa is?" Erin asked as she glanced into the hallway, not acknowledging Steve.

"Actually, she is moving the car out of the garage to the front of the house," said Jimmy.

"I told her to take the Mustang," said Rich.

"Where is your mum?" Jimmy asked Erin. "I haven't seen her tonight."

"I don't know. Dad, do you?"

"Arlene is at the neighbor's house and won't be home for a while," Rich replied as he waved them off. "Don't worry about me. You kids go have fun."

Steve and Jimmy got up, following Erin out the front door. They saw Lisa waiting in the driveway with the car running.

She put the window down when she saw them. "Come on, time to go."

Steve opened the passenger door, moving the front seat so Erin could get in the back. She climbed in and he sat down next to her. Jimmy put the seat back and got in front with Lisa.

Erin tried to make small talk to ease her discomfort. "So do either of you drive when you're in the United States?" she asked, looking from Jimmy to Steve.

Jimmy and Steve broke into laughter.

"Well, I very strongly recommend that Steve not be allowed to drive," said Jimmy. "One time when we were here he took out a whole row of mailboxes."

"Thank you very much indeed for bringing that up, Jimmy." Steve turned to Erin. "I gave up driving in the United States after that. I can't seem to get the car thing right over here. You people drive on the wrong side of the road."

Erin couldn't help but laugh at Steve's remark, and she became a little more relaxed. This rock star couldn't figure out how to drive in the United States.

"So do you like being a doctor?" asked Jimmy.

"Sometimes. I just have to figure out where I want to work."

"I want you to move somewhere close to Jimmy and me and find work there," Lisa whined. "I've missed you so much the last couple of years. It seems like we only talk on the phone now."

"I know."

Lisa turned the Mustang into the small parking lot of the bar and pulled into the last available spot. "This is the closest thing to an English pub in this area."

The boys were eager to get out of the car and go in. Three plastic green tables with chairs and umbrellas were set up outside the bar, but customers were sitting at them. Lisa opened the front door and they went in. The place was so small there was only one aisle going from the front door to the back. You could hardly see where you were walking until your eyes got used to the darkness. Little white lights were strung up all over the tiny bar, and it was noisy and smoky.

"You guys are in luck," said Lisa, looking at the beer menu on the wall. "They have Guinness."

"Fabulous," echoed the boys.

They looked around and saw one empty booth. Erin made a beeline for it and sat down, with Steve sliding in quickly next to her. The waitress came over within a few minutes, wiped down the table and took their drink orders.

"Erin," Lisa said, "we have to meet with the seamstress next Tuesday for your alterations. I have a picture of the dresses at the house that I forgot to show you. Silly me." She put her palm against her forehead and shook her head. "I think you'll really like them. They're real girlie, just the way I like things."

"All right," Erin said slowly. "How high are my heels?"

"Only about two inches," Lisa said, confident that Erin would be happy with lower heels.

"Good."

Erin wasn't trying to listen to the table behind them, but the people were talking pretty loudly because of all the noise around them. The jukebox was playing and the television had a baseball game going.

"My doctor said that I need a coronary bypass done. He's going to send me to a cardiologist next week for an evaluation," said a man.

"How could your doctor know that you'll need surgery if you haven't even been evaluated yet?" asked a female voice.

"We were wondering that," said another female voice. "Tim has to quit smoking by then, too. Don't you, Tim?"

"All right," said Tim as he blew the smoke over Erin's head.

Erin saw the smoke and waved it away. It was definitely an interesting conversation in the booth next to her. What was going on with all that? She was deep in thought until she felt all eyes at her table upon her. "Sorry, did I miss something?" She looked from face to face, feeling embarrassed.

"Erin, did you hear what Steve said?" asked Lisa.

"No. I was accidentally eavesdropping on the table behind us. I'm sorry." She looked at Steve, waiting for him to speak to her.

"I asked you if you would mind helping the best man pick out a gift for the wedding couple. Jimmy isn't worth a toss for ideas."

"What?" Jimmy frowned.

Steve kicked him under the table as he spoke. "Now Jimmy, don't get your knickers in a twist. Perhaps Erin will help me."

"Sure, I'd be happy to," Erin said, but she wasn't sure if she wanted to be alone with him again.

"All right then. When?"

She acted like she hadn't heard him. "I can't believe the wedding is less than three weeks away," said Erin, changing the subject and looking at her sister.

"August 24. I can't believe it's getting so close," burst in Lisa. "You know that the reception will be in a tent in Mom and Dad's backyard. It's huge. Mom suggested illuminated ficus trees and candles to be the only light throughout the tent during dancing. Before that, the tent will be well-lit."

"And aren't you getting married underneath the archway in the backyard?" asked Erin.

"Yes. Jimmy, Steve and the other guys will be waiting down there. The archway will have white roses and English ivy intertwined all through it. We'll walk down a white walkway trimmed in white rose petals and leaves."

"That sounds beautiful. Refresh my memory as to who else is in the wedding."

"You know my friends Carrie and Angela, and then there's Jimmy's sister Charlotte. The guys are Steve, Jimmy's brother Neil, and their other bandmates—Sid and Clive. Everyone will be in town a couple of days before the wedding so you'll meet them then."

The group ordered another round when the waitress came back. The table behind them turned up the volume as the whole bar got noisier.

"I just may start going to a different doctor altogether," Tim said loudly. "I don't feel like going to that cardiologist. My problem is my stomach, not my heart. That's what I kept telling him."

"Quiet, dear. The beer is talking now," said one of the women.

Erin was listening again and wanted to know more. Hearing some movement behind her, she knew that someone had gotten up.

"You know that lavender is my main color for the bridesmaids dresses and most of the decorations," Lisa was saying.

"Excuse me for a moment. I have to go to the restroom," said Erin, getting up and not hearing Lisa at all.

Lisa looked at Erin in astonishment as she walked away from the table. "What's wrong with her?" Lisa asked Jimmy.

"I don't know," Jimmy said.

Erin followed behind a short woman with a ponytail as she walked swiftly to the restroom and into a stall. Erin went into the next stall over. They relieved themselves, got out of the stalls, and began washing their hands at the same time. Erin caught the woman's eye and smiled.

"I couldn't help but overhear you at the table. I was sitting right next to you," said Erin.

"I'm sorry. I didn't know we were so loud."

"That's okay. It sounds like you're going through a stressful time."

The woman was guarded. "Yes, some things are coming up soon that my husband and I are worried about. He starts talking about it too much after a couple of beers."

"Sounds like you don't know for sure that he'll need surgery," said Erin.

"Well, Dr. Carroll seems pretty sure about it. Tim is going to the cardiologist next week." The woman dried her hands and smiled at Erin. "I need to get back."

"Good-bye." Erin smiled at her. Her smiled faded after the woman left. "Hmm." Erin walked back to the table, looking at the woman, her husband, and friend as she sat down with her sister and the boys.

"Erin, the guys want to know if we want to go dancing," Lisa said. "What do you think?"

Erin looked from face to face as she was on the spot again. She just couldn't keep up tonight. "Sure, let's go."

The group left the little bar and moved on to a more crowded dance club a few miles away. Erin thought that Steve seemed to press himself closer to her than he needed to. She tried to overlook it, as everyone appeared to be crammed together throughout the place. They ordered their drinks, but there was nowhere to sit, so they went and stood over by a ledge near the lighted dance floor. The bar was noisy, with people talking, and the bass in the music was turned up so loud the windows were vibrating. Lisa was smiling and gyrating in front of Jimmy and it wasn't long before they went out onto the dance floor.

Steve leaned over and put his arm around Erin as he spoke into her ear. "When do you want to go shopping with me for our cute couple's wedding gift?" he asked.

Erin could feel his warm breath on her neck. He was so close it made her feel uncomfortable. She tried to think of her sister and her schedule and ignore her discomfort. The only things she had to do were go to work every day and to the seamstress next Tuesday night. Time was running short, though. She didn't have any plans for the weekend. "Are you here this weekend?" she asked, facing him so he had to remove his arm.

"I don't know, actually. Let me think. We'll be in St. Louis on Friday night and Kansas City on Saturday night." He was squinting as he was thinking. "Des Moines on Sunday. I'll be back here on Monday and Tuesday, then we are off to Minneapolis, I believe."

"Your schedule must be hard to keep track of."

"It is. I can only remember five or six days at a time."

"I guess we should probably go shopping on Monday night after I get home from work." She glanced into those eyes again.

"Monday it is." Steve said, grinning at her. "I'll put it in my mental calendar."

The music changed to something slower.

"Would you like to dance?" he asked.

Erin looked out on the dance floor. Jimmy had Lisa pinned up against a wall, kissing her neck, making her giggle. She didn't have any excuse to say no. "All right."

Steve took her hand and led her out to the dance floor, walking through the throng of people. He put an arm around her shoulders, pulling her close to him, and squeezed her hand as he held it up. Looking into her blue eyes, he smiled.

Erin put her arm around his back and found herself looking up into his face. He had treated her very respectfully tonight and didn't mention the boat incident. Maybe Lisa had been right and Erin was the one jumping to conclusions. She smiled back at him. Relaxing, she found herself not caring how close he was to her, and that in spite of herself, she was having a good time.

CHAPTER 5

MICHELLE'S office building was in a newer part of town on a main thoroughfare. The road itself had just recently been updated to four lanes with a left turn lane in the middle. Dilapidated older buildings had been bulldozed and contemporary establishments had been erected. Large strip malls with grocery stores, coffee shops, phone marts and pizza places could be seen about every three to four miles. There were no empty lots and the area was in constant motion.

The office itself was a two-story building of brown brick, built in the shape of a rectangle with large round windows throughout. Recessed lighting could be seen underneath the overhang of the second floor. A special floodlight shone on the sign. A large red heart with the name of the practice: Mercury Cardiac Care. This office was definitely first class, and at night the special lighting and the building was admired by passing cars.

The first floor held the offices of Michelle and her partner, Dr. Phil Richards. Phil had been in practice by himself and planned on retiring in a few years. He had liked the hotshot young cardiologist with all her energy and ideas for the practice. She came to him, asking to form a partnership, but he didn't know her and she had finished her training at a hospital he hadn't been associated with. Calling some of her references, everyone said how impressive she was with her dedication and skill. Michelle Campbell. "You'd be a fool not to take her on," they said. When he and Michelle had their initial meetings together, they talked about how various heart ailments should be treated. Even though Michelle was new to cardiology, they weren't too off-base from each other on what they saw as the proper treatment. That was very important when forming a partnership. When she wanted them to move from his old office into a new building, he tried to talk her out of it at first, but ultimately moving to the bustling road was a stroke of genius. They were getting so busy that he thought they might even need to bring another partner into the practice. Michelle was resisting the idea of another partner so far, saying she could handle the extra workload as long as she was compensated for it. Wanting to do most of the heart catheterizations and angioplasties, Phil didn't really mind, as he preferred to see patients in the office setting and stick to reading the cardiac testing.

The second floor of the office building contained the cardiac testing equipment. EKG's were done there, as well as the different types of echocardiography and stress testing. The second floor was a goldmine. Most insurance companies paid for the testing without question, and those tests were very expensive. Michelle split the money from the second floor with Phil, even though she did most of the test ordering.

Michelle was starting early this morning. One morning a week she had patients come in at 7 a.m. so they could get their doctor visit in before work. She put her hand in her white lab coat pocket to make sure she had her stethoscope, prescription pad, and pen. Mrs. Harper was her first patient, and Michelle studied the chart for a moment outside the door. Mrs. Harper had had a cardiac cath done last week, but the blockages in her arteries weren't bad at all—not even as bad as some of the other patients whose cardiac catheterizations were modified. There were three blockages, but not a high enough percentage to meet health insurance company criteria for surgery approval. Michelle knocked on the door and went in.

Mrs. Harper was a middle-aged, overweight woman, with gray hair and wrinkles and sorely in need of time off from work. She was in constant stress at her job, working in an office building cafeteria. Her manager treated her badly and the physical labor was getting to be too much, but she had excellent health insurance and benefits, and that was what kept her there.

"Good morning, Mrs. Harper," smiled Michelle. "You're here early."

"This works out good for me, Dr. Campbell. I'll be too beat by the end of the day to do anything except go home and get in a hot bath. I really need some time off and I almost hope that you're going to tell me I need surgery."

Michelle thought for a moment. What she had planned to tell Mrs. Harper just changed. "I may as well tell you, Mrs. Harper. You're going to need a coronary bypass and you should get it done as soon as possible."

Mrs. Harper breathed a sigh of relief. "I'm not surprised or upset. Somehow, I thought I needed one."

"I can give you eight weeks off work. How does that sound?"

"I would love to have time off work. Eight weeks? I can't even imagine it. I would get disability, too, while I was off, so I wouldn't lose any money. These operations are very safe now, aren't they?"

"There is always a risk with any operation, but Southeast is known throughout the Midwest as a hospital with excellent outcomes for coronary bypass. Studies have shown that a hospital having a high volume of any specific surgery is associated with better outcomes."

Mrs. Harper nodded as she tried to understand what Michelle was telling her.

"Coronary bypass is now one of the most commonly-performed operations in the country, and I can honestly tell you that if I needed one, I would have it at Southeast."

"That is very reassuring, Dr. Campbell."

"Patient safety is a high priority at Southeast, too. You'll find the nursing staff is excellent and your care is very important to them. Quality counts at Southeast."

"My heart thanks you," Mrs. Harper, said putting her hand over her heart.

"Have you had any angina pain since your cath last week?"

"No, I've been fine. No pain. When should I have my surgery?"

"I'll give the cardiovascular surgeon's office a call and see when they can fit you in. They'll give you a call to discuss the date."

"The sooner, the better. I want to get it over with as quickly as possible, now that I know I need it. There are a lot of heart surgeons at Southeast, Dr. Campbell. Who is going to do my operation?"

"His name is Dr. David Keller. He's very experienced, and I'm sure you will like him."

"Okay," Mrs. Harper nodded. "I'll trust whoever you send me to."

"I'm glad you're taking this so well. Not all of my patients do."

"Once I've made up my mind on something, I'm ready." Mrs. Harper opened up her purse to look at her prescription bottles. "Should I stay on the same medications?"

"Yes. Do you need any refills?"

"No. I should be good until I see you again. Thanks for being so good to me, Dr. Campbell."

Michelle smiled.

"Should I let my primary care doctor know?" Mrs. Harper asked as she slowly climbed from the table, sliding down one hip then the other until she stood in front of Michelle.

Michelle opened up Mrs. Harper's chart and studied it. "Dr. Edward Carroll is your doctor, right?"

"Yes."

"Give his office a call so they can let him know you're going to have surgery."

"Okay." She shook Michelle's hand. "Thank you, Dr. Campbell."

"Good-bye," said Michelle as she opened the door and left the room. She went into her office and sat down at her large oak desk, making notes on the official chart of the patient. It usually wasn't that easy getting a patient to agree to surgery, but Mrs. Harper had wanted it badly just to get time off from work. What was Michelle supposed to do? That one was just too easy to say "no" to. This unnecessary surgery would ultimately give Michelle and her associates thousands of extra dollars. She took out her Palm Pilot and made a note to call Dr. Jeff Elliott to adjust Mrs. Harper's cath.

The next patient was someone she didn't know very well. Jeb White. He'd just had a stress test done last week and was here for his results. His insurance was Triangle, and Michelle was going to schedule him for a cath. She knocked on his door and went in.

"Good morning, Mr. White," Michelle shook his hand and sat down on a stool near the table Mr. White was sitting on.

"Hello, Dr. Campbell," said the patient.

"I have your stress test results right here. As you know, the purpose of stress testing is to find out if your heart is getting enough blood when you are working it. We worked your heart on the treadmill."

"I started having chest pain," he said, shaking his head.

"Let me read you the report. 'Patient exercised five minutes to a heart rate of 130 beats per minutes. Complained of chest discomfort. Images suggest a small area of inferior ischemia.'"

"Is that bad?" asked Jeb.

Michelle stopped reading and looked up at him. "Do you know what *ischemia* means?"

"No," he said.

"*Ischemia* means your heart is not getting enough blood. There is some kind of obstruction in your circulation."

"So what can we do about it?"

"The first thing that needs to be done is a cardiac catheterization, Mr. White."

"I was wondering if I was going to have to have something like that," he said, shaking his head again.

"Yes, you do. I think I can fit you in next week. Would that be a good time for you?"

"It will have to be, won't it, Doctor?"

Michelle smiled. "Schedule your cardiac cath with my medical assistant on your way out. She has an explanation sheet to give you and can answer other questions you have. I will go over everything with you right before the catheterization."

"If my catheterization is bad, will I have to have open heart surgery?"

"You might. We'll discuss your options after the cardiac cath."

Jeb looked down at the floor.

"Do you have enough nitroglycerin to get you through until after your catheterization next week?" Michelle asked. She stood up and waited for him to answer.

"No, I had better get more."

Michelle took the prescription pad out of her lab coat and wrote him out a new prescription and handed it to him. "I think we're all set. I'll see you next week."

Mr. White nodded.

Michelle went back into her office and updated the patient's chart and her Palm Pilot in a matter of minutes. She went out to the front desk to check how many patients she still had to see. "Stephanie, how many more for this morning?" she asked.

Stephanie picked up the scheduling book and counted as she twirled her long red hair around a finger. "It looks like six more."

"Okay, fine. Is Phil coming in at all today?"

"No," Stephanie said. "He has nothing scheduled."

"Good. After I see the rest of my patients I'm going to run upstairs and read the electrocardiograms before I go to the hospital. Anybody else here yet?"

"Two already waiting to see you."

Michelle turned around and went back down the hall. She was only gone about fifteen minutes and was back at the desk with the two patients right behind her.

"Mr. O'Connell needs to be scheduled for a cath next week," said Michelle setting down their charts on the desk. "Mrs. Cheng needs an echo."

"All right," said Stephanie.

"I'm going upstairs. I'll be back." Michelle smiled at Stephanie.

"Sure, Dr. Campbell." Stephanie couldn't believe the schedule Dr. Campbell kept. She was always busy and never seemed to slow down.

Michelle went to the stairwell and stretched her legs. Taking two steps at a time, she was upstairs in her cardiac testing facility in moments. She wanted to keep her heart in good shape. She had a lot of living to do.

Her technician, Trudy, handed her the four electrocardiograms that needed to be read.

Michelle took them over to the small dictation office. She picked up the first electrocardiogram and reviewed it herself instead of relying on the machine's interpretation. "Abnormal electrocardiogram, normal sinus rhythm, rate 72 beats per minute. Patient has a complete left bundle branch block with T wave abnormality," she dictated. Finishing that one, she went on to the next. She picked it up, studied it and dictated. "Normal sinus rhythm, left ventricular hypertrophy, rate 80 beats per minute." Reading the last two, she dictated and took them out to Trudy. "How many stress tests for today?"

"I have four people scheduled," Trudy said, looking at her list.

"Good. Don't forget that this is my weekend out of town. I'm off tomorrow, too."

"Sure, Dr. Campbell." Trudy knew not to ask any questions. Dr. Campbell had a very ill mother and went to see her once a month for a long weekend.

Michelle left and did a repeat walk back downstairs.

Stephanie was holding up the phone. "Dr. Campbell, you have a call. It's Dr. Patton."

"I'll take it in my office." She walked into her office and closed the door. Sitting down in her black leather office chair, she leaned back as she picked up the phone. "Hello, Charlie."

"Hey, baby, one of your early mornings?" he asked.

"You're up pretty early yourself. I take it you didn't have a late night," Michelle said, reaching forward and getting out a nail file from her top drawer.

"Not too late. I was a good boy. You know Dean Peach, don't you? The internist for Triangle that works over on Harbor Lake Road?"

Michelle was filing her nails and admiring how perfect they looked. She frowned as she thought. "Yes, I know him. Haven't had much from him lately. Why do you ask?"

"I think something may be wrong. He's gotten worse with his referrals. Only two for July. He was doing much better earlier in the year than he is doing now."

"What are you going to do about it?"

"I may give him a call today and see what's up. That reminds me, are you still going away this weekend?"

She stopped what she was doing. "Charlie, why do you even ask that?" She got irritated when he asked her the same question every month.

"I know. I just don't understand why I can't go meet your mother some time. Tell me the truth. Is it because I'm white?"

Michelle grinned as she started filing her nails again. "Yes, she would probably be upset about your lack of color."

"How about the age thing? I am a few years older than you, after all."

Michelle raised her eyebrows. "A few years? How about twenty years, Charlie?"

"You don't have to say it that way. It's not like I'm decrepit. I could help you take care of her."

"I don't believe that for a minute. It's never a fun visit there. I just spend time with her and make sure she has everything she needs. Prescriptions usually need to be refilled and doctor appointments made." Michelle heard a knock on her office door. Tilting the receiver away from her mouth, she called out, "Come in."

Stephanie opened the door. "Dr. Campbell, sorry to interrupt you, but Mr. Mitchell is here. He is in room seven."

"Great. Thanks, Stephanie. I'll be right out." She put the receiver back into position. "Charlie, got to go."

"Okay, doll. Talk to you later." He hung up the phone.

Michelle put down the phone and her nail file and got up to see her next patient.

The clock radio alarm clicked on, playing a song that Erin had never liked. She lifted up her hand and quickly hit the "snooze" like she always did. She gave herself enough time in the morning to be able to hit the snooze twice before she needed to get up and shower. Staying awake, she lay dreamily in bed until the radio went off for the second time. Making herself get up, she put on the blue robe she had thrown over the foot of the bed and tied it. As she opened the bedroom door, feeling half asleep, and stepped out into the hall; she felt a jolt as she ran into another person.

"Well, good morning," said Steve to Erin as they both recovered from the accident.

"Good morning," she said, glancing up at him and immediately wondering what she looked like. "Excuse me, I should have looked before I rushed out of the door." She tightened her robe around her and felt self-conscious.

He looked at her tousled hair and sleepy eyes and thought that she looked good, even in the morning.

As Erin pushed her hair out of her eyes, she noticed that she had smacked right into Steve's impressive looking chest. Her eyes stayed focused on it a moment, and not able to stop herself, she imagined what it would feel like to touch it with her hands—her fingers. She looked at the rest of him and realized that he didn't have much on. Just a pair of blue plaid drawstring pants. Erin was becoming more awake and realized what she was actually doing. *Oh no*, she thought. She hoped he didn't notice her staring at him.

But he did. Leaning up against the wall outside of Erin's door, he stretched his chest and back, encouraging her stares.

"Did you have a good time last night?" he asked, watching her out of the corner of his eye as she tried to avoid looking at him.

"Yes." She wanted to change the subject immediately and get away from him. "Are Lisa and Jimmy up yet?" Looking up the hall, she saw that their door was closed.

"No, I don't think so."

"I have to get ready for work, Steve."

"You'll need the bathroom then. All right. I'll just go downstairs to the toilet, then I'm going back to bed. I'm just going to be a lay-about today. Perhaps we'll see each other later. Jimmy and I will be leaving again tomorrow."

"I don't know if I'll see you anymore today, but I really have to go now." Erin held her robe tightly near her neck and hurried down the hall into the bathroom, locking it. Normally she was so confident. It took her awhile to calm down, and she couldn't understand why.

After going to the toilet downstairs, Steve walked back upstairs, looking toward the bathroom. Erin must still be getting ready for work, as the door was shut. Jimmy and Lisa's door was now cracked open, so he went over to it. Knocking slightly, he pushed it open. They were lying in bed, talking.

"Can I come in?" he asked. Without even giving them a chance to answer, he came in and closed the door. "Sorry, but I want to talk to you a moment." He sat down on the edge of the bed as Lisa moved over to give him room. "Lisa, do you think your sister likes me at all?"

"I'm sure she likes you just fine." She looked at him and waited for him to continue.

"I thought we got on swimmingly last night, but she seemed to be running away from me today."

"We know you're not used to that, Steve." Lisa put her hand over her mouth, stifling a yawn. "Normally they're running toward you, aren't they?"

"So you fancy her then?" asked Jimmy, realizing what the conversation meant. "Lisa's sister? What a bit of a giggle that is."

Jimmy and Lisa looked at each other and grinned, while Steve frowned. Lisa got out of bed and pulled up her nightgown strap that had fallen down. She was very comfortable being around Steve and didn't care how he saw her.

"So Erin was right. You were taking advantage of her on the boat," she said, looking him in the eye.

"If you could have seen her through my eyes, you would know I couldn't help myself. She's beautiful, you know." He smiled as he remembered the day. "I actually couldn't believe my luck with her having too much to drink and all. A beautiful, drunken girl right in front of me. Not like I haven't seen that before." He chuckled. "But I was sorry when she fell asleep for the evening."

Lisa's face registered shock and she smacked him in the shoulder. "I defended you when she complained about your behavior."

"Now wait a minute! I had also been drinking. Maybe I had too much to drink and didn't realize what I was doing," he said, grinning.

"Right." Lisa said and shook her head. "Well, I know your history with women, and I don't know if I want my sister to become a part of it. You can't be trusted. I've talked to some of your girlfriends before."

Steve stopped smiling. "Seriously, Lisa, I really would like to know her better. Believe me, I found her utterly fantastic both on the boat and last night."

Lisa sighed. "Do you want me to tell her you're interested in her?"

He paused and thought for a moment.

Lisa was putting on her robe and stopped. Her mouth dropped open. "Steve, you're in luck because I have an idea. The band is in St. Louis on Friday and Kansas City on Saturday. Are you staying at a hotel on Friday or getting right on the tour bus after the concert to go to Kansas City?"

"The band is staying at a hotel after the St. Louis show. It will only take us a few hours to get to Kansas City the next day if we leave early," Steve said.

"How about if Erin and I come to the concert in St. Louis on Friday and spend the night? That way she can meet Sid and Clive and see our Steve in action. You can impress her with your stage presence."

Steve nodded as he thought about the suggestion.

"She might like to see how you play the audience and then she can remember the way you played her on the boat." Lisa looked at him out of the corner of her eye.

Steve scowled.

"You know how you do it during a show. Telling the audience they're louder than the city you were at the night before. Persuading them to clap more, cheer louder, just because you say so. If they don't do it to your liking, you just shake your head at them until they scream even more for you. Don't take that microphone away from Steve until he's ready to give it up and don't take the spotlight off of him at any time."

Jimmy laughed. "She knows you, doesn't she, Steve?"

"Don't slag me off. My behavior is all in fun and just a part of the stage show. I'm the front man and the audience enjoys it. You know that."

Lisa raised her voice. "The bottom line is, don't be a scoundrel to my sister. She just ended a relationship. If I try to help, I expect you to treat her good."

"I will. I promise."

"Are you sure you want Erin seeing a show?" asked Jimmy, looking at Lisa. "You know how some of the girls in the audience get over him. It may not impress her at all."

"It's not like Erin ever suffered for lack of attention either," said Lisa. "Erin and Steve are both used to getting everything they want." She crossed her arms and grinned. "This might be quite interesting to watch."

"It should be a hoot," said Jimmy, smiling.

Steve glared at them. "Don't be so smart."

Lisa sat down on the edge of the bed, thinking out loud. "Erin and I will fly out after she gets home from work and get a room at the hotel you're staying at. We'll meet up with you at the venue for the sound check and stay for the show. Then we'll go back to the hotel and leave in the morning before you go to Kansas City." Her face brightened. "How does that sound?"

"Good," said Jimmy, nodding.

"All right," said Steve.

"Remember, Steve, you don't have much time to make an impression on Erin before the wedding. Once it's over, we're not staying at my mom and dad's house anymore. Who knows when you'll get to see her again."

Steve pondered this and nodded. "I'll do whatever it takes."

Hanging up the phone after talking to Michelle, Charlie started going through his email, deleting things that weren't important. Some days he must get fifty new ones, and most he had to just skim through because he never had the time to totally read them. He heard a noise and looked up from his work. It was Susan, standing in the doorway, leaning against it with one arm up, playing the vamp, just like in the movies. Her hair was up in a French twist the way he liked it and she had on a short pink dress and heels. She looked pretty good and was giving him the evil eye, but smiling.

"Charlie, you owe me money," she said in an even voice.

He sighed and was relieved to know that was her problem the last couple of days. It was his fault, as he wasn't very good at remembering child support. Charlie looked behind her for anyone within earshot. "Susan, get in here! Don't let anyone hear you say that."

She came into the office and stood in front of his desk with hands on her hips.

"How's the little rugrat?" he asked.

"He'd be better if his daddy would come visit him sometime."

Charlie paused and thought for a moment. Michelle would be gone this weekend. "I'll tell you what, Susan. I'll come and visit you and Trevor on Saturday. How's that?" Standing up from his desk, he approached her. He spoke a little softer now. "Maybe I'll even spend the night." Lifting up his eyebrows, he gave her a sly smile, thinking that would make her happy.

It did, but she couldn't help but be sarcastic. "We can pretend we're a family for the night."

"Oh, Susan, that really hurts." He put his hand on his heart and tilted his head.

"I want a check now, Charlie. If you don't start paying me on time I'm going to take you to court. I'll make you take a paternity test and we'll make this all official so I'll get my money on time."

"I don't think that's necessary right now, Susan. How much do you need today?" Charlie walked back to his desk and got his checkbook from his briefcase. He was facing the front of his office and thought he saw his boss, Bruce, outside. Bruce went around the corner and didn't stop at Charlie's office. Charlie sighed in relief. He looked at Susan for her answer.

She walked over to the same side of the desk he was on. "I'll take $1,000," she said without blinking.

"Didn't I give you $800 last time?"

"The economy is bad. I need the extra money."

He wrote out the check and handed it to her, all the while making sure no one walking by could see them.

"We can have fun Saturday, Charlie. Trevor and I will be looking forward to it." She folded the check in her hand and turned to leave. As she reached the door, she looked around at him and talked loud enough for a passerby to hear. "Doctor, the letters are almost ready for you to sign. I'll bring them in after lunch."

"Okay, Susan, thank you," Charlie said, going back to work, thankful that things would be all right with her for a while.

Erin was desperate to get started at work today. Her encounter with Steve had her so flustered that she needed to get involved in something right away to take her mind off him. He was all she could think of driving in, and she couldn't understand why. She kept replaying the hall experience over and over in her mind and couldn't believe she had embarrassed herself so badly once again. He had actually caught her staring at his body. Good grief, she felt like such an idiot! The elevator opened and she got on. Thankfully, it didn't stop until it reached her floor.

Going by her mailbox, she saw a big manila envelope from the Data department in it. This must be the information she had requested. Pulling it from the small rectangular box, she quickly walked to her desk and opened it. There were about fifty pages of lists of doctors and the drugs they had prescribed during the month of July. She began to boot up her computer and leaned down to put her purse in the bottom drawer of her desk. Erin didn't see the little lady walk toward her, down the row of cubicles, and stop until she looked up.

"Hi, Doctor, I haven't been introduced to you yet, so I thought I would do it myself." She was petite, round, and cute. A middle-aged lady with short, curly red hair and glasses.

Erin stood up and held out her hand. "I'm Erin Tyler. I just started here on Monday."

The lady smiled. "My name is Polly. My cubicle is at the end of the row," she said, pointing to it.

"And what do you do here?"

"Oh, I'm a nurse. I do special projects like what you're doing while you're here, but I'll be retiring next year."

"Well, I've always said, if you need to know something, ask a nurse. They know everything."

Polly laughed. "I don't know if this nurse knows everything or not, but I'll sure try to help you if you need it. Just ask me." She turned to leave. "Well, nice meeting you, Dr. Tyler." Polly walked down toward her own desk.

Erin thought of something. "Polly, I do have a question."

Polly turned around. "Yes?"

"I was wondering what happened to the Dr. Kramer that used to sit here. There are some papers and other things still in the desk that must have been his."

Polly walked closer to her and lowered her voice to almost a whisper. "What happened to Dr. Kramer is a big secret." She looked around the corner of their row to see if anyone was within listening distance and came back to Erin. "We really don't know what happened to him. One day he was here and the next day he was gone. We never got an explanation. It was all a little weird."

"Really?"

"Dr. Kramer had been acting funny for a couple of weeks. Looking nervous, you know, real jumpy. He was always wound too tight anyway, if you ask me. He was called away from his desk the last day he was here and he went into Dr. Patton's office for over an hour. When I came in the next morning, his personal items were gone. That was that. No one said anything. It was like he never existed." Polly threw her arms up in the air. "Oh, no! I shouldn't have told you this stuff. Aren't you Dr. Rich Tyler's daughter?"

Erin nodded. "Yes, I am, but don't worry. I won't say anything."

Polly put her hand over her heart. "Good. Thank you. Well, I had better get to work. See you later," she said, smiling at Erin as she sauntered back to her desk.

Erin had to remember to ask her father about Dr. Kramer, as she was sure he must know something. Putting her physician lists for prescriptions in a pile on her desk, she began her organization. She decided to start with the narcotics. The lists showed one doctor's name on the left and everything he had prescribed for the month. The names were in alphabetical order. A few things here and there for the same doctors. When she reached the P's, the only name listed was Peach, one of the primary care doctors. There were many prescriptions for OxyContin listed. She counted them: 24 prescriptions written for the month. Erin looked at the names of the patients and their ages. Many of the names were the same. He was writing prescriptions for a high strength and up to 180 pills at a time every couple of weeks. Some of patients were in their thirties and some in their eighties. That didn't make any sense. Why would so many of them be getting OxyContin? She looked through the other drug category lists, but didn't see anything that looked like it could be excess for Dr. Peach. The phone rang and she picked it up.

"Erin Tyler."

"Hi, Erin, it's me," said Lisa. "Are you working hard?"

"As a matter of fact, I am. And what are you doing?"

"Jimmy, Steve, and I just finished breakfast," she said. "They decided to leave early tonight and meet up with the rest of the band to practice a couple of new songs they have been working on. Anyway, we were talking and thought it would be fun for you to see the guys in action giving a concert. You need to meet the rest of the band, and it might be nice to meet them before the wedding. That way, when you see them again you'll already know them a little bit."

"When are you talking about doing this?"

"Tomorrow. They'll be in St. Louis. We can go there in the afternoon. You just have to leave work a little early."

"I just started this job. How can I leave early?"

"It's Friday. Doesn't everyone leave work early on Friday?"

"I can tell you haven't had a job with regular hours for a while. No, everyone doesn't leave work early on Friday. Lisa, I don't think I should. I certainly don't want anyone to think I get special treatment because I'm Dad's daughter."

"Can't you just come in a little early and not take a lunch?"

"Well," Erin contemplated, "I'll have to check with Dr. Patton."

"Great. It's a done deal. I already made plane reservations anyway. Our plane leaves the airport at 2:28 p.m. It arrives in St. Louis at 3:10 p.m., their time. It's an hour earlier than here."

"It seems you weren't giving me a choice in the matter. What are we going to do when we get there?"

"We'll check in at the hotel, go to the sound check, and then the concert. We're leaving the next morning, because they're going to Kansas City early," Lisa explained.

"All right. I guess I'll go, but I can't talk any longer now. I'm trying to work. I'll see you tonight.

"Bye," said Lisa.

Erin got up from her desk and walked around the corner and down a short hallway to Rich's office. His office was right next to Charlie's. Looking up from his desk when she entered, she noticed he was on the phone. He motioned for her to come in.

"Okay, Charlie, sure. All right. Good-bye." Rich hung up the phone. "That was Charlie, delegating again. One of his strong points," he deadpanned.

Erin laughed. "He's really quite a character." Changing to serious, she said, "Dad, I still think it was him I saw that day we were going miniature golfing. I know we were driving away and I didn't really have a good look, but I swear it was him."

"Like I told you that day, he was at an evening meeting in Detroit. It couldn't possibly have been him," Rich reiterated. "So did you come in just to visit, or did you need me for something specific?"

"A couple of things, Dad. Do you know what happened to Dr. Kramer?"

Rich leaned back in his chair and put his palms together, thinking back to the day Dr. Kramer left. "Erin, I'm a little hesitant talking about this with you. These things generally aren't discussed. I know Charlie wasn't happy with Dr. Kramer, as he complained about his lack of initiative and poor work performance a number of times. Dr. Kramer just never showed up again after being in Charlie's office one day. We assume he was fired. These things happen in a big office like this. People are fired, just not very often."

Erin still thought there was more to the story, but she would let it go for now. "Dad, I found a doctor who seems to be prescribing an awful lot of OxyContin in a month. It is one of the most expensive drugs we have, and as you know, has a high street value and is extremely addictive. Do you know Dean Peach?"

"Dean Peach. Yes, I think I do. He's over near Mercury Memorial, I believe. Are you going to give him a call, or go over there?"

"Charlie wanted me to go over there. I think I'll have someone look up these patient's first and see what information I can find out about them in the computer. I want to be as knowledgeable as possible," stated Erin.

"True, but let me warn you about how careful you have to be. Don't accuse him. You have no proof of anything yet. Just say you're there collecting information. That you're concerned about how many of his patients need OxyContin, for example. See if he will volunteer any information. If not, we'll just send for his patients' medical records and scrutinize them here. He has to give us his records, because it's in his contract. Just let him know that confidentiality has always been strictly followed here, even before the government got involved in this issue. We take this responsibility very seriously, and when we're done with patient records, they're shredded."

Erin smiled. "Thanks, Dad."

She got up and walked out of his office and back to her desk. Polly showed her how to look up the patients on the computer system. Luckily, there were only two screens she needed to look at. The screens brought up their name, age, primary care doctor and last diagnosis. One of the thirty-year-olds got a total of 360 OxyContin tablets in one month for a diagnosis of back pain. No amount of back pain can justify 360 OxyContin a month. There was definitely a problem with that one. Another one of the patients was 86-years old and his address was in a nursing home down the street from Triangle. He was Medicare primary with Triangle as his secondary insurance. Why would a man with a diagnosis of pulmonary disease who was living in a nursing home need OxyContin? And then Erin saw something else. He had an end date for his insurance and a code by it. She got up to ask Polly for help again.

"Need something, Dr. Tyler?" asked Polly as she looked up from her work.

"Yes, Polly. I just want to know what something means."

They walked back down to Erin's computer. Erin pointed to the three-letter code of DEA after an end date of 2/15.

"That code means death," said Polly. "The member died on 2/15."

CHAPTER 6

ERIN was on the road in her father's black Mustang, enjoying the swift ride it provided. What a fun car to drive! She could see why he loved it. As she neared Mercury Memorial Hospital, she squinted and saw it at a distance, with its old, tall brick chimneys stretching to the sky. Lisa had put the new Odyssey compact disc in the car for Erin to listen to, and she liked what she had heard so far as she drove. She turned it up louder. Steve did have a really good voice. It was such a strange feeling to realize she knew the band and one of them was going to be her brother-in-law. She was so glad she hadn't run into Steve again last night. He and Jimmy had already left by the time she'd gotten home from work and she was able to relax with her family again.

Nearing the older, run-down part of town where Dean Peach's office was, she looked at the address again on her notepad. 31456 Harbor Lake Road. Glancing out the window as the addresses went by, she knew she was getting close. She saw a small, dark building up ahead on her right. It appeared to be three stories high, but it looked aged and unkempt. Erin looked at the sign out in front, displaying the businesses inside. A bank, an auto insurance company. There it was! Dr. Dean Peach, Suite 210, Internal Medicine. She turned into the splintered parking lot. It looked as if it had never been resurfaced, as there were weeds growing through the cracks and multiple areas where the asphalt was totally crumbled. What a mess! Parking at the front entrance of the building, she sat in the car a few minutes, trying to get up enough nerve to go in.

Calling Dr. Peach's office yesterday afternoon, she had talked with Sara, his receptionist. Dr. Peach got on the phone and was very pleasant to her when she told him she was visiting on behalf of Dr. Charles Patton. "Please visit," he said. Telling him that she just wanted to come over and ask him a few questions, he didn't seem to mind at all. She wasn't really sure what she was going to say. It would come to her when she started talking to him. Forcing herself to get out of the car, she looked all around her. Pawn shop on one side of the building, car graveyard on the other... Definitely locking the car doors in this neighborhood. She walked inside the building and saw that the wallpaper was peeling in a few areas and the carpet was dirty. There was not a soul around. Afraid to get on the elevator alone, she decided to walk up the stairs instead. His office was right off the stairway, and she opened the door and went in.

There was one elderly man in the small waiting room, slouched down in his chair, watching television. Sara was behind the sliding window at the front desk. She looked up at Erin when she walked in, but looked back down to her desk again and didn't open the window. Erin went over to it and waited for a moment, staring at Sara, hoping she would look up again.

"Can I help you?" asked Sara, finally glancing up and opening the window.

"I'm Dr. Erin Tyler from Triangle Health Plan. I talked with you and Dr. Peach yesterday. He told me to come at 11 today."

Sara confirmed the time on her clock on the wall. "Let me go ask Dr. Peach if he can see you now. Please sit down." Sara got up and disappeared out of sight.

Erin sat in a hard chair and looked around the office. Everything about the place was disagreeable. The waiting room was so small that Erin didn't know how more than three or four patients could even fit in there. She noticed a wall socket without a cover and a lamp with a torn shade. She looked up as Sara called her name.

"The doctor can see you now. His office is down there," Sara said, pointing to a cubbyhole at the end of a narrow hall.

Erin walked into the tiny office and a skinny man got up from behind an old metal desk, stacked with patient charts and medical magazines. His hair looked oily and was parted down one side and combed over to the other. He had small, horn-rimmed glasses and a rumpled, dirty white lab coat on. Putting his hand out for her to shake, he smiled at her. She somewhat reluctantly shook his hand.

"Please sit down." He motioned for her to take a chair angled toward his desk. He sat back down, but seemed to lose his balance somewhat. His backside almost missed his chair. "Hello, Dr. Tyler. Dr. Peach here. So how's old Charlie?" He gave her a toothy grin.

"Dr. Patton is fine," Erin said evenly, not knowing how to begin.

"I imagine that he did send you. I was wondering when I was going to get a call or a visit from him, as he doesn't have the time now to check up on his people. When did you start working for him?" Dr. Peach asked.

"I just started last week at the office. Perhaps you know my father, Rich Tyler. He's a medical director at Triangle."

"Only met him once or twice," said Dr. Peach. Changing the subject, he said seriously, "I'm doing the best I can, you know. I don't have many patients, especially ones I can send to Michelle."

Erin didn't know what he was talking about. She was totally perplexed. "Dr. Peach, I'm not sure what you are referring to."

"You know." His voice began to rise. "Do I have to spell it out for you?" He looked at her, frowning, then what color he had in his face seemed to drain as he realized what he had done.

"I am here, Dr. Peach, to talk to you about prescription writing practices." Erin stared intently at Dr. Peach and waited for a response.

It seemed to take a few moments for the sentence to sink in. He stood up from his desk, looking quite shaky, and hissed at her. "Get out!" He pointed toward the door and came around to her side of the desk.

Erin was afraid he was going to strike her. He didn't have to tell her twice to leave. She got up quickly and exited the room, office, and building as fast as she could. There was no looking back. Getting into her car, she locked the doors and drove off the premises as quickly as possible.

Charlie sat at his desk, quietly contemplating his moves for the weekend. Michelle would be leaving for Boston to see her mother, so she was out of the picture. *Maybe I'll hit a casino with David Keller,* he thought, breaking into a smile. He would have to give David a call later on today. Charlie took a finger and tapped it on his cheek, thinking. He planned on spending the night at Susan's house on Saturday, so that night was booked. Michelle would be back on Sunday afternoon, but she was always really tired when she got back from her mother's and never wanted to see him that night. Maybe he should stay home on Sunday anyway and do some laundry. The silence was broken by the phone ringing.

"Dr. Patton," he said picking it up.

"This is Dean Peach. Charlie, what the hell are you doing?" Dean was furious.

"Dean, ol' boy, settle down. What are you talking about?" Charlie was confused.

"You sent that girl to see me. What was her name? Tyler, that's it."

"Erin Tyler was out to visit you? Why?" Charlie truly didn't know for a moment.

"Obviously here to nose around. She said she was sent by you."

"Erin is working on a project for me. A prescription project. Did you give her a chance to tell you what she wanted?"

"Er, I let a few things out before she said that."

"Dean, you're an asshole! What did you say?" Charlie was now getting worried.

"I told her that I didn't have many patients I could send to Michelle. She didn't seem to know what I was talking about and I realized that, so I shut up."

"Obviously not quick enough. Hopefully she won't retain that information. Did she ask you any specific prescription questions?"

"No, I didn't give her a chance. I threw her out."

Charlie could only shake his head. What a son-of-a-bitch this man was. "Well, I was planning on calling you anyway. You're numbers are down and I was wondering why."

"I just haven't seen many patients with potential cardiac problems, that's all."

"Just tell your patients anything to get them into Michelle's office. I don't care what you do. Get them over there!"

"All right."

"What drugs are you over-prescribing that Erin would be coming to your office about?"

"Don't know. I can't think of anything out of the ordinary."

Charlie thought he sounded evasive. "That tells me nothing. So is that the story you're sticking to?"

"Yes. I have nothing further to add."

"I'm sure that Erin will be coming to me with this information. You're lucky that you let me know about it. I am keeping track of everything you do, you know? You have to work for your money like everyone else. If you don't perform, you're out. Have I made myself perfectly clear?" Charlie was firm.

"Yes."

"Good-bye, Dean. Let's not have any more incidents like this again." Charlie hung up the phone. He hoped that Dean hadn't really screwed things up. Erin seemed pretty sharp.

After leaving Dr. Peach's office, Erin started driving back to Triangle, but decided to make a quick stop at the drugstore to pick up a few things for her trip.

She didn't feel like going back to the office, as she had been there since 7:00 a.m. and had been working steadily until she left for her visit with Dr. Peach. Thinking she should give her dad and Charlie a call to update them about Dr. Peach's behavior, she made her purchases and got back into her car. She took her cell phone out of her purse and called her father.

"Dr. Tyler," he said, picking up his phone.

"Dad, its Erin."

"How did your visit go?"

She proceeded to tell him what happened.

"I think he definitely requires more investigation. We'll send him a letter, explaining why we want the charts, and pull the ones on your list into the office. He has no choice but to comply," said Rich. "We can also request the nursing home patient chart. Then we can see if the charts of the Triangle patients that he wrote prescriptions for detail why he wrote the prescription, and for how much of the drug. We can then assess the situation better and decide if something is suspicious."

"I'm concerned that he seemed dizzy, or maybe uncoordinated, trying to get into his chair. Do you think he may be using the OxyContin?"

"I don't know. It can be hard to tell."

"What do you think of the other things he said about 'sending patients to Michelle?' Who is Michelle and what patients is he sending her?"

"Probably just minor referral issues. I don't think he has a busy practice. We are definitely going to do more investigation on him, though, for the drug issues. You should probably update Charlie. Are you coming back to the office now?"

"I don't want to. Our plane leaves soon and I need to get to the airport at least an hour early." She looked at her watch. It was noon and she hadn't packed her carry-on yet. "When I call Charlie, I'm going to ask him if I can just go home now."

"Okay, you girls have fun. We'll see you tomorrow," Rich said.

"Bye Dad."

Erin hung up from him and called Charlie.

"Dr. Patton," he answered on the second ring.

"Dr. Patton, its Erin Tyler."

"Hello, Erin. How are things going?"

"Not so good." She told him the full story of Dr. Peach, including the part where he almost lost his balance sitting back down. She left out the part about Michelle, as she decided that would require further investigation. Something just didn't seem right about the conversation.

"That certainly didn't work out well for you. I apologize for Dr. Peach's rude behavior. We will investigate him, of course."

"Dr. Patton, I have a favor to ask."

"Yes?"

"I'm going to St. Louis this afternoon, and I was hoping I wouldn't have to come back to the office now. I still have a few things to do before my flight." Erin was crossing her fingers.

"Sure, go on home. Have a nice trip."

"Thanks, Dr. Patton. I really appreciate it." Erin hung up the phone, relieved. She wasn't going to think of work anymore for awhile as she turned on the car and started driving back to her parents. When she arrived, she could hear talking in the kitchen. Her mother and Lisa were discussing the wedding.

"The tent is white. Is that okay, honey?" asked Arlene, looking at her list.

"Sure, Mom, that's fine. I don't know if I told you, but I picked up the lavender candles last week. They're all in boxes in the back of the garage. I want to smell lavender throughout the tent."

Erin walked in on them.

"Wedding planning, I see." Erin smiled. "If there's anything I can help with, let me know."

"Thanks, Erin." Lisa looked at the mantle clock. "You're home a little early, aren't you?"

"Yep. I'm running upstairs to take a shower and get packed. Are you all ready?"

"I'm always ready. I've done this quickie trip thing more than I like to admit. It's a pain sometimes, but I'm used to it."

"All right. I'll be back down within the hour and we'll leave." She raced upstairs to get ready. When she got to the top of the stairs, she wondered why she felt so excited.

The plane arrived in St. Louis without incident. The sky was somewhat overcast, but the guys were playing at an indoor venue, so rain wasn't a worry. Erin and Lisa took a cab and checked into a historic downtown hotel. Erin went up to her room to leave her things and briefly freshen up. Jimmy had already been up to the room he and Lisa were sharing and had left their backstage passes there. Erin and Lisa put the laminated rectangular passes around their necks and were off.

As they took a cab over to the venue, Lisa started to quiz Erin.

"What do you think about Steve?"

"He was nice to me when we went out to the bar the other night."

"So you've forgotten about the pontoon boat day?"

"I'm trying to."

"Do you think he's cute?"

Erin thought a moment before she answered. "I guess, but there's something about him that makes me nervous."

"Don't let him. He's okay. By the way, he told me he thinks you're beautiful."

Erin looked at Lisa out of the corner of her eye, but didn't say anything.

Arriving at the venue, Lisa paid the cab driver and they went up to the locked front door. She rang a doorbell located on the right side of the door as they waited for someone to let them in. It was 4:00 p.m. and it would still be a few hours until the show started. An elderly man with a cigar hanging out of the corner of his mouth opened the door, checked their passes, and let them in.

Erin followed Lisa, who seemed very comfortable in a place she had never been to before. As they walked down the center row of the venue toward the raised stage, they saw Steve and two other men emerge from a closed door to the right of it. Steve saw them, whispered something to the other men and rushed over.

He smiled at Erin and spoke. "I'm glad both of you made it. Lisa, the caterers just brought the food, and Jimmy is in the back eating." He motioned his head twice toward the exit at Lisa.

Lisa understood the signal. "I'm going to find Jimmy," she said as she took off, leaving Steve with Erin.

Steve tried being friendly right away. "Would you like to meet the rest of the band? That's them talking to the roadies by the stage." He gestured to the two guys he had come out with.

"Sure."

They walked over to the stage and the band members turned around.

"Erin, this is Sid, our drummer," Steve said, nodding to Sid.

Sid shook hands with Erin. He was thin and tall, with multi-layered dark brown hair and black glasses.

"Hello," he said and smiled cordially. "It's great to finally meet you. We've heard quite a bit about you." He looked at Steve and suppressed a laugh.

Steve scowled at Sid.

"You have?" asked Erin, thinking that Lisa must have talked about her before. "Nice to meet you, Sid."

"And my other mate here is Clive, who plays bass," said Steve.

Clive came over and shook Erin's hand, too. He wasn't as tall as Sid, but had dark hair that hung in loose curls that any woman would love to have. "Hello," he said nodding at her and smiling.

It was getting noisy, as the roadies were moving in the rest of the equipment from the three huge tractor-trailers that hauled it from town to town. Erin saw large black and silver cases being brought in and opened. What looked like thousands of feet of cable was being run on the stage. She looked up and saw lighting trusses being hung above the stage.

Steve directed Erin over to the door that led backstage to the dressing room.

"When we have a show day, the whole day revolves around the show. You tend to think about it all day. I like to keep busy to get my energy level up for the evening performance. If I have the time, I really like to look around the town I'm playing in. I was hoping I could persuade you to go with me for a bit."

Erin took a deep breath and let it out slowly so she could relax. Her heart was racing. She looked back at him. "What's there to do in St. Louis?"

"If there's a chance for sightseeing, I look up the city on the Internet, and there are plenty of things to do here. The most notable thing is the Gateway Arch that I'm sure you saw on your way here."

"I saw it. It looks huge."

"According to the website, it is 630 feet high and is the tallest national monument in the United States," said Steve, trying to impress her with his knowledge. "There are also brewery tours, an historic district, botanical gardens, and many other things. We can do whatever you wish."

Erin decided to go with him. He had done some homework on the city and was being easy to get along with. "All right. I'll go."

Steve also planned a horse and carriage ride as a surprise for Erin. They had a few hours before the show started, which he thought was plenty of time to do at least a couple of things.

"Why don't you go in the back and get something to eat? The catered food is usually very good. I have to check on a few things and then I'll meet you backstage," said Steve, motioning toward the door.

She walked over to the backstage entrance and was directed to the Odyssey dressing room by a man in jeans and an Odyssey tee shirt. Looking around, she saw Lisa and Jimmy talking in a corner, so she went over to them.

"How's the food?"

"Good," said Jimmy, taking a bite of a sandwich. "Where's Steve?"

"He said he would be back in a minute," said Erin, looking around at the people in the room she didn't know.

Steve came through the door with a distressed look on his face and walked over to them.

"I apologize, Erin, but I'm not going to be able to show you around like I had wished to. Some of our equipment broke loose in one of the trucks and our people are trying to fix everything. Must have been the dodgy road surfaces. The band will have to do the sound check earlier than usual so the problems can be fixed. I can't leave."

Erin smiled at him. "That's okay. Don't worry about it."

"Thanks for being so agreeable. I'm very disappointed that we can't see the city." He turned to Jimmy. "Come on. We have to go."

Jimmy nodded as they walked out of the room.

"Let's go sit down in front and listen to the sound check," said Lisa. "I think you'll enjoy it." She pulled on Erin's arm, only giving Erin time to grab a piece of cheddar cheese from a deli tray, and dragged her from the dressing room.

They walked down many rows of chairs, bolted to the floor, as Lisa tried to figure out where she wanted to sit. She settled on the second row center area. Other people that Erin didn't recognize sat down in various areas near the front of the venue. Erin saw one man tape something to the floor in four places.

"What's he doing?" asked Erin, pointing to the man.

"That's one of the roadies, taping the set list on the floor for each member of the band. Roadies are some of the workers that are hired by the band for the tour. It's a very hard job. They move the equipment from the trucks to the stage and set it up. After the show is done, they break everything down as quickly as possible and store it back again on the trucks."

Erin nodded as she watched what was going on.

"There are also instrument technicians that are needed for the tour. Each band member has someone to take care of his equipment, so there is a guitar tech, a bass tech, and a drum tech," Lisa explained. "Lighting people, sound people, tour manager, tour accountant, production staff. In each city there are local stage hands, electricians, security, and caterers at whatever venue they're at. I hope I'm not missing anybody, but I know I am," Lisa said.

"There's a lot more to it than I thought," said Erin. She looked at the back of the stage at the huge stacks of speakers and the other equipment sitting on the floor at the front of the stage. There were also boxes of varying sizes with interconnected wires sitting on the floor.

"It's hard to believe the amount of technology that goes into making a concert possible. Look, here comes the band." Lisa pointed as Odyssey came from backstage.

The guys walked onstage and after a few words that Erin couldn't hear started playing one of their songs. Erin was just starting to enjoy it when some problems with the sound developed. All the signal lines for every microphone and instrument were played through in the house and monitor systems. There were still some problems. Some tense moments followed as the guys started to bicker.

Lisa whispered. "Erin, lets go backstage again. I don't want you to see everyone argue." She stood up, knowing that it was probably for the best that Erin didn't see them that way at her first concert, especially if Steve was trying to impress her.

"Why are they fighting?"

"They're perfectionists and the sound isn't right, but they'll figure out what's wrong. Everything is tuned precisely to each venue every day. I should have known better than to bring you out here to listen when they were aware there were already problems. It's my fault."

They walked down the row to the aisle and started their walk backstage.

"Hi, Glenda," said Lisa to a girl that walked past them.

"Hello, Lisa," said the girl and smiled. "Nice to see you."

"Who was that?" asked Erin, looking back at her.

"That's the band's wardrobe mistress. She takes care of all of their clothes."

They found their way back into the dressing room again and sat down on a green leather couch.

"Things have calmed down backstage from what they used to be," said Lisa shuddering. "You wouldn't believe some of the stories I've heard."

"What do you mean?"

"Events, occurrences backstage with women—I think the band has finally grown up. Jimmy said they got tired of the debauchery. How long can you really keep that up? I wouldn't have stayed around if it was like it used to be. The last few years have made a big difference, I hear."

"That's nice to know."

"Until the show starts, I just watch television or walk around the venue. The boys can't do that."

Lisa turned the set on with the remote control, leaned back, and tried to relax.

Erin started thinking again about Dean Peach and what he had said. Something really sounded familiar. He was talking about Michelle and Charlie. Yes, Michelle and Charlie. What did that mean? What was the connection? Who is Michelle? Where have I heard about her before? Then the connection hit her. On Erin's first day at Triangle when Charlie had taken her to lunch, Michelle had called him on the phone. Erin thought Michelle might have been Charlie's girlfriend because of the way he had talked to her. She wondered if this was that same Michelle.

"Wake up, silly. You look like you're in a daze," said Lisa, hitting Erin's arm. "It seems like we've been in this room forever. Let's go out in front and see how many people are here."

Erin and Lisa got up and slipped down a hallway out to the front of the venue. They could go where they pleased with their backstage passes. Walking outside the venue, they saw a line of people stretched around the block that were slowly being let in the establishment. Erin noticed that the band's name was in lights on the marquee. *That must be exciting to see if that's your band,* she thought. When they went back into the lobby, they saw that it was already filled with people who were buying drinks and concert memorabilia. They looked at the things for sale for a few minutes. The tee shirts showed pictures of the guys, with dates and towns of the concert tour listed. There were also posters, wall hangings, and compact discs. Erin hadn't been to a concert in quite a while, and she was beginning to find herself energized to be here.

"Remind me to show you the inside of one of the band's tour buses tomorrow morning. Since the band is spending the night at the hotel, the buses are parked on a side street nearby. If they were leaving directly from the concert venue, the buses would be parked here next to the crew buses and equipment trucks behind the building," said Lisa.

Erin nodded.

Lisa looked at a clock on the wall. It was almost 8, and the first band would be going on in a few minutes. "We had better get backstage. I sure hope they got the sound problem fixed. Come on."

The Odyssey dressing room was overflowing now with the members of Odyssey, the warm-up band, and both bands' management. Everyone was wishing each other a successful show and many pleasant remarks and joking about could be heard, now that the equipment was working properly.

A man came in and got the first band. They left to go on stage and Erin soon heard the crowd applauding as they started to play.

Erin walked around backstage, alternating between listening to the first band playing and hanging around in the dressing room. She liked the way Steve looked with his purple sleeveless tee shirt, black leather pants, and black leather athletic shoes. He was talking to someone Erin didn't know.

Steve saw Erin looking at him and came over to her. "I'm locking myself away for a bit until the show starts. I have to get my voice ready."

"Okay," said Erin, not knowing what else to say because she never knew a singer had to get their voice ready before a concert.

He smiled at her and left the room.

Erin looked all around, immensely impressed with everything she had seen so far. It appeared that everyone was just waiting for the time to pass until Odyssey went on.

Lisa was fixing one of Jimmy's earrings that had come out and was putting it back in for him. Sid was throwing his drumsticks up in the air and catching them, trying to get in the way of Clive, who was watching an old television show.

"Piss off!" yelled Clive good-naturedly at Sid.

The first band ended their set after about forty-five minutes and their equipment was moved out of the way. Erin could hear the audience talking and the speakers playing louder music in preparation for the headlining act until it was finally time to go. Steve was back and everyone left the dressing room, going over to stage right. Lisa motioned for Erin to stand next to her because they would be on stage right throughout the show. The lights were turned down in the auditorium and the manic roar of the crowd began. Sid went out in the dark first and began a hard drumbeat. Clive then started on his bass and Jimmy on the guitar. Steve had his microphone with him and walked out from stage right. White lights suddenly flashed on, illuminating everything on the stage.

"Hello, St. Louis!" Steve bellowed, holding one arm outstretched to the ceiling. The roar in the auditorium was deafening as Odyssey started playing their first tune.

Erin was amazed at the view from stage right. When the auditorium lights lighted up the audience, she could see people of all ages standing, cheering, and singing. Some of the girls in the first few rows were dancing and staring at the respective band member they liked the best. There were quite a few watching Steve's every move.

Lisa saw Erin watching the girls. "If Steve were your boyfriend, you'd have to get used to that. I'm able to ignore it now. Jimmy always has a fan club, too."

Erin made no comment.

Lisa stared at Jimmy and smiled. "Just look at him, Erin."

Erin looked at Jimmy.

"Isn't he sexy?" Lisa put her palms together and watched Jimmy. "One thing I love about him is that he's always so happy. When he's onstage, he is having such a good time, and it shows."

Erin watched Jimmy as he danced around with his guitar, smiling at the audience and throwing an occasional guitar pick. "He's quite fit, isn't he? I didn't notice that when we were out on the boat."

"You were drunk on the boat."

"Don't remind me. Anyway, Jimmy sure is cute." Erin watched Jimmy for a few minutes, moving around the stage in his tight blue jeans and gray tank top and going over to sing into Steve's microphone with him. When Jimmy left Steve's side, Erin watched Steve. The audience responded to everything he said and did. He was quite a showman and Erin could tell he knew it, too. "He's very sure of himself."

"Steve? Yes. He has attitude. Attitude and charisma. You've got to have those things to be a great lead singer. It pours out of him—in buckets." Lisa looked at Erin. "And he's used to getting everything he wants."

The band played for an hour and a half and had two encores. Erin enjoyed it tremendously and surprised herself when she knew more songs than she thought. After the second encore, they came off stage and Erin and Lisa went with them back to the dressing room. Everyone was exhausted, but wound up from all the excitement. The guys all had towels around their necks, as they were perspiring from the lights and physical activity.

Steve came over to Erin. "What did you think?" he asked her, feeling very confident that she liked the show because the band always did the best they could every night.

Erin looked at him and said sincerely, "I think you guys were great!"

He smiled. "All right, then," he boomed as he faced everyone. "Let's go get pissed on a few pints!"

The band, the girls, and the tour manager Ian left in a beautiful white limousine and were taken back to the hotel. A few of the roadies and techs came to the bar after they loaded the band equipment and others went back to the crew buses, where they slept and lived as they traveled. There were other people in the bar who seemed to be waiting for the band to get there. They must have been fans, as they started asking for autographs and getting their pictures taken with various members of the band. Erin found herself near Steve many times over the next couple of hours. He even put his arm around her shoulders a few times as he talked to her, and she didn't mind. At one point, two girls came up to Erin and asked her if she were Steve's girlfriend. She said "no," and they walked away, whispering to each other. It was getting late and the crowd was thinning.

"Is it always like this?"

"The adrenaline is flowing and it can take a long time to come down from a show. They don't always party. Sometimes they'll just stay up and watch a movie in the hotel or on the tour bus."

"Is he always the center of attention?" asked Erin, noticing how people were still trying to talk with Steve, even at such a late hour.

"Yep," said Lisa. "Ian, the tour manager, directs him if there are people he needs to speak to. Steve is the lead singer and the one everyone wants. Sometimes it seems like it's the King Steve show."

Erin nodded as she watched. "Well, I want to go to bed. I've had an exhausting day." She yawned.

"I think I'm going, too." Lisa said. She turned to Jimmy. "Jimmy, Erin and I are leaving now. We're tired."

"I'm ready." Standing up, he looked around. "I see the lift over there." He started walking toward the elevator.

Erin and Lisa followed Jimmy. Steve was at the bar, talking to a man and a woman, and didn't notice they were leaving. Sid and Clive were sitting at a table with a couple of ladies they had met and looked like they had no intention of bidding farewell yet.

Steve glanced up and saw Erin exiting with Lisa and Jimmy. He had wanted to say goodnight to her properly, and really hadn't gotten to spend as much time with her as he wanted. The people kept talking, and Steve tried to get away. The elevator was just outside the bar and Steve watched as Erin, Lisa, and Jimmy got on and the doors started to close.

Erin saw him looking at her as the doors were shutting. "Thank you," she said, smiling at him, uncertain if he could tell what she was saying from so far away.

Michelle's red Cadillac convertible had two large suitcases in the trunk. One was filled with $50,000 in cash, wrapped within many of her clothes, and the other suitcase held her compact discs, books, and various other personal items that she had decided to take on this trip. On every trip, she took more of her favorite things from home to place in her new apartment. She turned into the valet parking area at the International Terminal and the valet ran over and took her keys. Checking in her suitcases without any problems, she went upstairs. She usually carried about $2,000 cash in her purse, and that was not unusual when security checked, as many people took cash when traveling. Having no problem walking through security, she sat down in the seats at Gate 2 to wait for boarding.

Every month since January, she had been going to Paris, not Boston to see her mother as everyone thought. She was planning on making the move to Paris when CAP was over. Charlie didn't have a clue what was going on, and that was the way she planned on keeping it. She knew he was in love with her, which was even more to her advantage. Michelle was the brains behind the operation, but let him think he was in control.

She had realized she didn't want to be a doctor during medical school, but knew she should continue, due to all the time and money that had gone into her education thus far. Medicine would still be the easiest way to make a lot of money, and she would have to figure out some way to make big money in a short period of time. Cardiology was the gold mine she was looking for.

Her account overseas was now over three million dollars. Swiss banking was wonderful, as they cared about a person's privacy and had a very stable economy, so her money was safe. Large deposits sometimes required personal appearances, but she didn't have to go to Switzerland on every trip, as she was able to wire money into her account in Switzerland from her bank in Paris. She also had her offshore debit and credit accounts through CAP and was listed as the second person on some of Charlie's accounts. One thing she still needed to do before her final move to Paris was get his password.

She had rented an old-fashioned private apartment on the Right Bank in Paris. She had no long-term plans yet, just to get out of the United States before CAP was discovered. After her move to Paris she would figure out what she wanted to do, which would probably include an identity change. She found this so exciting. Everytime she came to visit, it was harder to go back to the United States.

She loved to walk down the *Avenue des Champs-Elysees* from the *Arc de Triomphe* to the *Place de la Concorde*. That was her favorite walk so far. The beauty of Paris could be overwhelming at times. *Notre-Dame* to the *Tour Eiffel* and strolling along the Seine River… It didn't get any better than this.

People spoke English more than ever there, too. She was happy about that, as her French was not very good and she hadn't had the time to take French lessons yet. Nothing had been a problem so far, and everything was falling perfectly into place. It was just too easy.

The announcement over the speaker system called for her plane to begin boarding. She got up to stand in line. Her plane left at 9:30 p.m. in Michigan, but didn't arrive at Charles De Gaulle Airport in Paris until 11:15 a.m. Saturday morning. Trying to sleep all night on the plane, she wanted to be awake in Paris all day. Luckily, her bank was open on Saturday and she could get her business done. Then she continued her search for the perfect pastry as she always did on these trips and shopped at the big designer houses. She loved her Saturday nights in Paris, as all the bridges, monuments, cafes, and signs were illuminated. There were so many choices of nightlife that exceeded many other cities she had visited in the past. It was lonely sometimes, but she would find someone to spend her time with in the future. When she left for home on Sunday afternoon, all the time changes were difficult, especially going back to work the next day—almost 12 hours each way, from Detroit to Paris, and then back again. She always went to bed when she got home on Sunday, and Charlie could never understand why she was so tired when she got home from her mom's house. She just made excuses to him. And then Monday came—a full day of work when she was still way too tired—but the end was in sight. Greeting the flight attendant, she stepped over the threshold and onto the plane.

CHAPTER 7

DAVID had just finished going over the bypass operation with Dale and Jean Michaels, and Dale was now in the operating room getting prepped. David had told the Michaels that Dale's three blocked coronary arteries would be detoured by a portion of a blood vessel from his leg or chest to restore adequate blood flow to the heart. The operation would relieve his chest pain and hopefully improve his quality and length of life. It could take from four to seven hours, depending on how well things went.

An incision would be made from his neck to his navel and David would saw through the breastbone and open up the rib cage to view the heart. Dale would be hooked up to a cardiopulmonary bypass pump, which would take over for the lungs and heart during the surgery. The heart would be stopped and a special cold solution injected into it to lower its temperature. The bypasses of the diseased coronary arteries would be done with the new grafts sewn in place. When David was finished, the patient's heart would be electric shocked to start it pumping again. The heart and lung pump would be turned off and the blood returned to the normal body temperature. Dale's chest would then be closed up.

Dale would be in the surgical ICU for a couple of days. He would be on a ventilator for a few hours, until he was stable, and would then begin normal activities over the next few days. Cardiac rehab, diet, exercising would be taught. He would probably go home in three to four days if he didn't have any problems.

Finishing his electronic charting, David typed notes about discussing the risks and potential complications of the surgery including postoperative bleeding, irregular heart rhythms, infection, stroke, and death. He looked over Michelle's cardiac cath report and the heart films. Dr. Jeff Elliott did an excellent job of altering the reports. Since the cardiac cath was done at Mercury, none of the surgical staff at Southeast would know what had really gone on with this patient. Everything had been changed to show that Dale needed heart surgery, even the actual films that had been sent over. If the reports had included digitized images from the cardiac cath, this patient would not be having surgery at all. The films would have been sent from a Mercury technician to Southeast by a secure website and Jeff wouldn't have been able to change them, but Mercury didn't have cardiac digital imaging like Southeast did. Traditional x-ray film was still used. Michelle was the only cardiologist at Mercury who still did cardiac caths there. Sure, she did some of her caths at Southeast and even admitted that she enjoyed the most advanced cardiac equipment available, but Mercury counted on her to bring in revenue. She did it for the hospital, she said—and a little business called CAP.

This patient didn't have blockages that warranted a coronary bypass, but the conditions were right, as Michelle said. Dale Michaels was basically a healthy man with the mere onset of angina. It could be years before he needed surgery, if ever.

It was all for the love of money.

"Dr. Keller to OR #7," said a woman's voice over the loud speaker in the surgery area.

They were ready for him. Looking at the clock at the surgical desk, it said 7:10 a.m. He got up and walked to the operating room.

Michelle had just finished two cardiac caths at Mercury on this Monday morning before coming to Southeast. She was still exhausted from her trip to Paris and really wasn't in any condition to do surgery, but thanks to caffeine, she was able to function. She knew that David was in O.R. #7, and she wanted to talk to him before she went to her office. Seeing that it was 11 a.m., she decided to have one more cup of coffee. She went to the kitchen and poured another cup and sat down.

Looking at her Palm Pilot, she jotted down a couple of things she wanted to go over with David. Michelle couldn't believe all the money she was making for herself. Almost every patient that came to see her would get a stress test, echo, and cardiac cath ordered. The cardiac cath cash went to CAP if it was a CAP referral from one of the primary care doctors, but she had her own patients, too, that had nothing to do with CAP. These were referred by other physicians. Some patients had legitimate heart problems, and others didn't. Usually, she could at least get some cardiac testing cash from them.

David came out of the O.R. at 11:30 a.m. She saw him walk by.

"David," she called out.

He heard her voice and backtracked his steps.

"David, I'd like to talk with you a moment. Let's go into one of the staff rooms down the hall." Michelle got up and motioned for David to follow her to a small room that was reserved for dictation as they sat down.

"How are you, Michelle?" He looked very tired.

"I'm fine. Let's get right to the point, shall we? I'm sure you're as busy as I am." She set down her Palm Pilot so he could see the screen.

"I just finished a bypass on a man who didn't need it."

"You're not telling me anything I don't know, David. Don't forget that I did his cardiac cath and workup at my office. Think of all the money you just made that you wouldn't have if not for that unnecessary bypass." She was irritated with him already.

David looked down at the table, waiting for her to continue.

She looked at her figures. "I do most of my cardiac caths at Mercury, and at least half of them are now CAP cardiac caths. It looks like you should have at least ten more bypasses this month." She looked up at him and smiled. "Congratulations. As you know, the bypasses are the most expensive, and that will be a new CAP record on your first month."

"Didn't Doug Altman do a lot before he died?" David was somewhat confused. Dr. Altman had been the cardiovascular surgeon in CAP before him.

"Sadly not. He wasn't carrying his weight after he signed on. We were going to let him go anyway."

"That was too bad about his car accident. I didn't know him well, but he seemed like a nice fellow. It makes for one less cardiovascular surgeon in town and another reason why I'm so busy."

Michelle changed the subject. "We've been gradually increasing the amount of coronary bypasses that are done, or someone might get suspicious. Remember that the hospital keeps figures on all the surgeries that are done and what their outcome is. It's all good, David. Remember, CAP is only for a limited time." She looked down at her notes. "Your compensation will be deposited in your accounts later this month, as soon as the insurance checks start rolling in. You'll be surprised at how many thousands of dollars it will be."

David nodded. He could really use the money, as his gambling was getting harder and harder to hide from his wife.

"Do you know how the percentages go for CAP?"

"No, I don't remember. The day we met was pretty intense for me."

"You get 40% and I get 30% of the CAP profit for each month, since we have the greatest risk and do the most amount of work. Charlie gets 10% for doing the depositing and paperwork. Jeff Elliott gets 10% for alterations. The other five primary care doctors involved in CAP each get 2%. Your amount seems fair, doesn't it?"

"Sure, as long as I make the most. I have the hardest job."

"The hospital gets their regular fees that are separate from the physician fees, as you know. The important thing is to have your staff bill immediately so you get your insurance checks as quickly as possible. Fortunately, the health plans in our area all have agreements with the doctors to pay claims within thirty days or they get a hefty fine. The health plans are all striving to pay those claims in thirty days, and I have to say, they are doing a great job at it."

"That's a quick turn-around time," said David.

"The health plans don't even have a chance to really look at the bills well enough to know what they are for. That's why I never get questioned on my cardiac testing claims."

"So when my biller receives the insurance check for the unnecessary surgery, what does she do with it?"

"She would just put it in your regular office account like all your insurance checks. Charlie is aware of what the insurance company would pay you for the surgery, so that amount would then be sent to CAP. He will let you know what amount to tell your biller, who would then write out a check to CAP and mail it to CAP's post office box on a monthly basis. Charlie will deposit your percentage of the check into your offshore accounts and everyone else's percentage into their accounts. If your biller asks questions, just make up something like you're paying off a condo in Aspen. By the time she really starts thinking about this, CAP will be finished so there will be no questions about any checks," Michelle said. "She shouldn't ask questions anyway. Your biller works for you and should just do what you say."

"All right," David said, nodding.

"Our CAP primary care physicians all work together. Two of them actually practice in the same office. All the doctors take a variety of insurance, and before the health plans could possibly catch on to this, it will be over. There's really not that much overutilization of services when you look at all the members. The number of patients who actually have surgery is very small." Michelle loved to rationalize their behavior.

"I see," said David.

Michelle was getting excited. "Look at us. Look at the incentive we have! No one can keep track of health care fraud like this."

"You're probably safe for a while, but eventually someone will catch on."

"That's why we decided not to keep doing this. We don't want to get caught, and we won't." Michelle was adamant.

"I have to check on my patient now, Michelle."

Michelle kept talking. "Don't forget that Southeast should be real happy with you for a while, David. The CEO here has said that more coronary bypasses were needed. Surgical ICU beds have not been full and the extra staff needed for the surgical suites and surgical ICU was causing hospital costs to go up. See, CAP helps everyone," said Michelle happily.

David thought she was nuts. He heard his beeper go off and looked at the number; he saw that it was the surgical ICU. Dialing the number, he listened as the clerk talked a few minutes. "I'll be right there." Something had gone wrong with Mr. Michaels. "Michelle, I have to go to the surgical ICU. It's the new bypass." He got up to leave.

"I'll go with you."

They walked quickly over to the surgical ICU, dodging a group of nurses on their way down to the cafeteria for lunch and a man buffing the floors. Down one hallway to the left, then one to the right. Entering the SICU double doors, they saw a gathering outside of SICU #2.

Southeast had critical care physicians—or intensivists—that worked in the intensive care units of the hospital on a full-time basis. They provided critically ill patients with continuous supervision and gave the other physicians caring for the patient a consultant that could coordinate their patient's care while in the intensive care unit. This was another thing that Southeast did to increase patient safety at the institution.

The day shift intensivist, Dr. Page, looked up as David and Michelle arrived. He spoke to David first, since he had been the surgeon. "It looks like he has had a stroke. A pretty bad one."

David let out a heavy sigh and shook his head. "I was afraid he might have had some atherosclerosis in his aorta. Some of the material must have broken loose during the surgery and caused the stroke."

Michelle didn't say a word. She just stood there, thinking that this was David's problem, not hers. But this problem could become hers if the patient died and had an autopsy. The pathologist would see that the patient didn't have the blockages in his coronary arteries that were documented in her cardiac cath and on the heart films.

"We've already started standard treatment protocol, but we haven't told his wife yet about his stroke. I figured you'd want to tell her. She's in the waiting room." Dr. Page motioned his head to the right. "Sorry, Dr. Keller. Don't blame yourself. You know there was nothing you could do."

David didn't say anything. Not looking at Michelle, he walked heavily down the hall to give Mrs. Michaels the bad news.

"Not good," said Michelle, staying with Dr. Page.

"No," said Dr. Page, shaking his head.

"Wish we were having a better outcome on this one. Speaking of outcomes, how are my patients doing?"

"They're doing great. Everyone's stable right now. I think Vivian Young can be moved out this afternoon."

Michelle nodded. "I'll go take a look at her since I'm here." She looked at her watch and saw that it was noon, and she had to pick up Charlie for lunch. "Dr. Page, I'm on my beeper if anyone needs me."

"All right, Dr. Campbell."

Michelle walked down the hall to visit Vivian Young. She found the intensivists to be annoying. Preferring to write her own orders and be in total charge of her patients, she thought them to be intrusive and bossy. She liked it much better at Mercury, where she was the manager of everything that went on with her patients. Knowing that the intensivists were probably more knowledgeable about a wider variety of abnormalities and were able to intervene earlier than she was, since they were physically at the hospital, didn't matter to her. It was simply a control issue.

Erin was at the office early on Monday, as she had to work on pulling the charts in for Dr. Peach. She had Polly show her a letter that had been sent out in the past requesting charts from a doctor's office and duplicated the letter, but added in that a study was being done on these patients and the charts were needed within a specified time frame. Stifling a yawn, she remembered how busy her weekend had been.

She felt bad that she hadn't gotten to talk to Steve much the morning after the concert in St. Louis. On Saturday morning Erin, Lisa, the band, and a few of the techs went out for a quick breakfast. Everyone had piled in at once to the tables and took whatever seat they were near and Erin and Steve ended up not being near each other. They looked at each other a couple of times and smiled. Breakfast was quick and so were the good-byes because the boys had to get on the tour bus to travel to the next city and the girls had a plane to catch. Erin was going to make it a point to be more personable to Steve when she saw him tonight on their shopping trip for a wedding present. Lisa briefly showed Erin one of the tour buses before they left for the airport. Erin was shocked at how luxurious the huge black bus was. Besides having a living room area, there were roomy bunks with small televisions, a kitchen, dining area, bathroom, satellite dish system, and DVD players. A home away from home it definitely was, and all the comforts were there.

All of the Tylers had a fun time together on Saturday and Sunday. Erin found out more details of the wedding and it was going to be great if everything went as planned. The bridesmaids, Carrie and Angela, came over on Saturday night. Erin hadn't seen them in years, but the girls started drinking wine and reminisced over old times. It was like they had never been apart. They decided to get into the hot tub on the first floor and turned the heat down so it was more like warm bath water. With the air conditioning on in the house, it was very relaxing. Having had a great time, Erin felt the effects again of having too much wine on Sunday morning and allowed herself to lie around all day. Erin yawned again and got up to take the letter to Susan for mailing. Walking around the corner of her row, she saw Susan at her desk, wiping her eyes and appearing to be crying. Erin approached the desk and Susan looked up.

"Excuse me, Dr. Tyler. I had a bad weekend and I can't quit thinking about it," said Susan as she looked at herself in her purse mirror. "This morning has been no better."

"Is there something I can do, Susan?"

"No. I just have to make some tough decisions, that's all."

A door was slammed farther down the hall from Susan's desk. It was either her father's or Charlie's office. Erin looked down the hall and saw her father coming toward her. He stopped at Susan's desk.

"What's all the commotion out here? Charlie just slammed his door."

Erin shrugged her shoulders. "We just heard it, too, but Charlie wasn't out here."

"No, thank goodness," sighed Susan. "I've had enough of him."

Erin and Rich both caught that remark and looked at each other. They heard a noise as Charlie flew out of his office and over to Susan's desk. He was holding up an ivory piece of paper.

"Why didn't you give me this letter sooner?" he yelled.

"I stamped the date on it as last Friday when I received it," she said evenly. "It was on your desk on Friday afternoon and you just missed it."

"This is from the State of Michigan. A patient has made a complaint about us to the Attorney General's office and I needed to know about this the moment it came in," he growled at her.

Erin and Rich were surprised at Charlie's outburst. The letter was received on Friday afternoon. Today was only Monday morning.

"When I saw you this morning I was going to tell you, but you didn't give me a chance," stammered Susan. "You just started yelling at me right away."

"Susan, we have to talk. I want you in my office in five minutes." He turned to leave and walked back to his office but spoke loud enough for everyone to hear.

"You know what they say. 'If it's got tits or tires, you're going to have trouble with it.'" He shook his head and went into his office.

Erin and Rich's mouths dropped open in shock.

Rich was the first to speak. "That was a total breach of decency. I'm sorry you ladies had to hear that from our chief medical officer. I personally apologize for his behavior." He pulled Erin aside. "I have to call Bruce about this. What he said is disgusting and will not be tolerated."

"You have told me his behavior has been getting worse," said Erin.

"Definitely. It's become erratic. Outbursts, mood swings. I think I'm going to start writing these things down. In fact, I'm going to make out an incident report on this. It's going to make waves, but this was intolerable." Rich shook his head and turned to Susan. "I'm running upstairs for a few minutes to Bruce's office. I'll be back shortly." He left the two women alone at Susan's desk.

Susan looked at Erin, with a pleading look on her face. "Dr. Tyler, I think I need some advice. I know we don't know each other very well, but you seem nice and I feel like I can trust you. I have always liked your father and he has always treated me with respect."

Erin touched Susan's arm and said softly, "Susan, what's going on?"

"I'll tell you. Just let me go see what the jerk wants first. I don't want him looking for me when my five minutes are up." She got up, gave Erin a weak smile, and walked toward Charlie's office.

Erin heard the door close and wondered what was going on between Charlie and Susan. She heard Charlie yelling, but it was unclear as to what he was saying. It was only a few minutes until Susan was back at her desk.

"I've had enough. Come on, Dr. Tyler. Let's go find that conference room." She stuck a "Be Right Back" sign on her computer and they left Susan's desk.

They walked down a hallway on the opposite end of the building from Charlie's office. There was a small conference room with a table and chairs inside. It was empty and the light was turned off. They went in and shut the door.

Erin sat down first. She would wait for Susan to start talking whenever she was ready.

She started talking even before she sat down. "He's Trevor's father, you know."

Erin tried to disguise her initial shock. She had no idea. "I didn't know that, Susan."

"Yeah, I was Charlie's girlfriend for almost two years. I couldn't let anyone know about it, of course. It wouldn't look good if everyone found out the chief medical officer was banging his administrative assistant." Susan took out a tissue from her sweater pocket and dabbed at her eyes.

Erin was listening.

"We hid it so well. He would come over to my house and spend the night on some work nights and one night every weekend. I knew he had other girlfriends, too, but I didn't care." Susan started crying softly. "I was in love with him, so I was just happy when he was there. He spent money on me and took me out to eat at nice places and bought me gifts. The only gold jewelry I have came from Charlie." She lifted up her wrist and showed Erin her pretty two-tone gold bracelet.

Erin was disgusted at Charlie. Her first impression of him had been right. He was a pig.

"Then I found out about the drugs." Susan started talking even quieter. She looked up at the door, as if expecting it to open.

"The drugs?"

"Yes. He uses cocaine. I'm not sure when he first started, but after a while he began doing it in front of me and he wanted me to participate. I don't know how much he really uses, but when we were at my house he started snorting cocaine whenever he was over. He would just pour out a little pile on a mirror and use a razor blade to make a line or two, then he would snort it up his nose with a gold tube. He would do it about every half-hour or so until we went to bed. I didn't have any complaints—at first. I even did it sometimes myself, but I guess I didn't like it as much as he did. I had trouble falling asleep. It seemed to put him in a good mood, though. He drank his scotch and water, then we would watch movies or talk about places he wanted to travel to. But I think he started using too much."

"Why do you think that?"

"If the cocaine ran out while Charlie was at my house, he would get mean. I almost got hit a few times. Things would get thrown around my house and he even broke a kitchen chair once. He started getting paranoid and would think that someone was watching him through my front window. I had to always have my curtains closed when he was there. And then I got pregnant."

"The beginning of the end?"

"Yes. He asked me to have an abortion. Triangle covers abortions and no one knew about Charlie and me anyway. It would be easy, he said. I refused. I have always wanted a baby. I was 35, Erin. My chances of meeting the right guy and having a child before my fertility was over were slim. I felt this would be my only chance at ever having a baby."

Erin nodded her head in understanding.

"Charlie started coming over less and less. He still flirted with me at work and sometimes he came over to my house just to have sex. Then I found out he had another girlfriend he was serious about. I confronted him about it one night. All he would tell me was that her name was Michelle and that she was better than I was—smarter, prettier… That really hurt."

Erin hated Charlie now. She didn't know how she was going to be able to look at him again.

"I was getting bigger and bigger. I finally had Trevor, and it was the happiest day of my life. Charlie had stopped coming around at all by that time. He would give me money sometimes, but not on a regular basis. I didn't push it too much, as I make enough for Trevor and me to cover most of our expenses. When I need money, I flirt with him a little and he gives me some. He doesn't want to go to court."

"You need to sue him for paternity," Erin said.

"When he came over this weekend, all we did was fight. He was still using cocaine and he didn't care about Trevor at all. Sex was expected of me. I refused and he got angry. He threw the mantle clock on my fireplace at me and it just missed my head. Charlie was only over for two hours, total. Two hours too long."

"Susan, you need to take control of this situation right now. You can't let him come over anymore. He's done. You need to talk to a lawyer. When we go back to your desk, I'm going to ask my father who he would recommend. Maybe you even need to look for another job and get away from here. Please think about that, too." Erin was disturbed over all the new information.

"I'll think about it. That's all I can tell you for now. I can't think of anything I missed. We had better get back." Susan got up. "Thanks Erin. I feel better, telling someone about what's been happening to me."

Erin hugged Susan. "I'm going to help you. I'll get you a lawyer's name today. Okay?"

"Okay." Susan smiled.

They walked back to Susan's cubicle and Susan sat down to work. Erin went over to her father's office. Charlie was not in his, and Erin was glad she wouldn't have to see that disgusting creep right now.

Rich was sitting at his desk, but he looked up when he saw Erin. "How are things with Susan?"

"Dad, you wouldn't believe how much she spilled to me." Erin proceeded to tell him everything.

"Charlie is worse than I thought. I feel like I must take some responsibility for this. All of us at work have enabled his behavior from the start. He's my boss, so I never said anything, even when I knew he and Susan were having an affair. I suspected that Trevor was his child. I didn't know about the drugs and the abuse, though." Rich was shaking his head.

"Dad, you can't blame yourself. Let's just try to help Susan and Trevor now. We'll have to brainstorm on how we're going to deal with Charlie."

"The drug issues are just allegations. We can't do anything about that."

Erin nodded. "Do you have a name of a lawyer Susan can call?"

Rich thought for a moment. "Yes. Alex Hutchence is a good friend of mine. I'll give him a call about this. He'll help her out." He looked through his Rolodex and pulled out a card. "Why don't you give this to her?"

Erin took the card. "I'm going out of the building to pick up something to eat for lunch in a few minutes. Do you want anything?"

"I don't have much of an appetite now."

"All right. I'll be back shortly." She left his office, stopping by Susan's desk and handing her the lawyer's card.

Susan smiled and put the card in her purse. "Thanks, Dr. Tyler."

Erin went back to her desk to get her purse, walked to the elevator, and left the building. As she walked to her car, she saw a red Cadillac convertible standing in front of the South doors to the building. Erin was hidden by some cars as she was walked by, so she didn't think anyone in that car could see her. Charlie was getting out of the car, and he turned to the driver.

"Bye, Charlie," said the woman with the shoulder-length black hair in the driver's seat.

"See you later, Michelle," he said loudly. He walked toward the entrance without looking back.

Michelle hit the accelerator and pulled away from the door without even checking to see if any people were near her.

Steve and Jimmy were back by the time Erin got home from work on Monday. As soon as she walked into the house, she saw Steve. He was sitting on the couch at an angle so he could see the front door. It made her wonder if he was sitting there waiting for her. He must have been, because when he looked up and saw she had arrived, he came over to her immediately.

"Hello," he said, smiling at her. "Did you miss us?"

"I believe I did," Erin said, surprising herself with her answer as she looked at him and kicked off her shoes. "Are we still going shopping tonight?"

He nodded. "How about if we go out for a quick bite to eat first. I'd like for us to talk and get to know each other better. Are there any places at the mall you would like to go to?"

"There are plenty of places to eat there. When do you want to leave?"

"As soon as you're ready."

"Let me run upstairs and get out of my work clothes. I'll only be a few minutes." She hurried up the stairs and rummaged through her closet, trying to find something that she thought he might like. Trying on a couple of things, she settled on a short jean skirt and sleeveless, yellow knit top. Putting on a pair of braided leather sandals, she brushed her hair and touched up her makeup. This was starting to seem like a date to her and she decided she didn't mind at all. Walking back down the stairs, she looked for him in the hallway and living room, but he wasn't there. Searching through the first floor, she found him talking to Jimmy in the kitchen.

"Well, here she is." Steve looked at Erin as she entered the room. He couldn't help but stare because she always looked good to him.

"Are you ready to go?"

"Yes," he said, smiling.

"Have fun, you two," said Jimmy. He raised his eyebrows at Steve, and grinned, as he could see Steve was smitten.

Erin and Steve walked out of the house and got into the Mustang. She backed out of the driveway and headed out on the main road toward the freeway. It would take about twenty minutes to get to the mall.

"I've always liked how your motorways have so many lanes," Steve said. "It has to be much easier to drive that way. You can move around as much as you want."

"It looks good now, but at rush hour in the morning or the evening it doesn't matter how many lanes you have. They all seem to be full. That's one problem with working so far away from where you live; you're stuck with an awful drive every day."

Steve nodded. "We've been stuck in traffic many times while on the tour bus. I'm glad I'm not the one doing the driving." He looked at her. "So did you have fun in St. Louis?"

"I did," she said, feeling his eyes upon her. Her skirt was pretty short and when she sat down, it went up even higher.

"You'll have to come out for another gig. Maybe we'll have better luck seeing the city next time." He turned his head and looked out of the window for a bit.

Erin thought of something she had wanted to ask him. "Steve, aren't the words for a car's trunk and hood something different in England? I thought I heard Lisa mention it before?"

"Yes. The 'boot' is the trunk and the 'bonnet' is the hood."

"The boot and the bonnet." Erin smiled as she looked ahead at the road. "I love some of your English words."

Steve sat back, feeling quite satisfied with himself. At least he knew she finally liked something about him.

Erin saw the mall up ahead and turned into the parking lot. Easily finding an empty spot close to the door, she pulled in and parked. The mall wouldn't be busy now. It was dinnertime for most people, and the crowds wouldn't be back for another hour or two.

"Where would you like to eat? We have a variety of places here." She turned off the car and took the keys out of the ignition.

"I don't know, actually," Steve said. He couldn't think of a place that he would rather be right now than here with her, so where they ate didn't matter to him.

They got out of the car and walked in together. Erin pointed to a restaurant over to their right.

"This place has a great menu and salad bar that I just love," Erin said. "Would that be okay with you?"

"Right, then. Let's go there."

They went into the restaurant and the hostess showed them to a booth where they had no neighbors. Sitting down, they studied the menu.

"I already know I'm going to get the salad bar like I usually do here. Do you know what you want?" She looked up at him.

"I believe I do," Steve said as he scanned her face. He thought her to be an ethereal, blue-eyed, blonde beauty, and it took him a moment before he was able to refocus on the menu. Feeling already entrapped by her, he was shocked at his own behavior. It was totally unlike him to want someone so bad. "I think I'm just going to have a chicken sandwich and a Guinness."

The waitress came over and took their orders. She was back in a few moments with their drinks.

"Do you know how long you're going to work with your dad?" asked Steve, trying not to stare at her. He remembered that he would only be seeing her for a couple more weeks at her parent's house.

"I don't really like my job, but I haven't told him that. Lisa wants me to move near her and Jimmy. It looks like they'll move somewhere around New York City, as Lisa wants to get a job in the Garment District there for a couple of years before they go back to London."

"They've told me as much. She worked at a house of fashion in London near where they lived. I've seen some of her designs and she really is quite talented," said Steve.

"I agree," said Erin, smiling. "She designed her wedding gown and all the bridesmaid's dresses. I'm going for my fitting tomorrow."

"So if you move near Lisa and Jimmy, where would you work?"

"I'd like to work at a clinic again. Nothing fancy. Maybe a temporary doctor's position. They generally provide great perks and benefits such as furnished housing, and sometimes the positions even include a car. That way I won't be forced to make any major decisions yet about settling down in one place."

He nodded, liking the way things were open-ended in her life.

The waitress brought Steve's sandwich, so Erin went up to the salad bar to get her meal. Steve watched her every move, looking at her cute bum as she walked. A man in line started talking to her as she made her salad and talked with her all the way down the line of the salad bar. Whatever he said made her smile, and Steve actually found himself getting jealous. He wanted to be the one to make her smile. She was back in a few minutes and they ate their meal and talked. Steve thought they got on quite well and he enjoyed being with her. They finished eating, Steve paid the bill, and they left the restaurant and went out into the mall.

"Have you bought Jimmy and Lisa anything yet for their wedding?" he asked as they strolled and glanced into the stores.

"I had a photo album custom made with their names and the date of wedding inscribed on it. It's very beautiful. I hope they like it."

"I'm already giving them a seven-day trip to Carmel, California. We were there once and found it to be a marvelous place to visit, but I wanted to give them something they could keep, too."

Erin nodded. They walked past a travel store that carried luggage and traveling supplies. Erin thought she heard a voice that sounded familiar. It was raised and angry. Glancing into the shop, Erin saw a woman with straight black hair who could be the Michelle that she had seen with Charlie this morning. Looking very fashionable and without a hair out of place, the woman was talking to the clerk at the register. Erin took Steve's arm and quickly directed him into the shop.

Steve didn't resist, because after all, she was touching him. "Where are you taking me?" He looked around, but didn't care what store they were in.

She pulled him close to her and talked very low. "I want to listen to what that woman at the register is saying. I don't want her to see me, because there may be a chance she might recognize me."

Steve nodded his head and glanced at the woman Erin was talking about.

"I know this is confusing," said Erin. "I'll explain later. Let's just go over near there, but I'm going to keep my back to her. I want you to listen, too, in case I miss something."

They walked over near the row that held comfort supplies for airplane rides. Nonchalantly, they started looking through the eyemasks and head rests as they listened to the woman as she talked to the store clerk.

"I just bought this package of electric adapter plugs last week," the woman said. "It is supposed to contain the plugs needed for all parts of Europe, but this plug did not work in Paris over the weekend. This is the one that is supposed to work for all of France. It says so right on it." She held up a plug and the young man took it from her.

He looked at the plug and the label on it. "Maybe these have been labeled wrong. Did you try the other plugs to see if one of them was the correct one?"

"I'm not going to just start plugging anything into a wall socket. What the hell is wrong with you?" The woman was getting loud, but she obviously didn't care. She saw two people out of the corner of her eye and turned around to glance at them, but it was a couple browsing and they weren't paying any attention to her. Not giving them much thought, she turned back around to the store clerk.

When Erin saw the woman start to turn around, she quickly put her arm around Steve's lower back and turned her body into his to hide herself.

Steve didn't mind at all, and he picked something off the rack to look at. He thought things were looking better and better.

The woman took her credit card out of her purse and threw it at the young man behind the counter. "I want you to take these plugs off my credit card! I'll not buy another thing at this store."

"All right," said the store clerk as he picked up the card and began the process.

The woman did another glance at the couple behind her and saw that they hadn't moved, then she turned back around to the store clerk.

The store clerk finished the transaction and had the woman sign the receipt, holding up her card to see her name. "Sorry for your trouble, Ms. Campbell."

"That's *Doctor* Campbell," the woman snapped. She grabbed the credit card from him, put it in her purse, and left the store.

Erin could hardly contain her excitement. She watched as the woman exited the store, then put her arms around Steve and hugged him tightly. "That's her, Steve! Michelle Campbell. The name I needed." She turned around and looked, but could no longer see Michelle. Erin thought maybe they should follow her and leave the store immediately. "Feel like doing a little detective work?"

"I'm yours for the taking," he said happily.

She grabbed his arm and led him out of the store. Looking to the left, she only saw mallwalkers. To the right, no one. Erin started to panic. "Steve, do you see her?"

Steve scanned the people near and far. He saw mothers with children and teens traveling in a group. "Didn't she have on a brown outfit?"

"Great," said Erin, impressed that he'd noticed that. "I didn't even think about what she had on." She started looking for a woman in a brown top and pants and straight black hair. Erin squinted her eyes and thought she saw Michelle over by the sunglass kiosk in the center of the mall, and she grabbed Steve's arm.

They walked toward her briskly, slowing down as they got closer. Michelle was trying on various kinds of sunglasses, having the clerk bring out two and three at a time. She settled on three new pairs. Paying for them with cash, she continued walking in the mall. Michelle went in and out of a couple more stores, browsing but not buying anything. The last store she went in was a leather store. Michelle looked at quite a few new belts and bought two new ones, as Erin and Steve observed from the outside of the store. Putting her new sunglasses into the bag that held her belts, she went back out into the mall.

Erin and Steve continued to follow her. It seemed like she was ready to leave the mall as she opened up her purse and took out her car keys. She began walking toward one of the exits. They didn't want to get too close, as not many people were leaving at this exit, so they stayed back and let her get well ahead of them. The automatic door opened for her and she went outside. Erin and Steve got up to the door and saw her walking in the parking lot. They went outside and down the next row, away from her. She got into a red Cadillac convertible, started up the car, then left.

Erin was so happy that she wanted to jump up and down. The information she had gained was very valuable, and what she saw as a puzzle was starting to fit together a little more.

"I never followed anyone around before today. That was kind of fun," said Steve, smiling at her.

Erin laughed, feeling almost giddy, as she hugged Steve again. "I guess we had better go back in the mall and get your present. Thanks for helping me."

"Right. So the pressure's off then," said Steve, "but I don't know what I did, actually. You were going to explain to me who that woman was."

"Oh, I'm sorry. Let me tell you," said Erin, and she began.

They walked back into the mall and Erin told Steve everything that was going on at Triangle Health Plan so far. He listened intently and nodded his head as she talked.

"Interesting," said Steve. "You'll have to keep me informed and if you need me to play detective again, I will be glad to."

"Thanks," Erin said, smiling, as they continued to walk through the mall.

Seeing an upscale gift store up ahead, they went into it. Erin looked at porcelain picture frames.

"I think a picture frame would be a great gift from you," said Erin. "They could put in a wedding picture, or maybe a picture from the Carmel trip you are giving them. Let's find the perfect one."

Erin and Steve walked up and down a few rows, browsing. Steve found a white 8 x 10-porcelain frame with a raised vine design on it. It was trimmed in platinum.

"This looks like English ivy, doesn't it?" he asked, holding it up.

"Yes, it does. Do you like that one?"

"I think I do."

She saw a matching bud vase next to it and picked it up. "Why don't you get this, too?"

Steve nodded and took the vase from Erin.

They went up to the register and Steve paid for the frame and vase. He wanted them wrapped, and he picked out the wrapping paper he wanted. The clerk took the paper and gift into a back room behind the register and was back in a few minutes with a beautifully wrapped package. Placing the gift in a store bag, the clerk handed it to Steve.

Erin and Steve left the mall and started the ride back to her parent's house. She turned on the radio and Steve noticed that she appeared deep in thought, so he didn't say anything. They arrived at the house and Erin parked the car and turned to him.

"Thanks, Steve," she said, giving him a smile. "I had such a good time with you tonight." Without thinking, she found herself leaning toward his face as she put her hand on his cheek.

He had wanted for her to make the first move, and this being it, he turned his face down to hers.

She closed her eyes. He left his open. It wasn't a very long kiss, but it was exciting for both of them. They got out of the car and Steve put his arm around her as they walked in the front door of the Tyler home.

"I'm going upstairs," she said as they stood in the foyer together. "I have to work tomorrow morning and I have a few things I need to get done tonight."

"Goodnight," he said, smiling and touching her hair.

She turned and walked up the stairs. He stood with his hand on the rail and watched her until she was out of sight.

Steve went into the living room where Jimmy and Lisa were sitting watching television. They noticed right away the look of exhilaration on his face as he sat down on the couch with them.

"Steve," said Jimmy, trying to get his attention.

"What?" said Steve, not looking at Jimmy but handing him the gift bag.

Jimmy looked in the bag and then back to Lisa. "This must be our wedding gift," he said, grinning.

Lisa smiled and turned to Steve. "Steve, honey, we're not supposed to get our gift until the wedding day," she said softly.

Steve just stared straight ahead.

"Lisa, I remember when you were totally reluctant for Steve to even think about seeing Erin," said Jimmy.

"I was only worried about him treating her badly," she said.

Jimmy motioned his head toward Steve. "Look what she's done to him. You don't need to worry about that anymore."

"Looks like he's on a natural high. Erin generally makes an impact on men, but I'm shocked that she has had such an effect on our Steve." Lisa waved a hand in front of Steve's face.

"I don't believe I've ever seen him speechless."

"She might be a match for him."

Jimmy sniggered as he looked at Steve's face again. "You had best get out your lyric book, mate, and start writing down what your face is saying. I think we could get a song out of that."

Lisa nodded her head in agreement as she squeezed Jimmy's arm and grinned.

Steve acted like he didn't even hear them.

CHAPTER 8

ERIN liked getting to work early, before a lot of people were on the floor. The office was quiet so she could think without distraction. The pile of charts that Erin was supposed to be scrutinizing for Utilization Management continued to grow, and she knew that she should be working on them. This afternoon she would definitely start.

She thought a lot about Dean Peach. He was such a slimy character and something just wasn't right about him. Her father had told her that the OxyContin investigation wouldn't really start until Dr. Peach's charts were looked at closely, so there was nothing further she could do with that issue. There had been no member complaints about the man and his physician file was clean. She thought about what Dr. Peach had said about "referrals to Michelle." This Michelle character seemed to be someone important, as she had come up in numerous conversations. Erin started reasoning about what she knew about her. Yesterday Susan had mentioned Michelle as being Charlie's girlfriend. Charlie had talked to Michelle on his cell phone in the bar on Erin's first day at Triangle and seemed to be very cheerful talking to her. There were no harsh words to each other, and it seemed he was comfortable talking to her. Erin couldn't remember what their conversation was about, except that it was short and Charlie seemed happy. After last night at the mall with Steve, Erin knew that Michelle's last name was Campbell. She didn't know what kind of doctor Michelle was, but she had to be a specialist if doctors were referring patients to her. Erin had a few questions and looked down at Polly's desk, but she wasn't in yet.

Gradually, commotion could be heard as people came in and starting talking to one another and their phones started ringing. Polly walked down the aisle and went to her desk.

"Good morning, Dr. Tyler," Polly said, smiling.

"Hello, Polly." Erin thought she would let Polly get settled in before she questioned her.

Polly went to get a cup of coffee and checked her phone messages. She turned her computer on and got out her projects from the day before and looked to see where she had left off.

Erin walked over to her, and Polly looked up. "Polly, is there a way to pull up what kind of physician someone is?"

"Oh, sure. There's a screen code we put in." Polly typed in the code on her computer and a screen came up with an area to write in a physician's name. "What's the doctor's name you're looking for?"

"Michelle Campbell." Erin was very excited as Polly typed in the name and hit the enter button.

"Cardiologist" showed up on the screen immediately.

"She's a cardiologist?" asked Erin out loud.

"Yes," said Polly. "I recognize her name. She's on the other side of town from my cardiologist. I know she has a large practice with another doctor, but I don't know anything else about her."

"Is there any way we could get a print out of Dr. Campbell's member referrals for any given month and who referred them to her?" Erin asked.

"Sure. That is something the Data department can do for you."

Erin frowned.

Polly smiled. "Everything seems to have to go through them, doesn't it?"

"Yes, and every request takes two days. It's sure frustrating when you want information right away." Erin wasn't happy.

"It's the insurance company red tape, and as you can see, it even affects us. But I have no doubt that you know how to fill out that form. Anything else, Dr. Tyler?"

"No, thanks." Erin walked back to her desk and found the correct form to fill out on one of her computer drives. After filling it out, she emailed it to the Data department. Another stumbling block and another wait.

Her phone rang. She picked it up on the second ring.

"Erin Tyler," she answered.

"It's me," said Lisa. "You know we haven't talked about your shopping trip with Steve last night. I just wanted to tell you how bewildered you had him. He looked like a love-struck teenager last night when he came home. What did you do to him?"

Erin thought back to the night before and how enjoyable it had been. "We got along very well, Lisa." She took a deep breath and let it out. "We kissed each other in the driveway."

Lisa laughed. "That must have been some kiss! Steve was dazed and confused for quite awhile, just staring at the television and not even talking. Jimmy and I stopped trying to get any information from him, because it was no use. He even tried to give us our wedding gift."

"Really?" Erin hadn't realized she had made such an impression on him.

"I have to admit that I'm shocked by it all. It's just not like him. Anyway, I just wanted to remind you that your dress alterations are tonight. We need to get over to Cheryl's by 7 p.m."

"No problem. I'll come right home after work." Erin started thinking about Steve again. "Are the boys still here?"

"Until tomorrow. They go to Minneapolis Wednesday and Milwaukee Thursday, then they're back for the weekend."

"I can't believe how close your wedding is."

"Me, either. I'm really getting excited. One week and I'll be a married woman!" squealed Lisa.

"Okay, I should go and get back to work. We can talk later." Erin smiled as she hung up the phone. Lisa was so cute sometimes. Erin thought about Steve for a few minutes, reminding herself how well they had gotten along last night. Could she be falling again so soon? He was easy to talk to and incredibly handsome. And according to Lisa, Erin had an effect on him last night. She sighed as she got up from her cubicle and walked around the corner of her row. Her ex-boyfriend, Chris, was becoming just a bad memory now, but Erin knew she would have to be careful. She needed to take things very slowly. Seeing Susan sitting at her desk going through some papers, Erin went up to her. "Did you make that phone call?"

Susan looked at Erin and smiled. "Yes, I did. I have an appointment with the attorney next week. I'm not saying anything to Charlie. In fact, I'm going to be so sweet to him, he'll wonder what's wrong with me. I'll just let the attorney contact him."

"That's great. Just be professional in your dealings with him from now on."

"I plan on it. Thanks again, Dr. Tyler."

"I hate to bring up a sore subject, but what do you know about the Michelle character Charlie is seeing?"

"Nothing, really. She usually calls his direct office line when she calls here. I don't think I have ever talked to her on the phone myself."

"Is Charlie in yet today?"

"He's here, but his door is closed. If you need to talk to him, I'll call in there and ask him if you can go in. Is that what you want?"

Erin rolled her eyes. "Unfortunately, yes."

"Okay." Susan dialed a number and waited as it rang.

Charlie picked up the phone on the second ring. "What do you want, Susan?"

"Dr. Erin Tyler is at my desk and needs to talk to you. Is now a good time?" Susan looked at Erin and made a face.

"Sure. Tell her she can come in." Charlie hung up the phone.

"He's all yours," said Susan sarcastically.

"Thanks." Erin grinned. She went back to her desk and grabbed the stats on Dr. Peach and proceeded to Charlie's office, knocking on his door.

"Come in."

Erin walked into the office and bit her bottom lip. She hadn't seen Charlie since Susan's revelations yesterday and had to try to be as amiable as possible. "Good morning, Dr. Patton."

"Hello, Erin. Please sit down." Charlie motioned for her to take a seat in front of his desk. The phone was cradled in his neck and he put his forefinger up to indicate it would just take a moment for him to finish what he was doing. He glanced down at his briefcase on the floor, realizing that the CAP disc was lying there on top of the briefcase—exposed, unprotected. She probably couldn't see it from her angle, though, and she wouldn't know its importance anyway. Then he saw some white powder on his desktop. That wouldn't do at all. He nonchalantly brushed it off.

Erin looked around the room, trying to get personal information about him. There was a palm tree in front of one of the windows that needed attention. It looked like it hadn't been watered in a month. He had a small lamp on his desk that was turned on, instead of the full fluorescent lighting from the ceiling. Charlie must like the cozy look, although he was anything but cozy. His credentials were on the wall, as well as a couple of landscape pictures. Nothing exciting. No portraits of any people. Michelle's presence was nonexistent in this room. She had to think of a question to ask him about her.

"All right. Will do. Thanks," he said, hanging up the phone. His attention went to his computer for a moment as he made some notes, then got out of the program he was in and gave Erin his full attention. "So what do you have on Peach?"

Erin handed him the printouts showing the OxyContin prescriptions in July for Dr. Peach. "You can see here that this 30-year-old received 360 OxyContin 40 mg tablets for a 30-day period. That would average out to 12 pills per day. We both are aware that no one would be taking that many, no matter what the diagnosis was."

Charlie shook his head, studying the information.

Erin continued as she moved the papers around. "Look at this elderly man's information. He lives in a nursing home with a diagnosis of pulmonary disease and is also on large doses of OxyContin. According to other information I have received, this patient may not even be alive. What are we talking about here? Fraud? Is Dr. Peach taking these drugs, or selling them, or both?"

"Doesn't look good, does it?" Charlie was ready to kill Peach, and this wasn't the first time. Charlie had caught on before the government did once before and stopped Peach before he got exposed, but now he was doing it again. Peach was the resident doctor for the nursing home down the street from his office and sometimes didn't file the death certificate with the government but kept billing for services not rendered, as the patients were already dead. Charlie thought Peach must be hooked on OxyContin. Maybe he was splitting the prescription with the younger man and getting the prescription filled himself for the older man. He was really messing things up. Charlie had been concerned about him from the start, but Peach was the one doctor in CAP that was already so dishonest that he could easily be recruited. He was becoming detrimental to the works, though, and Charlie didn't know what he was going to do. Peach had already blabbed to Erin, although she might not have caught on to the Michelle thing that Peach had mentioned. Charlie looked up at her.

"I've already sent for these records, so the investigation will start as soon as we receive them," Erin said. "I've heard these things can take months."

"This could take quite a while to sort out before we can be sure what's going on."

Erin stood and picked up the papers. "Do you want copies of these for your files?"

"That would be great. You can just give them to Susan to copy."

Erin started to walk out, but turned around right before she was at the door. "Dr. Patton, I saw you with a woman yesterday. Was that Mrs. Patton, by any chance?"

Her question caught Charlie by surprise. "What woman?" Then he remembered being with Michelle. "Oh, her. I'm not married, Erin. She's someone I'm seeing," he said offhand as he turned back to his work again.

Erin was trying to sound interested in his personal life. "That's nice, Dr. Patton. What's her name?"

Charlie didn't look up from his desk. Erin had him on the spot. "Michelle," he said. Charlie wasn't happy at all that Erin had this information.

"Well, she was very pretty. I'd like to meet her sometime." Erin walked out of Charlie's office. That was the confirmation Erin needed to know that Michelle and Charlie were an item. She went over to Susan's desk and Susan looked up. "Charlie wants a copy of these papers when you get a chance." She set down Dr. Peach's paperwork.

"Sure, Dr. Tyler." Susan looked down the aisles around her desk to see if anyone was near. Not seeing anybody, she lowered her voice. "Remember when Charlie was upset yesterday about the letter from the Attorney General and he yelled at me about it?"

"Yes."

"I have it right here and you might be interested in reading it, because it mentions Michelle and it questions the way a couple of doctors are doing business. Do you want a copy?"

Erin knew she should probably decline, but she couldn't help herself. She nodded. "Yes, I want a copy."

"I'll bring it over in a minute with your other papers." Susan got up, arms loaded with records, and headed for the copy room.

Erin walked back to her desk, wondering what the letter was about that had made Charlie so upset. She sat and waited.

It only took a few minutes for Susan to come down Erin's row. She gave Erin a knowing glance and casually left all the paperwork.

Erin sifted through each page in the pile until she found the letter. She read it over very carefully. It appeared to be a member complaint about a primary care doctor named Edward Carroll, and the Attorney General's office was letting Triangle know about it. The members—Tim and Eliza Collins—claimed that Dr. Carroll told them that Tim was going to need a coronary bypass before he was even evaluated by a cardiologist. Dr. Carroll had referred them to a cardiologist by the name of Dr. Michelle Campbell, who said the same thing. She had scheduled him for a cardiac catheterization next week. Tim kept telling the doctors he thought it was his stomach, but no one looked into that. They filed a complaint with the Attorney General, as they thought something was wrong with the way the doctors were doing business.

Erin couldn't believe what she was reading. Michelle Campbell. This was incredible. *Charlie has to know what's going on*, she thought. *Could it be possible that Charlie was in on this? And for what reason?* She picked up the phone and called her father. His voice mail answered, so she left a message.

"Dad, its Erin. I need to talk to you as soon as possible. Call me when you get back." She hung up the phone.

Something about the member's letter rang a bell with her. She thought back to the week before. When she and Lisa and the guys were at the bar, Erin had been listening to a conversation about someone's doctor wanting them to have a coronary bypass. She tried hard to remember, and it soon came to her. The man's name at the bar was Tim, and the man in this letter was Tim. She looked at the letter again.

The return address was in the same city where the bar they had been at was located. She wondered if this could this be the same people. Erin dialed Susan.

"Susan, do you know where my dad is?"

"He went to Detroit for a meeting. I don't think he's coming back to the office today," Susan said. "Did you get a chance to read that letter?"

"Yes, I did. Thanks for giving it to me, and don't worry. I won't say anything."

Erin hung up the phone. She had gotten some good information today, but she didn't want to stop. Looking down her row, she saw Polly getting up from her desk.

"Polly, can you come here, please?"

Polly walked over to her. "Need something, Dr. Tyler?"

"The doctor screen you showed me this morning, am I able to pull it up, or do you have to have special clearance?"

"You can do it." Polly showed her what to do with the computer and wrote down the screen code and a couple of additional codes to get physician information so Erin could do it herself.

"Thanks," smiled Erin as she eagerly began to type. She put in the name of Edward Carroll and found him to be an internist. Erin looked up his address and printed the information. Doing the same for Michelle, she found that their offices weren't too far away from each other. They both had hospital privileges at Mercury Memorial and Southeast, and they obviously knew each other if Dr. Carroll was referring patients to Michelle. Getting out her drug utilization reports, Erin looked for Dr. Carroll's name, but he didn't appear to be a high utilizer of expensive drugs. Erin figured she had gotten a lot of facts so far today, but she had to make herself stop. She had other work on her desk to do. Placing the Attorney General letter into a manila file, she put it in the very back of her file cabinet, leaving the subject tab blank. She put the addresses of the two doctors in her purse.

Erin continued to go over the drug utilization reports and wrote down the physicians' names to go visit. There were quite a few. She hoped that the next few visits would go better than the Peach visit. Get the worst one over with first. She hoped so. The rest of the day was spent making appointments with doctors and getting directions to their offices.

Charlie was starting to get a little worried. Erin knew Michelle's name, but hopefully nothing else. She was sharp and may have remembered what Peach had said about Michelle. What was really worrisome was the Attorney General letter he had received. The State would be doing their own investigation, and the only good thing about that was anything the State did would take a long time. Michelle hadn't received her letter yet, but perhaps she'd gotten it today. Collectively, Michelle, Ed, and Charlie would have come up with some kind of a story to make the members look bad. Nothing would be documented in the member's records about the issue the members discussed, so it was just the member's word against two well-respected doctors without a prior history of problems. He looked at the clock. Michelle would probably be at the office by now. Dialing her number, he waited for the receptionist to answer.

"Mercury Cardiac Care. How may I direct your call?"

"Stephanie, this is Dr. Patton. Is Dr. Campbell available?"

"I'll let her know you're on the line. One moment, please," said Stephanie.

It was just a few moments until Michelle picked up.

"Hi, Charlie," she said.

"Did you get your Attorney General letter today?"

"Yes, and so did Ed. He has already called me. The letter is just asking for a copy of the member's record to be delivered to them within the next sixty days. We have plenty of time, and I really don't think we need to worry. You know our charts are clean, and if they request the cath from Mercury Memorial, it will be clean, too." She sounded very confident.

Charlie liked what he heard. "Great, honey." He relaxed a little. "Just wait till the last minute to send the chart. I'll call Ed and tell him the same thing. One more thing, Michelle. Did I tell you about one of our doctors here in the office who seems a little nosy?"

"No, you didn't."

"Her name is Erin Tyler and her father is one of our medical directors. She's just temporary here until she finds a job she wants. Anyway, she must have seen us together and she asked me about you. She had also just been at Dean Peach's office on business and he let your first name slip when he shouldn't have."

"That's not good, Charlie. We don't have to worry about her like we did Dr. Kramer, do we?"

"I'm not sure." He laughed. "Do you think Kramer needs company at the bottom of the Detroit River?"

"We might have to consider it. Keep tabs on her," said Michelle, sounding a little unhappy.

Changing the subject, he asked, "Do you feel up for some company tonight?"

"Not tonight, Charlie. I'm still tired from the weekend and being so busy on Monday. How about if I come over to your house tomorrow night? Would that be okay?"

"Sure, doll. Remember to bring something special to wear for me. We haven't spent the night together in a while," he crooned. "You know I like my women a little trashy."

"I'll be sure to wear something I know you'll like. See you tomorrow night." Michelle made some kissing sounds into the phone.

Charlie laughed as he hung up the phone. He had been a hit with the ladies his whole life. He dialed Ed Carroll's office.

"Dr. Carroll's office," said Chrissy.

"Good afternoon. This is Dr. Patton calling to speak to Dr. Carroll."

"One minute, Dr. Patton." Chrissy put him on hold.

Charlie tapped his pencil against his desk impatiently while he waited.

"Hey, Charlie," Ed said, picking up the phone. "What about that letter?"

"I just got off the phone with Michelle. We've decided not to worry about it right now. Don't send the patient's chart until the day before it's due. The State will be happy that they even received it near their time frame."

"I reviewed the chart again this morning. There is no suspicious documentation." Ed sounded very self-assured.

"With all the fuss about patient safety now, I'm more concerned with the State thinking there was a diagnostic inaccuracy from the very beginning and what they may see as a lack of documentation. The member thought he had stomach problems and that was why he came in to see you. I'm sure your medical assistant wrote that on his record. Did you work him up for that first?"

"Of course not. He was a good candidate for coronary bypass."

"Unfortunately, he is one of those consumers who asks questions. He wants to have a bigger role in his health care than most. Maybe you should have done a work-up on him, Ed."

"I don't know, Charlie. Maybe."

"I'm going to swing by tonight about 8 to have a look at that chart. Is that a good time for you? All your patients and staff gone?"

"That's fine. I'll be here alone."

"See you then," said Charlie.

"Good-bye." Ed hung up the phone.

Charlie got out his cocaine and snorted a spoonful. He wasn't going to be bothered about anything right now. Everything was fine and dandy.

Lisa and Jimmy had been finalizing the wedding details with her mom. Everything seemed to be ordered and confirmed. Deliveries would be the last thing on the list.

"All right," said Arlene, as she checked things off in their wedding planner book, "who has the rings?"

Lisa and Jimmy stared at each other with gaping mouths.

Lisa gasped first, then spoke. "They're still in London at our townhouse, locked up in the safe."

"I can't believe we forgot them," said Jimmy, shaking his head. "What are we going to do?"

Lisa was very distressed. "Mom, there is no one to pick them up, either. Jimmy's parents are way north of London and they are flying out tomorrow with his sister and brother. They're going to stay a couple of days in New York City before coming in here on Friday. Then they're going to see the guys do a show next week and I will be entertaining them the rest of the time."

"I don't see how we can retrieve them," said Jimmy. "We are working the whole week of the wedding, but next Friday is the rehearsal dinner and the wedding is on Saturday."

"There is an alternative," Arlene said, looking at the two of them with raised eyebrows. "You can get married without them."

The look on Lisa's face said it all. They would not get married without the rings.

Steve had been on the backyard deck reading the newspaper and relaxing. He sauntered into the kitchen to get a soda and saw everyone's face staring at him from around the kitchen table. "What's going on here?" he asked uneasily.

No one said anything.

"Don't everyone speak out at once."

"Steve, we need your help," Lisa said with pleading eyes.

"Help with what?"

Lisa explained the situation as Steve listened.

"So, when is it that I'm supposed to fly seven hours to London and back again before the wedding?" Steve asked, not thinking it could be done.

Lisa's mind was racing as she stood up. "I've got it! Steve, you guys have this weekend off. You can go to London on Friday and return on Sunday. Your next show isn't until Monday night."

"I was rather looking forward to the weekend off," Steve said, as he had been hoping to see Erin over the weekend.

Lisa could see that Steve needed additional prodding. She nudged him with her elbow. "What if I talk my sister into going with you?"

This peaked his interest and he looked at Lisa. "Who's going to ask her?"

"I will," said Lisa, smiling. "She has a passport and I know she has always wanted to go to London. Just show her around the city and be your usual impressive self." Her eyes narrowed as she watched him. "Remember that I'm wise to you. You want to know her a lot better than you do now."

Steve nodded. "I've been quite obvious about that."

Lisa walked around him in circles. "Just think about it, Steve. You and Erin, alone together for the entire weekend."

He raised his eyebrows.

Lisa stopped to look Steve straight in the eye. "I'm almost giving her to you. If Mr. Cool can't make progress in a weekend, then he no longer deserves the title."

Steve scowled at Lisa. "There she goes, slagging me off again."

"Is that enough persuasion for you?" She grinned.

He smiled back. "It's all I need. When is the flight?"

Lisa gave Steve a hug. "I'll go on the Internet and get the tickets, then I'll call Erin to tell her she's going to London on Friday. She can't possibly turn it down, especially if I tell her I already bought the tickets." She happily left the kitchen.

"Thanks, mate," said Jimmy, patting Steve on the shoulder. "I knew you would come through for us."

"Never a moment's rest for the weary," Steve said, shaking his head. Then he started thinking about having Erin to himself for the weekend and felt not so weary after all.

Erin arrived home from work for the day, not believing that she had been talked into a trip to London for a weekend. The plane ride would be exhausting and it wasn't enough time to do London justice, but she wanted to help her sister and Jimmy, so she hadn't put up a fuss when Lisa had called. At least Steve was going with her. Walking up the stairs, she heard a guitar playing softly as she reached the top. Erin stepped down to the door at the left of her room, and seeing it was half-open, she peeked in.

Steve was sitting on the side of the bed with an open-bound book next to him. He had jean shorts on and an unbuttoned cotton shirt. Playing a few notes on the guitar, he would then write something in the book.

He looked up at her. "Erin, how nice to see you."

"Hello," she said, smiling. "You and I are going to London together on Friday night, I hear."

"I'm sure your sister didn't give you much of a choice. It was most kind of you to agree on such short notice," he said, fixing his eyes on her. "I know we're doing it for Jimmy and Lisa, but we'll have a bit of fun and I'll be happy to show you as much of the city as we have time for."

"I know we won't be there very long, but I was hoping to see the Tower of London." She realized she liked his eyes more and more and wondered why she was having difficulty breathing.

"The Tower of London it is. I'll take you to some of our favorite pubs, too. There are quite a few around the corner from Jimmy's townhouse." Steve was quite excited for Friday to come, and he was unable to take his eyes from hers.

"When are you leaving for Minneapolis?"

"Tomorrow morning."

"Lisa and I are going to get my dress fitted for the wedding tonight. I hope to be back early, so I guess I'll see you if you're here."

"I'll make sure I'm here."

Erin felt herself blushing as she smiled at him again and turned to leave. The tension was undeniable, and her heart was pounding. She had better get a grip of it and fast, because something was definitely going on between them. Walking into her room, she changed into something more comfortable for the trip to the seamstress and then put her ear to the wall because she thought she heard him singing while he played his guitar. He was, and she liked hearing him again. Walking down the stairs as she calmed herself, she saw her mother and sister coming out of the master suite located on the first floor.

Lisa saw her on the stairs. "Erin, I finished my dress today," said Lisa excitedly. "Do you want to see it?"

"Yes. Where is it? In Mom and Dad's room?"

Lisa nodded. "Come here," said Lisa, almost whispering. "Jimmy isn't supposed to know it's here. You know he can't see it before the wedding." They crept into the master suite and over to her parents' walk-in closet.

On a large hanger was a floor length silk faille gown. It was strapless on the left side and had one strap wrapping over the right shoulder, with a small lavender bow tied around itself. The dress started out as white, but gradually turned into lavender by the time it reached the floor. A long, white silk tulle veil hung next to the dress and lavender platform shoes sat on the floor.

"Lisa, this is gorgeous! I don't know how you can sew like this."

"Thanks. I love it, too," Lisa gushed. "It has taken me six months to make it."

"You girls had better get going," said Arlene, looking at the clock. "It is almost 6:30."

The girls grabbed their purses and headed out the door. Lisa drove their dad's car this time, as Erin wasn't sure where they were headed. They drove down a busy four-lane highway with a left turn lane in the middle. Turning down a two-lane street, they went right into a subdivision and into the driveway of a gray wood contemporary house. Lisa parked in the driveway and they went up to the front of the house. A slender, short-haired girl answered the door right away.

"Erin, this is Cheryl," said Lisa. "She's been helping me with the dresses."

Cheryl smiled at Erin. "Nice to meet you. Come on in."

The girls all went into the spacious living room, where Cheryl had Erin's bridesmaid dress hanging in a portable closet with wheels. This was the first time Erin had seen her dress and she gaped at it.

"Wow! My compliments, ladies."

The dress had one strap wrapping over the right shoulder like Lisa's wedding dress, but was lavender chiffon and wrapped around the bridesmaid's body. It was tied at the waist on the left side and there was a loose ruffle down the front where it was tied. The bottom of the dress was also supposed to have a loose ruffle around the entire bottom and it fell just below the knees.

"Erin, you need to try the dress on so Cheryl will know where to sew the ruffle on," said Lisa. "We knew your basic size, just needed to finalize things."

"My family isn't home," said Cheryl. "If you don't mind, you can just change here."

Erin took off her clothes and put the dress on, tying it at her waist. She stepped up on a nearby platform.

"This feels very clingy," she said.

"It does have a lining, but there is something I didn't tell you," said Lisa. "Underneath the dress, you will only have on a matching lavender strapless lace bra and thong. No slip and no panty lines always create beautiful pictures with no worries about how you look."

"Thong? I hate those things." Erin made a face in distaste. "Lisa, why do you do these things to me?"

"Erin, the thong rules. You just haven't worn one enough to realize how comfortable they are. No one else has complained. Charlotte, Jimmy's sister, will be here from England this weekend, and she told me that she only wears thongs. Get with the times, girl. I bet you'll end up liking it." Lisa searched through a portable dresser that Cheryl had in the living room and found a package marked "Erin." She took out the underwear and held it up for Erin's inspection.

Erin picked up the bra and checked the size. It looked like it would fit her. Then she held up the thong. "All right. We'll see if 'the thong rules' like you say it does." She handed the underwear back and Lisa put it in the dresser.

Erin stood on the step so Lisa and Cheryl could pin on the bottom ruffle and cut the dress where the hem should be. Lisa walked over to the dresser again and took out a shoebox marked "Erin." In it was a pair of lavender toeless, backless slip-on heels.

"I don't suppose I will have stockings on," said Erin.

"Nope. The dress, bra, thong, shoes. That's it."

"I'm going to feel naked," whined Erin.

"Just drink more champagne, then it won't bother you," laughed Lisa. "Remember it will be at least 80 degrees outside. You might even feel comfortable. I'm the one with the big dress, so quit complaining."

Lisa and Cheryl finished pinning the dress. Erin took it off and Lisa hung it back up on the hanger.

"I think I need a drink right now." Erin sighed.

Cheryl went into the kitchen and came back with a chilled bottle of White Zinfandel and three glasses. "Everyone ready?"

They were. The girls sat down on the couch and drank the bottle of wine over the next hour while they discussed the wedding. Erin and Lisa thought they had better get back to the house, as they both wanted to see the guys and it was already almost 8:30.

"Thanks, Cheryl. It was so nice meeting you," said Erin. "When will we see you next?"

"I will be over the day of the wedding to help everyone get ready. I'm getting real excited for all of you," Cheryl gushed.

Erin and Lisa said their good-byes to Cheryl and got into the car.

"I want to take a little detour on the way home," said Erin, glancing at Lisa.

"Well, I don't. The guys are leaving tomorrow. I won't see Jimmy for three days."

"Let's call home and see what's going on."

"Call away."

Erin took her cell phone from her purse and placed a call to her parent's house. Her dad picked up the phone.

"Dad, its Erin. I'm sorry I missed you today. I have a lot to tell you."

"Erin, sorry I wasn't able to get back to you. I didn't pick up my messages until very late in the day, but we can talk when you two get home. Where are you now?"

"We just left Cheryl's house."

"Mom and I just cracked open a bottle of wine with Jimmy and Steve," Rich said. "We thought we would do a little celebrating tonight."

Erin could hear talking in the background. She was anxious to get home, but she knew she was close to Michelle's and Ed Carroll's offices and wanted to see where they were.

"We'll get there as soon as we can," said Erin. She hung up the phone.

"What's happening there?" asked Lisa as she watched the road.

"Mom and Dad are drinking wine with the boys," Erin said matter-of-factly, "but I really need a favor, Lisa."

"What?"

"I just want to drive by two doctors' offices that I think are only a few miles away from here. Please? It won't take long," Erin begged.

"All right, but I want to get home as soon as possible." Lisa was firm. "Read me the directions, and if I don't know where they are, then we're going right home."

Erin took the directions out of her purse and read them to Lisa.

"Okay, I know where they are. You're lucky. We're really close." Lisa turned left on the main highway and drove about two miles. "I think your first address should be around here on the left side of the road."

Erin started watching for the address. "Slow down, Lisa. I can't read that fast."

Lisa released the accelerator a little. They saw a two-story newer brick building on the left side. It was quite impressive looking.

"Mercury Cardiac Care," Lisa read on the sign. "Is that the one you want?"

"That's it." Erin examined the building. Quite a nice place Michelle had for herself. There were no cars in the parking lot. Office hours must be over for today.

"Are we finished here?"

Erin nodded her head. "Yes."

"The other office might be down the road over here, but I don't know if it's north or south. I'm really not sure. We may have to turn back in the other direction." Lisa turned right at the next light onto Balsam Boulevard. She drove slower as she saw a gray brick office building on the right.

As they got closer, Erin said excitedly, "Lisa don't slow down or turn into the parking lot. Keep going down the road." Erin put her head down a little, but kept her eyes peeled on the building.

In the parking lot was a green Jaguar. The front door of the office opened and two men came out. Erin could see clearly that one of the men was Charlie. The other man must be Dr. Edward Carroll. He had a limp and short black hair. He and Charlie shook hands as Charlie got into the Jaguar and the other man got into a sport utility vehicle parked next to Charlie's. Just then Erin and Lisa passed the building and she couldn't see what happened next.

Lisa turned into a carpet store located in the next building down the road and stopped the car. "What do we do now? What's the problem? Are these doctors friends of yours?"

"It is very complicated, and believe me, you really don't want to hear about it. This has to do with Triangle Health Plan and some problems there."

"Can we go home now?" Lisa pleaded.

"Yes, let's go home." Erin's mind was racing. She had now placed Charlie, Michelle, Dr. Edward Carroll, and Dr. Dean Peach as being in on something together. What was going on? Maybe it was innocent and she was jumping to conclusions, but she didn't think so. Something was wrong. Were there any more doctors involved?

Lisa turned back out onto the road.

Erin looked back at Dr. Carroll's office as they passed it, but she didn't see anything. The cars were gone.

Lisa put on the radio as they headed toward home. An Odyssey song from the early 90s was on, but almost over. She turned the radio volume up high and started singing very loudly until it was finished. "Of course it's an old song. With the way that radio is now, you won't hear a song from the new Odyssey album. Even though they have a loyal fan base, new stuff just doesn't get played from older bands on the radio."

"Really? Something is wrong with that. It must have to do with money."

Lisa nodded. "It's always about money. If you're not the flavor-of-the-month or bringing in a zillion dollars a week to your record company, they hardly act like you exist."

Opening her purse, Erin took out her lipstick and looked in her compact mirror as she put it on. She briefly powdered her nose and combed her hair.

"Who are you getting ready for?" Lisa glanced at Erin and smiled.

Erin just shrugged her shoulders and grinned. She was already excited over what had just happened with the doctors, and now she couldn't wait to get home.

Pulling into the Tyler driveway, someone turned the porch light on and off. The girls looked at each other and smiled. Good. The party must still be going on. They got out of the car and quickly went into the house.

The compact disc player was on shuffle and playing throughout the house. They heard talking in the kitchen, so they headed that way. Two empty bottles of wine were sitting on the kitchen counter. Rich was just getting ready to open up another.

"Girls, you're finally home. We've been waiting," smiled Rich as he turned the corkscrew opening the bottle of wine. "I just turned the porch light on for you, I think." He frowned, trying to remember. "Two more glasses, dear," he said to Arlene.

"I was hoping you two would be home soon. How did the fitting go?" Arlene set the two glasses on the counter for Rich to fill.

"Great," said Lisa. "Erin is all set, aren't you?" She turned to Erin and nudged her arm.

"Yes, everything is just dandy," said Erin, picking up her filled wineglass and taking a long sip. She looked around for Steve right away and saw him and Jimmy sitting at the breakfast nook sipping their wine.

He was already watching her when he caught her eye. They just stared at each other from across the room and smiled. Steve pulled out the empty chair next to him.

Erin took a deep breath and let it out. She refused the breathlessness that was trying to take over. Never breaking his gaze, she strolled to the chair and sat down by him.

"Did anyone tell Dad about the London trip on Friday for Erin and Steve?" asked Lisa, looking around from face to face.

"I have been informed," affirmed Rich. "I think that it's great they have agreed to take such a long trip in a short length of time. Thanks, you two, for doing this for Lisa and Jimmy." He raised his glass to them.

"Thank you, Erin and Steve," Lisa said, running over to hug each of them. "Jimmy and I really appreciate it."

Jimmy nodded his head appreciatively.

Erin and Steve smiled and glanced at each other again. Erin had no idea why, but she felt a little daring. Knowing Steve's shoe was next to hers, she lifted up her foot, wrapping her lower leg around his, underneath the table. She knew the wine was relaxing her, and she wanted to touch him. He looked at her, unsure of her intentions.

"Dad," Erin grimaced, looking at Rich, "we were supposed to talk about work tonight, but I don't want to. Can we just have fun?"

Rich laughed. "Quit whining, Erin. We'll talk about work tomorrow. Come to my office when I get in."

The next hour was spent discussing the wedding day and drinking another bottle of wine. Erin found herself looking for any excuse to touch Steve. She leaned across the table to pick up a napkin and had to touch his leg with her arm. Another time she touched his hand while talking. Everytime she looked at him, his eyes and mouth seemed to be smiling at her. Reluctantly, Erin forced herself to look up at the kitchen clock when she knew it had to be late. It was almost midnight, and 5:30 a.m. was her wake-up time. She didn't want the night to end, but she knew she needed some sleep.

She looked at Steve, apologizing. "I'm sorry, but I have to go to bed. Work comes very early for me."

Arlene was wiping off the kitchen counter. "I'm sure we'll all be turning in shortly. Honey, just go to bed. Don't worry about us."

Erin stood, but looked at Steve.

He got up, yawned, and stretched his arms. "I think I'm going to sleep as well. What time are we getting up, Jimmy?"

"We're leaving at 9 a.m.," Jimmy said.

"All right, then. Goodnight, everyone," smiled Steve. He followed Erin out of the kitchen.

"We'll talk in the morning, Erin," said Rich. "Goodnight."

Erin put her hand around Steve's arm and they slowly walked up the stairs without turning on the upstairs light. They stopped outside her room and Erin leaned up against the wall. The light cast from the downstairs foyer was barely shining up on where they were.

She felt reckless and wild—not terms generally used to describe Erin Tyler. "I guess I won't see you until Friday," she said softly. Being in the dark and a little intoxicated from the wine helped her talk, so she just said the next thing to come to mind. "I want you to kiss me. Now."

It took only seconds for him to put his arms around her shoulders and bend his head down. They kissed once and broke apart, staying just inches from each other's faces. Starting to grin, they realized this felt really good to each of them.

"Don't stop," Erin whispered.

Steve squeezed her tighter and she put her arms around his neck. The second kiss was unhurried and arousing and continued for an extended period of time. They reluctantly stopped when they heard talking at the bottom of the stairs.

"Goodnight, Mom and Dad," called out Lisa.

Lisa and Jimmy were starting up the stairs, talking loudly. Erin and Steve breathed heavily on each other while still in a clutch.

"I'll call you this week," Steve said in a low voice.

Erin nodded as they unwillingly let go of each other. She went into her room and shut the door, leaving Steve breathless in the hall as she heard Lisa and Jimmy reach the top of the stairs.

CHAPTER 9

DAVID sat at the surgical ICU desk at Southeast, looking over his patient's electronic charts. Wednesday mornings he was on call for Michelle. This was her coronary angioplasty day at Southeast, and a cardiovascular surgeon needed to be available in case a patient crashed during the procedure and needed immediate open heart surgery. Since he had started covering for her, no emergencies had happened during the procedures, but he supposed there would be a first time. Michelle wasn't able to make angioplasties a CAP surgery, but they didn't generate as much revenue as coronary bypasses anyway, so it probably didn't matter.

David still wasn't sure if his heart was in CAP. When his patient Dale Michaels had expired in the surgical ICU after his unnecessary coronary bypass and subsequent stroke on Monday, David started to have real doubts as to why he had let himself get involved in CAP. He thought about why he became a cardiovascular surgeon in the first place. It was a grueling profession, of course, but it had monetary and intellectual rewards. Being well respected by the hospital staff and his peers, he had never had any regrets about the specialty he had chosen. But what he was doing was wrong, and he knew it. The gains he was making would be so he could pay off his gambling debts and for money he could play with for the future. Michelle kept reminding him that CAP would only be for a limited time, so he would reap the benefits while they were available.

His involvement in gambling had basically come out of boredom. Needing to be busy at all times, he was unable to relax like some people by watching a movie or going out to eat with friends. There was boredom in his marriage—he and his wife had differing interests—and their children had already grown up and moved out. An educational convention in Las Vegas changed everything for him. He discovered gambling and his game of choice was poker. Having a lot of money available to him, he quickly acclimated himself to the lifestyle. The fun was there, but he did find himself unable to stop sometimes. Even on a losing night, he always thought he could turn it around. He was well known at the high roller tables in the local casinos and never had trouble getting in on any game he wanted. The gambling debt that he had could be easily turned around with all his CAP money, and he planned on being more careful in the future so that debt would not accumulate again. His wife had started getting suspicious about missing money and he had to account for it. Now that he was going to have a lot of money in private offshore accounts, things would be easier to deal with at home, and he could still have his fun.

David heard some commotion and looked up as a new patient was being wheeled down the hall on a stretcher.

Michelle and an operating room nurse were pushing the stretcher into the surgical ICU. They had come right from surgery and still had scrubs on. Michelle stopped in front of SICU #4 and spoke for a few minutes to the ICU nurse. The three of them talked as they wheeled the stretcher into the room and moved the patient to the bed. Monitors were hooked up and the patient was made comfortable. Everyone liked the fact that Southeast had plenty of nursing staff to handle the direct patient care. The nurses were happy here because they had a safe and manageable patient workload, making them able to truly enjoy their profession and provide a high quality of care. They were compensated well and burnout was a problem of the past. Michelle left the room as the nurses finished up and walked over to David.

"Good morning, David," she said and smiled at him. She pulled the elastic hat off her head and combed her hair with her fingers. Untying the surgical mask that was dangling in front of her chin, she threw both of them in the trashcan by the desk.

"I trust everything went well?" he asked as he closed out the electronic chart he had been daydreaming over.

"Yes, her angioplasty went fine and I expect discharge tomorrow. When is your next bypass?"

"I have one tomorrow morning," he said.

"One of ours?" she asked.

"Yes."

"Very good. My surgeries are done for today, so you don't have to worry about my patients needing you. Thanks for being available," she said.

David couldn't believe what a good mood she was in. He had never seen her so pleasant.

"I have a couple of patients who will be making appointments with your office. They will be candidates for coronary bypass. Hopefully, you can fit them in in the next couple of weeks." She sat down at the desk and put her password in the computer to chart, but stopped and looked at him. "David, I am making a change in CAP. I want you to do the patient's surgeries as quickly as possible. Don't schedule them in three weeks. Schedule them next week if you can. Understand?" she asked. The doctor that Charlie had told her about was starting to worry her more than she would like to admit.

"Fine," David said, shrugging his shoulders. He stood up to leave.

"It's a good thing the Michaels family refused an autopsy after his death. We would have been in big trouble with that one."

David nodded.

"All right, David. See you soon." Michelle looked up and smiled at him again.

David walked out of the surgical ICU and down the hall. He had no office hours today. An air of relaxation came over him as he decided to go to the casino, his usual Wednesday afternoon haunt. Maybe he would run downstairs and grab a quick lunch in the hospital cafeteria before the drive downtown. His office also might need a quick call to see if anything was going on. He took his cell phone out of his pocket and dialed.

"Dr. Keller's office," answered Becky.

"Hi, Becky," he said.

"Hello, Doctor," said Becky, sounding cheerful.

"Anything going on that I need to know about?" he asked.

"Not a thing. A couple of referrals from Dr. Campbell came over today and we took care of them. You'll be seeing those patients in a couple of days. That's about it," she said. "We'll be closing down at 1 p.m. for the day, unless you need anything."

"That's fine. I have a bypass tomorrow morning, so I won't be in the office until about 2 p.m."

"Yes, we know. Patients start at 2:30 p.m. tomorrow."

"Great. See you then." David hung up the phone, and with a spring in his step, walked downstairs to the cafeteria.

Erin had a terrible headache this morning as she sat at her desk. Opening her purse, she took out a few ibuprofen to get rid of the throbbing. She couldn't handle late night drinking and getting up early, but last night had been an exception. It had been great fun with her family and the guys. She knew that she had been drinking a lot since she had been back in Michigan, but the partying would probably slow down after her sister's wedding. Those close family things seem to happen few and far between, the older you get. You have to enjoy the time you spend with the people who are important to you in your life.

Swallowing her pills, she could now admit she felt strongly about Steve. He didn't know it, but she had almost dragged him into her room because she didn't want to stop kissing him. Maybe she should have. Smiling, she knew he had enjoyed himself as much as she had. When she left her room this morning, she looked down the hall to her right to see if his door was open, but it wasn't. She felt disappointed because she knew she wouldn't see him for three days, but she hoped he would call her like he said he would.

Turning to the business at hand, she got out her planner to see what was going on today. She would meet with her father when he arrived. She had appointments with Dr. Mike Fabian and Dr. Jane Marshall for the late morning. They were two internal medicine primary care physicians who worked together and had quite a few patients on the expensive drug lists that she had been checking. Her phone rang.

"Dr. Tyler," she answered.

"Well, this is Dr. Tyler, too. How are we feeling today?" asked her dad.

"A little rough. I need a nap."

Rich laughed. "Come on over. We can have that discussion now."

"I'll be right there." Erin hung up the phone. She got up from her desk and rushed to her father's office. Peeking in the door, he motioned for her to come in.

"Close the door," he said.

Erin closed the door and sat down at the table. She put her feet up on the seat of the other chair at the table and leaned back. Rubbing her temples, Erin let out a deep breath.

"There is something going on at Triangle, Dad. I'm not sure what it is yet, but I will find out."

"What have you found out so far?"

"On my first day, I went out to lunch with Charlie. He talked on the phone to someone named Michelle whom he seemed close to. I thought at the time it could be his girlfriend because of the way he was talking to her, so I really didn't think anything was suspicious."

"Go on," said Rich.

"When I was at Dean Peach's office, he talked about a Michelle that he wasn't sending enough patients to. He thought Charlie had sent me. You didn't think it was anything, Dad, but Peach was acting funny. I suspect he is taking OxyContin, but there was something else going on. Then he got angry and threw me out of his office."

"So whatever it is going on, you suspect Charlie is a part of it?"

"I think so. I saw Michelle on Monday with Charlie. He was getting out of her car. Susan said Michelle was Charlie's girlfriend."

"Susan is also a woman who has been scorned by Charlie. You have to take that into account," said Rich.

Erin sat up straight now. "Oh, I do. That brings me to the next thing. I don't want to get Susan in trouble, so you can't say anything about what I am about to tell you." Erin looked at Rich for a response.

"All right."

"Susan gave me a copy of a letter from the Attorney General. The letter is a member complaint that names two doctors. One is Michelle Campbell and the other is Edward Carroll. Do you know either of them?"

"I know Ed Carroll. Good guy. He is on our Ethics Committee," said Rich. "I see him once a month."

"I have a feeling he doesn't belong on the Ethics Committee. He is involved in whatever is going on. Charlie was at his office last night. Lisa and I drove by it on our way home from the seamstress."

"Erin, he and Charlie are close. That could have been a social visit. Be reasonable," Rich pleaded and shook his head.

"Dad, hear me out," Erin begged. "Steve and I saw Michelle Campbell at the mall two nights ago. She is the same Michelle that Charlie was with. I looked her up in the computer today and she is a cardiologist. Since I heard Dean Peach talk about not having many patients to send to Michelle, I assume he was talking about referring patients to Michelle. She is a specialist and would need a referral from a primary care doctor in order to see a member with Triangle insurance."

"That would be correct."

"I requested a report from the Data department with all the referrals that have been given to Michelle recently. It should come tomorrow."

"Erin, I'm sorry. Let me stop you now. I don't see anything that is suspicious so far. So what if Charlie has a physician girlfriend that takes Triangle insurance? As far as the member complaint issue to the Attorney General goes, members complain all the time about their doctors and their insurance companies. That letter doesn't prove that the doctors did anything wrong. An investigation will be done."

Erin was quiet. He didn't believe her.

"Have you finished the real assignment Charlie wanted you to do? The pharmacy issues?"

"No."

"How about the utilization charts you are helping me with?"

"No."

"I think you may be jumping to conclusions on a number of issues here. Go ahead and look at the Data department information when you get it, but try to be more objective. Just because you don't care for Charlie doesn't mean he's involved in anything illegal or otherwise. The issue of Dean Peach and the drugs will be dealt with. You have already started the ball rolling on that one." Rich looked at Erin for some kind of affirmation.

Erin felt terrible. She thought he would be excited as she was. Maybe she was jumping to conclusions. After talking about it out loud with her father, she could see how there was really nothing concrete to grasp on to. Just suspicions so far. She needed to go back to bed and take a nap.

"Why don't you put your personal investigation on the back burner for now and deal with the issues you are supposed to be dealing with? Have you talked with any other doctors yet about their prescribing patterns?"

"I'm going later this morning to see Jane Marshall and Mike Fabian."

"Good. Just deal with those things for now. You've got to remember, honey, that you haven't been here very long—not even two weeks yet. Don't get caught up in something you're not sure of."

Erin sat and listened.

Rich continued. "You're going to London this weekend and the wedding is next week. There is a lot going on with our family right now and we need you to help with those things."

Erin felt like a child. "All right. I guess I'll go now." She got up to leave.

Rich came over to her and hugged her. "I'm sorry if I was a little rough on you. I also stayed up too late. Forgive me?"

"Sure, Dad." She smiled at him and walked out the door.

Charlie had walked past Rich's office earlier and had seen Erin. He wondered if she was discussing him and the others in any way. Things didn't seem quite right any more, because he had a feeling the girl was suspicious. He got up from his desk to walk by Rich's office again. Erin was gone and Rich was working. Charlie looked farther down the hall and saw Erin at Susan's desk, so he walked up to them.

Erin turned and smiled. "Dr. Patton, can I talk to you for a moment about something personal?"

"Sure," he said, wondering what she wanted. "Let's go back into my office."

He and Erin walked back to it and he directed her to sit down.

"I'm sorry, but I need to leave early again this Friday," she said, looking up at him.

"Again?" he asked, frowning.

"I'm going to London for the weekend. I have to pick up my sister's and her fiancee's wedding rings from their townhouse. There is no one else who has free time to get them before the wedding next week."

"London for the weekend," said Charlie chuckling. "That's going to be a difficult Monday. After hearing your explanation, I would seem like an ogre if I said no to that one. Of course you can leave early. In fact, take the whole day off. I'm sure you have plenty of things you need to do before your flight."

Erin's face registered shock. "Thank you so much, Dr. Patton." She thought maybe he wasn't such a bad guy after all, but immediately regretted that thought.

"Anything else going on I need to know about?" He sat back in his chair, trying to look comfortable, but instead looked like someone under stress.

"Not a thing. Thanks again," she smiled as she got up to leave.

Charlie smiled at her until she was out of sight, then looked at his watch. He remembered that he had an appointment he needed to get to as he walked over to Susan's desk. "I'm going out, but I'll be back in a couple of hours. If anything comes up, beep me."

"Sure, Dr. Patton," Susan said, trying to be as polite as possible.

Charlie left the building and got into his car. He drove about ten miles away from the office until he came to a large, two-story wooden house located on the main road. Jane Marshall and Mike Fabian had bought this house for their practice. It had been renovated and really looked quite homey. It should have a barn with horses behind it instead of a concrete parking lot. He parked his Jaguar in an open space and went in the front door entrance.

"Hi there," he said to the receptionist as he leaned on the counter. She wasn't much to look at, and he was sure she knew it. "I'm Dr. Patton. I have an appointment with Drs. Marshall and Fabian." He gave her a slight smile, but there was no point in trying too hard.

"Yes, Doctor, let me see if they're ready for you." She left her desk and vanished out of sight.

Charlie looked around. The waiting room looked like someone's living room: couches and coffee tables with home and health magazines, flowery wallpaper and curtains to complete the atmosphere. He shook his head in appreciation. The décor certainly matched the house architecture. It really looked quite nice, even though he would never decorate that way. Country? Not for him. He preferred edgy, modern styles.

"The doctors will see you now," said the receptionist as she buzzed the door for him.

Charlie opened the door and sauntered down the hall. Mike Fabian met him halfway.

"Hello, Charlie," smiled Mike. He was a small, young man with short brown hair, and he always looked nervous. "We can go into Jane's office."

They walked around the corner and went into an office. Jane sat at her desk, her arms folded, and directed Charlie and Mike to sit at a small table near a window.

Charlie had always found her to be quite fetching, with her long brown hair and green eyes. He could imagine her dancing around a pole and smiling with very little on. A few years ago he had tried to date her, but she kept making excuses why she couldn't go out with him, so he dropped it. Michelle came along then, so he never tried Jane again.

"Jane," he said, "you look as lovely as I remembered you to be. I am aghast that we see each other so little."

"Ever the charmer, Charlie. What did we do to deserve your company?"

"Jane, Jane. I think you're doing just great. Looking at the amount of patients you refer is always a pleasure. There are no complaints on my side about you." He turned to Mike. "Mike, on the other hand, seems to be having some problems."

"I'm doing the best I can," Mike stammered.

"I know you're young and perhaps a little unsure of yourself. Your student loans are at $150,000 and that would worry anyone. That's the reason you're in CAP, correct?"

Mike nodded.

"In order to get your CAP payment, you have to do a little work. You don't seem to be doing that."

"I'm always encouraging him," said Jane. "I have been going through our appointment lists and giving him ideas on who to refer."

Mike nodded.

"Are you not taking Jane's recommendations seriously?" asked Charlie, somewhat exasperated with the young doctor.

"I don't know what I'm doing. Half the time, I'm not even sure if I want to be a doctor."

"Your feelings of inadequacy are not my concern," replied Charlie. "If you don't make referrals to Michelle, you don't get paid. I only saw two referrals on my list for July."

"I promise I'll try harder," muttered Mike.

"Don't make me come out here again."

Mike seemed to shrink in his seat, acting as if Charlie was going to strike him.

Jane frowned at Charlie's threat, but he certainly didn't intimidate her as he did Mike. "Why are you sending that other doctor out?"

"What other doctor?" asked Charlie, surprised at Jane's question.

"Dr. Tyler." Jane looked at the clock on her wall. "She should be here in about half an hour."

"What? She's coming here today?" Charlie couldn't believe his timing. He had to get out of there before Erin saw him. Now it was his time to stammer. "I have to leave. Dr. Tyler will just be talking to you about expensive drugs that you have been prescribing." He got up. "Don't say anything about my being here. I'll let myself out." He left Jane's office and got out of the building as fast as he could.

Erin got back to her desk and took out the file on Jane Marshall and Mike Fabian. Their office was about ten miles away from Triangle. Getting back on her computer, she found that they both had hospital privileges at Mercury and Southeast, and they were both internal medicine physicians. She looked at their prescribing patterns again. Many cholesterol-lowering drugs and anti-depressants. Not a lot of narcotics. Her talk with them should only last a couple of minutes. She didn't really like doing this and could see how other doctors wouldn't be happy with her telling them how to practice. At least she could use Charlie's name as her excuse. Getting up from her chair, she psyched herself up to get moving.

The office wasn't hard to find. It was an old Victorian house on her left. As she passed the office, she couldn't believe her eyes. A green Jaguar was in the parking lot. She didn't turn when she was supposed to, but kept driving straight, as she was at a loss of what to do. Charlie again? How could that be? After she drove a few more miles, she decided to turn around. As she got near to the office, she slowed down. The Jaguar was gone. Turning into the parking lot, she parked in the back and got out of the car. Erin entered the office and walked up to the receptionist.

"Hello, I'm Dr. Tyler from Triangle Health Plan. I have an appointment with Drs. Marshall and Fabian."

"I'll let them know you're here," said the receptionist. She disappeared from sight.

Erin knew that if she sat down on one of those comfortable couches she might even fall asleep. She decided to stand at the receptionist's window and wait. She tapped her foot and looked at her fingernails. It didn't take long for the girl to get back.

"Please come in," she said, buzzing the door open and showing Erin down the hall to an office in the back of the building.

Erin knocked on a half-open door.

"Come in," said a woman's voice.

Erin walked in and saw the doctors. Jane was sitting at a desk and Mike was sitting at a small round table in the room.

"Hello. I'm Dr. Erin Tyler from Triangle Health Plan. I'm very sorry to be bothering you, but I'll only be here a few minutes."

Jane stood up and held out her hand. She tried to smile. "Jane Marshall. Please sit down over there," she said pointing to where the other doctor was sitting.

He stood up as Erin approached.

"Mike Fabian. Nice to meet you." He shook Erin's hand and sat back down. Erin sat next to him.

"What can we do for you, Dr. Tyler?" asked Jane.

"I'm here on behalf of Charles Patton, chief medical officer of Triangle Health Plan. Pharmacy costs have become the biggest payout for all insurance companies. Some of the most prescribed drugs are the most expensive. I'm just here to talk to you about those drugs."

"Please go on," said Jane.

"Our Data department ran queries on some of these expensive drugs. I'm visiting those physicians who names show up as prescribing a lot of them."

"What kind of drugs?" asked Mike.

"For your office, it looks like cholesterol-lowering drugs and anti-depressants," said Erin.

"What does Dr. Patton want us to do?" asked Jane.

"Instead of just prescribing the cholesterol lowering drugs, he wants to make sure that the patients have tried to lower their cholesterol themselves by diet and exercise first. I also have a list to give you as to what each drug costs. If you must prescribe the cholesterol-lowering drugs and anti-depressants, he would like you to prescribe the lowest effective drug dose and least expensive medication. This is, of course, to avoid adverse drug events and to minimize the cost to the insurance company. If there is a generic available, please prescribe that." Erin handed each of them a list of drugs with their cost.

"Is that all?" asked Jane.

Erin was glad this was almost over. She breathed a sigh of relief. "Yes," she said, smiling, "that's all." She remembered that she thought she saw Charlie's Jaguar there. "How often do you get to see Dr. Patton?"

"I haven't seen him in months," Jane remarked, not skipping a beat. She stared intently at Erin.

Erin looked from Jane to Mike. He smiled at her, then looked away. Erin thought he looked nervous. There seemed to be an uncomfortable silence for a moment in the room, so she got up.

"Well, thank you for your time. I hope we meet again." Erin held out her hand and shook the doctors' hands.

Jane walked her out to the front of the building.

"Nice meeting you, Dr. Tyler," said Jane. "Feel free to stop in any time."

Erin smiled at her and left. Something about Dr. Marshall's demeanor just didn't seem sincere. She had denied seeing Charlie, but Erin felt quite sure it had been his car. There really weren't that many green Jaguars around. She got back into her car and left the premises.

Arriving at the office, she spent the rest of the day working on the Utilization Management charts she was supposed to be helping her father with. The charts were being reviewed to see if the patients had really needed to be in the hospital, or if their needs could have been met with home health care or other outpatient treatments instead. The cost of hospitalization days were getting so expensive that the insurance plans really had to keep track of unnecessary ones. The charts that Erin went through today really weren't very interesting, and she had trouble staying awake through the end of the day.

She made it home in record time; the house was quiet on her arrival. Quite a difference twenty-four hours makes. Only Lisa was home.

Lisa was on the phone throughout the evening. Jimmy's family had arrived in New York City and she was making sure everything was going okay with them. She had also talked to Jimmy a number of times to fill him in on everything going on with his family.

Erin made omelets for her and Lisa for dinner. After cleaning up the kitchen, she went upstairs and forced herself to pick up her room. Now it was time to relax. She took a shower, dried her hair, and put her gown on. Looking at the clock, she saw it was only 9 p.m., but she was exhausted enough that it didn't matter. She pulled down the covers and lay down in bed.

She heard the phone ring again. Thank goodness the ringing was elsewhere in the house and not in her room. Her eyes wanted to stay closed; the sound of the fan in her room added to her relaxation. It was only moments later that she heard Lisa walking up the stairs and talking to someone on the phone.

Lisa opened Erin's bedroom door. "Erin, do you want to talk to Steve?"

Erin couldn't get out of bed fast enough. She grabbed the phone and waved Lisa out of her room. "Steve, how are you?" she said, almost breathless as she sat on the side of the bed.

"Erin, hello. I had a bit of a lie-in this morning because of too much wine last night, but I'm better now. It was quite difficult to go to sleep. You make quite an impression, you know."

Erin laughed. "Do I?"

"Most certainly." He cleared his throat. "We're going onstage in half an hour, but I wanted to give you a quick call to let you know I'm thinking about you."

"I'm glad." She didn't really know what to say to him next. "How's the weather there?"

"It's raining a little. I hope it doesn't get any worse for the people sitting out on the lawn here. It doesn't look like we'll be getting wet where the stage is unless some rain blows underneath the pavilion."

Erin heard a lot of noise in the background. People were talking and she could hear loud music playing. She wished she were there.

"I'm looking forward to leaving on Friday. Should I take a jacket?" she asked.

"You had better. Even though it's August, England won't be as warm as what you're used to in the summer."

She paused a moment, trying to think of what to say. "Did you have fun last night?"

"I had a tremendous time with your family, but what I enjoyed most was being alone with you in the upstairs hallway. I could have gone on a bit longer than that."

Erin could feel him smiling through the phone, and she smiled back. "Me too." She heard Steve's name being called in the background.

"Excuse me a moment, Erin." Steve put the phone down.

Erin could hear him talking to someone.

"I'm sorry, but I have to go now." He delayed speaking for a second. "I'll see you on Friday then."

"Good-bye." She hung up at the same time he did. Taking the phone back downstairs where it belonged, she looked around for Lisa, but didn't see her. Bedtime would be easy now.

Michelle turned down Charlie's road as she had done many times before during the last few months. He lived in a large, sprawling condominium community. The condos were eight to a group and attached one to another. They were two stories of brown brick and basement, with each condo having a different facade. The windows were all trimmed in white, and every owner had a small cement stairway with a wrought-iron railing that led up to the front green door. The backs of the condos were like a walkout area. The garage was really half of the basement. Another entrance to the condo was to the right of the double garage door.

She pulled into a parking space in the front of the condo. Getting out of her car, she grabbed her overnight bag and walked up the stairs to the door. As she turned the knob, she found it locked. Since Charlie had gotten so involved in cocaine, he had become very paranoid. He used to leave the front door open when he knew she was coming, but not anymore. She impatiently rang the doorbell and soon heard him walking inside.

Looking out of the peephole and seeing it was her, he unlocked the door.

"You knew I was coming. Lucky for me it wasn't raining," she said as she walked in. She set her bag down in the foyer and unbuttoned her long jacket. Underneath, she had on a leopard teddy that left little to the imagination.

"That's my girl," said Charlie, smiling as he gave her a peck on the cheek. He carefully re-locked the front door and took her jacket. "Before we go upstairs, I want to show you something over here."

They walked over to the computer that was sitting in its permanent position on his kitchen table. A large pile of cocaine was sitting on a mirror next to the computer and a razor blade lay next to the pile. Not able to resist having a snort of it whenever he was near, he leaned over it now. After he finished, Charlie sat down on the oak chair. Michelle stood over him and rubbed his shoulders while she watched the screen. He was connected to the email system at Triangle. As he checked his queue to locate a specific email, he filled her in.

"I know that Erin Tyler, the nosy doctor I was telling you about, has been working with our Data department," he said, looking at Michelle. "After I decided that she might be snooping, I told them to let me know what she was requesting. Low and behold, I received this email today that I think you need to read." He moved his chair aside for Michelle to see the screen that he brought up.

"What is this?" Michelle asked, frowning.

"This is the form Erin had to fill out for her information request. The request is asking for all of the recent patient referrals given to Dr. Michelle Campbell and what doctor referred them to her."

Michelle was enraged. "How could this have happened again? You know this can't continue."

"I know," said Charlie, shaking his head and standing up.

"It looks like we're going to be in the same situation as last time."

"What do you want to do?"

"I have to think about this one for a while." She was thoughtful for a moment.

Charlie stood up and peeked inside Michelle's teddy. "Why don't we go upstairs? You can think later," he whispered to her.

She followed him up the stairs, remembering the real reason she had come over to his house tonight. This would be a good time to get his password for the bank accounts on which he had her listed on as a secondary owner. When she left the United States, she could clean those accounts out right away.

Charlie's room was large and messy. Clothes were strewn all over the floor and Michelle hated getting into his bed. Who knew the last time it was changed? He only had a maid come over once a month to clean his condo and whether bed linens were changed at that time or not was anyone's guess. This was one reason why she used to like it better when he came over to her place. She was meticulous about her house.

Although she and Charlie had started out as lovers and equal partners in CAP over the first few months, she realized that she didn't want to have a future with him. She was tired of Charlie and his habits and was bored having sex with him. She wanted someone closer to her own age that could give a little excitement to her life. That was when she had starting making the plans for herself and couldn't allow him to come over to her house for any length of time, lest he see that her move was already in progress. Michelle straightened the bed the best she could and got in. She left her teddy on, as he liked to be the one to remove her clothes.

He was in the bathroom, snorting more cocaine. She could hear him. A few minutes later he emerged, smiling and naked, with his arms outstretched. He strolled over towards her and climbed into bed.

"A little exercise would reduce that paunch, Charlie."

"But you like it, Michelle," he said as he got closer to her. "Come here, my little cup of hot chocolate."

It was always the same, and this time was no different. As he began to kiss her, she could taste the cocaine he always rubbed on his gums, and before long her mouth would go numb.

"Your little outfit is cute," he whispered to her, "but it has to come off." He took down each of her straps, pulling the teddy off and admiring her body. Charlie was quite happy with Michelle and thought the feeling was mutual. They had money and power as their like interests and he thought he could spend the rest of his days with her. He thought he was an excellent lover and his ego wouldn't let him think otherwise. The cocaine prolonged his performance and it was for her benefit, he thought as he puffed and wheezed on top of her. He sometimes felt like his heart would burst in his chest and it was during those times that he thought he was too old to be using the drug. As he now lay on his back, dripping in his own sweat, he concentrated on reducing his labored breathing.

Michelle realized this was the right time and nuzzled up to him as she tried to ignore the sweat. "Charlie, you never have told me the password on our accounts in Switzerland," she murmured. "You said you were going to tell me."

"Uh, huh," he mumbled through his closed eyes.

"Come on, Charlie." Michelle combed his hair back with her nails just the way he liked it. It was soaking wet and disgusting. She was getting irritated with him, and she was having to try too hard to get the information.

"Oh, that," he said, sounding uninterested. "The password is 'pressurized.' You know, like you, baby. Contents under pressure." Charlie smiled a little. His eyes remained closed and it wasn't long before he was asleep.

Michelle was ecstatic, since this was what she wanted. She lay there, close to him, with her hand on his chest until she heard him snoring. After getting up to take a shower and putting on the clean gown she always brought in her bag, she went downstairs and entered the password into her Palm Pilot. She sat down at Charlie's computer to read the email about Erin Tyler again and started to form a plan.

Charlie woke up a little while later and saw that Michelle wasn't next to him. He got out of bed and listened for her. Paranoia was becoming a way of life. Hearing a noise downstairs, he quietly crept down the stairs and let out a sigh of relief when he saw it was Michelle sitting at the computer. He walked over to her as she looked up at him.

"Did you figure out what we are going to do with Erin yet?" he asked her.

"I'm thinking that it shouldn't be her. You told me her father works with you?" asked Michelle, waiting for confirmation.

"Yes. Rich Tyler. He has been one of our medical directors for quite a few years."

"I think it should be him. If we get rid of him, she will leave the company. You told me she was just a temporary employee, so there would be no reason for her to stay. I'm sure that she would be so distraught that she would forget about anything she suspects about us."

Charlie contemplated this for a moment.

"Just think about it, Charlie. If we kill her, he would still be around. We don't know how much she has told him. He might start where she left off."

"You're probably right." Charlie had a problem with Rich anyway, due to the incident report Rich had filled out against him. The sexual impropriety Charlie had uttered in the presence of Rich, Erin, and Susan had caused Charlie to take a lot of flack from Bruce.

"Of course I'm right. I think that a massive digoxin overdose would likely do the trick." Michelle appeared deep in thought.

Charlie could almost see the wheels turning in her head.

"How would we do it?" he asked.

"I think I have enough digoxin at the office. You know what a powerful heart drug it is."

"Sure, I know about it. Digoxin makes the heart pump better and helps to control irregular heartbeats. It's easy for it to become toxic in someone's system if it's taken the wrong way," Charlie replied.

"Digoxin can cause death if it is taken inappropriately. We'll just give him about ten times the minimal effective dose." She picked up a pen and wrote a couple of numbers down, figuring out the dosage that she wanted to give Rich.

"I just remembered something. Erin is going out of town on Friday," Charlie said, thinking about her London trip.

"Then Friday will be the perfect time for his demise. Why don't you find some excuse to have him meet you for lunch or dinner and put the drug in his drink? I'll crush the tablets and have them ready for you."

"But if we're out in public won't someone notice if he starts acting ill?"

"Take him to that dark, quiet place you go to, and when something appears to be wrong with him, ignore it. When it seems like death is imminent, then call for help. Unfortunately, it will be too late."

"He'll have an autopsy performed, you know," Charlie commented. "This death would be classified as sudden and unexpected, with the patient having no history of natural disease. It would fall under the jurisdiction of the medical examiner."

"Yes."

"Erin is going to think his death is under suspicious circumstances. Everyone knows that Rich is a healthy man."

"I'll have a word with the medical examiner. He owes me a favor." Michelle didn't even know the name of the medical examiner, but Charlie wasn't aware of that. She realized that the medical examiner would send blood, urine, and a portion of the gastric contents to check for medicine, poison, and street drugs, but the results from the autopsy would take longer than a week and she would be gone by then. Although this turn in events was unexpected, a week would be plenty of time for her to do everything she needed to do. Her move to Paris would be one week from this Friday. After she left Charlie's place, she would have to make her plane reservations.

"I don't want to be implicated in any way," Charlie said, continuing to be troubled. "We didn't have to do the work when we got rid of Dr. Kramer or Dr. Altman."

Michelle was adamant and irritated. "Don't worry, Charlie. I told you I would talk with the medical examiner. There will not be a mention of digoxin toxicity in the autopsy report. Rich will have simply died from cardiac arrest."

CHAPTER 10

ERIN wasn't sure if she was happy because of Steve and their trip on Friday or because she'd be getting information back from the Data department today about Michelle's member referrals. It was probably both, she decided.

She turned on her computer and opened her email. Elated, she saw an email with an attachment from the Data department. She opened it and printed it. Erin laid the pages out and made a cursory inspection, just looking for certain names. There they were! Seeing the names of Edward Carroll, Jane Marshall, and Mike Fabian made her think she was on the right track, no matter what her father said. Looking quickly for any other names that really stood out, she found another one for the current month: David Keller.

Wondering what kind of physician he was, she got on the screens that would give her information on him. When she typed in his name, "cardiovascular surgeon" showed up. He would be given the referral from the cardiologist Michelle because if a patient needed coronary bypass, that was something outside of Michelle's expertise, and a referral to a cardiovascular surgeon would need to be done.

Another name she saw was Doug Altman. He didn't have any referrals for August, but for all of the previous months in the year he did. Erin found him to be a cardiovascular surgeon, too. Seeing Polly at her desk, she walked down to talk to her.

"Hi, Polly."

"Good morning, Dr. Tyler."

"I'm sorry to always be bothering you, but I need help again."

"That's fine. I've told you I'm retiring next year, so I don't mind working when I'm here." She paused. "Well, sometimes I mind working, but I don't mind helping you," said Polly, smiling.

"I need to know more about these two doctors." Erin showed Polly the names.

Polly went to her computer and put in a few different codes, looking for information.

"As you can see here, Dr. Altman is a cardiovascular surgeon who no longer works for us. He has an end date with the company of 7/19. That name sounds familiar, though." She tapped a finger on her cheek for a moment. "You know what? Let me give my friend a call." Polly picked up her phone and dialed for an outside line.

Erin just stood and listened.

"Hi, Marilyn." Polly was silent for a moment. "Sure I can go on Saturday. Listen, I have a question. Do you remember a doctor by the name of Doug Altman?" Polly was quiet again as she listened to what Marilyn was saying. "I thought so. Okay, thanks. Bye." She hung up the phone and turned to Erin.

"What did you find out?"

"He died in a car accident in July," said Polly. "Marilyn remembers reading about it in the paper. There was some kind of odd mechanical failure with his car and he went off a freeway overpass."

"That's awful," said Erin, thinking about it.

"Luckily it was in the middle of the night and there were no other cars near him when he went off the overpass. We all thought it was pretty strange."

"Yes, it is. What about David Keller?"

Polly checked a few screens for him. "I don't really know the name. It looks like he has only been with Triangle for a few months. He's probably getting more business since Dr. Altman died."

"I would imagine he is. Thanks Polly." Erin walked back to her desk. She would have to think about everything for a while and try to make some sense out of it. Having a few pharmacy visits for the afternoon, Erin thought she should try to at least do a couple of Utilization Management charts before she went out. Her visits would tie up the rest of the day, so she didn't plan on coming back to the office.

Her first chart must have been sent to her in error. It concerned a new mother who needed to stay in the hospital longer than normal; it was due to her asthma rather than something related to her delivery. The extra days were fine, as far as Erin was concerned, as the mother needed treatment that required a hospital setting.

The second chart was about a man who stayed longer after his surgery due to a wound infection. Erin got intrigued immediately. He had been at Southeast for a coronary bypass by Doug Altman in July. Looking at his chart from the beginning, Erin saw that he had his cardiac cath at Mercury by Michelle Campbell. A doctor by the name of Jeff Elliott reviewed the cath and the report was in the chart. The patient had extensive blockages in three coronary arteries and a note said the patient met criteria for the insurance company. She wondered what "criteria" meant in this context. Erin walked down to Polly again.

"Okay, Polly, I'm at your mercy. I know nothing about insurance lingo. What does 'met criteria' mean for coronary bypass surgery?"

Polly smiled. "Let me try to explain." She thought a moment. "Standards have been developed nationally to show if a surgery is medically necessary. We don't want people having surgery who don't need it. For coronary bypass, the arteries have to be blocked at a high percentage in order for it to be considered a medically necessary surgery."

"Polly, you're a wealth of information. How can they let you retire?"

"They don't have a choice." She laughed.

Erin went back to her desk and continued with the chart. The patient met criteria for the surgery at Southeast, which was done one week after the cath. The infection was in the saphenous vein, where pieces were taken to use for the coronary bypass. Erin didn't see a problem with the overstay at the hospital. The most common infections after coronary bypass are the saphenous vein infections and they can cause excess length of stay and readmissions. What Erin was wondering about was if Michelle always did her caths at Mercury and if Jeff Elliott always reviewed them. *Why doesn't Michelle review her own caths,* she thought. The chart said, "Procedure performed by Michelle Campbell, signed off by Jeff Elliott." That seemed very odd.

Erin got up out of her seat again and went walking down to Polly, who was on the phone. Polly looked up at her and motioned to Erin that she was getting ready to hang up.

"We'll meet there for lunch at noon tomorrow. Bye." Polly hung up the phone and smiled at Erin. "Need me again, Dr. Tyler?"

"Polly, I want to know if Dr. Michelle Campbell always does her cardiac caths at Mercury Memorial Hospital. Don't tell me I have to go through the Data department again."

"That's exactly what I have to tell you. If I had member names, I could look up what hospital they went to. I am unable to do what you are asking. Sorry."

"If I called over to the Data department, do you think I could avoid the formal request by email and get a rush on this?"

"I wouldn't bother. You'll just get in trouble for not filling out the form," said Polly, shaking her head. "There's really no way to get it quicker."

Erin went back to her desk, disgusted. She would not fill out that form again, and she decided to just call anyway and see where that got her. Getting on her email address book, she found a person located in the Data department and picked up her phone to call the number.

"Data. This is Regina."

"Hello, Regina. This is Dr. Erin Tyler. I'm a new medical consultant here and I'm in need of some information about one of our doctors."

"There is a form that needs to be filled out." Regina was unable to finish what she was going to say, as Erin interrupted her.

"I know there is a form. Is there any way to get information faster than the form?" Erin felt quite irritated.

"No."

"Thank you." Erin hung up the phone, feeling very defeated. She got on her computer and filled out the form. Deciding to look up Jeff Elliott on the computer, she typed in the name, but couldn't bring him up. Getting out of her chair to look for Polly once again, she saw Polly coming toward her.

"Dr. Tyler, I can see I'm just in time."

"I'm not finding this doctor. Why not?"

"It doesn't look like he's a Triangle doctor. We wouldn't have any information on him if he weren't. Anything else? I'm going out to lunch now."

"Is it lunch time already? I've got to get out of here. I have appointments to go to. Thanks for all your help today, Polly. I won't be here tomorrow, so I'll see you on Monday. Have a good weekend."

"You, too, Dr. Tyler. Good-bye." Polly smiled as she turned the corner toward the exit.

Erin shut down her computer and cleaned up her desk. As she put some papers in her top drawer, the sticky note that she had shoved back was up in front again. She took it out and looked at it. This was Dr. Kramer's note that she had found her first day at Triangle. Looking closely at it, she saw the name "Dr. Carroll" and "Dr. Fab." The letters after "Fab" were illegible. Could the first name mean Edward Carroll? Was the second name Mike Fabian? Erin couldn't believe her eyes. Did Dr. Kramer suspect something was going on at Triangle like Erin did, and was he fired for it? Or maybe firing wasn't what happened. Maybe it was worse than that.

Charlie was at his desk, writing up the figures for the July report that Susan was to type for Bruce. He picked up his phone on the first ring.

"Dr. Patton," he said.

"Good morning, Dr. Patton. This is Mary McDonald. I'm one of the managers over in the Data department."

"Yes, Mary. How can I help you?"

"We had a call today from one of your medical consultants, a Dr. Erin Tyler," said Mary.

"Yes." Charlie stopped what he was doing.

"She was trying to avoid filling out the data request form that is required to obtain information from our department. My analyst who answered the phone call thought her to be rude. Dr. Tyler was trying to get information about a doctor and wanted it quicker than two business days."

"Do you know which doctor?"

"No. The conversation didn't get that far. I just wanted you to be aware of the situation."

"Thank you, Mary. I appreciate the call and will take care of things on my end. Please accept my apologies." Charlie hung up the phone. The anger was starting to build again. That girl was definitely a thorn. He remembered that he needed to contact Rich about their special meeting on Friday. Dialing up Rich's number, he got his answering machine. Charlie slammed down the phone. He got up to walk to Susan's desk to give her the report to type.

She looked up as he approached.

He tossed the report across her desk. "I need this today. I'll take it to Bruce myself."

She picked it up and perused it quickly. "Dr. Patton, I hate to tell you this, but you're missing the summary at the end."

"It's good enough for who it's for. I'm not doing another thing with it," muttered Charlie. "Where's Rich?"

"I just saw him go back into his office."

Charlie turned from Susan and walked to Rich's office.

"Hey, Charlie," said Rich as he sat back down at his desk.

"Rich, I need you to do something for me next week."

"Sure, what do you want me to do?"

"I'm supposed to give a short speech at the Board of Directors meeting next Thursday night, but I'm going to be out of town. I was hoping you could give the speech for me."

"I'll be glad too. Have you already written it?"

"No. That's the problem. I just haven't had the time. Anyway, I was hoping we could go out to dinner tomorrow night and talk about it. How about you meet me at my favorite watering hole in Royal Oak about 8 o'clock. Sound okay?"

"Let me think a minute." Rich thought about how Jimmy's family would be getting in town tomorrow, but he would meet them right after work at his house. Lisa and Jimmy would then be setting them up in Birmingham and would be with them tomorrow evening. Erin and Steve would be leaving for London. Arlene? He didn't know what she would be doing, but she wouldn't mind if he had a business function. "I don't see a problem. I'll meet you there at 8."

"Great." Charlie turned to leave, then stopped. "You know the email that Bruce sent us earlier about a Dr. Armand?"

"Yes, what's that all about?"

"Armand is just a whiner. I don't believe anything he says."

"Do you know the Dr. Campbell that he is complaining about?"

"Oh, yeah, Michelle and I go way back. She's a great gal. A fantastic cardiologist." Charlie smiled and shook his head from side to side. "I wouldn't believe for a minute that she would make a patient do something they didn't want to do. She is one of our strongest specialists."

"Bruce wants one of the medical directors to investigate," said Rich.

"I'll take care of it. I'll talk to Bruce myself. The problem is that Dr. Armand is just an old milkshake who has seen his time. Now that's one that really needs to retire." Charlie pretended like his hands were shaking and he couldn't see in front of him. "Would you let this man diagnose you? I don't think so. He hasn't had a new book in his office for twenty years. Even his journals are old. He just rereads them. The poor old guy. He should be the one we get rid of."

Rich laughed. "All right, Charlie. Let me know if there's anything you want me to do with him. I'm a little bogged down with charts from Utilization right now."

"Hey, when is that lovely daughter of yours getting married?" asked Charlie. "I seem to be having a memory lapse."

"August 24. We've already received your RSVP."

"Right," said Charlie, putting his finger up.

Charlie left Rich's office and went back to his own. Looking at the clock, he figured Michelle would still be at the hospital. He dialed the number of Southeast.

"Southeast Regional Medical Center," answered the operator.

"I'm calling for Dr. Michelle Campbell," said Charlie.

"Who's calling?"

"Dr. Charles Patton."

"Hold on, please."

Charlie was placed on hold. He waited for about one minute before Michelle picked up the line.

"Dr. Campbell."

"Hi honey. We're all set with that special meeting I have for tomorrow night."

"Good. I'm getting ready to leave the hospital and I'll run the package over to you. Can you come out to get it when I arrive?"

"Just call up to my office and I'll come down."

"All right. Good-bye." Michelle hung up the phone.

Charlie looked at his schedule for next week. Too bad Rich wouldn't be around to give that speech next Thursday. Charlie could have really used him. He hated going to Board of Directors meetings. Talk about boring. Bruce wanted him to speak about things the health plan hoped to accomplish in the next year. He and Michelle wouldn't even be there all of next year.

Charlie put in his CAP disc to add up the scheduled surgeries for August. Looked good. With the month only half over, this would be their biggest take yet. It took about thirty minutes to go over all the numbers and the amount of money August would generate.

His phone rang.

"Dr. Patton," he answered.

"I'm here," said Michelle.

"Okay, be right there." He took out the disc and put it in his briefcase. Realizing he needed a pocket for the package, he put on his jacket and walked out of his office. Charlie didn't notice that Erin had gotten on the elevator before he reached it.

Erin had parked fairly close to the front door this morning. As she was getting into the Mustang, out of the corner of her eye she saw something red go by her, so she turned around. It was a red Cadillac pulling up to the entrance. Looking closely at it, she saw Michelle at the wheel. She crouched down a bit. Moments later, Charlie came outside the door and walked over to the driver's side. Michelle put the window down and handed Charlie something in a small white paper bag. They talked for a few moments, then Michelle sped away. Charlie put the bag in his jacket pocket and looked around for a moment before he returned to the building.

Wondering if she should make some excuse to go into Charlie's office, Erin sat in her car for a few moments, thinking. She wanted to find a way to check his jacket pocket and see what Michelle had given him. Then, thinking it was probably just Charlie's cocaine, she looked at her watch and decided she had better get moving to her appointments.

CHAPTER 11

THE Tyler home was bustling with excitement on Friday morning. Lisa had left for the airport to pick up Jimmy's family. Arlene and Erin were busy cleaning up the house and getting food ready. Rich left for work early, as he planned to come home before the group left for Birmingham in the early evening.

Erin had hardly slept the night before, due to the excitement she felt about the trip. She had already packed an overnight bag, but she kept changing her mind as to what she wanted to take, and she repacked several times. Steve and Jimmy would be in from Milwaukee around 1 p.m. and she couldn't wait until she could see them. She kept looking at the clock to see what time it was. Finally, hearing a car, she looked out the living room window just as the Yukon pulled into the driveway.

"Mom!" she yelled. "Lisa and the Emerson's are here."

Erin and Arlene got to the foyer just as Lisa opened the door.

"Hello," called out Lisa. "We're here."

The group was assembled in the foyer and Lisa started with the introductions.

"There are so many of us, I'm just going to say everyone's name. This is my mother Arlene and my sister Erin," said Lisa, smiling at them. "Jimmy's parents are Brian and Catherine Emerson and this is his sister Charlotte and his brother Neil."

Erin and Arlene starting shaking everyone's hands.

Erin thought that Jimmy and Charlotte really looked alike, both slim with blonde spiked hair. Neil looked more like his father, with brown hair and eyes. Brian and Catherine looked a few years younger than Erin's parents. Hearing their English accents made Erin smile and want to see Steve.

"If anyone needs to freshen up, feel free to use the bathroom. It is right down the hall here. Otherwise, please come into the living room and relax," Arlene said graciously.

Neil excused himself to use the restroom and the rest of the group went into the living room. Erin brought in some sandwiches and beverages. Conversation was made as everyone started to get to know one another.

"Does anyone want to see my wedding dress?" asked Lisa, looking around.

"I'd love to see it," said Charlotte. "Don't I have to get my dress fixed or something like that?"

"We'll be going on Monday to my friend Cheryl's house to alter your dress." Charlotte nodded as she followed Lisa into Rich and Arlene's room.

"I should go have a peek too," said Catherine, getting up and following the girls to the hallway.

"How was your flight?" Erin asked Brian as she took a sip of her iced tea.

"I think Catherine was trying hard not to go mad. She really doesn't like flying at all," he said. "At least this flight was quite a bit shorter than the one from England."

"I don't know if you've been told or not, but I'm flying to London today," said Erin.

He cocked his head toward her, looking interested and surprised. "I didn't know. How long are you staying then?"

"Until Sunday. Steve and I are going to pick up the wedding rings in Jimmy's townhouse."

"What? The wedding rings are in London?" Brian was shocked at the information. "It is quite nice that you two have agreed to travel that far for such a short time."

"I'm not surprised he forgot them," sniggered Neil as he returned from the restroom and took a sandwich from the tray. "Jimmy can be a little thick sometimes."

"Oh, rubbish," said Brian, admonishing him. "It could happen to anyone. Jimmy has been very busy."

Erin and Arlene couldn't help but look at each other and smile at the conversation. The women returned from seeing the bridal dress and sat down. Lisa had a huge grin on her face, looking deliriously happy.

"It is so beautiful," spouted Charlotte. She interlocked her fingers together and glanced toward her future sister-in-law. "Lisa, you must make my dress when I get married."

"If you ever get married," said Neil as he put up a forefinger to correct her. "Whenever you fancy someone, you just scare him off."

"Mum, make him stop," said Charlotte, frowning and looking to her mother for support.

"Now come on, Neil. Maybe if you have a bit to eat you won't be so difficult," said Catherine. She turned to Arlene as if to apologize. "My children haven't lived together in years, yet they still fight when they're together. You'd think they would have grown up by now," she said as she turned to her children and frowned.

Arlene tried to make everyone happy. "Please eat, Neil. I have plenty of food. If anyone needs a rest, I have a couple of rooms you can lie down in and another room to watch television in. Jimmy will be getting here in a little while and then he and Lisa will take you to your hotel. I know how difficult and out of sorts you can feel traveling and being so far from home."

Erin got up from her chair and started pacing, anxious for Steve and Jimmy to arrive. It was already almost 1:30 and they hadn't appeared yet. Hearing some noise outside in the front driveway, she rushed to the window and saw the boys getting out of a cab. She ran to the front door and opened it just as they were coming in.

"I'm so glad to see both of you," gushed Erin. She looked at Steve first as they put their arms around each other and smiled. Putting her face up to him, they gave each other a quick kiss. Turning to Jimmy, she gave him a big hug. "Your family is in the living room."

The boys walked into the living room with Erin following, and grinned when they saw Jimmy's family.

Brian stood first. "I see you two have been doing quite a bit of gigging," said Brian, shaking their hands.

"We're tired," said Jimmy as he ran his fingers through his hair. "I love touring so much, but I'm ready for a break after the wedding." Jimmy hugged his Mum and sister and slapped his brother on the back.

After Steve said hello to the Emerson's, he stepped back into the foyer and motioned for Erin to come out. She walked into the hallway and he immediately pulled her close to him in the corner by the front door.

"Do you still want to go with me?" he asked quietly, looking at every inch of her face and smiling.

"I'm ready." She put her arms around his neck and leaned into his body to kiss him.

He kissed back. "I've been looking forward to this all week. We'll leave for the airport at about 3. I'm knackered, but I'm going upstairs to pack now and take a quick shower. I'll be back down as soon as I'm able."

"Okay."

They kissed again and parted as Steve walked upstairs and Erin returned to the living room, anxiously waiting for the time to pass.

Since they were only going to be gone until Sunday, Erin and Steve would take a cab to the airport. It was in the driveway, waiting for them, a little while later as Steve ran down the stairs and they said their good-byes to the rest of the family. Just as they were walking out the door, Rich pulled up.

"You two have a good trip, just don't forget the rings," said Rich, smiling. "We'll see you on Sunday." He hugged Erin and shook Steve's hand as he went in the house to meet the Emersons.

The drive to the airport took longer than expected because it was the start of rush hour on a Friday. The freeway was like a parking lot with cars only a foot between each other's bumpers and four lanes deep. Anyone that was able to got off work early on Friday. Erin and Steve's cab finally made it to the airport without incident and they were dropped off at the International Terminal. Having no luggage to check, they went through security with their carry-on bags and sat down in the hard plastic chairs to wait for their flight to board.

"I realized today that I hardly know a thing about you," said Erin, looking around at the other people that would be on their flight. "Do you feel like telling me something?"

"What do you want to know?"

"Anything."

Steve thought for a moment, peering off into space as he squinted one eye. "Well, I'm from Bristol, in England's West Country, and so are Sid and Clive. Jimmy is from the Northwest."

"What is your family like? Do you have any brothers or sisters?"

"I have two brothers. One lives in Scotland and the other lives with his family near my Mum and Dad just outside of Bristol. My parents still live in the house I grew up in and I'm about an hour away from them. I'd like to show you, but we won't have the time to travel there on this trip."

"What do you like to do for fun?"

"I'm not much for the telly. I like football, but I'm starting to think it doesn't like me. It seems like I'm always getting hurt whenever I play. And I love to travel, so I have a good job for that. If I didn't like to travel, I would be in trouble. What do you like to do?"

Now it was her turn to think. She looked down to the floor for a moment. "I'm an avid reader and I love history, so I'm excited about this trip." She started to rack her brain again, then thought of something else to say. "When I lived in California, I liked going to San Francisco for fun and Yosemite National Park to hike and look at the scenery."

"I've been to San Francisco several times over the years," Steve grinned. "That place can get rather wild."

Erin smiled. She was anxious for the flight to leave and looked around the terminal, wishing they could board soon. "Do you like London?"

"I can tolerate it for a while, but it's really not my cup of tea. Too busy. Everything moves so fast. If you don't pay attention, you'll get knocked down on the street. It does seem like I'm there a lot, though. Jimmy and I write quite a bit together in his townhouse." Steve took out the tickets from his pocket. "I have to apologize for these not being in first class. They were already sold out when Lisa tried to get them."

Erin laughed. "That's okay. I've never flown first class anyway. I won't know what I'm missing."

"If you see first class, you'll know what you're missing."

The announcement came over the speaker system for their section of the airplane to begin boarding. Erin and Steve got up and went over to the gate entrance to stand in line, holding out their tickets and passports for the flight attendant to look at them. Passed through, they began to walk down a long hallway showing their tickets and passports again as they crossed the threshold into the plane. They were directed down the right side of the plane and found the location of their seats, which were about halfway down the plane in a row of only two seats.

Steve lifted up the armrest between their seats so they could be more comfortable and could get closer together. Blankets and pillows were distributed by the flight attendants to all the passengers to make them comfortable. After a smooth takeoff, Steve and Erin watched the in-flight movie while trying to get relaxed enough to go to sleep.

A petite woman with short blonde hair and glasses came up to their row and stood looking at them for a moment.

"Excuse me, but aren't you Steve Robinson?" she asked, smiling.

Steve glanced up at her. "Yes, I am."

The woman cleared her throat. "I just wanted to let you know that I've enjoyed your music since I saw your first concert in Detroit many years ago. Can I please have a picture taken with you?"

"Sure." He turned to Erin as he sat up straighter in his seat. "Erin, can you take the picture?"

Erin took the camera from the woman, who was grinning from ear to ear. The woman stood next to Steve's seat as Erin focused the camera and took the picture.

"Please, take another one," said the woman, not moving from her spot next to Steve. "In case the picture doesn't come out."

Erin smiled and took another picture, then handed the camera back to the woman.

"Steve, can I get you to sign a CD?" the woman asked, pulling one out from behind her back that she had hidden.

"No problem."

She handed him a copy of his latest CD and a black Sharpie marker.

"What is your name?" Steve asked looking up at her.

"Linda."

Steve wrote and spoke at the same time. "To Linda, kind regards, Steve Robinson. Anything else I can do for you, Linda?" He smiled as he handed the CD and marker back to her.

"Look for me at the end of September when you play in Detroit," said Linda, with a twinkle in her eye. "Thank you and have a good trip." She grinned at Steve and Erin and left.

"She was real nice," said Erin as she watched Linda walk back down the aisle of the plane, wondering what it must be like to have fans.

"I enjoy talking to the people who like our music," Steve said. He turned to Erin and raised his eyebrows. "You never told me if you like our music."

"I like it a lot." She paused, then her eyes gleamed at him. "How could I answer otherwise?"

He smiled as he spread out the blanket and covered himself and Erin with it.

Kicking her shoes off and putting her pillow behind her back, she snuggled up against Steve, laying her head and hand on his chest.

"I'm going to sleep now," she said.

"So am I. It will be Saturday morning when we land." He bent his head down toward her and kissed her forehead, then leaned back and closed his eyes.

Charlie was at the restaurant a little earlier than 8 and got his usual quiet, dark booth in the back. He was feeling a little nervous. After all, he usually didn't do the dirty work and he had known Rich for a long time. Trying not to feel guilty, he thought he had better start drinking to help himself relax. He motioned for Laura, whom he saw was working tonight.

She walked over to him and smiled. "Dr. Patton, I haven't seen you in a few days."

"I've just been too busy to go out. What are you doing working these late hours?" he asked, as he fidgeted with his tie.

She shrugged one shoulder. "I'm just working a double tonight because we had a sick call. What can I get you? Your usual?"

"No. I think I'll have a Budweiser. Draft."

"All right, Doctor. I'll be right back."

Charlie didn't even look at her backside like he usually did when she walked away. Didn't even think of it. Moments later, she brought him the beer and set it down on a napkin.

"Are you dining alone tonight?" she asked as she held four menus in her hand.

Charlie picked up his beer, taking a long drink from it, then set it back down. He let out a deep breath. "No. My guest should be arriving soon. Just set down the menus and we'll order when he gets here."

Laura nodded and set down two of the menus before she walked away.

Charlie looked at the menu, making his selection, then laid it back down. He took a writing tablet out of his briefcase and started making a few notes. Checking his watch, he saw it was 8 exactly, and looking up, there was Rich coming over to him, right on time as expected.

"Hello, Charlie," said Rich, sliding into the booth and taking off his jacket. "Did you already order?"

"No, just a beer. I was waiting for you."

Rich glanced at Charlie's drink. "Beer? Sounds good." He looked at the menu.

Laura was dropping off drinks at another table near them and noticed that Charlie's guest had arrived. She walked over to the table and smiled.

"Are you ready to order?" she asked, looking to Rich first.

"I'll just have the club sandwich," said Rich, closing the menu back up and handing to Laura. "And a Budweiser."

"Cheeseburger and another beer," said Charlie, smiling at Laura and handing her his menu as she walked away.

"Are you ready to start working?" asked Rich.

Charlie frowned at him. "Rich, don't you ever relax? Let's have a beer first." He drained his first beer and remembered what a perpetual drag Rich was. Seeing Laura leave the bar, she was coming toward them already with their new beer.

She walked over and set them down. "Anything else until your dinner comes?" she asked, looking from one to the other.

"No, thanks," said Rich, smiling.

Laura turned and walked away.

"Did Erin get off to London?" asked Charlie, gulping his drink.

"She's gone. It's too bad they have to come back so soon. She'll hardly get to see the city." Rich took a sip of beer.

"What a shame. All that way for a weekend. Is your other daughter's wedding all set?"

"Just waiting for the day. Her fiancee's family arrived today and Lisa and Jimmy are showing them around for the weekend," said Rich.

Charlie saw Laura glancing at their table and nodded to her as he held up his almost empty mug.

"I guess we should get started," said Charlie, reluctantly picking up his pen.

Rich took out a pad of paper from his briefcase and a pen from his pocket.

"Okay, the speech just needs to be only about fifteen minutes or so. I think you know most of the Board of Directors," said Charlie, looking at Rich.

"I do."

"Bruce wants the speech to focus on what managed care organizations are facing now and for the future."

"So, problems with costs, of course."

Charlie nodded. "I just got word today from Bruce that we had to raise our rates again."

Rich shook his head. "That's too bad. Let me see. Pharmacy, delivery of care, government regulations." Rich was making notes.

"Of course," said Charlie, writing down what Rich was saying.

Rich stopped and wondered why Charlie was writing things down if he was going to give the speech. "What are you doing? I thought I was giving the speech?"

Charlie shrugged. "Old habit, I guess. I'm so used to taking notes on everything."

Rich looked around. "Charlie, we should have picked a brighter spot to meet. This place is dark. I can hardly see my paper."

Charlie ignored the remark.

"I think I'll run to the bathroom before our food comes," said Rich as he set down his pen and got up.

"I'll get you another beer."

Rich walked around a corner towards the men's bathroom and out of sight.

Charlie was still having a twinge of guilt. He knew this was the right time and he had to overcome his feelings. Knowing what a lucky man Rich was made it even harder to do the deed. Rich had a wonderful family and was an all-around nice guy, but this was necessary. It was now or never. Rich would only be gone a few minutes. Reaching into his pocket, he took out the small envelope Michelle had given him with the crushed digoxin. Pouring it into Rich's half-full beer, he stirred it with a knife, wadded up the envelope, and placed it in his pocket. Drying off the knife with a napkin, he set it back down on the table just as Laura was bringing over their meal and Charlie's beer.

"Here you go," said Laura, smiling as she set the food down. "Sorry it took so long."

"No problem," grinned Charlie. "Another beer for my friend here." He saw Rich coming around the corner, returning from the restroom.

"Time to eat, I see," said Rich, sitting down and taking a sip of beer. He turned to Charlie and made a face. "The beer seems to taste a little bitter," he said, picking up his sandwich.

"I noticed that too. Maybe we got a bad batch," said Charlie as he started to eat.

While they ate and talked about Triangle over the next thirty minutes, Laura came back with Rich's second beer. He had already finished his first and gave her the mug. After they cleaned their plates, they leaned back against the booth and relaxed for a few minutes.

"That cheeseburger was almost too big for me," laughed Charlie. "It must have been a pound of meat. I'll have to let my belt out a notch."

"Well, my sandwich didn't sit too well. I feel a little nauseated."

"I'm sure that will pass," said Charlie, looking at Rich more closely.

"Now back to business." Rich looked at his pad of paper again. "Another big concern for managed care organizations is quality. There is overuse and underuse of services, and I know there is misuse going on too."

Charlie glanced at Rich quickly, but Rich wasn't looking at him.

"There can also be too much variation in services, depending on the physician and what kind of physician group he is in." Rich took a sip of the new beer and wrote down a few things.

"Quality," wrote Charlie. He looked at his watch. It would take at least thirty minutes for Rich to start having symptoms and it had been forty-five minutes already. The nausea could have been the first one.

"You know, Charlie, I've been doing a lot of reading about electronic record systems. Since Triangle is growing, I also think we should look into giving more incentive to physicians who use them. It's real easy to just flip through pages and pages of patient history, and I think our physicians would be more likely to comply with preventive measures if they have more support. If a flag came up that it was time for a diabetic to have their dilated eye exam or bloodwork done, the physician would be more likely to order it."

Charlie nodded and made a note. "Sounds like a good idea."

"We can't expect our physicians to remember everything on their own. The amount of new medical studies released every year showing what treatments work is astounding. System support is real important and we need to help our physicians as much as we can, thus increasing quality."

"Southeast has electronic medical records."

"Yes, I know. From what I hear about Southeast, it must be a great place to work," said Rich.

"I know their system cost millions of dollars, but it does hook up with every aspect of their health care delivery system which includes some of the physicians affiliated with us. I'm not sure how many Triangle physicians that would comprise, though."

Rich looked up from his pad of paper. "Funny. My vision seems a little blurry." He looked across the restaurant trying to focus. "Everything looks kind of green and yellow. Is it the lighting in here?"

Charlie didn't say anything.

Rich cleared his throat and let out a deep breath. "We need to somehow make it easier on our physicians to follow our rules, too. Too many of them are upset with the insurance company process."

"Rich, slow down. Your speech is looking longer than fifteen minutes," Charlie laughed. "We're not giving a day-long seminar."

"Charlie, I'm not feeling well." Rich turned his head from side to side, looking around. "I feel dizzy."

Charlie kept writing on his pad of paper. He looked out of the corner of his eye at Rich.

"My head feels heavy. I can hardly hold it up," said Rich almost inaudibly. "I feel like I'm going to pass out." Rich's voice trailed off as his head fell down toward his right shoulder and he started to slump over to the table.

Charlie nervously looked around the bar. No one was looking at them. The corner they were in wasn't very well lit and there were no other patrons near them. He tried to set Rich up and lean him back against the booth. Checking Rich's pulse, he found it to be slow and irregular. How much longer it would take, Charlie didn't know. He kept his head down and pretended to be writing. Seeing Laura starting to come their way, he still didn't look up. Maybe she wouldn't come over there either. But she did.

"How are you guys doing?" she asked, walking up to them. "How about I take away those dirty dishes to give you more room?"

"Fine," said Charlie, barely looking up. "We're working on business."

Laura looked from Charlie to Rich. He appeared rather odd, she thought. Something just didn't look right about him. She went around to Rich's side of the table. "Sir, can I get you anything?"

He didn't answer her and there was no acknowledgment that he even heard her at all.

Laura's voice showed concern. "Dr. Patton, I think something is wrong with your friend." Laura touched Rich's shoulder. "Sir, are you okay?"

Rich fell down against the table.

Laura jumped back and screamed. "Someone call 911! Someone call 911!"

A number of people in the restaurant could be seen getting out their cell phones from purses and pockets and pushing in numbers.

Charlie had to show his concern immediately. "Oh no! Rich, what's wrong?" He lifted Rich's torso from the table and laid him gently back against the booth.

Taking his pulse, he still found it to be slower than before and quite irregular. Rich might be in heart block now. Charlie saw that Laura was watching everything going on so he needed to put on a good show.

Two young men ran over to the table. "Do you need any help?" one of the men asked.

Charlie looked at the two men in front of him, then realized that the entire restaurant had quieted down. All eyes were on them. Charlie put his fingers through his hair. "We should put him on the floor," he said, starting to feel a little shaky himself.

The men helped Charlie lay Rich down flat. Charlie rolled up Rich's jacket and placed it under his head, looking Rich over again. Rich was breathing and still had a pulse, but he was unconscious. There was nothing that could be done until the paramedics arrived. Charlie remembered that he still had the small envelope that had contained the digoxin in his pocket. He had to get rid of it as soon as possible. He glanced around the restaurant. The few minutes of waiting seemed like an hour.

Laura looked up as she noticed some commotion toward the front door. "I think the paramedics have just arrived."

Charlie saw a woman and a man quickly coming over to them with their supplies.

"What happened?" asked the woman as she placed a blood pressure cuff on Rich.

"We were just here working and he slumped over," said Charlie, trying to explain. "We're both physicians and we work together. Rich said he was nauseated and dizzy right before he passed out. His pulse is slow and irregular and I'd say it's running around thirty to forty beats per minute. He only had a couple of beers and dinner while he was here with me. I don't know if he is on any regular medications or not."

The paramedics started working on Rich. One of them put oxygen on him and established IV access. The other one placed him on cardiac monitoring and saw that he was in second degree heart block.

"Look at the monitor, Cecelia," said the male paramedic.

She looked at it for a moment, eyes looking serious, then turned to Charlie. "Does he have a family?"

"Yes, I'll call his wife. He'll be going to Mercury Memorial Hospital, I presume," said Charlie, also seeing the cardiac monitor and trying to formulate a new plan.

Cecelia took Rich's blood pressure before answering. "It's the closest emergency room. What's his name?"

The other paramedic was removing equipment from his supply chest and placed an external pacemaker on Rich. Medication was given through Rich's IV.

Charlie watched him for a moment, then addressed Cecelia. "Richard Tyler. I'm sure his wallet is in his pocket with his driver's license." He ran his fingers through his hair again and let out a deep breath. "I don't know who his doctor is, but I'll call Dr. Michelle Campbell to take a look at him when he gets to the emergency room. She's a cardiologist who works out of Mercury."

"His pacemaker isn't capturing well," said Cecelia to the other paramedic as she watched the monitor. "We'd better get moving."

The male paramedic moved the stretcher next to Rich and he and Cecelia lifted him up onto it. Strapping him down and securing the equipment, they nodded to Charlie as they wheeled Rich out of the restaurant.

Laura looked at Charlie. "I hope he's going to be all right." Noticing that Charlie appeared frazzled, she asked, "Are you okay? You don't look so good."

Charlie touched his forehead and noticed he was perspiring. Patrons of the restaurant were still looking over his way and whispering. It was time to make himself scarce. "I don't feel so good. Excuse me while I go to the restroom." Charlie nodded and left Laura, quickly walking to the men's restroom. Going from stall to stall, slamming the doors open as he peered in, he had to make sure no one else was there to witness what he was going to do. He was alone. Breathing heavily, he went back into the first stall and locked it. Taking out the small envelope he had hidden in his pocket he opened it up again and looked inside. Hiding down in the corner, almost unnoticeable was a clump of the crushed white drug. Damn! Charlie shook his head in disbelief, because Rich hadn't gotten the fully-intended dose. He tore up the envelope angrily and flushed it down the toilet. Taking out his cell phone, he made the call to Michelle.

"Charlie," she said picking up on the first ring.

He let out a deep breath. "Things haven't gone as planned."

"What happened?"

"Everything was going fine. In fact Rich was already unconscious and I had everything under control, then the damn waitress noticed something was wrong with him."

"Is he alive?"

"He's on his way to Mercury as we speak. I told the paramedics you would take a look at him in the emergency room, so ER may page you. It looked like he was in second degree heart block and they placed an external pacemaker."

"I'm on my way." She paused. "You're going there, aren't you?"

"Yes. I'll call his wife and give her the news." He paused a moment. "Michelle?"

"What? I'm in a hurry."

"He didn't get the complete dose. I don't know what happened. The envelope still contained some digoxin when I checked it."

Michelle hung up the phone.

Charlie cleared his throat and starting thumbing through his cell phone address book, looking for Rich's home phone number. Thompson. Trenton. There it was. Tyler. He dialed the number, thinking how much he dreaded this call as it began to ring.

"Hello," Arlene answered.

"Arlene, this is Charlie Patton." He couldn't help but sound somber.

"Is something wrong?"

"I don't know where to begin, Arlene." He sighed. "Something happened after dinner with Rich. We're not sure yet. He said that he was nauseated and dizzy and a few minutes later he passed out. It looks like it's his heart." He paused. "The paramedics came and they took him to Mercury Memorial Hospital."

"Why didn't you have them take him to Southeast?"

"Mercury is closer, and I know for a fact that one of the best cardiologists around is over at Mercury tonight. Her name is Michelle Campbell." He paused again. "I was only thinking of Rich. I'm sorry if Mercury wouldn't have been your first choice."

"That's all right. I'll go right over there."

"I'll meet you in the emergency room, Arlene. I'm very sorry."

Arlene hung up the phone.

Feeling stunned, she ran upstairs to grab her purse. She tried to concentrate on what she needed to do, but she couldn't think straight. Walking into the bathroom instead of the bedroom where her purse was, she redirected herself upon realizing her mistake. She was trying to remember where Mercury Memorial was and couldn't. Then it came to her. She hadn't been in that part of town in a long time. It would take about thirty minutes to get there and she could call Lisa on the way. Grabbing her purse off of the dresser in her bedroom, she ran out to the car and started the engine. As she pulled out of the driveway, she took out her cell phone to call Lisa.

"Hello," Lisa answered cheerfully.

Arlene tried to focus on the road as she drove. "Honey, something's happened to your father."

"What?" Lisa's voice changed to one of concern.

"He's in the hospital. I'm on my way there now."

"An accident? What happened?"

"I'm not sure. He passed out in a restaurant. His boss, Charlie Patton, was with him and says it might be his heart. I don't know anything more than that."

"I'm going there," said Lisa, sounding like she was going to cry. "Which hospital?"

"Mercury Memorial. Do you know where it is?"

"Yes, I think so."

"Where are you now?"

"We're still at the Townsend Hotel with Jimmy's family, but we were getting ready to leave anyway."

"All right. I'll see you there." Arlene hung up the phone and tried to stay centered on the drive.

The ambulance arrived at Mercury Memorial Hospital, screeching to a halt in front of the emergency room. Rich's stretcher was pulled from the back of the ambulance and wheeled through the double doors by the two paramedics.

"ER#2," a voice yelled to the paramedics from the desk.

Rich was pushed into the appropriate spot as a physician and nurse, both dressed in blue scrub clothes, ran toward his stretcher. In a well-practiced hospital scene, the paramedics and emergency room personnel moved Rich from the ambulance stretcher to the hospital stretcher in a single fluid move. The nurse, Sally, hooked him up to the hospital's oxygen and cardiac monitor as quickly as she could, freeing the ambulance equipment so it could be returned to its rightful place. The physician wheeled in the red metal crash cart that held the emergency room equipment and drugs next to Rich's stretcher, keeping his eyes on the cardiac monitor. Cecelia started giving an oral report to the physician while Sally began to take vital signs. Rich was still unconscious as they pulled the curtain around him and began the next round of treatments.

"Let's give him Atropine 1 mg ," said Dr. Roth, seeing the second-degree heart block. "His pacemaker's still not capturing well."

Sally proceeded to give the dose of Atropine through Rich's IV. They now had to wait a few minutes to see if it had any effect. Meanwhile, Dr. Roth put on his stethoscope to listen to Rich's heart. A technician came around the curtain to do an electrocardiogram and everyone moved back to give her room and to watch the monitor.

"So we don't know if he has taken any medications?" asked Dr. Roth, looking at the paramedics.

"We don't know anything about him except that he started complaining of nausea and dizziness before passing out," said Cecelia, looking at her clipboard.

"The patient is Richard Tyler, according to his driver's license. I've been told that he's a physician. Dr. Michelle Campbell is supposed to be coming in to have a look at him."

"Great," said Dr. Roth, with a determined stare at the cardiac monitor. "Michelle can take over when she gets here." The technician left and he listened to Rich's heart with his stethoscope again.

Sally took Rich's vital signs and they all watched the cardiac monitor, hoping for a change in the heart rhythm. There was no change.

"Sally, give him another dose of Atropine," said Dr. Roth, looking at his watch. "I wonder if we are dealing with an acute overdose or an accidental ingestion of something. Let's draw some blood and check out a few things."

Sally gave the Atropine and went outside the curtains to get the glass tubes that would hold Rich's blood.

"Thanks," said Dr. Roth, nodding to the paramedics.

The paramedics dropped off their paperwork at the desk and started to leave. The double doors opened just as Charlie entered the emergency room, deep in his own thoughts. He recognized them immediately.

"Is the man you brought in still alive?" he asked, turning around to look at them as he hoped for the worst.

"Yeah. He's over in ER#2," said Cecelia, as the doors closed behind her.

Charlie shook his head in disbelief as he hurried over to the emergency room desk to speak with the clerk who was just hanging up the phone.

"Excuse me, I'm Dr. Charles Patton," he said impatiently. "I was with the man that was just brought in. Can I see him?"

"No," said the emergency room ward clerk, a round woman in her 40s who was used to rejecting requests. "Dr. Roth is with the patient. Are you family?"

"No, I'm not, but his wife is on her way."

"The patient is currently being treated and can't have any visitors."

Charlie expected that answer. "Has Dr. Campbell arrived yet?"

"No, she hasn't. You'll have to go out in the waiting room now, sir." She took her pen and pointed toward a single door, wanting her request to be obeyed immediately.

Charlie knew he had no choice but to go. He briefly looked around the emergency room just as Michelle walked in through the outside doors. Rushing over to her, he ignored the clerk who was calling to him loudly.

Michelle saw him, but kept walking toward the desk. "Charlie, I haven't even seen him yet. Back off and let me work." She pushed her hair behind her ears and frowned as she began to read the barely assembled chart the clerk handed her.

Charlie figured there was nothing he could do now. Everything was out of his hands. Thinking of how much he hated having no control over a situation, he roughly pushed open the waiting room door and sat down on the green vinyl couch to watch television with the dregs of society who frequented this emergency room.

Michelle was pointed to ER#2 by the emergency room ward clerk, and she went over immediately. She pulled open the curtain a little and saw Sally drawing Rich's blood. Knowing that they would suspect digoxin, due to what Rich's cardiac monitor was showing, she had to think hard about what she should do. Her first thought was just to slip over to the medication room, grab some potassium chloride from a bin, inject him when no one was looking, and be done with it. The potassium chloride would kill him quickly and wouldn't show up on autopsy, but a rational plan was needed instead.

"Hello, Paul."

"Michelle. Glad to see you," said Dr. Roth, who turned from the cardiac monitor to Michelle.

"I think we'll skip the drugs and go right for the temporary transvenous pacemaker," she said, making her first decision in taking over Rich's care. Watching as Sally took the blood out of the emergency room to the lab, she pursed her lips in dread.

"Do you want to wait for some lab work before you do the pacemaker?" asked Dr. Roth.

"No, I don't want to wait."

"I think this might be a drug ingestion, but since he already has toxic manifestations, I'm concerned about inducing vomiting or passing a gastric tube," said Dr. Roth.

"Yes." Michelle listened to Rich's heart for a moment. "Paul, can you have the clerk call ICU and get a bed? As soon as I'm finished, we'll take him over there." Michelle looked up at the monitor and saw that Rich was still in second-degree heart block.

Dr. Roth left the room as Sally returned with the temporary pacemaker and the other equipment needed for the procedure. Sally expertly set up the area and helped Michelle put on her sterile gloves, surgical mask, and gown.

"Need any help?" asked Dr. Roth as he peeked back into ER#2.

"No, I think we're fine," said Michelle, not looking up, as she started to work.

"Good. I'm needed elsewhere. Thanks, Michelle." He let the curtain fall back and left.

Michelle placed the temporary pacemaker through the internal jugular vein without difficulty and watched the cardiac monitor stoically a few moments to check for problems. The pacemaker was now taking over for Rich's failing heart and it was performing as it should.

Sally let out a sigh of relief upon seeing the cardiac monitor. "We can move him to ICU anytime, Doctor. The bed is ready."

Michelle nodded. "Let me chart for a few minutes in the physician charting room. Call me after the chest x-ray and electrocardiogram are completed. I'll help you move him to ICU."

"Sure, Dr. Campbell," said Sally, smiling as she opened the curtains around Rich's stretcher.

Michelle took Rich's chart and walked into the windowless charting room near the desk, closing the door behind her. She quickly looked at the orders Paul had written and took them off the chart. Folding the paper, she placed it deep in her pants pocket, then looked up when she heard a knock on the door.

"I have Mr. Tyler's lab work," said the emergency room ward clerk as she opened the door in the room.

"Thanks, I'll take it." Michelle took the papers from the clerk and the clerk closed the door. She studied everything. The digoxin toxicity showed up, as was expected, but it wasn't as high as she had hoped for. It could go higher in a few hours after more of it was absorbed, but of course he didn't get all of it anyway. The other drug screens were negative and the lab work was good. She placed the digoxin report in her pocket and put the other drug screens and lab work on the chart. Writing her own physician orders, that didn't include digoxin screening, she was ready to help move Rich to ICU. Leaving the chart room but never letting go of Rich's chart, she walked over to the stretcher. "Can we move him now?"

"Sure, Dr. Campbell," said Sally. "Testing is completed."

Michelle and Sally rolled Rich's stretcher down the hall to the ICU. He moaned but never opened his eyes. The ICU nurse helped them move him into the bed as they hooked him up to the ICU cardiac monitor and placed his IV on a pole. Sally starting giving the ICU nurse a report on the patient as Michelle went over to the desk.

"I've written my orders," said Michelle to the ICU ward clerk. "I'm going to the ER waiting room to talk with his wife and I'll come back to check on him before I leave the hospital."

"Okay, Dr. Campbell," said the ICU ward clerk, smiling at her as she took the chart from Michelle and started to process the physician orders.

Michelle walked back down the hall to the emergency room. She peeked through the small square waiting room window and saw Charlie sitting on a couch, talking to a redheaded woman. She assumed the woman was Rich's wife. Taking a deep breath in and blowing the air out, she opened the door and walked over to them. Michelle held out her hand for the woman as she approached the couple.

"Mrs. Tyler?"

"Yes," said the woman.

"I'm Dr. Campbell." Michelle shook Arlene's hand and sat down in the green vinyl chair next to her.

"How is he?" asked Arlene, staring at Michelle straight in the eyes.

"He's in critical condition, I'm afraid. I placed a temporary pacemaker, as his heart was in a rhythm that could have caused cardiac arrest. We will just observe him now and see if his heart gets better on its own. If it doesn't get better," she paused and took a breath, "then we can discuss other options for treatment." Michelle tried to hold Arlene's gaze, but couldn't and looked away for a moment.

"What caused this?" Arlene asked, her eyes never leaving Michelle's face.

"At this point, I'm not sure. Does he take any medication on a regular basis?"

"No."

"His blood was checked for a number of drugs, but everything has been negative thus far. Mrs. Tyler, we are in a wait-and-see period now. That is all I can tell you. The ICU will let you in to see him whenever you want to go back." Michelle stood up to end the conversation as Lisa and Jimmy rushed into the waiting room, running over to Arlene. Michelle ignored them and continued speaking. "I'll talk with you when there is further news." Turning to Charlie, she frowned. "Dr. Patton, may I have a word with you?"

"Sure," he said as he stood up and followed Michelle to the hallway beyond the waiting room where they could be alone.

Michelle was angry, but cognizant of where they were, and kept the volume of her voice down to a loud whisper. "Nice going, Charlie. Unless something unexpected happens, he's probably going to pull out of this. I will not take any more chances while he's in the hospital and will do everything in my power to save his life."

"Great," said Charlie as he put his fingers to his temples. "We're screwed this time. Did the ER doc order a digoxin screen?"

"Yes, but I intercepted it. The digoxin was positive in his blood, of course, but not as high as I had hoped. The chart now has nothing in it about the order or the lab work. I put new orders in."

He tried to smile. "You're right on top of things, Michelle." She was truly amazing and that was just one reason why he loved her. "So we might be free and clear on this?"

"It's still too early to predict. I'm going back to check him again then I'm out of here. We'll talk tomorrow." She turned away from him and left.

Charlie looked over at the Tylers, huddling together, and reluctantly walked back to them. He couldn't wait to get out of the hospital. There had been quite enough activity and stress for one day.

Arlene looked up when she saw him. "Charlie, this is my daughter, Lisa, and her fiancee Jimmy. I know you met her a few years ago," said Arlene as she took a tissue from her purse and dabbed at her eyes.

"Nice to see you again, Lisa. Hello, Jimmy." Charlie nodded at them and turned back to Arlene. "I'll wait and go back with you to see Rich if you like."

"That's okay, Charlie. We'll be all right. I'm going to get his paperwork done for admitting now, and then we'll go see him," said Arlene. "Thanks for your caring. I appreciate it."

"I'll call you tomorrow, Arlene. Oh, it's already Saturday," he said as he looked at his watch. "I'll call later this morning. Take care." Charlie glanced at all three of them, exuding his most serious look of concern, and left the emergency room.

Arlene glanced at Lisa and Jimmy. "I guess they have Rich's drivers license and Triangle insurance card at the counter. I'm going up there to see what else they need." She grabbed her purse and walked up to the admitting desk.

Lisa lay against Jimmy's shoulder and started crying. "Jimmy, I'm so scared. We need to let Erin and Steve know."

Jimmy patted her on the head, trying to console her, then looked at his watch. "Darling, it's 1 a.m. here but 6 a.m. there. It is still a while before their plane lands. Didn't Erin say she would ring you?"

"They were going to do some sightseeing and she was going to call me later this morning." Lisa sat up as the tears streamed down her face.

Jimmy put his arm around her. "We should have more information by then."

"You're right. Erin was going to call me at home around 10 in the morning, our time. We'll just make sure we're there to get her call." Lisa wiped away the tears that were running down her cheeks and tried to regain her composure.

Arlene walked back to them and let out a deep sigh before speaking. "He's in ICU bed #5. I guess it's down this hall to the left," said Arlene as she motioned to the door that would take them to the correct hallway.

Lisa and Jimmy got up from the couch and started their somber journey with Arlene down the hall. Their footsteps echoed as they walked though the quiet hospital. The bright lights of the hallway made everything seem surreal, and when coupled with apprehension made their walk even more daunting. They pushed the square silver button on the right side of the ICU doors, which opened automatically. Arlene went in first and walked up to the desk that was right inside the doors.

"I'm Arlene Tyler. My husband, Richard, was just brought in here."

The nurse looked up at her from the desk with caring concern. "Hello, Mrs. Tyler. I'm Theresa and I'll be your husband's nurse for the rest of the night. Please come with me. I'll take you to his room." Theresa looked at Lisa and Jimmy as she stood up.

"This is my daughter, Lisa, and her fiancee, Jimmy," said Arlene. "We would all like to go in."

"No problem."

They followed Theresa around the corner from the desk. The ICU unit was only five beds, so Rich's room wasn't very far away from where they had started. Although they could see other people in the ICU beds, they could only focus on one.

Lisa gasped as they got closer and could see inside Rich's room. He was lying in bed with a cardiac monitor at his bedside. There were many wires that appeared to run underneath his hospital gown. He had an IV hanging on a pole and didn't appear to be awake.

"How is he?" asked Arlene, looking at Theresa as they followed her into the room.

Theresa walked over to the foot of Rich's bed. "A little while ago, he tried to talk, but he didn't open his eyes. It seemed like mumbling and he just moved his head from side to side. Those wires are to his pacemaker and the cardiac monitor that you see there," she said pointing at them. "He is getting IV fluids, but no other medications."

"Do you know why this happened?" asked Arlene.

"We're not sure what caused this abnormal heart beat he is having. It almost seems drug-induced, but nothing has shown up on his drug screens," said Theresa.

Arlene, Lisa and Jimmy just stared at Rich in disbelief.

"There is a waiting room across from the double doors where you came in," said Theresa. "Feel free to stay in there. Visiting hours here are only every four hours for fifteen minutes at a time. The times are listed on the waiting room doors. I'll leave you with him now. Please let me know if I'm needed." Theresa touched Arlene's arm and left the room.

Arlene showed no emotion. Her eyes were fixed on Rich's face.

Lisa clung to Jimmy. "I wish Erin was here," she sobbed.

CHAPTER 12

ERIN woke up and tried to stretch her legs out under the seat. She was surprised how well she had slept on the plane. There wasn't any noise during the night, as most of the other passengers also wanted to sleep and the plane ride had been very smooth. Lights were turned down low, and thank goodness there had been no crying babies. She ran her hand over Steve's chest. Finding him very cuddly didn't hurt her sleeping either. Not knowing what time it was, she bent down and grabbed her purse from the floor. Taking out the watch that she had changed to the correct time zone before the trip started, she saw that it was 6 a.m. There was more activity in the cabin and Erin looked up to see what the commotion was. The flight attendants were pushing the breakfast carts down the aisles of the plane and other passengers were waking up.

The captain's voice came over the intercom. "Good morning. This is Captain Dunn speaking. We will be landing at Heathrow within the hour. It should be bright and fine in London today, with a high temperature of 22 degrees Centigrade. We hope you had a pleasant flight and that you will fly with us again soon."

Erin turned toward Steve. He looked like he was still sleeping. She lifted her head up to his and gently kissed his mouth. "Wake up, sleepyhead," she whispered into his ear. "It's time for breakfast."

He opened his eyes and smiled at her. "Now that's the way to wake up. Just have a pretty girl kiss you."

She hugged him. "Did you get some sleep?"

"Actually, I did."

The flight attendants reached their seats. Erin and Steve sat up straight and pulled down the trays in front of them as they took their breakfast from the flight attendants.

"This doesn't look too bad," said Steve as he peeked at his bran muffin and pulled the lid off the strawberry yogurt.

Erin was starving and dove into her breakfast right away.

"After we go through customs, we'll need to look for the ride Lisa ordered us. A man will be holding up a sign that says 'Tyler,' and he will take us to the townhouse," said Steve.

Erin nodded her head in agreement as she took the last bite of her breakfast.

The flight attendant walked around to see if anyone needed more beverages. She stopped at their row as Erin held up her coffee cup.

Erin thought that she had better have all the caffeine she could get in order to stay up all day, so she took another cup. Steve wanted tea with milk. By the time they had finished their beverages, the plane was descending and it wasn't long before they landed.

The customs line was short and soon they were in the greeting hall, looking for the man who would take them to Lisa and Jimmy's townhouse. The hall was crowded and loud, with people talking and luggage carts screeching by. Erin thought she saw a man holding up a sign with her name on it toward the back of the hall. She grabbed Steve's arm as they filtered through people and walked over there.

"Hello," she said, looking at his sign and seeing her name. "That's us."

"Very well," said the man. He nodded to them curtly. "I'm parked outside here." He pointed toward a door near where they were standing that was opening and closing at a frantic pace from so much activity.

They walked outside to his waiting car and the man opened the back door for them. Erin got in first and Steve followed, closing the door behind him. The driver and Steve briefly discussed directions to the townhouse.

Erin thought it seemed a little chilly outside, but it was early in the morning. "The pilot said it would be 22 degrees Centigrade today. Does anyone know what that is in Fahrenheit?" She looked from Steve to the driver.

Steve frowned and appeared to be thinking. "If my calculations are correct, it would be about 71 degrees Fahrenheit."

"Well, that's better than I thought." Erin looked out through the window as they exited the airport roadways.

There were three lanes for each traffic direction and each lane was crowded; this must be the London equivalent of rush hour. Erin didn't know if she could drive on the opposite side of the road and could understand how Steve had difficulty with it when he was in the United States. She loved how everything appeared foreign to her, from the way the rows of identical buildings looked to the advertising signs. Some of the cars seemed very small and they darted in and out of traffic at a hectic pace. She shuddered as motorcycles flew in between the cars, only inches away, but acted as though they had the right of way. It didn't take very long before they got to an area where the roads were a little different. Businesses and restaurants were evident, and the roads seemed to intersect more. Going down to two lanes with parallel parking on each side of the street, there were now traffic lights and she could see what she thought must be a subway station.

Steve saw her looking at the station. "Over here, we call that the 'underground' or 'tube.' While we're here, we can take a cab."

"I want to ride the tube," Erin said, turning to him. "It has been years since I last rode one when I was in Toronto. Unless you mind, of course."

"I don't mind." He smiled at her, relenting. "You want to ride the tube, we'll ride the tube."

She squeezed his arm. "Thanks."

"Up here on your left you'll see Kensington Palace," said Steve, nodding and looking up ahead. "I know that was something you said you wanted to see while you were here."

Erin saw the palace behind a long, wide walkway and beautiful, well-tended green gardens. It was a large, impressive-looking red structure with two stories of lengthy windows and an ornate gold and black gate surrounding the complex. She looked at it until it was out of sight.

It took only a few minutes more until they arrived at Jimmy and Lisa's three-story home. The street contained what looked like continuous townhouses, with one townhouse hardly looking different from the next one except for minor architectural differences. The only thing separating the townhouse from the street was the sidewalk. The driver pulled up in front of a corner brown brick one with white-trimmed windows and a black wrought-iron fence on each side of the black front door. Getting out of the car, they collected their bags and Steve paid the driver. Erin looked in anticipation as they walked the few steps to the cement porch and Steve opened the door with the key he took out of his pocket.

The living area was a light-filled room of high ceilings and large windows with elegant, modern furniture and a polished, wooden floor—just the sort of place Erin could see Lisa living.

She set down her bag and walked around in a circle, taking in everything.

"This is great. I love it," she said enthusiastically.

Erin saw a picture of herself on an oak end table and walked over to pick it up. She was standing in a breathtaking setting of mountains and greenery.

"I remember when this was taken. This is at Inspiration Point in Yosemite National Park. I love it there. There's El Capitan, Half Dome, Full Dome, and Bridalveil Falls," she said, looking at the picture. "Lisa and my parents had come out to California to visit me. She was living with Jimmy and told me all about him, but he wasn't able to come on that trip." She frowned, trying to remember. "I think you guys were working on the new album." Erin's face darkened and she set the picture back down quickly. It made her think of her breakup with Chris.

Steve saw the look on her face, so he went over and picked it up. "I, too, have a story to tell you about this picture," he said, gazing at it.

Erin looked up at him, waiting for him to continue.

"When Lisa moved in here with Jimmy, she set that picture up on this table. Everytime I came over here, I was drawn to it. They would have thought me totally daft if they knew. I've been looking at it for over a year, wondering if I would ever meet you." He looked at Erin, then set the picture back down. "When I found out I was actually going to meet you, I couldn't believe it."

Erin smiled. "Steve, that's so sweet." She put her arms around his back and gave him a squeeze.

"Now let's go get those rings before we forget," he said, grinning at her and remembering why they were in London. "Come on."

He led her up the stairs and down a hallway to Lisa and Jimmy's room. It was a luxurious master bedroom in cranberry and navy. The room had large windows on two sides, and when Erin walked over to the back window, she had a view of a brick patio with a small but lovely garden surrounding it that couldn't be seen from the front of the townhouse.

"I don't know how they could leave this place," she said. "I'd love to live here."

Steve opened up the closet and moved a shoe rack. Behind it was a wall safe. He took a piece of paper from his wallet and proceeded to open the safe with the combination. Taking out two ring boxes, he closed the safe back up and put the shoe rack back into its proper position.

"Well, here they are." He opened up the boxes to reveal two matching platinum wedding bands.

Erin picked up one of the boxes. "This ring is gorgeous," said Erin, looking closely at it.

"They were crafted locally," said Steve. "Lisa has a jewelry store she goes to all of the time."

"No doubt," said Erin as she gave Steve back the ring and smiled.

"Getting back to other matters, there are two bedrooms for you to choose from." He led her back out into the hallway and walked her by the two rooms, hoping that whatever room she picked he would be a guest there tonight.

The first room was in pastel colors and white wicker, but Erin liked the traditional bedroom that was beige, mocha, and pewter, with oak furniture.

"This will be the one," she said as she went in and sat on the bed and looked around. Lisa's style overflowed into the room, from the accent pillows to the window coverings. It was very comfortable and it was all Erin could do not to lie down now, as she was so tired. "Let me freshen up and I'll be right with you," she yawned.

"I'm going to put these rings away. Now don't go to sleep," he said firmly as he walked back down the stairs.

Erin felt like she needed to change the shirt she had slept in on the plane. Taking it off, she opened up her bag. Choosing a white cotton blouse, she put it on and buttoned it. It was tight, with a low neckline showing just a hint of cleavage, and it looked good with her low-cut stretch blue jeans. She glanced at herself in the mirror and turned from side to side briefly. This was just the way she liked to dress when she wanted to be noticed. Over the shirt, she put on a little pink hooded jacket, but left it unzipped. Walking over to the bathroom across the hall, she brushed her teeth, touched up her makeup, and combed her hair, which was somewhat unruly from the long plane ride. She was ready for Steve—and for London.

She walked out into the hallway, admiring the art Lisa had on the walls, and then down the stairs to the living room, looking around at Jimmy and Lisa's beautiful home all the while. Steve was just walking out of another bathroom, combing his hair as he moved.

"What's on the third floor?" asked Erin, looking up.

"It's just storage right now."

Erin nodded.

"Do you want to eat first or go to the Tower of London?" he asked, putting his comb in the back pocket of his jeans.

"I think the Tower of London first. I'm not hungry yet."

"All right then. Let me think of where the nearest tube station is." He appeared to be deliberating for a moment, then went over to one of the end tables in the living room and opened the top drawer. Inside was a tube map. "Aha! I thought I remembered one in there," he said, opening it up and studying it. "Looks like we can get on the Circle Line at Notting Hill Gate and take that all the way to Tower Hill. Sounds good."

They left the townhouse and started walking down the street. It was a sunny day and Erin looked at everything around her as they walked from the residential area to the business area. A red phone booth, with a man in a tweed jacket, talking and waving his hand. A grocery store that seemed so much smaller than the ones at home. And the shops: designer blouses, coats, shoes, dresses, and accessories that appeared never-ending. Display windows full of London's treasures. Walking fast to keep up with Steve, she could see the tube station with the red circle and the blue horizontal bar on a building up ahead.

Steve bought their tickets for the journey to Tower Hill and back again from the machine in the station entrance hall and they walked down the stairs to wait for it.

Erin saw an illuminated sign that said two minutes until tube arrival. Scanning the walls around her, she could see advertisements for plays and television shows. Hearing a noise, she felt a rush of air. The noise got louder and she could see the tube coming from the dark circular tunnel. Being much longer than she thought, it stopped and the doors opened immediately. She and Steve went in the closest door with a few other people and sat down just as the doors closed. There were padded seats on both sides and poles and handles to hold onto if the seats were full. Advertisements continued on these walls and a map for the Circle Line reminded you of where you were. An English woman's voice over the intercom announced each stop as it was made until their destination was announced: Tower Hill. As the doors opened, they sprang off of the tube and up the stairs into the sunlight. As soon as they rounded a corner, Erin saw it.

It was a medieval brick fortress that was so much larger than Erin had imagined it to be. They walked down the hill and crossed over the street. Erin couldn't help but stare at it the closer they got because it looked so amazing. There were many different buildings and architecture from various points in history, with a high wall surrounding the entire place. A city within a wall. Looking like it didn't belong in modern London, the Tower looked as though someone had plucked it out of history and just stood it there on the edge of the Thames. It was so hard to believe it had been there for so many hundreds of years and the rest of London had been built around it.

There were many different areas to examine, so Erin took a map at the entrance and started reading it while Steve paid the entrance fee.

"Do you have a preference as to where we go first?" she asked him.

"I haven't been here in years. Let's just start exploring." He held his hand out for hers and they started walking.

They went through building after building. Each one was built at different times in history and had different stories to tell. Some of the goriest events in England's history happened here. From the scaffold site where two of Henry VIII's wives were beheaded to the Bloody Tower where two young princes were murdered, the Tower of London was simply an astounding place to visit. The crowd was thin, as Erin and Steve had arrived early on this Saturday morning and they saw quite a bit over a one-hour period.

They began to feel physically tired from the plane ride and time change and Erin's feet hurt. Seeing a sign that said "Jewel House," they went inside the building. An employee of the Tower was standing there to let them know that no pictures were allowed in this area. Leaving the employee and entering a small, dark room, they saw many chairs with high backs on them, all connected together. Each chair had a different monarch of England listed on it.

Steve started reading. "Henry VII 1485-1509, Henry VIII 1509-1547, Edward VI 1547-1553. Enough of that." Sitting down in the Henry VIII chair, he leaned back and watched Erin as she looked at all of the monarch names. Liking the way that she moved and the way she was dressed and how she brushed her blond hair away from her face, he thought she was completely gorgeous. He was surprised at the restraint he had been showing, but it was getting too hard. "Erin, please come over here."

Erin turned around and saw him watching her. She walked over and sat down on his lap and put her left arm around his neck, running her fingers through his soft hair. Placing her right hand on his chest, she felt his heart beating beneath her hand. She smiled as his eyes burned into hers and she didn't look away. Gazing into each other's eyes, face to face, their breathing seemed to synchronize. As he parted his lips, she leaned toward his face and they kissed each other.

The hard, wood chair was small and not very comfortable, so they moved a little to find a better position. Steve put his left arm around Erin's shoulders and she leaned back against the arm of the chair as the kissing intensified for a few minutes. He then left her mouth and started kissing her chin, slowly working his way down her neck. Reaching the top button of her blouse, he lifted up his head and undid the first three buttons with his right hand. As the buttons let loose, the blouse opened quite a bit, exposing a low cut pale blue bra and considerable cleavage. He looked up at her and saw no objections as her head stayed back against the chair and her eyes were closed. Bending his head down, he lingered, kissing her cleavage and touching her exposed skin until he heard her moan. Taking his time, he kissed her all the way back up to her mouth, then laid his cheek against hers.

"What do you want to do now?" he asked in a low voice into her ear.

"I want to go back to Jimmy's," she whispered, almost unable to breathe.

Lifting his head and kissing her mouth again, he helped her get up. She stood and faced him while he stayed in the chair. Putting his hands around her bum, he watched closely as she buttoned her blouse and he realized he was barely breathing. They were both startled when they heard talking as some tourists walked into the room. It was time to go. Steve stood up and put his arm around her back as they left the room, going back out the way they had come in.

Not speaking as they left the Tower and keeping a brisk pace up the hill back to the tube station, they saw that the tube wouldn't be there for four minutes. Sitting down on a bench close together, Erin put an arm around his neck and her hand on his chest as they stared at each other again. They laid their heads back against the wall, gently kissing each other over and over again, not caring that other people were assembling to get on the tube when it arrived. Not stopping until they felt the wind from the oncoming tube, they got up and walked over to get on. He put his arm around her after they sat down and she laid her head against his shoulder.

"Erin, I was thinking. Let's get business done first. Why don't we stop at Victoria Station on the way back to the house? It's one of our large rail stations. You can ring up your sister there and I can pick us up a Travelcard for the tube. When we go out later tonight, we won't have to keep buying individual tickets each time we ride. I don't want anything to delay our pleasure when we get back to Jimmy's. How does that sound?" He looked at her, waiting for an answer.

She turned towards him and placed her hands on his shoulder, looking him straight in the eyes. "Whatever you want."

He laughed. "You're making me crazy."

There were quite a few stops before they reached the Victoria stop, where they got off. Erin was amazed at how crowded the area was. People were walking fast in all directions as different tunnels and stairs went to different tube lines and another tunnel would take you to the actual Victoria Rail Station. Looking at the signs, they found their way there.

A man and woman walked by them quickly. "Hello, Steve," the man said, not stopping to chat as they continued to walk.

Steve turned to look briefly at the people, but didn't know them, and he kept walking.

"Who was that?" asked Erin, looking back.

"I don't know. Sometimes I get recognized and people say hello." He motioned. "There it is up ahead."

The tunnel they were in stopped at the entrance to an immense building. A large open area with a cement floor gave way to benches, ticketing windows, and food marts. A high, rounded ceiling with rows of windows at the top let in sunlight, but the outermost part of the building was open to the elements and Erin could see many railroad tracks leading into it. This was Victoria Rail Station, and it was even busier than the tube.

"I see a phone booth over there," Steve said, motioning over to their left. "You can use the phone card Lisa gave you. I'm going over here to the ticketing window to get our Travelcards."

"All right." They separated and Erin walked over to the area where she saw a few phones, dodging people right and left as she moved. She went into an open booth and got out her phone card. As she looked at her watch, she noticed that she would be calling an hour sooner than she had planned. Hopefully someone would be home and awake. She dialed the number to her parent's house.

Lisa answered on the second ring. "Hello."

"Hey."

"Erin, I'm so glad you called. Are you having a good time?"

"I'm having a great time with Steve! He's turning out to be something special."

"I'm sorry to have to bring you down, but something terrible has happened," started Lisa.

"What?" Erin didn't know what to think.

"It's Dad."

"What's happened to Dad?"

"He's in the hospital, Erin." Lisa started crying. "He's in critical condition."

Erin couldn't believe what she was hearing. "Lisa, what put him in the hospital?"

"He was having dinner with his boss."

"Charles Patton?" she said, interrupting. She immediately started to seethe.

"Yes. Dad was nauseated, got dizzy, and passed out. They say that his heart is in a block or something, and they put what they called a temporary pacemaker in him."

Erin spat out the words that she dreaded to ask. "Who put in the pacemaker?"

"Her name is Dr. Michelle Campbell."

Erin started breathing fast. Wanting to yell and cry at the same time, she heard a loud roar and turned to see two trains coming into the station. "Lisa," she said talking louder, "I'm at the train station and a couple of trains are coming in. Stay right there. I'll call back in a few minutes." She hung up the phone, took a deep breath, and let out a scream that would have been heard all over Victoria Station if the trains hadn't been roaring in. It took her a few minutes to calm herself and to think properly. Michelle and Charlie had tried to kill her father. Erin hit the glass in the phone booth with her palm in frustration and anger. She looked up and saw that Steve was still in line, so she dialed home again.

"Erin?" Lisa answered.

"It's me. Tell me as much as you can. How is Dad acting?"

"He's acting drugged or something. Mumbling, not making any sense. He had his eyes open for a while early this morning, but that's all."

"How long has he been in the hospital?"

"Not even twelve hours yet."

"So he has a temporary pacemaker?"

"Yes."

"What else is he hooked up to?"

"A heart monitor and an IV."

"Is he getting any drugs?"

"I don't think so, but I'm really not sure."

"How's Mom doing?"

"Okay. She hasn't left the hospital. Jimmy and I were there most of the night with her, and we just came home to get some sleep. His family is here now and we're supposed to take them to Comerica Park to a baseball game today. Maybe we shouldn't go. I don't know what to do."

"I want to call Dr. Campbell and the hospital. What hospital is he in?"

"Mercury Memorial Hospital."

"Mercury?" Erin would have preferred for him to be at Southeast where they had the intensivist on duty at all times that would collaborate with Michelle. At Mercury, Michelle would be the only doctor writing her Dad's hospital orders, and that was not a good thing. Charlie and Michelle had probably planned it that way.

"Yes, hold on a minute and I'll get the phone numbers. I'm putting the phone down."

Erin heard Lisa's shoes click clack away from the phone. Cradling the phone between her shoulder and neck, she opened her purse and took out a little blue spiraled notebook and black pen she had in the corner. She heard Lisa's footsteps as she came back, and she was ready to write.

"Erin, here they are."

Erin wrote down the numbers that Lisa gave her. "I'm going to make some phone calls. I'll see you tomorrow. I love you."

"I love you, too. Bye." Lisa hung up.

Erin opened the door of the phone booth and saw Steve walking over to her with a spring to his step. He was now a man with a mission. An elderly gentleman with a beret stopped him for a moment and she saw Steve speak with him and then point toward the tube. The man hobbled off in that direction and Steve turned her way again. She hated to tell him what had occurred. Things were starting to go so well between them, but he would understand. He just had to.

Steve could tell immediately by the look on her face that something was wrong. "Erin, what's happened?"

Erin sat down on a green bench in front of the phone booth, feeling overwhelmed and so far away from home. "Steve, my father is in the hospital and is very ill. I'm not sure what's going on yet, but I think Charlie and Michelle tried to kill him."

"Let me try to get us an earlier flight back." Steve went into the phone booth and Erin could see him flailing his arms about as he talked loudly. He came out about ten minutes later. "There is only one direct flight each day to Detroit, and it's already left. We would have quite a few layovers and planes to change to if we leave today, but if that's what you want to do, we'll do it."

Erin thought about it a moment, then shook her head. "No, we'll just leave tomorrow as planned. I guess I should make the phone calls to try to get more information."

"You can make the calls at Jimmy's. They don't have to be done here."

"I'm here now." She stood up.

Putting his arms around her he said, "Right then. Do whatever you need to do. I'll just sit here and wait." He turned from her and sat down on the green bench, concentrating his view on a large group of people who were talking to a train conductor.

A determined Erin went back into the phone booth, and using the phone card dialed up the hospital.

"Mercury Memorial Hospital," the operator answered.

"Could I have the ICU, please?"

The operator connected her.

"ICU, Pat speaking."

"My father is a patient there. His name is Richard Tyler. I'm his daughter Erin, and I'm calling from England to find out about his condition."

"His condition is critical," Pat answered.

"I need more information than that. I'm a physician. Can't you please tell me more?"

"If you're a physician, then you know that I can't give medical information over the phone. I'm sorry. Do you have any family in the waiting room that you might wish to speak with?"

"Yes, my mother should be there. Can you check?"

"One moment." Pat put the phone on hold.

A few minutes later, someone picked up the phone.

"Erin?"

"How's Dad?"

"I don't know. He doesn't seem much different than when he got here."

"He hasn't gotten any worse, has he?"

"No, they haven't said that. Everytime I get to see him, everything is calm. There just isn't much going on."

"I have to tell you something, Mom. Please listen carefully to me, and don't repeat anything I say. I don't want to alarm you, but I think Charlie may have done something to Dad. Dr. Campbell is Charlie's girlfriend and they are up to no good."

"What?"

"There are some problems going on at Triangle. I'm telling you, I don't trust Dr. Campbell or Charlie, and you have to believe me."

There was silence on the phone.

"Mom, I don't want Dad leaving his room for any testing. Do not sign a consent for any procedure. He cannot leave his room for any reason at all. I'll be back tomorrow afternoon and will come directly to the hospital from the airport."

"Are you sure that's the right thing to do?"

"Yes. I'm thinking that this illness may be drug-induced and when the drugs wear off, Dad should get better."

"They said there were no drugs in his system."

"Hmm." Erin thought for a minute. Dr. Campbell may not have ordered testing for the drug that was given to him. "Please, Mom. I feel very strongly about this. Any procedure can wait until I arrive tomorrow. Then they will have to convince me that it's needed."

"Okay, Erin. I'll do what you say. I had better get off their desk phone in case they need it."

"I'll see you tomorrow. I love you, Mom." Erin hung up the phone and started crying. She went outside the phone booth and sat down with Steve. Leaning against him, she let the tears pour down her cheeks, feeling like her heart had been crushed. Life without her father had just become a consideration, and she wasn't ready to deal with that yet.

"Are you ready to leave now?" he asked. He rubbed her back, trying to console her.

"No." She paused. "I have one more phone call to make," she said, barely able to talk. Erin cried for a few more minutes until she couldn't cry anymore. Feeling stronger, she got up and went back into the phone booth, taking a deep breath as she dialed.

"Answering service for Dr. Campbell," the voice said.

"My name is Dr. Tyler, calling for Dr. Campbell."

"Can I take your number and have her call you back, Doctor?" the operator asked.

"No. I will hold. I'm calling from England."

"Very well, Doctor. Hold on, please."

Erin waited for almost five minutes before she heard a pick up.

"Dr. Campbell," Michelle answered pleasantly.

It was Michelle. Erin felt outraged just to talk to her. She tried to remain calm. "Dr. Campbell, this is Erin Tyler. I'm Dr. Richard Tyler's daughter."

"Oh, yes, Dr. Tyler. Dr. Patton has told me about you."

Erin was sure that Charlie had told Michelle about her. "I'm calling to get information about my father."

"Well, he's in ICU on oxygen, IV fluids, and a cardiac monitor. I put a temporary pacemaker in while he was in the emergency room due to second-degree heart block unresponsive to Atropine. I'm not sure yet if he will need a permanent pacemaker. That is a possibility."

"What kind of lab work did you order?" asked Erin.

"We checked him for a variety of drugs, from calcium channel blockers to beta-blockers, because we didn't know if he took any regular medications. Of course we checked his electrolytes, cardiac enzymes, thyroid, BUN and creatinine. Everything looks fine so far. We are taking good care of him. There is no need for you to worry about that."

Erin shook her head in disbelief. She didn't want to question Michelle too much and make her angry. "Well, thank you, Dr. Campbell, for speaking with me. I'll be back there tomorrow. I look forward to seeing my father and meeting you."

"Same here, Dr. Tyler. Good-bye."

Erin hung up the phone and laid her head against the glass of the phone booth. She started hitting it gently, then harder.

Steve heard the noise and got up. "Are you all right?" He looked concerned.

"I'm fine. Let's go."

"Where to?"

"Beer. I want beer."

Leaving Victoria Station, they went out into the sunlight with the crowds and the noise and started walking. Erin had no idea where they were, and she didn't care. Steve was thinking more sensibly.

"We haven't eaten all day. Do you mind pub food?" he asked.

"What's pub food?"

"Nothing fancy and not a large food menu."

"Fine. Is that a pub over there?" asked Erin, pointing at a corner establishment that had large, oval etched windows trimmed in wood and its name printed in gold lettering on the front and sides.

"Yes, it is."

The pub had small wooden tables and chairs with a few booths. Pictures of brightly-colored parrots were all over the dark red walls, and a clock with Roman numerals hung high above the pictures. Huge mirrors hung from the wall behind the bar and reflected the numerous beers on tap in front of it. A blackboard near the bar had a large menu that featured the variety of beer the pub had and another smaller menu that listed the food.

"Do you know what kind of beer you want?" asked Steve as he looked at the menu.

"No."

"Pint or half pint?"

"Pint."

He walked over to the bar to order. "One pint of Guinness and one of London Pride," he said to the bartender as he waited, then paid. "Cheers," he nodded to the bartender as he left the bar.

Erin thought that it seemed so long ago since they had gotten off the plane. Too much had happened since then. She tried not to think about her dad, but he kept coming back to her mind.

Steve brought the beer over and sat down. "I believe I could eat something now," he said, looking up at the food menu. "A meat pie sounds good."

Erin looked at the food menu. "What's a jacket potato?"

He laughed. "It's just a baked potato cut in half with toppings on it."

"I guess I'll have the jacket potato with white cheddar cheese and vegetarian baked beans," she said, reading off the menu. "Do we have a waitress?"

"No, we order our food at the bar, too, and the bartender will bring it over to us. I'll go order." He went back up to the bar and placed the order.

Erin couldn't believe how pleasant he was. "Steve," she said when he returned, "thanks for being so understanding. I'm sorry that I don't feel like going back to the house now."

"You've had quite a shock, haven't you? It's all right. Don't worry about it."

They drank their beer while watching the other people in the pub. It wasn't long before their food arrived and they ate in silence. After the next beer, they decided to leave.

"Where do you want to go now?" Steve asked.

"Let's just walk."

They moved soundlessly. The walk turned into blocks, until Erin looked up and saw a familiar site. It was a lavish clock tower within a beautiful Victorian Gothic Revival building. Erin stopped and stared.

"That's Big Ben and the Houses of Parliament. Did you know that Big Ben is really the main bell, and not the clock itself?" asked Steve.

"No, I didn't," she said, squeezing his arm and trying to smile.

They started down a street named "Birdcage Walk," where they saw more beautiful gardens and then what looked to be a gigantic gray building with a black and gold fence and a large paved area in front of it. It was a somber looking place without much color, but it was impressive nonetheless.

"Let me guess," said Erin. "Buckingham Palace?"

"Right. Many people come here just to see the Changing of the Guard, but it gets much too crowded here for me," said Steve.

"Can we go have another beer?"

"Why don't we take the tube first and get closer back to Jimmy's." He looked at the tube map he had in his pocket and directed Erin down another street.

They walked for a few minutes until they reached the tube station. Hearing it howl through the tunnel as they went down the stairs, they broke into a run and hopped on just before the doors closed. Laughing as they sat down, Erin laid her head against Steve's shoulder until they reached their stop.

"There is a pub right down the street here that you might like. In fact there are three pubs on this street, not very far apart. They all know Jimmy and Lisa by name. I don't think they'll remember me, though."

Walking until they reached the first one, they went up to the bar and ordered. The bartender did recognize Steve and nodded to him. They sat down in a corner on upholstered stools and drank their beer. By the time they finished their third beer, it was dark outside.

"I think I've had enough for one day. Do you mind going back now?" Erin asked.

"It's always been your choice as to what we do. I have to say, I'm rather exhausted myself."

Erin and Steve trudged back to the townhouse and wearily went in. Steve started walking around, turning on a few lights, then locked the front door.

Erin went up to her room. She took off her jacket and shoes and laid down on top of the covers on her side, unable to do anything but stare at the wall. She felt so helpless. Charlie and Michelle had their hands in this, she just knew it. They did something to her dad, but what? They must have drugged him. But what drug was it? And why would they want to hurt him? Were they trying to get to her? She didn't have enough information to even make an educated guess.

Steve came upstairs into the room and sat down on the edge of the bed. "I'm sorry. We'll get back tomorrow and hopefully everything will be okay." He took off his shoes and lay down on his side to face her. Moving some of her blond hair that had fallen in front of her face, he got as close as possible to her putting his cheek against hers.

Erin thought that Steve was showing himself to be a wonderful, caring man. There was no one better that she could have fallen for. She draped her arm over him and started to move her face so they could kiss. Then, remembering that her Dad was ill, the mood was ruined and she stopped, but left her lips on his cheek so she could still be close to him for a few more moments. "I can't do this tonight," she whispered to him as she pulled away. Without saying another word, she turned over on her other side, away from him.

After a few minutes, he got up from the bed and picked up a blanket that was folded on a nearby chair. Spreading it over her, he turned out the light and started to walk out of the room.

"Steve," she said softly.

He stopped, but didn't turn around.

"Please don't go. Stay with me."

He turned around and climbed back onto the bed in the dark. Getting under the blanket, he snuggled up behind her until they were both comfortable. It wasn't long before they were asleep.

CHAPTER 13

THE light coming through the window woke Erin up, or so she thought as she turned away from it. It couldn't have been that she had this big, beautiful warm man sleeping next to her or the bathroom call her bladder was giving her. Then the real reason why she needed to wake up hit her. *Dad!*

Dragging herself out of bed, she looked at her watch. 7 a.m. She stepped across the hall to the bathroom and turned the shower to hot. Forgetting her fresh clothes, she walked back into the bedroom and saw him lying there. She stopped and stared at him for a moment. Still asleep. Still someone she wanted. Taking her clean clothes out of her bag, she went back into the bathroom, shaking her head and letting out a deep breath of regret at what hadn't happened. *Maybe next time,* she thought. The shower felt wonderful and helped her focus on what she had to do today. It was going to be a very long and arduous day. She dressed quickly and opened the door to the bathroom to let the heat out. Rummaging through a bathroom drawer she found a hair dryer and turned it on. She sat down on the toilet and closed her eyes as her hair dried, not hearing him come in.

"You could have woken me up for your shower. I would have agreed to watch you or even joined you," he said, smiling.

She opened her eyes, turned off the dryer and grinned. "You were asleep. I wouldn't have woken you up for that."

"I'm telling you now to please wake me up for that," he begged. "So, do you want to watch me take a shower then?"

She considered it for a moment. "No, I had better not this time. Next time." She set the dryer down on the bathroom counter and stood to put her arms around him. "I'm sorry things didn't turn out the way we wanted them to."

He looked back into her eyes. "Next time." Kissing her quickly, but not letting his passion take over, he released her and turned on the shower.

Erin made a hasty retreat from the bathroom and went back into the bedroom to pack. Not much to do really. She folded the blanket they had used on the bed and held it close to her. It was still warm. She put it back onto the chair next to the bed. The comforter just needed to be fluffed, and it looked as good as new. Walking out into the living room, she looked around again. Lisa and Jimmy had a beautiful place and she wanted to come back soon. London was already calling to her again, and she hadn't even left it yet.

It didn't take long for Steve to get ready, and he walked out into the living room. "I see you've already tidied up the place," he said. "We had better get breakfast before our driver comes."

They walked down the street, arm in arm, and got a bite to eat at an open restaurant, then hurried back to the townhouse to wait for their ride to the airport. A car pulled up within a few minutes of their return. The driver got out and opened the door for them. It was the same driver they'd had for the ride in yesterday.

"I see you've only had a short trip," he observed. "At least you had a good day." He looked up to the darkening sky. "The rain is moving in now."

Erin and Steve got into the car for the ride to the airport. She took in all the sites as they drove, trying to piece together the large map that was London. When she came back next time—and there would be a next time—she wanted to see everything and go everywhere.

Check-in time and wait time went by quickly at the airport, and before they knew it they were on their way to Detroit. The flight back was nothing like the flight over. Everyone seemed to be awake and fidgeting. She and Steve were in the middle of the airplane, with noisy people all around them. When Erin tried to sleep, she was awakened by the snoring of the man next to her and who was crowding into her seat space. Children sitting in front of her started throwing playing cards at her and one of them spilled apple juice in her lap. Things weren't going well this time, and she couldn't wait for the ride to end.

There was a thunderstorm in Detroit as they landed and the plane dropped in huge increments at a time as it got closer to the ground, making her feel sick to her stomach. When they finally landed, Erin felt like she needed to sleep for a week, but Steve seemed unfazed by it all. They ran through the pouring rain to get to a taxi as quickly as they could and were on the road to the hospital.

"I wonder if I should call and let them know we're on our way," she said, trying to decide what to do as they turned onto the freeway. Erin opened her purse, then combed her damp hair and freshened her makeup.

"How long will it take us to get there?"

"About forty-five minutes." She thought for a moment. "I don't think I'll call, because I don't want to hear any bad news."

They drove in silence and Erin was reminded of how tired she was. Even the ICU waiting room chair sounded good right now. Something to look forward to, she supposed. Pulling into the hospital parking lot, the taxi driver dropped them off at the front entrance of the hospital. Steve paid their fare and took their bags out of the cab.

With the apprehension building, Erin and Steve walked into the lobby and were directed to the ICU waiting room on the first floor. They saw Arlene, Lisa, and Jimmy sitting there as soon as they walked through the door.

"Erin," burst Lisa, "you don't know how good it is to see you two!" She jumped up and hugged both Erin and Steve.

"How's Dad?" asked Erin, looking around for an answer.

Arlene smiled. "He seems to be doing better. The last time we were able to visit him, he woke up and talked for a few minutes. Dr. Campbell was here a couple of hours ago and said that his heart is starting to beat more normally now."

"Really? She didn't ask to do any procedure on him?"

"No."

Erin thought that Michelle probably didn't want to take any more chances while her dad was in the hospital. "Well, I didn't get enough of London, but I'm glad to be back to see Dad."

"So how was your trip, dear? Did you get to do everything you wanted?"

"No," said Erin, not looking at Steve but feeling guilty for even thinking about him at this moment.

"Are you sure you don't want to go home and sleep?" asked Arlene. "You can come back tomorrow. I'll be all right here for another night."

"Go home, Mom. I'm staying," said Erin. "I don't want to miss Dr. Campbell in the morning." She had decided that she should stay with her dad and being there all night would allow her some snooping time when the hospital was at its quietest. The answers to many of Erin's questions were here at Mercury, she just knew it.

"Steve, did you remember that we have to do four days in a row this week because of the wedding this weekend?" asked Jimmy. "Cleveland, Cincinnati, Indianapolis, and Chicago. We won't be back until Friday morning."

"I know," he said, shaking his head. "We'll have a very busy week. My voice will be shredded. I can't remember if we ever did four consecutive days before."

"Friday!" exclaimed Erin, turning around to face Steve. "You won't be back until then?"

"I'm sorry, Erin."

Lisa and Jimmy looked at each other with raised eyebrows at Erin's outburst.

"We best be going," said Jimmy, getting up. "I want to go to sleep early."

"Steve, do you want to ride back with Mom to keep her company?" Lisa asked, looking at him.

He was gazing at Erin. "Yes."

"Erin, call us later with an update," said Lisa, noticing how neither Erin or Steve seemed to be listening as she and Jimmy walked out.

Arlene got up from the couch easily, observing that something was going on between Erin and Steve. "Erin, I'll tell the nurses I'm leaving and you're staying. I'll be back in a few minutes."

Erin put her arms around Steve as soon as her mother left. "I'm going to miss you so much! I don't want you to go." She kissed his cheeks, his forehead, his mouth…

"You're making this very difficult." He pulled her close.

"I should have wiped off my lipstick." She saw imprints of it on various parts of his face. She rubbed some of it off with her finger. "I don't want to get it all over you."

"That's all right. I want you all over me." He grinned.

She grinned back. "Will you think about me while you're gone?"

"All the time," he said, staring into her eyes.

"Will you call me?"

"Everyday." He kissed her. "Erin, I'm crazy about you."

"I know." She smiled at him.

"Be particularly careful. I don't want anything to happen to you."

"All right." Erin heard the clicking of her Mom's shoes on the hospital tile. They kissed each other one last time before they separated.

Arlene came back into the waiting room. "Erin, the nurses said to go on in and see your father, even though it isn't visiting hours yet." She walked over to the couch, then paused. "I did want to tell you how excellent the nursing care has been here. All the nurses make it a point to keep us updated and they have been very sensitive to our needs. I've been very pleased. I guess Southeast isn't the only good hospital around." Arlene grabbed her things off the couch and looking exhausted, turned to Steve. "Are you ready to go?"

"Yes, I'm ready." He turned to Erin and raised his eyebrows. "I'll call you."

After they left the room, Erin plopped down in one of the hospital chairs for a few minutes, telling herself to focus on what was important. Four days wasn't really that long and she just had to accept it. She would now be able to help take care of her dad and could work on her investigation. Having plenty of things to keep her busy until she saw Steve on Friday, she tried to put loneliness out of her mind as she got up to see her dad. She pushed the button to open the automatic door of the ICU and went up to the desk.

"Hello, I'm Erin Tyler. Someone said I could see my father," she said, looking at the people at the desk waiting for someone to acknowledge her.

"He's over there, Ms. Tyler," said a busy-looking man pushing a medication cart and motioning to Rich's room. "I'm Anthony, his nurse tonight. Go on in for a few minutes."

Erin walked quickly to her father's room and went in. Looking at the cardiac monitor right away, she saw that his heart appeared to be beating normally. There were no signs that the pacemaker was needed to make his heart beat. She felt elated at this information. His head was lying on its side and his eyes were closed.

"Dad," called Erin quietly, "can you hear me?"

Rich opened his eyes and tried to focus on the voice. "Erin, is that you?"

"Yes, it's me. How are you doing?" Erin smiled and got closer to the bed.

"I think I'm better." He turned his head to look at Erin and tried to move himself to sit up.

"Wait, let me help you." Erin found the controls to his bed and put the head of the bed in more of an upright position. "Is that better?"

He was able to sit up and Erin propped his pillows behind him to help him get comfortable.

"Yes, that's better," he said. "Fine time for my heart to go out on me. Right before your sister's wedding."

"Do you feel like talking?"

"I'll talk your ear off," he said, raising his voice. "I have to get strong as soon as possible. I'm dancing on Saturday, you know."

"Dad, what do you remember about the night you became ill?"

He frowned. "Charlie and I met at that restaurant he likes in Royal Oak. You know, the one he took you to."

Erin nodded.

"We were working, then we ate dinner. I started feeling sick after that."

"Dad, do you recall getting up from the table at any time and leaving Charlie there alone?"

Rich was thoughtful. "I don't remember. Why?"

"I think Charlie may have drugged you."

"How can you say that?" He looked at her face and saw how serious she looked. "Let's not go down that road again."

"You've been a healthy man, Dad. For you to suddenly go into second-degree heart block while you were with Charlie makes me very suspicious."

"All of my testing was negative."

"Dr. Campbell may have only tested what she knew would be negative."

Rich didn't speak. He didn't want to believe this.

"I want to see if I can get the nurses to tell me what was ordered for you, then I should be able to tell what wasn't ordered. Do you have any objections to that?"

"I guess not." Rich turned around and hit his pillow a few times. He leaned back and let out a breath. "All right, Erin. Do what you will."

"I'll be back." She walked out of the room, going over to the circular desk.

A nurse sitting at the desk watching the cardiac monitors looked up at her. "Can I help you?"

"Hi, I'm Dr. Tyler's daughter. I'm also a physician. I was wondering if someone would let me look at my father's chart." She knew they wouldn't let her, but she thought she would give it a try.

"I'm sorry, but you have to ask Dr. Campbell if she would go over the chart with you and we would need written consent from your father."

"Perhaps you could just look up something for me then." Erin smiled. "I just wanted to know what type of drugs Dr. Campbell checked for when she did my father's drug screens."

"I suppose I can tell you that." The nurse stood and picked up Rich's chart from the rack, pulling up the correct tab. "I'll just let you look through the labs yourself instead of reading them all off." She set the chart on the counter and watched as Erin thumbed through each page of labs.

"Thank you so much," said Erin, closing the chart and handing it back to the nurse. "Do you have a drug book here that I could borrow? I'll bring it right back."

"Sure," said the nurse. She put the chart back in the rack and reached for one book among many on the small bookshelf at the ICU desk. Handing it to Erin, she smiled and sat back down in front of the cardiac monitors.

Erin took the book back to her father's room and sat down. She turned to the index and looked up the drug that was missing from the labs ordered.

Rich watched her. "Well?"

"Dr. Campbell checked for many different drugs that can cause heart problems like the various beta-blockers and calcium channel blockers. She also did thyroid studies and has been checking your electrolytes. It looks like a very thorough work-up, but there is one drug missing that should have been checked for."

"What?"

"I just wanted to look the drug up to confirm what I thought." She turned the pages until she found the right one in the book and started to read. "It says that overdosage can put you into abnormal heart rhythms such as second or third-degree heart block. Some of the symptoms are visual changes, confusion, nausea, decreased consciousness, dizziness." She looked up at him. "I know you had some of those. This drug is a big one, and it is very obvious."

Rich shook his head and looked solemn. "Digoxin. That son-of-a-bitch Charlie tried to kill me with digoxin."

"I'm sorry, Dad." Erin got up from the chair as she closed the book and sat down on his bed.

Rich's nurse peeked his head into the door. "Ms. Tyler, I'm sorry, but I have to ask you to leave now. It really isn't visiting hours. You can come back in at 10 p.m., though." He smiled at Erin.

"I'll leave. Thank you, Anthony." Erin looked at her dad. "If you continue to do well tonight, I'm sure you'll get moved out to the regular floor tomorrow and may even get to go home tomorrow or Tuesday if you don't have any problems. Keep that heart beating normally and I'll be back at 10." Erin stood up and bent over to kiss his forehead.

"I think I'll nap for awhile. See you later." Rich took his bed control and put it in the "down" position and moved his pillows around.

Erin left his room and returned the book to the ICU desk. She knew her father needed to rest, but he had a lot of thinking to do, too. Realizing how exhausted she was, Erin went to the waiting room. Someone had turned the television up very loud and it was immediately annoying. There was no one around, so she turned it off. Lying down on one of the couches, she closed her eyes and her fatigue took over.

A ringing sound seemed far away but was relentless. Erin could hear it in her mind, but when she opened her eyes she realized it was a phone ringing. Looking around and seeing no one else there, she had to pull herself off the couch. Feeling like it was taking forever to get to the phone, she finally made it over to the other side of the room to answer it.

"ICU waiting room," she said.

"Erin?"

She smiled. It was her Englishman. She sat down on a small folding chair in front of the pay phone and closed her eyes. "It's me."

"How's Rich?"

"He's doing well. Since the drug overdose is wearing off, his condition is changing dramatically. I think he'll be able to go home tomorrow or Tuesday." She yawned.

"So that was his diagnosis—drug overdose?"

"That's my diagnosis. Dr. Campbell didn't test for the drug she overdosed him on."

"Can you prove she did that?"

"No, she's gotten away with it this time, but there won't be a next time."

"I'll inform everyone of the fantastic change of events. Erin, since we have been getting on so great, I thought I would ask you something."

"Yes?"

"Would you be interested in going on holiday with me for a few days after the wedding? Lisa and Jimmy will be on their honeymoon, so we aren't playing for two weeks. I have to spend more time with you."

"I'm supposed to work, but I'm thinking of leaving the company anyway. I really don't think I'm cut out for that type of job, but I can't make any plans until I see how my dad does." Erin leaned her head and the chair back against the wall so it was balancing on two legs, her eyes still closed. "What did you have in mind?"

"How about the Caribbean?"

She smiled. "You and me in the Caribbean. That sounds wonderful. Lying on the beach, listening to the waves and drinking Margaritas."

Erin didn't hear someone come into the waiting room and walk over to her. The person stood and stared at Erin for a moment, listening to Erin's conversation. Then she spoke.

"Are you Dr. Tyler?"

Startled, Erin opened her eyes and found herself looking directly into Michelle Campbell's face. Putting the chair flat down on the ground again, she stammered into the phone, "Steve, I'll call you right back. Dr. Campbell is here." Erin's manner went from playful to serious in a heartbeat as she hung up the phone. She stood and held out her hand.

The tension was thick as both women regarded each other with suspicion. They shook hands and started sparring.

"Yes, I'm Dr. Tyler. May we talk?"

Michelle nodded. "Would you like to stay in here?"

"Fine," said Erin, directing Michelle over to the couch as they sat down in unison. "My father seems to be doing great now. I don't anticipate any more problems. Do you?"

"No, I don't," said Michelle. "In fact, I just removed his temporary pacemaker. I plan on discharging him tomorrow evening if nothing further develops."

"That's what I was hoping. So what is your final diagnosis, Dr. Campbell?" asked Erin, staring at Michelle.

"Second-degree heart block, cause undetermined."

"Cause undetermined?"

"Yes."

"Such a healthy man who has never been on any medications. That's rather odd, isn't it?"

"It is. But as you know, medicine is not an exact science." Michelle was inching toward the edge of the couch.

"Yes." Erin paused as she chose her words carefully. "Just so that you're aware, Dr. Campbell, we plan on being extra vigilant now for any problems."

Michelle stood up, her face expressionless. "He'll be moved to a regular floor in the morning. Increasing his activity will greatly help his strength. I will be by to see him in the afternoon. Can I expect to see you too, Dr. Tyler?"

Erin stood and nodded. "Yes. I'm not leaving the hospital until he does."

Michelle nodded back. "Goodnight." Turning her back to Erin, she left the waiting room.

Erin sank back on the couch and sighed. The confrontation with Michelle could have gotten much uglier, but would have led to nothing. There was no proof of attempted murder. Knowing that the answers to her other questions about Michelle had to be here at Mercury Memorial Hospital, Erin thought about later tonight, when the hospital would be quiet and she could snoop. She was confident that she would find something. First, she had better call Steve back before he worried. Getting up from the couch and going back to the pay phone, she dialed her home phone number.

"Hello," answered Lisa.

"Hi, it's me."

"How's Dad?"

"Probably going home tomorrow."

"That's so great! I can't believe it. Erin, we got lucky."

"I know. Update Mom for me and tell her I'll call her in the morning." She paused. "Can you get Steve for me?"

"I knew it. I thought something must have started between you two. Are you sure you're ready for this so soon?"

"I wasn't looking for it. It just happened."

"This relationship is going to be a lot different than being with an architect."

"I know."

"You have to get used to being away from him when he's on tour."

"I know."

"There's always going to be other women who want him. You have to think about that. It's not easy being the girlfriend."

"Lisa, you could be a little more supportive. I thought you wanted me to like him."

Lisa sighed. "I'm sorry. I just want you to know that it's not easy. He's a great guy. Hold on. I'll get him." She put the phone down.

After a few minutes, Steve picked up. "Erin, I'm glad to hear you're all right. So did you put her in her place?"

"I tried."

"How agonizing for you. Can you go to sleep for a while now?"

"That's my plan. I wanted to get back with you about the trip. You have to give me a few more days to make a decision."

"All right then."

"I'm going back to sleep now. I'll miss you."

"I'll be back in a few days." He paused. "I'll call you from the road."

Erin reluctantly hung up the phone and went back into the ICU. She stopped at the desk.

"It's not 10 yet," said Anthony, looking at the clock. "He's doing fine. The pacemaker is out and he's sleeping."

"Good," smiled Erin. "I'm going to sleep in the waiting room. If there is any change, please let me know."

"Okay." Anthony nodded.

Erin went back to the waiting room and sat back down on the couch. Seeing shelves that she hadn't noticed in a corner of the room, she observed blankets and pillows stacked on each row. She took one of each and put them on the couch. Then thinking about how hungry she was, she looked around the room for something— anything—to eat. There was a wicker basket on a table by the pay phone with what looked like food poking out from the top. Getting up and walking over to it, she saw a little card stuck in the basket that said the basket was an ongoing donation from a local church. *How nice*, she thought. Erin saw some apples, bananas and packages of peanut butter and crackers. She eagerly took a banana and a package of the crackers and devoured them in minutes. She yawned. The makeshift bed was calling to her and she answered willingly.

Michelle got into her car and started the drive to her house. She wasn't surprised by what Erin had said to her. Erin was too smart not to have figured it out, and it wasn't all that hard anyway. Michelle was glad there was still paper charting at Mercury. Tearing paper and depositing it in the wastebasket continued to be the easiest way to dispose of things you didn't want anyone to see. Thank goodness Rich hadn't gone to Southeast. If he had, there wouldn't have been any way to erase the digoxin result in his electronic medical record. The intensivist would have seen it and there would have been many more questions that demanded an answer. Michelle felt very confident that she was home free on this one. Maybe it was for the best that Rich hadn't died. She didn't know why she had felt so strongly about it when she and Charlie were making their plans. Her plane reservation was in five days and she would be gone. She didn't care what happened to anyone else. It was all about Michelle now. Actually, it had always been about Michelle. If Erin figured things out after Michelle was gone, so what? She didn't care. She would be gone and untraceable. But what if all hell broke loose before she left? That was something Michelle refused to think about.

Erin woke up, feeling quite refreshed for having slept on an old couch for three hours. A few people had arrived in the waiting room and the television was turned up again, waking her. She took her purse and walked into the bathroom, splashed cold water on her face, then combed her hair. *Time to see Dad anyway*, she thought. She went into the ICU and walked over to his room.

He was sitting up and looking at her as she entered his room. "Got rid of my wires. Dr. Campbell said I can increase my activity."

"I know. Dr. Campbell and I had a conversation in the waiting room."

"She was actually quite nice to me."

"I would think she would be very nice to you. So do you believe me now?"

"I'm trying not to, but I'm coming around."

"Do you want to sit up in a chair for awhile? It will help with your strength."

"Sounds good." He moved himself to the edge of the bed and without any difficulty threw both legs over the side.

Erin smiled. "Slow down, Dad. Just sit there a moment and take a couple of breaths. And let me help a little." She took his IV pole with one hand and grabbed his upper left arm with her other hand and eased him up and out of bed. They walked slowly over to the chair.

"Not bad," he said as he sat down. "I think I'm just a little dizzy from being in bed for a day and a half. I've got to get my strength back quickly."

"I'm sure you will." She paused. "Dad, I'm not going to work tomorrow. I plan on staying here all night and tomorrow until you go home. I'll go to work Tuesday."

He looked up at her. "Okay. Call Charlie and tell him in the morning."

She rolled her eyes and let out a breath. "I don't want to talk to that man. He tried to kill you."

"Call him. Just get it over with. There is no real proof, Erin, even if we believe it to be true."

"I know."

"When you talk to him, tell him I still plan on giving that speech to the Board of Directors on Thursday."

Erin's mouth dropped open. "What? Are you crazy?" She couldn't believe how stubborn he was. Shaking her head, she remembered it was a Tyler trait to be stubborn. They all were.

"Charlie is going out of town. I told him I would give a short speech for him on Thursday."

"Dad, please."

"Erin, you do what you want and I'll do what I want. And I want to give a speech to the Board of Directors on Thursday night. I would like for you to join me there."

Erin rolled her eyes in exasperation. "Okay, I'll go."

Rich put his hand over his abdomen as he heard his stomach growl. "Dr. Campbell gave me the okay to eat, and I'm famished."

"I'm sure they ordered you a tray."

"Do you think I could get anything to eat around here?" Rich asked loudly, looking outside his room for a nurse. "You know I've been given the all clear to eat now."

Anthony was just outside the door and poked his head into the room. "Food tray has been ordered, Dr. Tyler. Won't be long."

"Thanks, Anthony," said Rich. He leaned his head back against the chair. "So what are you going to do here tonight?"

"I told you that I suspect Michelle, too. Something is up with her cardiac caths. I think she does most of them here and has another doctor do the cath report. Why doesn't she do the report herself? She has a large cardiac testing facility at her office and I'm sure she takes care of all of the reports there, yet she doesn't for her own cath reports here at Mercury. Something is just not right with that. I'm going to look around and see what I can find out."

"No, that doesn't sound right. Be careful," Rich cautioned as he looked out his door again. A food tray had just been set on the counter at the ICU desk. Rich turned on his call light as soon as he saw it.

Anthony picked up the tray and came toward Rich's room. "Is this what you were calling about?"

"A person could starve around here."

Anthony set the tray down and opened it up. "Liquids tonight, regular foods tomorrow." He turned off the call light.

"At least it's something. Thanks, Anthony." He picked up a spoon and started sipping his broth as Anthony left the room.

"I'm going to make my first run around the hospital to figure out where everything is," said Erin. "I won't see you until the morning, so you get some rest."

"All right, Erin." Rich didn't look at her. He seemed more concerned with his gelatin.

Erin smiled as she left the room. It was great to see her dad getting back to normal. She walked out of the ICU and turned left. Farther down the hall, Erin could see four or five single doors in a row. Getting closer, she saw the Radiology Department. Looking all around her and seeing nobody, she cautiously opened the doors. X-ray machines were in a couple of the rooms, but the lights were out because the department was closed at night. There would probably be only one or two people working during the night to do portable x-rays that might be needed on an emergency basis in the hospital. She would have to be careful not to run into those people.

Reaching the end of the hall, she had to turn to the right. The first closed door she reached was an office. On the door the sign said, "Jeff Elliott, Radiologist." Dr. Elliott was a radiologist? Looking all around her once again and seeing no one, she slowly turned the knob on the door. It was unlocked! Thinking that she should wait until later in the night when the hospital would be as quiet as the morgue, she let the door close fully again. Continuing to walk down the hall, she saw double doors that read "Cardiac Catheterization." Opening one of the doors, she saw a large x-ray camera above the patient table and several television screens that would show views from the x-ray camera for the doctor during the cath. There were heart monitors and other special equipment all around the room and a door to the left that looked like it went into Dr. Elliott's office. She exited and closed the door again. Making another turn when she reached the end of the hall, she saw doors that led into the kitchen area of the hospital and the adjacent cafeteria. She walked to the cafeteria and went in.

"We're getting ready to close until tomorrow at 6 a.m.," said a woman, wiping the counter.

Erin smiled. "Okay. I'll be back in the morning. Thank you."

Erin left the cafeteria and completed her circle around the first floor, which included the emergency room and visitor entrance, and then she was back to the ICU and waiting room. Realizing she had absolutely nothing to do, she figured she might as well go back to sleep. She knew she would wake up in a few hours from discomfort, then she would go back to Dr. Elliott's office to look around. The other visitors had left the waiting room, so she made her bed up again and lay down to sleep.

Waking up to a loud grinding noise, Erin assumed it was the sound of the portable x-ray machine being pushed into the ICU. She peeked through the ICU doors, just to make sure it wasn't for her father. Breathing a sigh of relief that it wasn't, she looked up at the wall clock and saw that it was 4 a.m. Having slept longer than she thought, she went into the bathroom to freshen up again. She even put on some makeup after combing her hair, as she figured she wouldn't be going back to sleep. It was time to do a little detective work.

She walked down the hallway back towards Dr. Elliott's office, keeping watch all around her. Knowing the x-ray technician would be coming back this way, she wanted to get there as quickly as possible. Opening his door, she glanced around the office and saw an overhead light above his desk. She slipped in and closed the door behind her. She was in total darkness as she felt around for the switch. Finding it, she turned it on and light flooded the tiny office. She started quickly opening drawers in the desk. Nothing exciting—files of radiology magazines and drawers with extra office supplies. As she tried to open the large bottom drawer in the desk, she found it locked. Knowing that most people keep their desk keys somewhere near or on their desk, she looked at every possible place where a key might be hiding. She went through his desktop calendar. No key. She looked through his office supply drawer. No key. She looked in a little jar on his desk. Still no key. She looked underneath the overhead light, and there it was! A magnet with a key attached to it. Not believing her luck, she took the key down and stooped to open the drawer.

She hit the jackpot! The first large file she pulled said "CAP" on it. *What is CAP?* she wondered. Looking through the file, she saw many cardiac catheterization reports, all in alphabetical order. The names of the patients didn't mean anything to her. Their type of insurance was listed in the lower left corner and not only did she see "Triangle Health Plan," but other insurance companies as well. As she glanced through the cath reports, she noticed that all of these patients had extensive blockages listed in their coronary arteries that would meet insurance company criteria for medically necessary surgery. Large manila envelopes with the patient's names on them held their cardiac films and were behind their cath reports.

Leaving the CAP file, she went into additional files in this drawer. Erin found more heart films with patients' names on them. As she started going through these, she recognized some of the names from the CAP file. Seeing one for Larry Cinda and recognizing the name as having been in the CAP file, she compared a couple of the heart films that had the same date on them. Erin held up two of the films to the light under Dr. Elliott's desk; they were of the same coronary artery. Mr. Cinda didn't have an extensive blockage on his left anterior descending artery film from the file in the back of the drawer, but he did on the film that accompanied his cath report in the CAP file. She also thought the anatomy looked a tiny bit different. Erin's mouth dropped open as the reality of the situation hit her.

Were the cardiac cath reports and films from the CAP file the ones sent to Southeast for surgery? Looking quickly in more files, Erin saw dozens of cardiac films. As she held them up to the light in the office, she found no names on these films. What Dr. Elliott must have done was make copies of cardiac films of patients who had extensive blockages. When a patient was picked for surgery, Dr. Elliott decided what films he wanted to use. He picked films where the anatomy was close to the actual patient's anatomy. Putting the patient's name and date of their cath on the copied films, he then did a fraudulent cardiac cath report. The report was sent to Southeast for the surgery, and Erin was sure this meant the cardiovascular surgeon was involved.

Michelle did her cardiac caths here at Mercury because she had someone working with her to change them so the insurance companies would accept the surgery as medically necessary and pay for them. The patient didn't need surgery, but they got it anyway. Unnecessary fraudulent surgery that put a patient's life at risk. For what reason? Money? At what price do you sell your integrity? There were always people out there who never had enough money, and a degree of dishonesty can exist in every profession—even medicine. Don't a cardiologist, cardiovascular surgeon, and radiologist make enough money? Erin knew they were part of the highest-paid group of specialists, but people can always find a way to rationalize anything.

Erin thought about Mercury Memorial Hospital. It was a small, older hospital, dwarfed by the modern technology of Southeast. Michelle did her cardiac caths here because the hospital wanted her to and because it worked to her advantage.

Sometimes patients who undergo cardiac catheterization need to be hospitalized immediately due to a critical heart problem or unexpected complications of the procedure. These patients would go to Southeast, and it was close enough that a patient could be transferred there whenever needed. Erin was sure that Michelle was greatly respected and wanted here, and Dr. Elliott was her cohort. She did the caths, somehow it was decided upon who would be a candidate for surgery, the reports were falsified, and the patient later had surgery at Southeast.

Dr. Kramer must have found this out, and who knows what happened to him. Michelle and Charlie tried to kill her father because she was getting close to exposing them. But what part did Charlie play in this? The ringleader, perhaps? What about the other internal medicine doctors she had found behaving rather oddly? Were they a part of this, too? Not able to piece everything together yet, Erin had to figure out what she was going to do about this hard evidence.

It was time to make some quick decisions. Should she try to copy a few of the reports? Was she doing something illegal? She didn't know. What she did know was this would be her only chance in this office and she had to try and get proof of wrongdoing. Taking the CAP cardiac cath report for Larry Cinda out, she also decided to take the two films of his left anterior descending artery. She then went through the CAP file and picked out two more Triangle insurance patients, taking their cardiac cath reports out, but decided against taking their actual cardiac films. Those two of Larry's should be enough, as it might be hard to hide them. Figuring that the ICU must have a copy machine, she would go there and copy the cath reports. She would come back here and put the reports back before Dr. Elliott came in for morning. Looking at the clock on his desk, she saw that it was almost 5 a.m. *Not good*, she thought. She had better get moving. Locking the file up and placing the magnet key back up under the light, she picked up the reports and the two films. Turning off the light in the office, she slowly opened the door that led into the hallway, looking both ways to see if anyone was around. Not seeing a soul, she walked back down the hall to the ICU. Entering the double doors, she glanced over at her father's room and all looked well. She walked over to the desk.

"Excuse me, Anthony, but could I use your copy machine for a few minutes?"

"Oh, sure. It's over there." He motioned to a small room to his right, not really paying any attention to her, as he was doing his charting.

Erin got over to the copy room as quickly as she could and made her copies, folding them and putting them into her purse. She walked out of the copy room and glanced at Anthony. He was absorbed in what he was doing, so she walked by her father's room. Rich appeared to be sleeping. Going in the room and over to his closet, she slid the two cardiac films down the side of his patient belongings bag. She had to get the cath reports back into Dr. Elliott's files, so she left the ICU.

Walking back down the hall toward Radiology, she saw the x-ray technicians pushing the portable x-ray machine into a corner of the hallway. They looked up at her as she walked by. She turned the corner where Dr. Elliott's office was located, but she knew she couldn't go in there now. The technicians could peek around the corner at any time. Erin saw a bulletin board across from Dr. Elliott's office that held job postings for open positions in the hospital. Standing there reading the job postings, she decided to wait until they left. What happened next was totally unexpected and certainly not in the plan. Erin heard a voice coming from around the corner.

"Good morning," the voice said to the x-ray technicians.

"Good morning, Dr. Elliott," said one of the technicians.

Erin froze. She looked down at the papers to make sure he wouldn't be able to tell what they were and kept her eyes focused on the bulletin board.

Dr. Elliott came around the corner and opened his office door. Noticing the attractive blonde woman standing outside of it looking at the bulletin board, he didn't go in. "Can I help you?" He waited for her to look at him.

She turned around and gave him a big smile. "Hello. I'm just looking at the job postings."

"Looking for a job here?" He was intrigued when he saw what she looked like.

"I'm always in the market."

"What do you do?"

Erin only had seconds to decide to lie or not. She knew she was not a good liar, so she just said it. "I'm a physician."

He came over to her side of the hall. "A physician?" He looked her up and down. "Do you have a position now?"

"Yes, I do."

"What are you doing here in this hospital?" He found her quite appealing.

"My father is in the ICU."

"I'm sorry."

"He's doing fine and will be moved to the floor today."

"Glad to hear it. I was just getting ready to go to breakfast. Can I interest you in going with me? The cafeteria is just around the corner," he said, smiling at her. "I'm Dr. Jeff Elliott."

Erin thought that this would probably be her only chance to get rid of the papers. "All right." She paused. "Why don't I meet you there? I want to run back and check on my father. I'll just be a few minutes."

"Sounds good." He thought the day was starting off quite well, with a lovely dining partner for breakfast. "I'll order for you. What would you like?"

"How about coffee and a toasted cheese bagel, if they have them? Otherwise, any bagel will do." She smiled at him again.

"And your name is?"

"Erin."

He nodded. "I'll be sitting in the back of the cafeteria by the window, Erin." He closed his office door and started walking away from her.

Erin pretended like she was going to walk back to the ICU, even going around the corner toward it. The x-ray technicians were gone and she didn't see anyone else. As soon as she turned the corner, she stopped and looked back down the hall, making sure he didn't come back. Not seeing him, she hurried over to his office and opened the door. Finding the drawer key again, she opened it and carefully put the cath reports back into their proper files. It seemed like it took forever to find the correct file and she was afraid she would be caught. Everything went fine, though, and she locked the drawer again, putting the key in its proper hiding spot.

Now she had to go to breakfast with him. Maybe this would be a good opportunity to get more information. She walked around the corner and entered the cafeteria. Hardly anyone was there yet, as it had just opened. The workers were still putting out the fresh juices and checking to see the dispensers were full. Seeing him in the back of the cafeteria by the window like he had said, she took a deep breath and starting the walk back there, noticing that he was watching her every move.

"That was quick," he said. "Your father still doing well?"

"Oh, yes." She smiled. "Thank you for getting my food. How much do I owe you?"

"Nothing. It's on me." He started buttering his toast. "Who is your father's doctor?"

"Dr. Campbell."

He stopped what he was doing momentarily. "Did your father have to have a cardiac cath?"

"No."

He nodded his head and continued to butter his toast. "That's good. So tell me about yourself, Erin."

Erin didn't want to give him any personal information. "You know, I think I'll get hot tea instead. Excuse me a moment." She walked back into the cafeteria and took her time getting herself a tea, and then reluctantly returned to the table. "Dr. Elliott, what do you think of Dr. Campbell?"

"Please call me Jeff. Dr. Campbell is an excellent physician and highly respected. She can do no wrong."

"That's great to hear," said Erin eating her bagel as quickly as she could. "I thought I saw a cath lab here. Does Dr. Campbell do all of her caths here?"

"Yep, except for an occasional one at Southeast. This hospital would be in dire straits if not for the money generated from her caths. She's queen around here, and can be quite bossy, I must add. The administration here will bend over backwards to do whatever she wants, so the cath lab is very well-equipped." He finished his toast. "Getting back to you, could I have your phone number and perhaps we could go out to dinner this weekend?"

"Actually, this weekend is pretty full. My sister is getting married." Erin stood up. "Well, thank you for breakfast, Dr. Elliott. I'm sorry, but I really have to run." She turned and left the cafeteria as quickly as possible before he could say anything else.

Walking back down to ICU, she had a few minutes left for visiting hours and went into her father's room. His breakfast tray had just arrived and he was sitting up in the chair, starting to eat.

"I'm going up to the floor after breakfast. They need my bed here anyway. Isn't that peachy?" He grinned at her.

"Wonderful."

"Did you find any information during the night?" He started eating his oatmeal.

"I found out that cardiac cath reports are being changed to make them appear worse than they actually are. Then surgery may be being done on patients that don't need it."

Rich shook his head. "Really?"

"I copied three cardiac cath reports and have two different cardiac films of the same artery that I removed from the radiologist's office down the hall. The films are in your bag in the closet. When I get to work tomorrow I'll see if they had the surgery done."

"I don't even know where to begin with this."

"Don't worry about it, Dad. Just get better. I'll try to get more information."

Anthony poked his head into the room. "I don't mean to rush you, but we need to move you to the floor in just a few minutes. Sorry."

Erin smiled. "Anthony, my family and I would like to thank you and the other nurses for the wonderful care my father has received here."

"Yes, thank you," said Rich. "I know I can be a pill at times, but I appreciate everything you've done for me."

"Would you please tell everyone for us?" asked Erin.

"I will," grinned Anthony. "It's nice to be appreciated."

Erin looked around Rich's room. He didn't have many items there that needed to go with him—the all-important patient belongings bag that contained the cardiac films and the clothes he came in with. He had his robe and slippers on and his watch was on the bedside table. She picked it up and put it on him.

"Dad, I see a wheelchair coming over here. They must need the room quickly for someone."

"Fine. I don't like it in ICU anyway." He pushed the bedside tray away from him.

Anthony brought the wheelchair in. Rich stood up and walked over to it as they started the trip upstairs. Erin followed behind them, wondering how soon it would be before Michelle showed up. There was no reason for her father to even be here any longer.

CHAPTER 14

MICHELLE had canceled her Monday morning cardiac caths last week. Today she would see only a few patients and cancel some more surgeries. She had told her staff that her mother had become increasingly ill and she didn't know if she would have to leave at a moment's notice. Telling her partner Phil the same thing, he was ready to step into the office to help out however he could. His presence would really be required starting next Monday, more than he could ever realize. Charlie had no idea what was going on at her office now. As far as he knew, everything was on schedule for August to be CAP's biggest month yet. Michelle walked out of her office and up to the front desk. "Stephanie, is my first patient here?"

"Yes, Dr. Campbell. Larry and Louise Cinda are in room two."

"Thank you." Michelle walked down to room two and took Larry's chart out of the rack. She had just done a cath on Larry last week and he was back for the results. Jeff Elliott had finished his paperwork and Larry would be a coronary bypass candidate. Michelle looked through the chart briefly and knocked on the door as she opened it. "Good morning," she said, smiling at the Cindas.

"Hello, Dr. Campbell," said Larry.

Michelle sat down. Since she no longer cared about CAP, she no longer cared if the patient had the surgery or not. Maybe she should be nice and not even recommend that he have surgery at all.

"So what's going on, Doctor?" asked Louise. "Does Larry need to have surgery?"

"We could try maximum medical treatment first, if that is what you prefer." Michelle looked at the two of them.

"Last week you seemed so sure that Larry was going to have the surgery real soon," said Louise, acting suspicious. "Has something changed that we don't know about?"

"Not at all. Larry just isn't having many symptoms of increasing problems, so I think it may be prudent to just wait a while and see how he does." Michelle acted like she was looking through his record.

"But we already made an appointment with Dr. Keller," Louise said. "Should we cancel it?"

"I would. If there aren't any plans for surgery, there is no reason to keep that appointment."

"Okay, Dr. Campbell. We'll cancel it. Should he just stay on the same medications then?" asked Louise.

"Yes, stay on the same medications. Make an appointment for six months from now and we'll talk again." Michelle smiled at them. "How does that sound?"

"Great," said Larry, with a nervous laugh. "I was getting a little worried."

"Thank you, Doctor," said Louise, smiling back at Michelle. "We were both more than a little anxious about him having surgery."

Michelle stood up. "See you in six months." She turned and left the room, closing the door and walked back up to the front desk. "Stephanie, let me see the schedule for Friday."

Stephanie handed her the schedule.

Michelle saw only a handful of office appointments for Friday. That would be fine. She could see a few patients at the office and run by to see the hospital patients, then on to the bank to close accounts. By the afternoon she would be all packed and would just be clock-watching until it was time to go to the airport. The excitement was starting to build within her.

"Is everything in order, Dr. Campbell?" asked Stephanie.

"Yes," she said, smiling. "Everything is fine. If we get any insurance checks today, make sure you make a bank deposit into the office account only. No other accounts." She wanted to be sure that any money due her would be cleared by Friday so she could cash out.

"Okay, Doctor," Stephanie said as she answered the ringing office phone. Michelle looked at her watch. She didn't feel like going to the hospital and seeing Rich Tyler or his daughter, but the pain wouldn't last long. Michelle was hoping that since Rich was doing so well, Erin would keep her nose out of things for the rest of the week. After that she couldn't care less. "Stephanie, I don't have any more appointments for two hours so I'm going to run over to Mercury and Southeast and see my patients. I'll be back as soon as possible."

Stephanie cupped her hand over the phone's mouthpiece. "All right, Doctor."

Erin was sitting up in a chair, watching television with her Dad. She disliked television and hoped that the torment wouldn't last long. Her time would be better spent reading or kissing Steve. She thought about him and smiled.

"Knock, knock," said a voice.

Erin looked up to see Jeff Elliott at the doorway. He had found her.

"Hi Erin," he said. "I see your father got transferred out of ICU. May I come in?"

"Sure," said Erin halfheartedly.

Rich looked at the person entering the room, then back at Erin. "Who's this, Erin?"

"Dad, this is Dr. Jeff Elliott. Dr. Elliott, this is my father, Dr. Richard Tyler."

Jeff walked over and shook Rich's hand. "I'm glad you're doing better, sir. ICU isn't a good place to be."

Rich glanced at Erin with a look of confusion as to who this person was and why he was acting so friendly to him.

"Let me explain, sir. I met your daughter downstairs and she ran off before she could give me her phone number." Jeff laughed. "We're going out this weekend."

Erin couldn't believe her ears. She was sure she had told him she had plans. "Dr. Elliott, I told you I was busy this weekend."

Rich interrupted and chuckled. "Erin doesn't usually go out with doctors. Personally, I don't know why. Erin, I'm glad to see that you're going to start dating again."

Erin felt like she was in shock. How could her dad do this to her?

"Erin told me that you have a daughter getting married," said Jeff.

"Yes. This weekend." Rich had a brainstorm and leaned toward Jeff. "You know, Jeff, that Erin doesn't have a date for the wedding."

"She doesn't?" Jeff raised his eyebrows at Erin and gave her a smile.

She felt sick to her stomach. This was a nightmare.

Rich motioned for Jeff to come over closer to him as he spoke in a low voice. "Why don't you ask her if you could be her date?"

"I think I will. Can you give me her phone number?" Jeff asked, as he took a pen and paper from his white lab coat.

"It's 643," Rich started.

Erin stood up. "Enough," she snapped.

"Hello, everyone," said a voice at the doorway. "What a cozy little group I see here."

Silence took over as all eyes turned to the door. It was Michelle.

Michelle glared at Jeff. "Dr. Elliott, may I speak with you outside for a moment?"

"Sure." He turned to smile at Erin. "I'll be right back." Walking outside the room with Michelle, they went a little farther down the hall out of the Tyler's hearing range.

"What are you doing here?" she asked him with controlled anger.

"I'm trying to get a date with that girl in there. In case you didn't notice, she is quite hot," said Jeff, somewhat irritated.

"Well, Dr. Elliott, it's obvious that you don't know that girl is also trying to bring CAP down. Did she get you so excited that you told her all of our dirty little secrets?"

He looked at Michelle with a disgusted look on his face. "No, I haven't told her anything. I just wanted to go out with her."

"I'm telling you no. You're not going out with her. Go put some ice in your pants and get out of here. When you get back to your office, make sure any important papers are secure."

Jeff paused for a moment, then spoke. "All right." He turned and marched back down the hall, away from the Tylers.

Michelle walked back into Rich's room. "Sorry for the interruption."

"Where did Dr. Elliott go?" asked Rich. "He seemed like a nice guy."

"Dr. Elliott had other business to attend to." She thumbed through Rich's chart quickly. "I'm discharging you, Dr. Tyler. You're doing fine. I don't think you'll have any residual problems from this incident." Michelle nodded and left the room, as she didn't want to be in there any longer than necessary.

"Well, that was short and sweet," said Rich after Michelle left.

"Dad, Dr. Elliott was the radiologist I was telling you about who is falsifying the cath reports."

Rich shook his head and let out a deep breath. "Erin, I'm sorry. I got a little carried away. It made me feel good that you were thinking about dating again."

Erin thought this might be the time to tell him briefly about Steve. "Dad..."

The charge nurse, Mrs. Hernandez, abruptly walked into the room. "Dr. Tyler, I know you just got here, but I have some good news for you."

"I'm going home?"

"Yes, Dr. Campbell just discharged you. You are free to go whenever you wish."

"Did she leave any instructions?" asked Erin.

"Regular diet. Activity as tolerated. No medications. Off work for one week. If you have any problems, feel free to contact Dr. Campbell," said Mrs. Hernandez. "Just put on your light when you're ready to leave and we'll call for a wheelchair."

"Great. Thank you," Erin said to Mrs. Hernandez as she left the room. "I'm going to call Mom and tell her to call up here when she arrives. She can just pull into the circular drive in front of the hospital. No reason for her to make a separate trip up here."

"Everything Dr. Campbell said sounds good," said Rich, "except for the part about not working for one week. I'll stay away from the office except for that speech on Thursday night." He got up from bed and took his personal belongings bag out of the closet. Lisa had brought him clean clothes on one of her visits, and he was happy about that as he took them out. Not seeing the cardiac films that Erin had slid inside his bag next to some paperwork, he placed his robe and slippers next to them.

Erin shook her head. He could be so exasperating sometimes. She called her mother, explaining the plan to her. As Erin hung up the phone, she noticed that her Dad had already changed out of his hospital gown and was all set to go.

"Did you ever call Charlie and tell him you wouldn't be in today?" Rich asked.

"No."

"Call him now."

"Okay," Erin said as she reluctantly dialed the number, but she hung up when he answered. "I'll try back again in a few minutes." She went to the nurse's station and requested a wheelchair for Rich, then went back to the room to wait for her mom.

Charlie sat at his desk, tapping a pencil. He had talked to Arlene Tyler on Sunday night and found out that Rich was doing much better. Erin would be staying at the hospital until he was discharged. Michelle had updated him that Rich would probably go home on Monday. Charlie's phone started ringing.

"Dr. Patton," he said, picking it up.

The line went dead.

He wondered if Erin would come in today. Getting up from his desk, he walked over past Susan's to the row where Erin sat. Her desk was clean, without any lighting turned on.

"Susan, have you heard anything from Erin Tyler?" he asked, stopping at Susan's desk on the way back to his.

"Yes, she just called me. She had been trying to reach you, but only got your machine. Her father just went home from the hospital and she'll be in later today."

"Good. Good. He's going home." Charlie frowned as he walked back to his office.

Rich received a hero's welcome when he arrived home. Lisa had his favorite dish cooking in the oven and she had gone to Arlene's shop and had gotten over a dozen brightly-colored balloons that were filled with helium and sticking to the ceiling in the living room, foyer, and kitchen.

"It's good to be home," sighed Rich. "Thanks, everyone, but I think I'm going to take a little nap first, then a shower should make me feel as good as new." He walked over to the master suite and went in.

Arlene followed to see if he needed anything.

Erin went to the kitchen and poured herself a glass of orange juice. "The boys are gone?" she asked Lisa, who was right behind her.

"They left about an hour ago."

Erin nodded. "So what are you doing today?"

"I'm going to pick up Jimmy's sister, Charlotte. The two of us are going shopping, then we have to go to Cheryl's house for Charlotte's dress fitting. What are you going to do?"

"First I'm taking a shower. I can't believe that I was in London 24 hours ago and the hospital ever since." Erin drank her juice. "I believe I need a nap, too, before I go to the office." She made a face as she thought about going there.

"I'm out of here. See you tonight." Lisa smiled and left the kitchen.

Erin went upstairs and got into the shower. She could have stood there for hours and let the hot water beat down on her. Her body was exhausted. She lay down in bed without even drying her hair and fell asleep immediately. Her sleep was not restful, as she dreamed of something she had always been afraid of since she was a little girl. Clowns. The two brightly made-up clowns were scary and started chasing her through a dark woods. She was screaming for help, but no one could hear her. When they caught her, they started whispering about how they were going to kill her. As they took off their makeup, Erin saw Charlie and Michelle. They started laughing and taunting her. Erin's body jumped and she woke up in a cold sweat. She felt horrible and got up to take another shower.

David had just finished his coronary bypass for the day and was typing out the pharmacy orders. Things had gone well, but he found himself dreading this whole week. He had four bypasses scheduled, and they were grueling. Many hours on his feet, many serious decisions to be made, but all for many dollars in his pocket. The insurance checks should start coming in soon. His first bypass for CAP had been two weeks ago and Charlie had said it wouldn't take long to get money put into his account. He looked up and saw Michelle coming toward him.

"Hello, David," she said, without smiling.

He nodded at her. The computer stopped him as he put in a drug dosage incorrectly and needed to fix it before he could continue. He had put in a potentially dangerous dosage, so it was a good thing the computer caught it. Adverse drug events here at Southeast were a thing of the past, due to the safety climate that prevailed throughout the hospital.

"How many do you have this week?" Michelle asked.

"Four," he said. "Are you busy?"

"Actually, I'm not going to be here much this week."

"The hospital is pressuring me to learn some new cardiac surgery techniques. I'll have to take some time off work and go away for a few days." He looked at her out of the corner of his eye.

Michelle didn't care; she had to keep business as usual so David wouldn't become suspicious. "You're too busy right now to take any time off."

David felt like he wasn't in charge anymore. Just wanting to finish his orders, he continued typing and hoped she would go away. He stopped paying attention to her for a moment as he finished what he was doing. When he turned around, she was gone.

By the time Erin arrived at the office, the afternoon lull was in full swing. The whole floor seemed quiet, as everyone was trying to stay awake and get their work done. Phones were not ringing, people were not talking, and clock-watching was now in session. Erin's desk was piled high with charts and her email was overflowing. She really wasn't up to this. Putting her purse in her bottom desk drawer, she looked down her row. By the way Polly was sitting, it appeared that she might be taking a nap. Erin smiled. Getting up, she walked over to Susan's desk to see how she was doing.

Susan pushed her glasses down on her nose and looked up at Erin.

"Nice to see you back, Dr. Tyler. I'm glad you're dad is okay. That must have been pretty scary."

"It was. Susan, my father will be giving a talk at the Board of Directors meeting on Thursday night. Where will that be?"

She pointed directly above her. "Upstairs in the boardroom at 7:30 p.m. I'm sure they would understand if Dr. Tyler wants to decline this month. It can probably wait until next month."

"He doesn't plan on declining. I'm sure he has already started to write it." Erin gave her a half smile.

"Charlie will be getting his letter from my attorney on Friday. It's being delivered here. I hope I get to see his face when he opens it." She grinned.

"I'd pay to see that. He's here?"

"No, but he should be back any time. I'm expecting to be yelled at today. He wasn't in a good mood Friday or today."

"I'm going to take a peek in my dad's office to see if there is something on his desk that needs to be done. I'll be right back." She glanced at Charlie's office as she walked by. His door was open and his light was on. That would be the place to look around. Did she dare go in there? *Not now, but maybe another day this week*, she thought. She remembered Charlie telling her about a code to get into the building after hours. Maybe her dad had that code. Getting to her father's office, she went in and sat down at his desk. Picking up a couple of charts on his desk to take back to hers, there wasn't much else except the mail for today. She looked through it and set it back down. Knowing her father, he would be back in this office as soon as he could. She walked to the door and stopped as she heard Charlie talking to someone, but she couldn't make out what they were saying. The door to Charlie's office was then closed.

"Well, that was a good lunch, Ed. I want to go back to that place soon," said Charlie as he sat back in his chair.

"Not bad. Cheap, too," said Ed.

"Can you close the door for a moment?" Charlie asked.

Ed got up from the chair and shut the door.

"I'm still worried about Erin Tyler finding out about CAP. Do you think we should do her in?"

"What? Kill her? Charlie, get ahold of yourself! You can't possibly be serious."

Charlie could tell by Ed's surprised face that he had pushed the boundaries too far. He gave Ed a big smile. "Of course I was only kidding, Ed. She really is becoming a pain in the ass, though."

"Why don't you just let her go. Her father won't be back for a week or so. You can make up some reason why you don't need her anymore and didn't want to bother him with details."

"Yes, that is a possibility. The only thing is, she has a big project to finish for Bruce and we are real backed up on chart reviews. With Rich gone, she'll be the only one working on charts, and they're stacked a mile high. Who's going to do the work?"

Ed thought for a minute. "Can't you send them over to the other medical directors—Dr. Hunter and Dr. Prakash?"

"No. Hunter's on vacation for two weeks and Prakash is overloaded with outpatient issues."

"Why don't you take away some of her computer access so she can't get any more information that way?"

Charlie shook his head, thinking. "Good idea. I could do that and deny any knowledge of it."

"I got it," Ed said, putting his hand up in the air. "Tell her that it is mandatory she has all of her work done by Friday. That way she'll be so busy she won't have time to be overcurious. After she turns in her work on Friday, let her go. Work done. Girl gone. Simple as that."

"Ed, you're a genius. That's why you get paid the big bucks." Charlie laughed as he got up from his desk and smacked Ed on the back.

Ed looked at his watch as he opened the door. "Charlie, gotta run. Talk to you soon." He shook Charlie's hand and left the office.

Erin heard a man leaving Charlie's office and peeked around the corner. She only saw him from behind, but she recognized the limp and short black hair. Edward Carroll!

"Susan," Charlie bellowed, "get in here!"

Erin left Rich's office quickly and tried to walk by Charlie's office as Susan walked in, hoping that he wouldn't see her. It didn't work.

"Erin, is that you? Can you come in here?"

Erin let out a deep breath and turned around. She entered the office after Susan and sat down in a chair.

Charlie proceeded to raise his voice at Susan. "I just found out I missed a couple of important meetings that I was supposed to attend. Why haven't you kept me updated?"

"I have, Dr. Patton. Everything is on the schedule I made out for you. It is sitting there on your desk. I will not take responsibility for you missing those meetings."

Erin was happy to see Susan standing up for herself. She was getting stronger. Charlie would really be in for a shock on Friday when that letter came.

"You need to remind me everyday of what meetings I have. I'm much too busy to remember everything myself. That's why I have you." He shuffled some papers on his desk. "That will be all, Susan."

Susan turned to leave and winked at Erin.

Erin put her hand over her mouth. She didn't want Charlie seeing her suppress a smile.

He looked over from his desk at Erin. "So how's Rich?"

Looking Charlie in the eyes reminded Erin how much she despised him. How could he have consciously poisoned her father? What a loathsome human being he was! She couldn't help but narrow her eyes at him as she spoke. "He's going to come out of this stronger than ever, Dr. Patton. Don't underestimate my dad's fortitude."

"I wouldn't dream of it." Charlie knew it was obvious he needed to get control of this girl right away. She made him nervous. "I'm so sorry about all those charts on your desk, Erin, but we're real backed up right now. They need to be done by Friday. Also, the pharmacy investigation needs to be completed by then, too. Bruce pushed up the timetable." He shrugged his shoulders. "Nothing I can do about that."

"Fine. Everything will be done." She stood up and didn't smile. "Anything else, Doctor?"

"No, Erin. That's all for now."

She left the office and walked back to her desk. Sitting down at her computer, she went through her email first and deleted everything she could. The first thing she wanted to do was look up those members whose cardiac caths she had taken from Jeff Elliott's office. Looking at the screen lists that Polly had made her, she typed in a few codes. A hospital screen came up. Typing in the name of Samuel Morrison, his most recent hospitalization appeared. He had been in Southeast for four days in July for a coronary bypass. She typed in the name of Allen Perry and found the same thing: a recent coronary bypass surgery. The last patient was Larry Cinda. She saw nothing listed for him in the past or future for coronary bypass. She only saw his cardiac cath in the system. His bypass surgery must not have been scheduled yet. Instead of feeling elated, she felt heavyhearted. Everything was true. Her father was going to make a few phone calls today to the state to see what they needed to do to get an investigation started.

Not happy at the pile of charts she needed to get done by Friday, she pulled out her pharmacy investigation to see if she could finish that up next. She had been out to talk to a number of doctors. It was all a matter now of writing everything up and summarizing it for Bruce. Having only met him twice and feeling confident that he was someone reasonable, she spread out everything on her desk and started working on her computer. Before she knew it, the afternoon was gone and she was done with the pharmacy project. Erin thought a moment. Should she send the report to Charlie today for him to review it before it went to Bruce? No way. Charlie would get it on Friday afternoon at the last minute.

Erin looked in her desk and found the blank manila folder in the back of her file cabinet with the Attorney General letter in it. Taking it with her, she walked down the aisle to say "hello" to Polly and left the office. She was delighted that she had gotten so much done in such a short time. There shouldn't be a problem getting the rest of the charts done by Friday.

Rich was sitting in the den, working hard on his speech for Thursday on the computer. He enjoyed public speaking and was glad to have been given the opportunity, even though he was sure that Charlie didn't want to do it. Already feeling better since his nap and shower, he was almost halfway finished.

"Rich, do you want to go with me tomorrow to get the alcohol and soda pop for the wedding?" asked Arlene, peeking her head into the den.

"Sure, dear. What else am I going to do?" Rich leaned over the computer to check his sentence structure.

"I'm running over to Cheryl's house to pick up my dress. Did I tell you that I'm wearing a hat for the wedding? Lisa wanted me to follow English custom of the bride's mother wearing a large hat."

Rich smiled. "I'm sure you'll love that."

Arlene grinned. "It's coming off right after pictures. Anyway, Lisa and Charlotte are over at Cheryl's now, and Erin should be home any minute. Will you be all right?"

"Sure I will. Quit treating me like an invalid. Damn! Where's that spell check button?" Rich took off his glasses for a moment and checked the toolbar.

Arlene left the room and closed the front door just as the phone rang.

Rich picked it up. "Hello?"

"Rich, this is Steve Robinson. I hope you're feeling well."

"Steve, I'm doing fine. Thank you. Where are you calling from?"

"We're in Cleveland."

"And how is Cleveland?"

"If we could get rid of this smudgy daylight, we would be doing fine."

Rich chuckled.

"Is Lisa there by any chance?" Steve asked. "Jimmy and I were wondering if we were supposed to pick up everyone's tuxes on Friday before we arrived at the house."

"No, Lisa's not here."

Rich heard Erin come through the front door.

"Well, is Erin there?" Steve asked.

"She just came in. I don't think she'll know the answer to the tux question, but you can ask her." He turned his head toward the door. "Erin!" he called out.

Erin came into the den. "Hi, Dad. How are you doing?" She bent over to hug him and handed him the Attorney General letter file.

"Fine. Steve is on the phone with a question. I told him I didn't think you had the answer to it, though." He handed her the phone and started reading the letter.

She took the phone and left the room. Not returning until about twenty minutes later, she smiled as she put the phone back down on the computer desk.

"So did you know the answer to the question about the tuxedos that he had?" Rich asked, looking at her.

"What tuxedo question?" Erin gave him a blank look as she turned to leave.

Rich was baffled. He wondered what they had talked about for twenty minutes if Steve forgot to question her about the tuxes.

Erin turned back around. "Dad, did you make any phone calls today?"

"Yes. The ball is rolling. I talked to the state licensing and regulatory agency and they will start their investigation. I'm sending them the cardiac films and the cath reports you gave me. If they feel a violation has occurred, they will move quickly."

CHAPTER 15

DAVID came out of the operating room, exhausted and depressed. This was the third coronary bypass he had done this week, and it hadn't gone well at all. There was much difficulty with bleeding during the procedure, and the patient suffered a heart attack and expired. He went to the operating room desk and sat down, taking off his surgical hat and mask. Going into the patient's electronic chart, he made a brief entry in the progress notes about what had happened during the surgery. He would dictate the full operative report after he talked with the family.

Getting up and walking to the surgical ICU waiting room, he saw her husband and teenage son sitting there, watching television. David always hated giving bad news and he had given his share over the years, but this death should have never happened. The reality of what he was doing was finally sinking in. Money wasn't everything. He was clearly abusing his professional power and was having difficulty facing the truth of what he had been doing. The time had passed when this surgery could have been prevented. He had failed in his responsibility as a physician and had shown an unmistakable lack of integrity. David went and sat down in a chair next to them.

"How is she?" asked Mr. Walker, seeing that the doctor's face looked grave.

David cleared his throat and looked at Mr. Walker. "I'm afraid I have some bad news for you. The operation didn't go as planned." David took in a deep breath and let it out as he continued. "There were problems with bleeding that we didn't anticipate. She had a heart attack; we were unable to resuscitate her, and she didn't survive. I'm very sorry."

Mr. Walker and his son put their heads down.

David wanted to get out of there as quickly as possible. "I'll call pastoral support if you'd like me to. They can come in and talk with you."

"That won't be necessary," said Mr. Walker. He looked up at David, his eyes defeated and his face drawn, while his son cried silently. "Can we have an autopsy, Doctor?"

David was shocked. He didn't think that they would request an autopsy, as he had explained what had happened during the surgery. The patient had been told after her cardiac catheterization two weeks ago that she had significant narrowing in all three major arteries. The patient and family had been informed when they signed the consent form that heart attacks do occur with this surgery and were the main cause of death.

"I've told you what happened during the surgery," said David, trying to remain calm. "She had bleeding problems and then had a heart attack."

"I know, Doctor. I think I would just feel better if I knew for sure."

"Of course. An autopsy can be done. I'll take care of the arrangements and get a permit for you to sign." David stood up. "My condolences to you and your family." He left the room and walked to the physician dictation room as his torment increased. Janice Walker had been a CAP patient and during her autopsy, healthy coronary arteries would be found.

Erin had been working hard all week. Her pile of charts was decreasing at a rapid pace, and she didn't think there would be any problem having them done by Friday. She had been avoiding Charlie as much as possible, and thankfully had only passed him in the hall a few times. All she had been doing was sitting at her desk, reading charts all day and looking forward to Steve's phone call at night. Steve had been trying to get her to come to Chicago with Lisa and the Emerson's for the concert tonight and had called her numerous times. She wanted to go very badly, but had decided that she would not be coming back to Triangle after Friday and she wanted to get all of her work done. Besides that, her father's speech to the Board of Directors was tonight and he wanted her to be there. Reluctantly, she turned Steve down.

Leaving the office at 4 p.m., she arrived home just as her father was taking a pizza out of the oven.

"Just in time, Erin. Looks like it's just you and me for a while. Your mother is at the shop, making sure everything is ready for delivery tomorrow. We really have a busy next couple of days."

"I'm so excited about the wedding." Erin got out the plates and put a slice of pizza on each one as she and Rich sat down at the table. "Dad, there's something I want to talk to you about."

"What?"

"I haven't told Mom yet, but I've decided to move out East with Lisa and Jimmy."

"I have to say that I'm very surprised, Erin. We thought you would take a little longer to make such a big decision."

"I know, but things have changed a lot for me the last couple of weeks."

"What kind of job will you get?"

"I have been looking into taking temporary assignments through an agency in New York."

"A temp agency? Why?"

"I'm not ready for anything permanent right now. With an agency, I'd have freedom to travel and to pick where I want to work. The pay is great and I wouldn't have to deal with the everyday problems of a practice. I'm still early in my career, Dad."

"I know, Erin. If that's what you want, then your mother and I support you."

"Another thing, Dad. I'm not coming back to Triangle after Friday. All of my current work will be done, so that is a good time for me to leave. You know I can't stand to be near Charlie now, so it's better that I just go."

"Have you told him?"

"No, not yet. And there's one more thing that I need to talk to you about." Erin took her plate to the sink and set it down as the doorbell rang.

Rich got up from the table and walked into the foyer to open the front door. There was a delivery for Lisa and Jimmy all the way from Ireland. Rich signed for it and took the package into the house, setting it on the kitchen table.

Erin went over and looked at the large brown package and picked it up. It was quite heavy and the return address said it was from the Ryans in Belfast. Erin was so interested in it, she forgot that she was going to tell her Dad about Steve.

"Wow! They've been getting deliveries from everywhere. How exciting to be so worldly. I'll go upstairs and put this in their room," she commented. "I think I'll get ready for the meeting, too."

"We need to leave at 6:30."

"All right." She put the package in Lisa's room and went into her own. Lying down on the bed for a few minutes, trying to nap, she decided that tomorrow night after the rehearsal dinner she would go to Charlie's office and look around. Before she knew it, she had slept for twenty minutes. Erin got up from the bed and went into the bathroom to freshen up for the meeting. Going downstairs, she found her father in the den with the computer printer going.

Rich took the pages off the printer and handed Erin his speech to look at.

Erin picked up the papers and started to read. The beginning of it focused on how Triangle and its members are paying more for their health care. Whether from the rising cost of pharmacy, increase in government regulations, to the actual delivery of care, the cost was up for everyone. He discussed how physicians are upset with the rules of insurance companies for referrals and procedures. How we need to work with our physicians more to help them understand why we do things and how we can help them do their jobs better so they are happier. He expressed how members need to take more responsibility for their health care because the physician can only do so much. It was up to the member to follow through. Rich spoke of why Triangle needs to manage their pharmacy better and educate physicians and members about the rise in drug costs. Triangle should think about having pharmacy and disease management programs to help with regulating costs. He talked about how Triangle needed to work to help prevent fraud. Smaller health plans have the most difficulty fighting abuse and fraud. There are health care providers out there that overtreat and undertreat patients, which drastically affects the quality of care their members receive. Lastly, Rich spent a few minutes on how the focus for the future of Triangle Health Plan should be on quality and safety for members. Triangle wants their doctors to put quality above everything else they give their patients.

"Dad, I think that's great. Nice job."

"You don't think it's overdone in any way?"

"Not at all. I can't wait to see the reaction of the Board Members." She hugged him. "I'm so glad you're back to your old self."

He raised his eyebrows. "I told you I'm dancing on Saturday."

Erin smiled at her father. He was so cute. "We had better get going."

Arriving at the office in plenty of time, they got out of the Yukon and walked over to the front door. Erin noticed the small keypad entry to the left of it.

"Is that the place you put a code in for after hours entry?"

Rich looked at Erin, eyes narrowing. "I don't like your question."

"I want the code. I'm coming to look in Charlie's office tomorrow night after the rehearsal dinner."

"I don't think that's a good idea. It could be very dangerous."

"I'll take someone with me so I won't be alone. Dad, can you please give me that code?" Erin begged.

Rich relented. "Okay, Erin. Quit whining. It's 92480. The outside doors are locked at 9 p.m. so you'll need the code after that. Are you happy now?"

"Yes, thanks." She smiled. "I'll be careful. Don't worry."

Rich gave her a look of concern as he opened the door to the building, and they went upstairs.

The Board of Directors meeting was only once a month in the boardroom of Triangle. It was an elegant-looking room with a large oblong oak table, oak arm chairs with upholstered gray seats, mauve walls, and a blend of gray, blue, and mauve carpeting. Coffee and tea were set out on the table as the members began assembling in the room. Erin recognized Bruce Washington, the CEO of Triangle, but no one else.

Bruce walked over to her and held out his hand. "Erin, how nice to see you again. I wanted to let you know that speaking for myself and for Triangle, we are very thankful Rich has made such a fast recovery."

"Thank you," smiled Erin, shaking his hand. "I'm glad, too."

"Your father is a remarkable man." Bruce nodded to her as he walked away and took his seat.

Her father had told her that community leaders, health plan physicians, and consumers were on the board. She put a chair in the corner near the exit to remain inconspicuous.

The business of the day was carried out, then it was time for Rich's speech. He walked up to the podium and addressed the room. She was amazed at the charisma her father exuded. Every eye in the room was upon him as he spoke. Erin found herself forgetting to listen to him because she was watching the people around the table. By the time she refocused on her father, he was almost done speaking.

"In closing, we here at Triangle Health Plan believe in managed care. We must make strenuous effort to deliver to every one of our members the kind of care that each of us would want for ourselves and our families." Rich closed his folder to an enthusiastic applause from the board members.

The meeting ended and Rich made small talk with a few of the members as they gradually filtered out. He was congratulated over and over again for his robust words and shook many hands. Bruce spent quite a few minutes talking to him quietly, while shaking his hand and patting him on the shoulder.

"We'll see you on Saturday at the wedding," smiled Rich as Bruce turned to leave.

Erin was very impressed. "Dad, you should have been a politician," she said as they walked out to the car.

"No, I don't think so," he said, laughing. "I'm happy with what I'm doing, thank you."

Erin could tell her father was pleased with the evening. He was humming to the radio and seemed completely relaxed on the drive home. She was very proud of him and happy that things had gone so well. Unfortunately, there was still the problem of Charlie and Michelle and however many other doctors were involved with them in their fraudulent schemes. Erin had gotten lucky at Mercury obtaining information. She hoped that the same good fortune would be with her when she went to Charlie's office.

CHAPTER 16

DAVID had a sinking feeling that today wouldn't be a good day. He had hated like hell to take the autopsy permit to the Walker's to sign. How could he possibly get away with what he had done? Unable to sleep for days now, the circles under his eyes had become obvious. He hadn't been taking care of himself properly. Bathing was something he had to remind himself to do and eating food just didn't seem important anymore. Not thinking clearly, it seemed like walls were closing in on him. Would he have the courage and the heart to face the truth of what he had done? Was redemption an option at this point? As he walked into the surgical ICU, he thought that some of the nurses were whispering about him, so he avoided eye contact with anyone. Were they talking about him because they knew what he had done or because he looked worse than they had ever seen him look before? He sat down at a computer to work, then glanced up when he saw someone next to him out of the corner of his eye.

"I heard about your death," said Michelle, staring down at him with narrowed eyes. "That's two deaths within a short period of time."

He didn't say anything, but he continued to look intently at the computer screen.

"This is not good, David. You know that the hospital will do an investigation. This makes their outcome numbers for coronary bypass look bad." Michelle noticed how bad David looked—unkempt and shaky—just like Dr. Altman looked before his unfortunate accident happened.

"I know."

"Did the family want an autopsy?"

David looked at his watch. "Yes, and it's probably already been done."

Michelle shook her head and sat down. "You're in big trouble." Looking at the large clock on the wall above the crash cart, she started counting down the hours until her plane left. She couldn't have picked a better day to leave.

"What are we going to do?" asked David.

"We? Don't even go there. It's every man for himself now. My advice to you is to just wait and see what happens. The pathologists will contact the Chief of Surgery, and he will want a meeting. You had better start thinking up a good story." Michelle knew that by the time they got around to trying to contact her she would be gone. She scrutinized David and almost felt sorry for him because he looked so awful. "Maybe you should give your attorney a heads up phone call today. Services will probably be needed."

David let out a deep breath. "What a nightmare. I don't know if I can handle this."

She scoffed at him. "Like you have a choice." Looking around the surgical ICU, she decided that she didn't want to be seen talking to him, although it didn't really matter. "Keep me updated on what happens today. Call me on my cell phone." Michelle got up from David's side of the desk and went over to the opposite end of the nurse's station and sat down in front of a computer screen.

David made his rounds quickly, then went back to the desk and finished his computer work, trying to avoid the intensivist, Dr. Page, at all costs. Luckily, Dr. Page wasn't around. David left the surgical ICU and stood outside the double doors for a moment, not knowing what to do next. Finally, deciding to walk down to the cafeteria to get a cup of coffee before he did rounds on the other floors, he saw the two hospital pathologists who would have done the autopsy on Janice Walker. They were in front of him in line at the cashier. David felt weak, as only five people separated them from him. His heart was brought to a standstill as he tried to decide if he should just turn around and leave or stay where he was. He tried to get his feet to move, but they wouldn't, so the decision was already made for him. Breaking into a sweat, he had to make a conscious effort to inhale and exhale as he stood in that line.

The two pathologists were talking to each other as they moved up in line. One of them turned around, looking through the line as he talked to the other doctor. His eyes stopped at David's face as he recognized him. He stared into David's eyes just for a moment, as if trying to peer into his soul. David broke the gaze immediately as he bent down to get his wallet out of his pants, but continued to look at them out of the corner of his eye. The pathologists whispered for a moment and the other one turned around to look at David, too, before they walked away from the register.

As he continued to stand in line, David wondered how the scenario had gone down in the autopsy room. During an autopsy, the pathologist is looking for the truth about how a patient really died. They would have glanced through the chart first and seen that it was written that the patient was having a coronary artery bypass and had a heart attack during the procedure. Although every organ would be looked at during the autopsy, the heart would be examined very closely. They would remove it and section the coronary arteries to see their interior. During the sectioning, they would see that the blockages weren't bad at all. "Why was this patient even having bypass surgery?" they would ask. One of them would open the chart again and look at the cardiac cath report. They would see that the blockages listed didn't equal the blockages that they saw with their own eyes. A discussion would then ensue, as they finally put two and two together. They would continue to question this horrifying discovery, even as they saved sections of the three coronary arteries involved and placed them in three separate jars of preservative solution. But in those jars of preservative floated the truth.

Erin set down her final chart and let out a deep breath. She was so glad she was done with this dreadful job. Even though she didn't know what kind of work she would have in the future, she knew it wouldn't be in an office like this. She wasn't ready yet to work in this type of environment. Looking at the clock and knowing Steve should be calling soon to tell her he was at the house, she didn't want to be too far away from her phone. She looked down her row and saw Polly returning to her desk from lunch. Deciding that it wasn't too far to hear the phone ring, she headed that way.

Polly was just sitting down in her seat as Erin arrived.

"Polly, I wanted to thank you for all the help you've given me while I was here and wish you a happy retirement. I didn't want to leave today without saying good-bye to you."

Polly looked surprised. "Today's your last day? Where are you going, Dr. Tyler?"

"I think I'm going to move out East with my sister and her new husband."

"You're moving next week?"

"Oh, no. Not yet."

Polly appeared confused.

"I'm going on vacation next week," Erin said.

"Okay. Where are you going?"

"The Caribbean."

"I love the Caribbean," said Polly enthusiastically. "What island are you going to?"

Erin blushed. "I don't know."

Polly smiled at her. "You're going to the Caribbean next week and you don't know what island you're going to?"

"No."

"Well, the company must be good."

"Very good."

"Then it doesn't matter where you go, does it?" Polly gave her an all-knowing look.

"Polly, you are very wise." Erin gave her a hug as she heard her phone ring. She hurried up the aisle back to her desk and grabbed it. "Dr. Tyler," she said into the phone.

"Is this *my* Dr. Tyler?" Steve asked.

"Yes, it is," said Erin, her heart fluttering.

"We just got back and I'm in need of you right away. Come directly upstairs to my room and please do not talk to anyone when you arrive."

"I'm on my way," said Erin, smiling as she hung up the phone. She was so excited that she could hardly think. He was back. Should she tell Charlie she was leaving? No. To hell with Charlie. Erin wanted to say good-bye to Susan, so the first thing she did was carry all of her charts over to Susan's desk. Not seeing her anywhere, Erin put a sticky note on the top chart that they were done and could be processed. She then wrote Susan a note, wishing the very best for her and her son, placing it in an envelope she found on Susan's desk and taping it to the computer. Rushing back to her desk, she emailed the pharmacy project to Charlie and shut down her computer. Waving good-bye to Polly, she slipped out of the office, feeling elated that she wouldn't have to go there any more.

Getting home as fast as she could, she pulled up into the driveway and parked with some difficulty. The circular driveway was full with the Tyler cars and two that Erin didn't recognize, but guessed that they were the other bridesmaids'. There was also a large truck that Erin believed must have held the tent, tables, and chairs for the wedding. Erin walked to the front door and turned the doorknob, trying to be quiet but knowing the door always made a squeaking noise. Listening for voices as she briefly stood in the foyer, she heard many of them coming from the kitchen area and living room. She turned to her right and started up the stairs, taking two steps at a time.

Charlie heard the familiar noise on his computer that indicated a new email had just been received. Minimizing what he was working on, he glanced at the sender and saw that it was Erin Tyler with the pharmacy project that was due today. He opened the email and ran through it briefly. It looked like she had done a good job. Too bad he had to get rid of her. He wondered if she had finished all of the charts she had been working on and figured it was time to see. Getting up from his chair, he walked out of his office over to Susan's desk.

Susan wasn't around, but there were two piles of charts sitting at her desk with a note. Reading it, he saw it was from Erin telling her that the charts she had been working on were completed. Charlie nodded his head. Erin had finished everything that had been required of her, but now it was time to let her go. He walked around the corner to the cubicle she sat at. She wasn't there. In fact, the desk was totally void of paper or anything else indicating someone sat there, and the computer and lights were off. Glancing down at Polly's desk, he saw that Polly was talking on the phone. Charlie frowned as he walked back to his office. *Where had Erin gone?* he wondered.

"Was that Erin that just came in?" asked Rich, nonchalantly. He was standing at the back window, watching Sid and Clive examine the pontoon boat that was tied to the dock.

Lisa was rinsing dishes off in the sink. "Maybe," she said, listening for the squeaky door.

Carrie and Angela got up from the kitchen table, where they had been sitting as they discussed the wedding with Lisa.

"Lisa, we're going to sit out on the deck and watch the guys from your mom's shop put up the circus tent," said Carrie, looking at Lisa for a response to her joke.

"Circus tent? Thanks a lot." Lisa pretended to frown, but then smiled.

"Well, where is she?" Rich turned his head to look toward the kitchen entrance, looking for Erin. "Perhaps she wanted to go upstairs first to get her work clothes off."

"I think that's a possibility," said Lisa, hiding a smirk and wondering where Steve was.

Reaching Steve's closed door, Erin gently knocked and opened it. The blinds were parted just enough to let a little light through. Steve was lying on his side on the bed with jean shorts on and an unbuttoned shirt that exposed his bare chest. A pillow was sitting next to him, and he started patting the space in front of it impatiently.

"Hurry up and get over here."

She smiled. "I'm glad to see you, too."

He watched her as she closed the door. "You look so cute in your little outfit."

"I don't like wearing suits." She made an unhappy face as she took off her jacket and set it down on a chair next to the bed and kicked off her shoes. "How are you?" she asked, looking at him.

"I'm much better now." His eyes burned into hers.

Seeing his chest reminded her of the time she'd seen him in the hallway and had imagined herself touching it. Now she could. Noticing his bare legs on the bed, she reached up under her skirt and pulled off her panty hose. Skin-on-skin sounded good. When she got to the bed, she quickly crawled over to his side. She laid down on her back with her head on the pillow and looked up at his face.

He leaned over and started kissing her right away. "I've been wanting to do this all day. I had no idea how much I was going to miss you this week." He held onto her face as he started slowly kissing the corners of her mouth.

"I missed you, too," she said, almost unable to speak when he kissed her like that.

"Keep talking. I'm just trying to breathe you in," he said, closing his eyes and continuing what he was doing for a few moments. "You are utterly fantastic. Has anyone ever told you that you have a beautiful mouth?"

Erin had her eyes closed and answered without thinking. "Yes."

He lifted his head to look at her, then lay down on his back. "That's not the answer I wanted to hear, but I guess I asked for it."

Turning on her side toward him, she put her arm on his chest and stroked it with her hand. It felt as good as she had imagined it would. Putting her left leg over his, she rubbed it with hers. "Is this better?" she whispered as she turned his head towards her and looked into his eyes. "I didn't mean to upset you."

"I must admit that you put me in agony for a moment, but I'm going to stop thinking about it." Leaning over to his right side, he opened the bedside table and took out a long, thin gold box and handed it to Erin. "I bought you something in Chicago."

"You did?"

They both sat up on the bed as Erin lifted the lid. Inside the box, resting on red velvet, was a sparkling, diamond tennis bracelet.

"I can't believe you bought this," she said, taking it out of the box, feeling quite surprised and excited.

"I'm not behaving like I normally do. You make me want to spend my money," he said as he stared at her face and smiled.

"How did you know that I've always wanted one of these?"

"Lisa directed me a bit. We were walking in downtown Chicago with Jimmy, Lisa, and the Emersons. The only thing missing was you. I wanted to go into a jewelry store to buy you something and I took Lisa with me for advice. She said you had always wanted one, so here it is."

"Can you put it on for me?" She held up her left wrist for him as he fastened the clasp. Lying back down on the bed, Erin held up her wrist, turning it as the bracelet glittered. "It's beautiful."

Steve positioned himself back down on his side and watched her. "Are you pleased?"

"Very pleased." She moved to face him again. "I'm free to go away with you on vacation whenever you want," she said, touching his cheek with her hand. "I quit my job."

"Excellent," he said and smiled. He leaned over to kiss her. "Is the Caribbean still all right?"

"Take me wherever you want to. I've never been anywhere and you've been everywhere."

"I'll make the arrangements for our holiday then."

"So is everyone here for the rehearsal?" She held up her wrist again to look at her bracelet and then looked back at him.

He bent over and kissed her again, pulling her toward him. "Yes."

"When do we have to go downstairs?"

"Now," he said, staring at her. "They're probably waiting for us."

Erin moved his hair out of his eyes as he bent down to her face and their kissing became heated. It was wonderful to be lying here on a bed together without any disasters going on around them, kissing and hugging and touching each other. Finally! They were relaxed and intertwined in each other's arms and it felt spectacular.

Steve stopped abruptly and turned over on his back, gazing at the ceiling, breathing heavily. "I'm losing control, Erin. We have to stop." He let out a lengthy breath. "We can't continue this or we won't get downstairs at all for the rehearsal."

Erin didn't answer for a moment. "I think they would miss the maid of honor and the best man. Lisa wouldn't be pleased. She'd come up here and get us." She paused. "I don't want us to be rushed."

Steve breathed a sigh of exasperation. "You have to go then. If I look at you anymore I won't be responsible for my actions."

Glancing at him and seeing that he was serious, Erin got up from the bed and collected her things. "I'll see you downstairs," she said as she left the room.

Michelle finished her rounds at Mercury and Southeast and was back at her office seeing patients. It was hard to believe this was her last day. She felt exhilarated, and she welcomed the change that was coming into her life. This was something she had been looking forward to for months.

"Stephanie, are we almost done?" she asked, picking up the appointment book and looking at Stephanie.

"Yes, we're done." Stephanie smiled as she twisted her hair around her finger. "Do you have to go see your mother this weekend, Dr. Campbell?"

"No, but I needed to keep my schedule open just in case." She looked at Stephanie and smiled. Stephanie had always been a pleasant girl to work with and had been a real asset to the office. "I'm going to leave in a few minutes. Have a good weekend."

"You too."

The desk phone started ringing and Stephanie picked it up as Michelle entered her office. She looked around the office briefly, trying to decide if she should take anything else. Plants that she didn't care about and a couple of books that could be replaced. Nothing else mattered. She picked up her purse just as her phone rang. "Yes, Stephanie?"

"Dr. Patton on line 1."

"Okay, thanks." She waited while the line clicked over. "Hello Charlie."

"Hey, Baby. What are you doing?"

"I'm finishing up my patients so I can go home. I haven't been feeling well."

"Do you need anything? I can come over tonight."

"No, that's all right. I just need to rest. I'll be fine." Deciding that he needed something to worry about besides her, she let the bomb drop. "David Keller had a death, and an autopsy was done today on the patient."

"What?" Charlie sputtered. "When was someone going to tell me?"

"I'm telling you now. I just saw David at Southeast a couple of hours ago. He doesn't seem to be handling it very well. He looks terrible. Reminds me of Dr. Altman near the end."

"I can't believe this," Charlie stammered.

"They're going to know, Charlie."

"And they'll be knocking on your door next. We have to find some way of making him the fall guy and getting you out of this mess. Do you have any ideas?"

"Not right now. Let me think about it. I have to go, Charlie. Patients are waiting."

"All right. I'll call you later." He hung up the phone.

Michelle smiled, as she knew that Charlie would immediately inhale the vial of cocaine he had in his jacket while he tried to figure out what to do. She would miss him, but not much. Looking around her office once more, she turned off the light and left for the bank.

CHAPTER 17

AFTER leaving Steve, Erin went to her room to quickly change out of her work clothes and get downstairs. She didn't want him upset like that, but he realized the necessity of stopping the encounter when he did. Their time would come, and it would be soon. Erin found her pink cotton halter dress and white leather sandals she had planned to wear for the rehearsal and put them on. She held up her beautiful new bracelet to the light. It was gorgeous, and she couldn't believe that he had bought it for her. Hopping down the stairs two at a time, she went through the kitchen and out onto the back deck, where she saw a lot of activity going on. The enormous white tent was erected, chairs were being set up on the lawn for the ceremony, and all the people she expected to be there were outside. Seeing Carrie and Angela, she crept up behind them and spoke. "Everyone lock up your sons. The wild women have arrived."

Carrie turned around and laughed. "Look, Angela, there's our drinking buddy. Are you up for some wine tonight, Erin?"

"No." Erin rolled her eyes. "The last time I drank wine with you two I felt terrible the whole next day. I better lay off of it tonight if I want to feel good for the wedding tomorrow."

"You have to learn to pace yourself," said Angela. "I'm already in a partying mode for the entire weekend. I plan on having a blast."

"Erin, I'm glad I didn't bring a date for the wedding. I kind of like that English guy with the curls," said Carrie, pointing to Clive, who was still on the pontoon boat. "I was already introduced to him, and I think I'm going to get to know him better this weekend." Carrie raised her eyebrows and grinned.

"Sid doesn't look bad, either," said Angela, nodding her head.

Erin laughed. "You guys are too funny. Just stay away from the best man. He's mine."

She walked away from them and said "hello" again to the Emersons, who were discussing seating arrangements with Lisa. Erin looked up and saw her dad stepping on the pontoon boat to talk with Sid and Clive. Jimmy was relaxing in a chair facing the lake and Steve was standing there talking to him. She kept her eyes fixed on Steve for a moment. He looked quite handsome, having changed his clothes to khaki pants and a sage-colored cotton shirt.

Erin went over to the tent to find her mother, who was directing the production. Arlene was inside with the men that were placing the floor down in interlocking pieces. Tables and chairs were sitting outside, ready to be taken inside the tent after the floor was done. Dozens of ficus trees were being unloaded from the truck, ready to have little white lights placed on them.

"Everything looks great, Mom," said Erin, scanning the scene.

"It's fine so far," smiled Arlene. "Most of the work will get done today. The flowers and cake will come tomorrow with the food." She looked at her watch. "We should start the rehearsal now."

They walked out of the tent and looked for Lisa. She was already over by the archway with the minister and Jimmy.

Arlene cupped her hands over her mouth and spoke loudly. "Okay everyone, we need to get started."

It didn't take long for the wedding party to assemble. Jimmy, Steve, and the groomsmen were positioned at the archway. Lisa, Erin, and the bridesmaids would be in the kitchen and come out from the door near it when the wedding started. The wedding party did a complete run-through with all the details being worked out. Erin and Steve made eye contact again as they went through the rehearsal, and she took his arm to walk up the aisle to the back of the house.

"Are you able to look at me now?" she asked him.

"Just barely, but don't get too close to me."

"I'm going to Triangle tonight to check Charlie's office. Do you want to go with me?"

Steve scowled as he looked ahead. "Are you sure you want to do that?"

"I'm sure."

"You are quite a stubborn girl, aren't you?" He turned to her. "Of course I'm going. I'd be totally daft if I let you go alone."

She smiled.

They finished the walk up the aisle and arrived at the back of the house. The Emersons were sitting on the deck chairs. Steve sat down with them as some of the wedding party wandered around the yard and others went into the house. Arlene and Rich walked over to the tent to see the update, and Erin went with them.

"When are we leaving for the restaurant?" Erin asked her father.

"In a few minutes. Your mother wants to make sure everything is fine with the people working in the tent."

Arlene started talking to one of the men, while Erin and Rich stayed at the entrance.

"Are you feeling okay, Dad?"

"I'm a little tired, but I don't plan on staying out late tonight. My energy will be saved for tomorrow."

"I'm still going to look around in Charlie's office tonight after the dinner."

"I was hoping you would change your mind. I really wish you wouldn't go there." He didn't speak for a moment. "Are you taking someone with you?"

"Steve."

"Good. I'm sure I don't have to tell you to be careful. Do you remember the building code?"

"Yes."

Rich nodded as Arlene came over.

"Looks beautiful, doesn't it?" She beamed at them.

Erin looked around. The round tables and chairs were set up. The ficus trees were positioned around the perimeter of the tent and a girl was putting the little white lights on them. The buffet and head tables were assembled. What a difference another 24 hours was going to make.

"Are we ready to go?" asked Rich. "I suppose we'll need to take all of the cars."

"I want the Mustang," said Erin.

"You always want the Mustang," said Rich, smiling.

They walked back to the deck and the group decided on the driving arrangements. When everything was settled, they took off for the restaurant.

Michelle had gathered the rest of her favorite things in the living room and spread them out on the floor. This was all that was left. Walking into the kitchen, she opened the refrigerator and took out her last chilled bottle of Cristal. This was the perfect time to drink it. Opening the bottle and pouring the pale, gold champagne into her favorite glass, she toasted herself.

"To me!" she said out loud, holding up her glass. "I've done it." She paused for a moment, thinking of what she wanted to say. "Let's talk about quality, shall we? The quality of being ingenious is mine. No one will ever find me. I am smarter than all of them put together. Sorry, Charlie. You picked the wrong bitch to get involved with. I guess I pulled one over on you after all. I'm rich, young, and beautiful, and the world is mine for the taking." She took a drink of the champagne and smiled.

She meandered back into the living room, carrying her glass and the bottle of champagne as she looked around. Sitting down on the couch for a moment, she thoroughly enjoyed two more glasses before sitting the bottle down on the end table. She saw the pile of clothes she had put on the recliner and decided it was time to fold them for packing. Getting up from the couch, she walked over to them, but paused when she reached the recliner. She picked up the clothes in her arms and danced around in a circle, throwing them wherever they landed. This was totally unlike her, and she knew it. Normally so meticulous, there was a new Michelle emerging—a Michelle who didn't have to be serious all of the time. One who could now care about frivolous things and enjoy the fruits of her labor. Laughing, she fell back down on the couch and finished the bottle of champagne. She didn't have much left to pack and could finally feel the freedom.

David sat at the high rollers poker table, betting larger amounts than usual. He just didn't care anymore. Nothing seemed to matter. The day had fallen apart since the very beginning, and he wasn't sure what he was going to do. Not at all surprised when he received a call from the Chief of Surgery for an 8 a.m. Monday morning meeting, he didn't bother to call Michelle and let her know, like she had requested. Holding up his empty scotch glass to the waitress, he looked around the casino. It was very crowded already on this Friday night and it was still early. As the waitress brought him another drink, he saw a familiar face across the room. Turning his head away, he hoped he wouldn't be spotted. Another hand had started and David was in on it right away. He forgot about the face as he contemplated removing two cards from his hand.

"I would get rid of those cards if I were you," said a voice behind him.

"Hello, Charlie," David said, without looking, as he dropped two cards and got two more from the dealer.

"Can we talk?"

The dealer won the hand and David threw in his cards.

"Sure." He picked up his drink and turned around to face Charlie.

"Let's go over to the bar." Charlie noticed immediately how ragged David looked.

They walked across the casino to the bar which was located in the middle of the floor and sat down at a small table with two chairs that was just being vacated. Charlie went up to the counter and got himself a drink as David stared blankly around him.

"Well, David," said Charlie as he sat back down, "what's the damage for today?"

"Pretty bad. Meeting Monday morning with the Chief of Surgery."

"Ouch." Charlie took a long sip of his drink.

David shrugged. "I don't know what to do anymore."

"Nothing much we can do until we see what the Surgery Chief has to say to you. Try to be optimistic. Maybe the pathologists didn't figure it out." Charlie drained his drink quickly and ordered another one from a passing waitress.

"Right," David said sarcastically. "The way they were looking at me today? They knew." He shook his head.

"Michelle and I will think things through over the weekend and get back to you."

"How did you know I was here?" asked David as he finished his drink.

Charlie looked at him and laughed. "Come on, David. Remember why you wanted in CAP to begin with? You have a problem that you thought no one knew about. I just had to drive by the casino valet lots to figure out which one you were in. There it was. A cream colored Lincoln Continental. Bingo! I'm at the right casino."

As David started talking, he seemed to have an internal struggle with himself rather than talking specifically to Charlie. "I should have never let you entice me to join CAP. Cardiovascular surgeons make a lot of money, but somehow I didn't think it was enough. Why? I sold my soul for a few extra thousand each month."

Charlie saluted him with his drink. "Quite a bit more than a few extra thousand, my friend. You've been doing most excellent with your surgeries. Don't think about it as selling your soul. It's much more than that."

"I can't believe the incredible suffering I have caused. How can I live with myself?"

"You'll be able to live with it better when you see your account next week. There will be a pretty penny in it. Try to relax a little until then, David." Charlie looked around him, hoping no one could hear David ramble.

"I was only concerned with financial gain and protecting my own interests."

"I don't see a problem with that."

"Charlie, this was wrong, and I'm going to come clean about it. Whatever happens, I accept it."

Charlie stared David straight in the eye as he started to panic. He put his hands out on the table while he pleaded. "David, be reasonable. You can't possibly be serious about that. There are way too many people involved. If you truly want out, we can discuss that after we get through this crisis. Come on, have another drink."

David pursed his lips and got up from the table, leaving Charlie. He walked through the casino until he reached the exit. Giving his ticket to the valet, he waited under the porch until his car was driven up for him.

"All ready to go, sir," said the valet as he got out of the driver's side of David's Lincoln.

David reached into his pocket and pulled out a wad of cash. He looked at it for a moment, then handed all of it to the valet.

The valet looked at the money briefly and could tell there were hundreds of dollars in his hand. He looked back at David, sure this was a mistake. "Sir, do you know how much money you've just given me?"

"Yes, I know." David didn't look at him as he got into the car. He had never felt more alone, and the emptiness was at the deepest level in his soul.

Downtown Detroit was aglow with lights as David turned out into the street. Darkness had just settled into the city on this humid August night and there were people walking around everywhere. He just started driving down streets in the downtown area, turning right at one and left at another, not paying any attention where he was. Horns beeped at him as he ran a red light, and another time as he almost hit a bus. Going through a large intersection and turning left, he realized he was on Jefferson Avenue. He passed Joe Louis Arena and the Renaissance Center, driving with the traffic at first, then swerving over onto the sidewalk that he drove on until he came to a large grassy area that faced the Detroit River.

Putting his window down and turning off his car, he listened to the sounds of the city. He could hear the woeful blaring horns of the barges going down the river. If he listened carefully, he could hear music coming from a couple of different areas around him. The clubs and concert halls were in full swing on this Friday night. Looking ahead, the lights of Canada could be seen across the river for what looked like miles. And the river itself—furious, strong water, moving at a fast pace. Lightless, hypnotizing water that could make everything all right.

Looking to his left, he saw a car a little ways down that looked like it was moving toward him in the dark. His eyes squinted as he stared at it. Blue lights flashed on. Turning to his right, he saw another vehicle with flashing blue lights coming toward him. It was decision time. David's last act of free will.

Starting his car, his headlights flashed on and he pushed the accelerator to the floor. The tires hesitated in the grass for a moment, then broke free. Moments later he hit the top of the fence at the river, but was going too fast for it to stop his car. As he became airborne, he looked around in wonder for the few seconds before his car hit the water.

CHAPTER 18

CHARLIE had another drink and wondered where David had gone. He looked all around, but didn't see David anywhere. He got up and went back to the poker table where David had been playing, but he wasn't there. David didn't like the slots, so Charlie didn't even bother looking there as he perused the rest of the floor. Going out to the front entrance of the casino, he looked around, but could no longer see David's car in the valet lot. Motioning the valet over to him, Charlie gave the valet his own ticket and waited for his car. After tipping him, Charlie pulled out into the street and drove aimlessly around a few blocks, looking for David's car and wondering where he had gone. Then he resigned himself to the fact that maybe David had just gone home, Charlie turned onto Jefferson Avenue to get on the Lodge freeway and head home himself.

He looked over towards the river, where he saw the lights of numerous police cars and a local television station broadcasting. Pulling over to the side of the road, he called to a man standing nearby.

"Hey, buddy, can you tell me what's happening over there?" Charlie asked, nodding his head toward the commotion.

"Someone drove into the river," said the burly looking man. "I was down there fishing and saw the whole thing." He shook his head. "It was a horrible sight."

"What kind of car?"

"Beautiful Lincoln Continental. Glowed in the dark until the water took it."

"Thanks." Charlie frowned. He put his window up and headed for the freeway as he dialed Michelle's number.

Erin and Steve slipped out of the restaurant without telling anyone else where they were going. Her father looked concerned, and he nodded at them when they left.

"I loved looking at those pictures Mrs. Emerson had of you guys when the band was just getting started. All of you looked like babies," said Erin as they walked to the car.

He glanced at her. "We were quite young, weren't we?"

As Erin got into the driver's seat, she started the car and put the top down. "Isn't this great?" She put her head back against the seat and looked up at the clear, black sky and the many shining stars that she could actually see twinkling.

Steve was staring at her, but turned away. Groaning, he settled into his seat and put the seatbelt on. "Let's go then," he said, looking straight ahead.

Erin heard him groan and turned to him, giving him a quick kiss on his cheek. She backed out of the parking space and headed for Triangle.

Upon arriving, she pulled into the north side of the parking lot. Not seeing any cars at all, she parked near some bushes that would hide the black car even more. They got out of the car and silently walked over to the entrance. Erin pulled on the outside door and found it was locked. She reached in her purse and took out the building code. Punching in the code, the door clicked and then opened. The low lighting on in the building made it difficult to see as they took the elevator to the 5th floor and went into the office.

Even though Erin knew they were alone in the building, she still spoke softly. "Steve, just follow me. We're going over to the Credentialing department to see if we have a file on Michelle."

They walked slowly to Credentialing as their eyes adjusted to the low lighting. Easing around the cubicle rows, she saw the small rectangular file room and tried to open the door, but it was locked. Going over to where the administrative assistant sat, she opened the top drawer of her desk and rummaged around until she found a small box with keys in it. She searched through them until she found a ring that had a sticker attached to it that said "file room." She took it out and they walked back to the file room, easily opened the door, and went in. Erin took a small flashlight from her purse. Shining the light, they looked up and down the rows of file cabinets until they found the ones that held the "C's" and stopped.

"C-a-b through c-o-r. It should be in the first drawer here." Erin opened the drawer and thumbed through the names until she came to "Campbell, Michelle." Pulling out the file, she opened it and found herself looking at a smiling picture of Michelle. She quickly went through the file, seeing where Michelle went to school and at what hospitals she had trained. Erin took a little notebook from her purse and wrote down Michelle's home address and phone number. Putting the file back in its place, she closed the drawer. They exited the room as Erin locked it back up and placed the key in the desk where she had found it.

They crept over to the other side of the building to Charlie's office. As they turned the corner by it, the green glow of his desk lamp could be seen outside in the hall. Erin turned to Steve and put her finger to her lips for him not to say anything. He frowned as he looked around behind him for a moment, not liking the turn of events. Erin tiptoed and peeked inside the office. Not seeing Charlie at all, she saw his computer screen gleaming. She squinted to read the screen and thought she saw names and money amounts listed, but she couldn't see them clearly. Her eyes focused on a pile of white powder sitting on the top of his desk. Cocaine! Erin's heart skipped a beat as she realized that he was somewhere close and hadn't left his light and computer on by accident.

A voice bellowed from behind them. "Yes, I'm here!"

Erin gasped as she and Steve spun around to where the voice was coming from.

Charlie ambled into view from around the corner and looked with disgust at Erin. "You meddling bitch! Both of you in the office—now—and sit down." He motioned with his head for them to go in.

They reluctantly walked into the office and sat in the two chairs positioned directly in front of Charlie's desk as they waited for him to speak.

He sat down at his desk and picked up a razor blade. Making a thick line of white powder with the razor, he picked up a small gold tube and snorted the powder up into his nose.

"Here," he said holding up the gold tube, "have some cocaine."

Erin and Steve both shook their heads "no."

"Suit yourself," said Charlie as he set the gold tube down and looked at them. "It's too bad you decided to come here."

"Right," said Steve, trying to act tough. "So what's this all about, Charlie? Let's have it."

Charlie raised his eyebrows and looked questioningly at Steve, then back at Erin. "Who is this guy?" he asked sarcastically.

"He's my boyfriend." Erin glanced at Steve and weakly smiled as he looked back at her.

"Well, boyfriend, you are going to be very sorry that you accompanied Erin here tonight," said Charlie. "Some things are better left alone, and your nosy little girlfriend just couldn't do that." Charlie stopped looking at them for a moment and closed what he had been working on in the computer. He took out the disc and placed it in his jacket pocket as he looked up at Steve. "So, boyfriend, you want to know what this is all about, do you?"

"The name is Steve."

"Very well, Steve. Listen and you'll hear everything." He turned his attention to Erin. "My dear Dr. Tyler, you're too young to know what it used to be like to be a physician. Gone are the days where you were just able to help your patients get better and get paid for your services. Now there are a myriad of different insurance companies with strict rules for payment: preapproval requirements for surgeries and treatments that differ with each health plan. You have to be a businessman as well as a physician, and the business side has become more important. A physician these days has overwhelming responsibility to know everything that is out there. That is one reason I left my office practice and came to work for the insurer."

"I know it's not easy to be a physician, Charlie," said Erin.

He snorted another line of cocaine. "The insurance end of it is no easier. We are in deep trouble, too. I'm sure Rich told you about the problems we're having. Pharmacy is one of our biggest headaches, as we discussed prior to your pharmacy assignment. As the baby boomers age, things will only get worse."

Erin nodded. "I agree with everything you have said so far."

"Now, national organizations and the federal government scrutinize the insurance company to no end. The demands they place on us are unbelievable. You must do this, you must do that. Collect data on this, collect data on that. Tell us how you're going to help your members with such and such diagnosis or we won't endorse your health insurance. Half the time an insurance company can't even look at claims properly due to government regulations or your own company telling you they must be paid within a certain length of time. As it turns out, this was one of the things that my little business was based on. The thirty-day claim turn around was the best thing that ever happened to a businessman like me."

Erin watched him and listened.

"I've seen how some physician office's tamper with claims. They keep altering the codes until they hit on something that the insurance company will pay for. They put in the codes that will pay the highest amount. The fraud that goes on with that is unbelievable. No wonder we have to keep raising our rates. Unfortunately, members don't care about physicians deceiving the insurance company. As long as the physician gets paid, they don't concern themselves with what had to be done for the payment to happen."

"I can see how all of these things have made you angry," said Erin, trying to placate him, "but I think that most physicians are honest and trying to do the best for their patients. Even in a well-managed practice, billing errors can happen. It doesn't mean they're intentional."

Charlie acted as though he didn't hear her. "Michelle and I met and found that we were of like minds. We were tired of the health care industry. The cost of malpractice insurance is ridiculous. Falling Medicare and Medicaid payments continue. Agreeing that we had no job satisfaction, we brainstormed and figured out a way to make a huge amount of money in a short period of time so we could just leave everything here behind and leave the country. We planned this venture to last one to two years. Our little business is called CAP. That stands for 'cash and physicians.' Simple as that. Recruiting wasn't easy, because we had to be very careful what we said and to whom, but we got our little group together and it has worked out fine, most of the time. Michelle and I have a nice bank account already."

"I can't believe so many other physicians would let themselves get involved in a conspiracy," said Erin, shaking her head.

Charlie got up from his desk and walked around to the front of it. He sat on the edge and studied Erin. "Everyone had their own reasons for getting involved. The internists were in it for the cash, and all they had to do was refer patients to Michelle. Their job was easy and they had no risk."

Erin started talking. "So the internists sent patients to Michelle who may not have needed a cardiologist at all. If they were found to be good candidates for surgery, their cardiac caths were altered at Mercury and the false report sent to Southeast, where their surgery was performed by a cardiovascular surgeon on CAP's payroll."

"Bravo, Erin." He laughed. "I knew you were sharp."

"How did Jeff Elliott get involved in this?"

"Jeff started getting much-reduced cash payments from insurance companies for his services, and that made him very angry. The amount he was paid made him feel that his services weren't worth anything. He couldn't wait to get involved in CAP and has been compensated very well, making over twice as much as the internists."

"Why did he sign off on Michelle's caths? He's a radiologist. It immediately made me suspicious."

Charlie raised his eyebrows. "I didn't know that. Chalk that one up to his ego."

"I find it hard to believe that a cardiologist and cardiovascular surgeon who are already two of the highest paid specialties would risk everything to do unnecessary surgery for cash," spouted Erin.

"Not everyone is able to handle it," muttered Charlie, thinking about David. "You know, Erin, that we are just little fish here. We are not corporate evildoers that illegally take millions and millions from its shareholders or customers. There are very few of us in CAP. We are not taking anyone's retirement or money from their children's college funds. The members are the casualties of war—the war against the system." He walked back behind his desk, sat down, and started shutting down his computer.

"What happened to Dr. Kramer and Dr. Altman?"

"More casualities."

Erin was getting angrier by the moment. "Tell me about the night my father became ill."

"Oh that?" said Charlie offhandedly. "Michelle and I thought that if we got rid of Rich, you would go away. Obviously, we didn't get rid of Rich and you didn't go away."

Erin was raging and wanted to lash out at Charlie. Not knowing what she was going to do, she got up quickly from her chair.

Steve saw her fury, but put his hand on her arm and spoke quietly. "Erin, don't."

She fixed her eyes on Steve and he stared back at her. Seeing how concerned he looked, she sat back down in her seat, deeply troubled. She took a deep breath before she spoke. "Charlie, you can't rationalize your behavior. You're a disgusting human being that has violated all moral standards. I am sickened to know that you're a physician."

Charlie shrugged his shoulders. "There will be no atonement for me." He bent down toward his desk and snorted another line of cocaine. Taking the razor blade, he scraped the rest of the pile into a bottle and capped it. Putting the bottle in his pocket, he looked up from his desk as if he heard something. Walking over to his office entrance, he listened momentarily, then went back to his desk.

Erin and Steve looked at each other blankly, not knowing what they should do next.

Erin rose slowly from her chair and turned to Steve. "Come on, we're leaving."

Steve started to get up.

"Not so fast," sneered Charlie. He took a small gun from his desk drawer and placed it on the desktop, facing them. "Sit down."

They sat down and glared at Charlie.

"Now what am I going to do with you two?" Tapping his fingers on his desk for a moment, he took out his cell phone and dialed a number. He leaned back in his chair, talking low off and on for a few minutes. He frowned, then ended the call. Getting up from the desk, he put his jacket on. He picked up his gun and turned off his desk lamp. "Let's go."

Erin and Steve got up from their chairs as Charlie directed them out of the office. Steve put his arm around Erin, then moved her in front of him as they walked. Turning the corner to get to the elevator, Steve put his right arm out and struck it backwards against Charlie with violent impact.

The hit took Charlie by surprise; he lost his balance and fell to the floor. The gun slipped from his hand, but he recovered it as quickly as Steve could turn around to face him. Charlie got up and slammed the gun into Steve's left temple, immediately causing a trickle of blood to start running down the side of Steve's face. As Charlie pointed the gun at his head, Steve put his hands up and the confrontation ended.

"Well, I didn't anticipate opposition from you," yelled Charlie to Steve. "I would suggest that you don't try anything like that again." He moved back from Steve, but still held up the gun toward him.

Erin moved swiftly to Steve to look at his head. Moving his hair back, she saw a small cut with blood oozing from it. She opened her purse and removed a tissue, wiping up the blood already running down his cheek, then holding the tissue to his temple. Looking at the cut closely, it didn't appear that it would need to be sutured. "Are you okay?" she asked him, her hands trembling.

He looked at her and nodded. "It hurts a bit, but I'm fine."

"Move it," said Charlie, motioning for them to start walking again.

Steve held the tissue to his head as he and Erin walked with Charlie to the elevator.

Michelle would be winging her way to Paris in just under an hour and the time waiting at the airport seemed to be endless. It was bad enough that David Keller had escaped his misery tonight by driving into the Detroit River. She was shocked that he had done that. He didn't even try to run away like she was doing. Her phone rang and she took it out of her purse. Looking at the number, she saw that it was Charlie. She decided not to answer it, and the call went to her voice mail. Waiting for a moment to see if he left a message and seeing that he didn't, she started to put her phone back into her purse.

It started ringing again and Charlie's number was showing.

She decided to answer it and talk to him for the last time. "Hello, Charlie," she said into the phone.

"We have a problem, Michelle."

"What?"

"I have Erin Tyler and her boyfriend here in my office. They were snooping around. What do you think we should do?"

The airport had gotten very noisy as a plane came in and its passengers were disembarking right in front of her. She hoped that Charlie couldn't hear all of the commotion. Getting up and going over to a corner where nobody was sitting, she could talk louder.

"Why don't you take them back to your condo and lock them in the wine cellar?"

"And then what? Are we going to kill them?"

"You could call up your drug dealer. Maybe he can set up something like he did for Kramer's cement demise in the Detroit River or Altman's fatal car accident."

"True. I'll give him a call. What are you doing now?"

"I'm trying to rest. I told you earlier that I haven't felt well today."

"Well, I want you to come over. We need to talk."

"Charlie, I don't want to come over. I'm in bed."

"I insist, Michelle. We need to discuss what we are going to do about the hospital situation coming down on Monday. Everyone will find out about David by then. You'll be the next in line to get the summons."

"Charlie…" she said, trying to think of another excuse and not finding one.

"Can I expect you within the hour?"

She lied. "All right."

"I'll lock up Erin and her boyfriend. See you soon."

"Bye." Hanging up the phone, she breathed a sigh, knowing that she was done with him forever.

She knew what the scene would be like at Charlie's condo. He would go back there and lock up Erin and her boyfriend. Waiting for her as he continued to snort cocaine, he would keep calling her phone and getting angrier by the minute at not being able to reach her. When he finally gave up at about 5 in the morning, he would lie down on the couch and fall asleep. Waking up in the morning with a hangover, he would realize she had never called or come to his condo. Driving over to her house, he would see her car in the driveway and not know something was wrong until he went in. It had been so long since he had been to her house, he had no idea she had been moving things for months to Paris. When he walked upstairs to check on her, he would see that most of the personal items in her bedroom were gone. When he realized the house was unoccupied, it would take him a few moments to think about what this meant. By the time he thought to check his bank accounts, they would be empty. What a staggering blow that would be to him.

She looked at her watch and decided to get a magazine for the plane trip. Walking over to the newsstand, she opened her purse and beamed at all the beautiful money she saw inside.

CHAPTER 19

ERIN, Steve, and Charlie took the elevator down to the first floor and went out the main door that led to the south side of the parking lot. Erin had parked on the north side of the building, and that was why she and Steve hadn't seen his Jaguar. She should have driven around before she parked, but hadn't thought that anyone would be there so late. *What an error on my part*, she thought.

"Boyfriend, get in front," said Charlie. "You're driving. Erin get in the back seat."

"I don't think you want me to drive," Steve protested as he got into the front seat. He found the power seat adjustment and moved the seat back to compensate for his long legs. He adjusted the mirror and put on his seatbelt.

Charlie looked at Steve irritably after getting into the car. "Please don't argue with me. I'm not in the mood." He put his gun into the pocket of his jacket, next to the CAP disc.

Erin climbed in the back seat and put her arms around Steve's neck, kissing his cheek. "Be careful," she whispered. She glanced at his wound, and seeing that it had stopped bleeding, took away the tissue. Sitting back in the seat, she locked her seatbelt.

Steve started up the car and drove out of the parking lot. As he pulled the Jaguar out into the far right lane on Woodward Avenue, he drove well for a few miles.

"I'm doing better than I thought," he said to Erin. He looked in the rear view mirror at her and tried to make an effort to smile.

"Turn right at the next light," Charlie said.

Steve was trying to concentrate as he turned, but it just didn't seem natural to turn that way and go into that lane. He still had not been able to adjust to the complete opposite traffic pattern of England. As he turned onto the two-lane highway, he went into the oncoming traffic lane, but didn't realize it, because there weren't any cars coming.

"Wrong lane!" hollered Charlie. "Get over into the right lane."

A car could now be seen coming over the hill at them, not very far away.

"Move over!" shouted Charlie.

"Get over, Steve," Erin said loudly.

Steve moved the car over into the right lane just in time for the oncoming car to speed by them. They all breathed a collective sigh of relief.

Charlie was extremely annoyed. He looked at Steve. "You don't know how to drive?"

Steve glanced at him with displeasure. "I think that's crushingly obvious."

None of them saw the police car hiding on the side street that had witnessed the wrong lane fiasco. A moment later, the blue lights were turned on and could be seen flashing in the dark all around the Jaguar as the police car pulled up behind them.

"Damn!" said Charlie, turning around to glimpse the lights. "Pull over to the right." Charlie quickly put on his seatbelt before the officer could see that he didn't have one on. "You two had better not say a word. Just do what the cop says and we'll be out of here quickly."

Steve moved over to the side of the road and put the car into park.

The police car pulled over behind the Jaguar. As the officer got out of his car, he shined his flashlight on the Jaguar's license plate and made a note. He walked over to the driver's side of the car.

Steve put the window down and smiled.

"Good evening," said the officer as he shined his flashlight into the car to briefly view its occupants. "License and registration, please."

Steve took his wallet out from his pants pocket and pulled out a folded piece of paper. It was his England driver's license. He unfolded it and handed it to the officer.

The office positioned his flashlight over the license. "You're from England?" he asked, looking at Steve again.

"Yes, Officer," said Steve.

"Where is your registration?"

"I'm looking for it," said Charlie, rummaging through the glove box's contents. "This is my car."

"And why are you in the United States?" asked the officer as he looked at Steve's license again.

"I'm a musician; I've been touring in the Midwest for about a month," said Steve pleasantly.

Charlie decided it was time to interrupt. Having found his car registration in the glove box, he passed it over to Steve to give to the officer.

"Officer," said Charlie, leaning forward so the officer could see him, "I apologize for the *faux pas* committed by my English friend here. I've been teaching him to drive while he's in the United States. Since it is so late in the evening, I thought this would be a perfect time for him to hone up on his driving skills." Charlie gave the officer a wide smile. "Obviously, I didn't use very good judgment."

"Are you Charles Patton?" asked the officer as he read through the registration. Charlie nodded.

"Where have you been and where are you going?"

"I am a physician and the chief medical officer at Triangle Health Plan, which is located about five miles away around the corner on Woodward Avenue. We had been at the office on business and were going back to my house," said Charlie slowly as he made up the story.

"What a complete load of old bollocks," Steve added quietly.

Charlie glared at Steve.

The officer didn't seem to hear Steve's remark. Appearing satisfied with Charlie's explanation, he shined the flashlight back at Erin, who smiled weakly.

"That's Dr. Tyler in the back seat. She works at the health plan with me," said Charlie. He grinned. "Would there be anything else we could do for you tonight, Officer?"

Before the officer could respond, Steve turned to Charlie and spoke loudly. "Charlie, I think I've had enough of driving for tonight. You had sportingly agreed to teach me, but Erin and I have made other plans." Steve gave Charlie a broad smile before turning back to the officer. "May I get out of the car, Officer?"

Charlie was unable to protest as the officer was still standing there. His anger was boiling over and there was nothing he could do.

"Sure," said the officer, moving back to let Steve get out.

Steve turned back to Charlie, looking him straight in the eye with disgust as he opened the car door. "Sod off, you bloody wanker."

Charlie frowned, but kept his mouth shut and stared straight ahead.

Erin turned her head toward Charlie. "Oh, Charlie," she sang out.

Charlie turned his head back at her.

"I no longer work for you. My boyfriend wants to take me on vacation instead." Opening her door and climbing out, she couldn't believe that it was so easy to get away from him.

"Thank you, sir," said Steve as he turned to the officer and put out his hand. "I promise I won't drive again while I'm here this time in the United States."

The officer shook his hand back and smiled. "Take care, you two."

He started walking back to his patrol car.

Charlie was left dumbfounded as he watched Erin and Steve hike quickly down the street back to Woodward Avenue. This was a heavily-populated area on a Friday night, and many people were out. Restaurants, bars and gas stations were teeming with patrons. The officer had returned to his own car, but was just sitting there and seemed in no hurry to leave. Charlie got out of his Jaguar, walked around to the driver's side and got in. He sat in his car a few minutes, thinking, but he knew there was nothing he could do about Erin and Steve right now. They had gotten away. Turning on his car, he started for home.

Erin and Steve walked as fast as they could toward the Starbucks they had seen down the road until they were sure Charlie had left. They stopped for a moment and put their arms around each other.

Erin buried her head into his chest. "I wonder what he was going to do with us."

"He's a bastard. Who knows what he would have done."

"How's your head feeling?"

"I have a headache, but it's not that bad."

She turned her face up to his and kissed him. "That was quick thinking on your part to get us out of that mess."

Steve smiled. "I'm surprised I pulled that one off. Shall I hail a cab to take us back to your car?" he asked as he looked around in the neighboring parking lots for a cab.

"We're not going to find a cab just driving around. We aren't downtown in the city. If we call one, it will take a while for it to get here."

Steve scanned up and down the busy highway and thought he saw a cab coming towards them. He squinted his eyes. "Erin, is that what I think it is?"

She turned to where Steve was looking. "I don't believe it."

They moved closer to the street off the sidewalk and waved their arms until the cab pulled over. The sign on it said "Airport Taxi." Someone must have had a cab take them home from the airport, which was about forty minutes away from where they were.

The cabby opened his window.

"Hello," said Erin, bending down to talk to him. "Can you take us for a quick trip only about five miles away? My car is parked in a lot over there."

"I'll give you an extra $20 for your trouble," Steve promised. "Can you help us out?"

"Sure. Hop in," said the cabby as he unlocked the doors.

They got into the back seat and Erin told him where they needed to go. She leaned over against Steve and let out a heavy sigh. "I need to call my father and let him know what's going on." She took out her cell phone and called her house.

Rich answered the phone.

"Dad, its Erin."

"Where are you?" he asked.

"Well, right now Steve and I are in a cab on our way back to Triangle to pick up the car." She told her father everything that had happened.

"I am shocked by all of this, but I'm glad that you and Steve are all right. I am going to call Bruce to let him know about Charlie, and then we should call the police."

"Steve and I are going to drive by Michelle's house. I got the address from her Credentialing file. Please don't call the police yet, Dad."

"Come on, Erin. Just come home now. You don't need to jeopardize your safety anymore. The police will take care of everything."

She didn't say anything for a moment, then spoke softly. "We're just going to drive by her house."

Rich knew there was no use arguing with her, but didn't believe that she was just going to drive by without stopping. She was, however, going to do whatever she pleased. He knew her well enough to know that. He sighed. "Call 911 if anything else happens. Leave your phone turned on."

"Okay, Dad. Bye."

The cabby arrived at the Triangle parking lot and pulled in. Erin made him drive around first to make sure Charlie wasn't in the vicinity before he let them off at the Mustang. Charlie must not have even thought about how Erin and Steve had gotten to Triangle in the first place or he would have come back to their car and waited for them. Must be the cocaine clouding his brain. Erin paid the cabby his fare and Steve handed him the extra twenty.

"You don't know where Mystic Lane is located, do you?" she asked the driver. "I know it's in this city."

"I sure do. I picked up someone earlier this evening from that street and took her to the airport." He explained how to get there to Erin and Steve as they nodded in understanding.

"Thanks for all your help." Erin smiled at him as he left.

She and Steve walked over to the car, continuing to look all around them as they got in. Erin even looked in the back seat of the car, just in case.

"So we're going to Michelle's house now?" asked Steve. "And what if she's there? Have you thought of that?"

Erin deliberated for a moment without speaking.

Steve put on his seat belt. "Even though I fancy the arse off of you, I have to say that I'm unsure that this is the right thing to do."

"Charlie told the police officer that we were en route to his house. I assume that Michelle would be going over there, too, to help deal with us, because he did call someone on his phone." She looked at Steve seriously for a moment, realizing that they may not be out of danger yet. Leaning over to him, she put her arms around his neck. "You are such a doll. I know we should probably go back to my house, but I can't stop yet. Please try to understand. We'll be more careful this time." She grinned. "I'll make it up to you."

"I'll hold you to that," he said, looking her in the eye.

Erin sat back and smiled as she started the car.

Charlie drove faster than he should towards his condo, but felt a need to get there quickly. He was pushing sixty miles per hour on this two-lane highway, but he didn't care about cops this time. Running red lights if there were no cars around him, he noticed that his hands were shaking as he tightly gripped the steering wheel. Picking up his cell phone from the console with his right hand, he dialed Michelle's cell phone and tried to watch the road the best he could. He wanted to let her know that Erin and Steve had gotten away from him and they had to discuss what to do next. Her phone rang and rang until the voice mail picked up. Trying her home phone, the same thing happened. He threw the phone down on the passenger seat, extremely irritated. Thinking that maybe she had already arrived at his place, he pushed the accelerator a little bit more until he arrived. Driving to the back entrance where the garage was located, he looked around for her car, but didn't see it. *She might have parked in front again*, he thought. Opening the garage door from his car, he drove into it and parked.

He turned the garage light on and walked across the cement floor to the wooden stairs. Looking around to make sure no one was behind him, he climbed the stairs to the entrance that led into the kitchen. After he opened the door, he did a quick walk through his house and turned on the lights. He peeked through the blinds to see if Michelle's car was parked in front of the condo. Not seeing it, he took off his jacket and hung it over the chair at the dining room table where his computer was sitting.

Not having a clue as to what he should do next, he sat down at the table and took the cocaine out of his pocket. Thinking of the paternity suit Susan had started on him wasn't bothering him at all. Susan and the rugrat couldn't get money from him after he disappeared in Europe. He poured the cocaine out on the mirror he

had sitting on the table, making two big lines out of the vial, and turned on his computer. Snorting them up deeply, he clapped his hands together once when he was finished. He shouldn't let himself get stressed out by details. Things always had a way of working out.

Following the cabby's directions, Erin drove to Michelle's house, which was located only a few miles from where they were. With hardly any cars on the dark two-lane road and with Erin being unfamiliar with the area and the absence of streetlights, it was difficult to see. Erin saw the subdivision of Mystic Hills to their left and turned into the entrance. Michelle lived in an upscale neighborhood with large brick houses that had very little yard to maintain.

"The cabby said Mystic Lane would be the first street on the right after we turned into the sub," she said.

Steve had the paper in his hand with the address. "There's the street," he said as he pointed.

Erin turned right onto Mystic Lane and started to go more slowly as they looked for her house. It was hard to see the addresses. The mailboxes were all clumped together on one part of the street and not all of the houses had addresses showing at their front door.

"Her house should be on the left," said Erin, looking at Michelle's house number.

"There it is!" exclaimed Steve. "29531."

Erin parked across the street from the two-story brick colonial and turned off the car. The red Cadillac was parked in the driveway and the garage door was closed. She could see lights on in the house and the front drapes were open.

"Are you ready to look in a window?" she asked Steve as she got out of the car.

He opened his side door. "Is there anything in your Dad's car that we can use as a weapon?" he asked, looking around in the back seat.

"My dad is always prepared. Let me check the trunk." She opened the trunk and they saw a heavy flashlight, tire iron, blanket and spare tire. She picked up the flashlight. "This flashlight should be enough. If it comes down to a fistfight, I should be able to take her." Erin smiled and made a fist with one hand and pounded it with the other.

"You're cute, but remember she might have a gun like Charlie did."

"Then we'll have to rely on your brawn again." She started walking toward the house.

"But it didn't work well the first time," said Steve, wincing as he remembered the confrontation at Charlie's office. He turned and followed Erin.

"Let's peek in the front window first," she whispered. Erin looked around briefly at the neighbors' homes to make sure no one was outside and could see them.

They walked in between the shrubs until they were close to the window, and peered in.

The living room was quite a mess, not what one would expect from Michelle. Clothes were strewn everywhere, toiletries were lying on the floor, and an empty bottle of champagne was sitting on an end table next to the couch. No noise could be heard and they didn't see her anywhere.

"Should we try the door?" asked Erin, glancing at Steve.

"No," said Steve. "Her car is in the driveway."

Erin opened her purse and took out her little notebook that had Michelle's phone number written on it. "I'll call her." She dialed the number on her cell phone.

"Are you sure that's wise? Won't she see your name on the caller ID?"

"I don't think she's home."

They could hear the phone ring, but Michelle didn't answer it and Erin's call was picked up by the answering machine, so she hung up.

Erin peered in the window again. "Let's walk around the house."

Grabbing Steve's hand, they started the journey around the house. Lights were on on the second floor in what Erin assumed was Michelle's bedroom. Erin wanted to go in the house really bad, and she truly believed that Michelle wasn't home. Then she remembered what the cab driver had said.

"Steve, the cab driver had known where Mystic Lane was because he had picked someone up from there earlier and taken her to the airport. I remember him saying 'her,' don't you?"

"Yes, he said 'her,'" said Steve, shaking his head. "Definitely."

"I think the person he took to the airport was Michelle, and she's probably already on an airplane going who-knows-where. I wonder if she plans on coming back." She paused. "Or did she leave without any thought of returning?"

"Erin, do you remember when we were at the mall and saw Michelle at that travel store?"

"Yes."

"She had talked about being in France. Do you remember?"

Erin thought for a moment. "You're right. So that's where she's gone," she said, squeezing his hand and smiling.

They had completely walked around the house and were back at the front. Erin climbed the stairs to the door and slowly turned the doorknob. To her surprise, the house was unlocked. Looking back at Steve, who now walked up the stairs, they opened the door and went in.

Listening for a few moments, they didn't hear any noise inside the house, so they started to look around. It appeared as though Michelle had gone on a trip. The clothes and toiletries lying on the floor confirmed that. The empty bottle of champagne on the end table was Cristal, which Erin knew was very expensive. Michelle must have drunk it before she left. They walked into the kitchen. Erin opened the refrigerator and didn't see much of anything in there, just some soda pop and milk. She went over to a bi-fold door and opened it. It held a garbage can, so Erin looked through it. Moving an empty juice container and bread wrapper, her eyes lit up. She saw some papers ripped in half that said "Mercury Memorial Hospital" on the top. Fishing them out, she laid them on the counter.

"Steve, look at this." Erin eyes opened wide as she read them.

Steve looked at the papers as Erin explained.

"I don't believe this. These papers are the proof that my dad was poisoned with the drug digoxin. Here are the physician's orders from the emergency room. They confirm that the doctor ordered a drug screen for digoxin." She picked up the other paper. "This is the lab result that confirms digoxin toxicity. Michelle must have removed these papers from the chart."

"Appalling!" said Steve as Rich's attempted murder was now confirmed.

Erin washed her hands and dried them with a paper towel from the counter. Going through the kitchen drawers, she found a plastic bag to put the papers in for safekeeping. She closed the bag and put it in her purse.

"I want to look at her phone." She glanced around and saw a phone sitting in a cradle near the door wall. Picking it up, she checked the caller ID.

"Anything good?" asked Steve.

"The call before mine was Charlie," she said, looking up at him as she placed the phone back into its cradle.

The phone started to ring. They watched as the caller ID revealed the name of Charles Patton. He didn't leave a message when the answering machine came on.

"Well, that's a bit of a giggle," said Steve. "He doesn't even know that she's gone."

"It appears that way, doesn't it?"

"Do you want to look upstairs before we leave?" asked Steve.

Erin nodded. "I want to look in her bedroom."

They listened again at the stairs, but didn't hear anything. Quietly walking upstairs, they peered in all of the other rooms before they went into the lighted one. It was Michelle's room, a huge master bedroom with exquisite oak furniture. Erin looked through the drawers of her dresser and bureau, but most were empty.

Seeing the walk-in closet, she and Steve went in. A few things were still hanging on the hangers, but what grabbed their attention was the gray safe sitting on the floor. It was wide open and empty.

Charlie was starting to get angry with Michelle. Not knowing where she was really bothered him. Why wasn't she answering her phone? She couldn't have gone to sleep, because she had promised she would go over to his house. He shook his head. That girl! He liked to think he was in control of her, but deep down he knew he had no say in anything she did. She was the one in charge. He looked down at the table. Out of cocaine! But there was more where that came from. Walking up the stairs to his room, he opened a dresser drawer and took out a rolled up plastic bag with an ounce of the drug in it. Knowing that he would break the bag down into smaller increments tomorrow, he would have to be careful that he didn't snort too much tonight. Sometimes greed got the best of him with cocaine and he found himself not being able to stop. His nose was numb tonight and he knew he was a little on edge. The episode with Erin and Steve had really upset him, and not being able to reach Michelle made things even worse.

He turned his head to the left and listened as he thought he heard a noise downstairs. He frowned. It sounded like someone trying to get in the front door. Never knowing if it was just paranoia creeping in again or really someone trying to get into the house, he had to force himself downstairs to check. Moving slowly down the stairs, he only took two steps at a time, then stopped and listened. Two more steps and he listened again. This continued until he reached the bottom of the stairs and he was in his living room. The front door was closed and he couldn't hear any noise coming from it. He breathed a sigh of release. A false alarm. Walking over to the front window blinds, he peeked through the slats again but didn't see Michelle's car.

"Damn her!" he said out loud as he walked over to the kitchen table. Opening the bag of cocaine, he poured a small pile of it onto the mirror, then closed the plastic bag and set it down next to his computer. Making himself a large line, he inhaled it quickly, deciding to check out his porn sites while he waited for Michelle. He went online and checked a few of his favorite places to see if there were any new pictures that he hadn't seen. Clicking his mouse with his right hand, the left hand was alternating between dialing Michelle's cell phone number and her home phone number. He couldn't understand where she was and why she wasn't answering the phone. Exiting the porn sites, he decided to check his email. Ed Carroll always sent him good jokes, and he was in need of a few laughs. Clicking on one of them, he read it and laughed, then decided it was time for another line of cocaine. After snorting it, he felt it draining into the back of his throat and he needed something to drink. As he got up to get a beer from the refrigerator, he thought he heard a noise in the garage.

"Hello?" he called out while he stood in the kitchen. He listened for a moment to see if anyone would answer.

Charlie tried to remain calm, but he felt his heart racing. He thought that his breathing was increased, too, but maybe it was just his paranoia again and not anyone in the garage. Walking over to the half-bathroom that was just off the kitchen to the left, he turned on the light and looked at himself in the oval mirror above the sink. He turned his head from side to side. Thinking that he looked rather pale and sweaty, he turned on the faucet and threw some water on his face, patting it dry with the hand towel.

Walking back into the kitchen again, he swore he could hear something in the garage and listened for a moment before panic overtook him. He didn't know for sure that he had closed the double garage door when he had driven in! The door could be wide open and he knew that he had left the garage light on. Those asshole teenagers who lived down the street would see his garage open. They might think that he had money and cocaine in the house, and they would be right. He thought that they had been watching him in the past, just waiting for an opportunity to come up. They could be trying right now to get his attention by making noise in the garage. If they could get him to come down, they would hide before jumping out and hitting him over the head with one of the bricks he had outside of the garage for decoration. He was not going to let that happen—not Charlie. Going over to the jacket he had hanging on the kitchen chair, he reached into the pocket and took out his gun. His heart was pounding and he was sweating again as he walked over to the kitchen door that led into the garage and opened it.

CHAPTER 20

ERIN and Steve were sitting outside of Michelle's house in the Mustang, contemplating what to do next. The car wasn't turned on and it was dark all around them. All was quiet. All was peaceful. He was ready to go home and call it a night. She wasn't so sure.

"I'd really like to go to Charlie's house." She glanced at him out of the corner of her eye.

"What?" Even in the dark, he could just see the wheels turning in her head. "I believe you're off your trolley. You highly intelligent people sometimes have no common sense."

She rolled her eyes. "Steve, it's there. That floppy disc that Charlie put in his jacket pocket. That disc has everything on it. All of the CAP information. All the rest of the proof."

"The police will find it."

"They might not. He could destroy the disc before they get their hands on it. We have to acquire it first."

"Erin, no. I don't think we should go there."

"We'll take more precautions. The tire iron from the trunk! We'll take that with us."

Steve shook his head. "I must insist that you call your father."

"All right." She picked up her phone and dialed her home number. "It's me," she said as Rich answered.

"What happened at Michelle's?"

She told him everything, concluding with the empty safe.

"I guess the physician order sheet and lab work from Mercury is the proof we needed," Rich said.

"I know you didn't want to believe it, but you have to now."

"And I think it makes sense to say that Michelle is gone. I informed Bruce about what happened at Triangle tonight. He was shocked, but glad to hear that you and Steve got away from Charlie. The police need to be involved now, Erin."

Erin crossed her fingers and let out a breath before she continued. "I want Charlie's address, Dad. We just want to drive by there and see if he's home."

"Are you nuts? Erin, I don't want you going there," he said sternly.

She didn't answer.

Rich couldn't believe how headstrong she was. "Erin, let me talk to Steve."

She handed the phone to him.

"Hello, Rich," said Steve.

"Steve, I'm relying on you to be the voice of reason. Erin's lost hers because she's so damn stubborn. I don't want you two going to Charlie's house."

"I'd prefer not to go there either, but you know that she can be quite persuasive," Steve said as he eyed her.

"Charlie is dangerous. You already know that."

"I agree. We did find a heavy flashlight and tire iron in your trunk that we could use for weapons if we need to, though."

Erin leaned over to listen to the conversation and started kissing Steve's neck. "I don't want anything happening to us," she whispered to Steve. She unbuttoned the first few buttons of his shirt, then bent her head down to kiss his chest. "We'll be very careful," she murmured.

"Can you talk her out of it?" asked Rich.

Steve was trying to listen to Erin and Rich. "I think that would be exhaustively impossible," he said as he leaned back against the seat, enjoying the attention Erin was providing him.

"I want you, Steve," Erin breathed.

"What?" Steve looked down at Erin.

"Well, let me give you the address and just pacify her by letting her drive by there. Call me after you're done," said Rich. "Are you ready to take the directions?"

Steve was frazzled. He shook his head from side to side. "One moment." He paused. "Ah, let me get a piece of paper." He put the phone down so Rich couldn't hear. "Erin, don't stop what you're doing. Just tell me where I can write down Charlie's address."

"He's giving us Charlie's address?" Erin stopped kissing his chest.

Steve groaned.

Erin sat up and got her little notebook out of her purse. She grabbed the phone away from Steve. "Dad, it's me. I'll take the directions."

Rich gave her the quickest way to Charlie's place from where they were.

"I'll call you back soon." Erin hung up the phone.

"So are you done with me then?" asked Steve, feeling quite disappointed as he looked down at his open shirt.

"For now," Erin quickly smiled. "Sorry, but we have to get to Charlie's." She put her seatbelt on, put the car in gear, and they were on their way.

Steve reluctantly buttoned up his shirt and put his seatbelt on.

They only had to drive for about fifteen minutes and Erin saw the condominium community where Charlie lived. She turned into it and promptly got lost. All the condos looked alike. Finally finding Charlie's street after getting turned around in the wrong direction for a few minutes, Steve located the correct condo and they drove by slowly. Every light in the place was on. Erin parked in a space at a condo next door to Charlie's, but left the car running.

"I'm just going to run up the front stairs and look in the window. I'll be right back," said Erin.

"I'm watching you," Steve cautioned. "Don't do anything else."

Erin quietly opened the car door and left it open. She crept up the cement stairway leading to his front door and tried to peek in the window through the slats. Not seeing Charlie anywhere or hearing any noise, she went back to the car.

"The lights are on. I didn't see anything."

Steve nodded.

"I want to drive around to the back," she said.

Pulling the car door shut, she slowly drove around to the other side of the condo. Charlie's garage door was open and the light was on. Erin parked across the street and turned off the engine. She gave her cell phone to Steve and grabbed the flashlight for herself. She opened the car door quietly.

"Slow down, Erin. You're not going in alone," said Steve, frowning as he put the cell phone in his front pants pocket. He opened the car door and got out.

Erin unlocked the trunk. "Here, Steve." She handed him the tire iron and closed the trunk.

They crept across the street, eyes peeled for any danger, and as they got closer to the garage crouched down as they moved. Entering to the left of Charlie's Jaguar, they heard a noise at the top of the stairs and looked up.

"All right, you hellions! I hear you down there!" Charlie screamed down the stairs. "I have a gun!"

A shot rang out. It struck the wall behind Erin and Steve. Looking at each other, they were unsure if an attempt should be made to move or not. Erin peeked just a bit over the car fender so she could see Charlie. He was standing at the top of the stairs, his body weaving from side to side.

"Something is wrong with him," she said, frowning. "He doesn't look right."

Trying to focus on where he heard the sounds in his garage, Charlie took aim toward his car and shot his gun again. Ignoring the heaviness he was feeling in his chest, he tried to take a deep breath to get out a voice. "No one here gets out alive!" he screamed as he let out two more shots. He could hardly breathe, and he felt dizzy. If he grabbed the railing he might be able to steady himself, he thought. As he reached down to grab it, he felt himself falling forward. Starting to tumble down the stairs, he was not able to stop himself. As he felt his legs and arms twist and turn in ways they shouldn't, he knew that this time Charlie Patton wouldn't come out smelling like a rose. When he saw the cement floor of the garage coming toward him at breakneck speed, he closed his eyes and waited for the impact.

Erin and Steve peeked from behind the car as they heard him fall. Erin started to go around the car and run over to Charlie, but Steve grabbed her arm.

"Let's walk slowly over there. You know he is untrustworthy," said Steve.

They took a couple of steps at a time, peering at him as they moved.

Charlie was trying to breathe, but the pain was unbearable. He knew he must have broken ribs and who knew what else. Lying face down, he saw blood in front of him on the cement floor. He turned his head. Looking at his right hand, he saw a mangled mess of flesh. The hand was blue with many cuts and appeared to be swelling right before his eyes. His right arm didn't look right. It was twisted in an unnatural position and he was unable to move it. His right leg was the same. Turning his head to the left, his left arm and leg looked better, but he was unable to lift himself up with them. He looked in front of him and saw his gun only a few inches away. Stretching his left arm out, he tried to reach it, but couldn't. He listened for the teenagers and wondered if they were still in the garage.

"We need to get that gun away from him," whispered Erin.

"We must be careful. I'm not sure if he's faking or not." Steve looked around the garage wall. There was a push broom hanging up. "This might work." He set down the tire iron and took the broom off the wall.

They crept closer to Charlie. His head was lying on the floor and he wasn't moving. Steve stretched out his left arm as he held the broom. He kept moving closer to the gun.

Charlie heard the noise and opened his eyes.

In a quick motion, Steve grabbed the gun with the broom bristles and pulled it toward him. It slid across the garage floor under the Jaguar.

"Call 911 and tell them we need a ambulance and the police," Erin said as she stood up and started quickly walking over to Charlie. "Call my dad, too."

Steve took the cell phone from his pocket and started the calls.

Erin reached Charlie. His skin was drained of color. His eyes were partially open and the pool of blood near his head was obviously caused by hitting the cement floor. "I don't think we need to worry about him getting up. Looks like he's in bad shape." She shook her head. "We'll just wait for the ambulance. There's nothing I can do for him."

Charlie opened his eyes wider as he tried to focus on Erin. "You," he said, almost inaudibly, as he recognized her.

Steve arrived at Erin's side. "They're on the way." He took his right foot and nudged Charlie with it. "Just give me a reason to shoot you, arsehole!"

"Michelle is gone," said Erin, looking Charlie in the eyes as she bent down to him.

He tried to lift his head but couldn't.

"She's left you."

He let out a breath and moaned as he closed his eyes.

It was only a few minutes until the police and ambulance arrived. Erin updated the officer in charge while the paramedics started working on Charlie. Rich pulled up in his Yukon a few minutes later and ran into the garage. He put his arms around Erin and explained to the police who he was.

"I'm reminding everyone not to touch anything," the officer said as they started walking up the stairs into the condo. He put latex gloves on and began looking around.

Charlie's bag full of cocaine and mirror with cocaine sitting on it were the first things they noticed.

"I think he had a drug problem," said Erin to the officer. "We saw him using earlier in the evening."

The officer nodded. "Looks like he may have been using a lot."

Erin saw Charlie's jacket hanging on the kitchen chair and could hardly contain her excitement. "Officer, can you check inside the jacket pocket for a computer disc?"

The officer placed his gloved hand into the jacket and pulled it out.

"Can you put it into his computer?" she asked. "You'll see how important it is."

The officer placed the disc into the computer and opened it up.

Erin gasped as she saw what was on the disc as the officer scrolled down the pages. There were the names of the doctors in CAP and the money they had made each month. Also listed were the names of all the patients who had unnecessary surgery and the dates their surgeries were performed. And last, the names of who had upcoming surgery dates scheduled within the next few weeks.

"Erin, you hit the jackpot," said Rich, finally admiring the tenacity that Erin had shown over the last three weeks as she tried to convince him that something reprehensible was going on. Rich quickly read through the information and shook his head. "I know we have many problems plaguing the health care industry that Charlie was unhappy about. He let the negative things about our system control him. This was Charlie's way to get out of it, and it is obviously an abuse and violation of the highest degree."

"Dad, I'm sorry. I know you really didn't want to believe it."

"I've known him for so long. He was always quite a character, but the last few years he seemed to change quite a bit."

"It's over now," she said.

Rich was pensive as he turned to her. "We need to keep what is good about our health care delivery system. And there are good things, Erin. Focusing on the areas that need improvement and improving them to everyone's satisfaction will be the difficult part."

She nodded.

Rich took a deep breath and then let it out. "Why don't you two go home? I'll handle things from here."

"Sounds good," yawned Erin. She opened her purse. "Here's the paperwork from Mercury that Michelle threw away."

Rich took the plastic bag from Erin and put his hand out for Steve. "Thanks for watching out for her."

"My pleasure," said Steve, smiling as he shook Rich's hand.

"Dad, I don't know if I told you or not, but Susan had started a paternity suit against Charlie."

"That's good to know," said Rich. "Thanks, honey." Rich turned around to talk to the officer again.

Erin and Steve walked back down the stairs to the garage and looked at Charlie once more as he was being loaded into the ambulance. Now it was Erin's turn to be reflective. "So long, Charlie. I can't say that it's been a pleasure."

A gloved officer was placing Charlie's gun into an evidence bag.

"I have an imprint of that gun on my face if you want a picture of it," said Steve.

"That won't be necessary," said the officer, smiling.

Steve put his arm around Erin. "Bloody great. Let's get out of here."

They walked across the street and got into the Mustang. Erin glanced at Charlie's condo once more and drove off.

Pulling up into the Tyler driveway at last made Erin and Steve realize how exhausted they really were. Someone had left one small living room lamp on and they peaked in to see if anyone was up. The room was empty and the mantel clock showed the time to be 1:30 a.m. Feeling very weary, they started up the stairs. Erin had her arm hooked through Steve's for support. The hall was dark except for the night light, and not a sound could be heard upstairs.

"Let's go in the bathroom," said Erin. "I want to clean your wound."

They walked into the bathroom and Erin put the toilet seat down for Steve to sit on. She started looking through the cabinets for supplies and found what she wanted. Cleaning his wound with antibacterial soap, she patted it dry and applied antibiotic ointment and a band aid.

She kissed the band aid. "There. I kissed it and made it all right. It doesn't look bad at all."

"Is your life normally this chaotic?" he asked.

"No. It's only been this way since I met you. Can we go to bed now?"

He looked up at her.

"My bed," she said. "We've had a rough night and I don't want to be away from you."

He let out a breath as he stood up and held her hands. "Erin, quit torturing me. I'm sure your dad will check on you when he gets home tonight. I respect him and don't want him to find me in your bed, as much as I want to be there. He has been through too much this week already."

Erin frowned. "You're right."

"Let's go to sleep now, because today will be a happy day," he said, thinking about what time it was. "I almost forgot that Jimmy is in my room tonight because he's not supposed to see Lisa until the wedding." He smiled. "Good thing the bed is large, because he moves around quite a bit."

"I want you to think about me when you go to sleep," she said, putting her arms around him and laying her head against his chest.

"I'll oblige you on that one. I've thought about you everyday since I met you," he said.

They walked down the hall, stopping at Erin's door where they kissed good night. Erin went into her room, took off her dress and got into bed. It wasn't long before she fell asleep.

Rich got in the house about 2:30 a.m. He was glad that after the dinner at the restaurant he had come home and rested awhile, because he had certainly needed that strength the last couple of hours. Charlie was now all packed up and on his way to the hospital. The police had been given all the information that Rich could think of and Bruce had also been updated. Rich couldn't wait to get some sleep. He thought he should probably check on Erin first and started walking up the stairs. Stopping halfway, he changed his mind. If she was already sleeping, he didn't want to take the chance of waking her. Turning around, he went back down and to his room.

CHAPTER 21

THE sun had been shining through Erin's window for a few hours, but finally moved over enough to hit her in the eyes and she woke up. Looking at the clock, she saw it was 10:30. She couldn't believe that she had slept so long. As she got up from the bed and stretched, she immediately thought of Steve. Thinking back to the day when she had first met him, he had said that if she ever needed anything to just knock on the wall and he'd come running. She walked over to the wall that adjoined his room and listened. She didn't hear anything. She knocked a few times on the wall and listened again, but heard no response. *Oh well,* she thought, *so much for that.* She went back over to her bed and sat down on the edge, rubbing her eyes and trying to wake up. Suddenly she heard the door to his room open. He had remembered! Elated, she stood up and rushed over to her door to open it.

There he was with tousled hair, in his drawstring pants and open robe and looking every bit the handsome rock star. Erin put her arms inside the robe and around his back as he leaned against the wall. His body felt warm and wonderful as she pushed herself up against it. They grinned at each other.

"How did you sleep?" she asked.

"Like a shipwreck."

She stood on her toes as they kissed each other.

"Well, I guess I did better than that," said Erin. "I don't remember anything after I hit the pillow."

"You must tell me, Erin. Did your dad check on you last night?"

"I don't know. If he did, he didn't wake me."

Steve groaned.

She smiled and moved his hair to look at his temple. "Let me look at your wound."

"It's all right."

"When you take your shower, just wash it with soap. Put the ointment and band aid on it when you get out. Your hair will hide it for the wedding."

"Okay," he said, not really listening as his eyes were scanning the little satin nightgown she had on.

She saw him studying her and grinned. He opened up his robe and pulled her into him wrapping the robe around her tightly.

"What are you doing?" she laughed. She was now just inches from his face.

He looked her straight in the eyes as he held her. "I'm trying to get as close to you as I can before you have to leave me again."

She stared back at those green eyes. "That's so sweet." Putting her fingers on his lips, she caressed them for a moment, then kissed them gently. She continued to touch them as they gazed into each other's eyes.

The door to Lisa's room opened and she peeked around her doorway. "Erin, is that you? It's time to start getting dressed."

"But I want to get undressed," she said softly. She smiled and kept looking at Steve.

Steve bent his face to kiss her and they began to slowly savor each other's mouths while continuing their tight embrace.

"Erin, I can tell you right now that I'm feeling a little stressed," Lisa said warning her. "Jimmy can't see me before the wedding and I know he's just down the hall a few feet from you and could open the door at any moment. It's time for you to come to my room to start getting ready."

There was no response from Erin as she continued to kiss Steve.

Lisa blew air up from her mouth, making her bangs move. "Hello? Reality check. Remember that I'm the bride and I rule today. Tell Steve good-bye and that you'll see him later. Steve, kindly unwrap yourself from my sister and leave." Lisa closed her door loudly in exasperation.

Erin and Steve stopped kissing but continued to gaze at each other.

"I guess I need to go to Lisa's room now," said Erin as she ran her fingers through his uncombed hair. "We don't want Jimmy to come out of the room and see her."

"Jimmy isn't in the room. He must be downstairs," said Steve, not releasing her a bit from his arms.

"I have to go. I'm going to hear about this as it is."

"All right then." He unwrapped her.

She put her hands on each side of his face and smiled at him. "Good-bye," she said, kissing him a few quick times. "See you at the wedding."

He stood there and watched her as she disappeared into Lisa's room.

The phone in the Tyler home seemed to ring nonstop all morning. It was the flower shop, then the caterer, then wedding guests who had last minute questions about directions or times. By 4 p.m. the flowers had arrived, the last minute food questions had been answered and all of the arrangements for the guests had been made.

Rich was already dressed and ready to walk his firstborn daughter down the aisle. He looked in the hall mirror at himself and adjusted his tie, thinking that he didn't look bad for 62 years old. In fact, he looked quite elegant and smart today for having had very little sleep. The phone rang and he picked it up.

"I'm just the bride's father," he remarked into the phone. "How can I help you?"

The caller laughed. "Rich, this is Bruce."

"Good afternoon to you, Bruce."

"What time did you finally get to bed?"

"Almost 3:00. I feel fine, though. Slept like a log."

"Good, good. I have additional news for you. David Keller, one of Triangle's cardiovascular surgeons that was involved with Charlie, drove into the Detroit River last night."

"I can't believe it," Rich remarked. "That's terrible."

"I agree. This whole thing is a nightmare. We're going to take a beating on television and in the newspapers about this, especially since our chief medical officer was the leader of the pack. Our next CMO has to be a person without a blemish on his record and one that our Board of Directors respects."

"I agree, Bruce."

"I have a few phone calls to make, but I'll be there on time for the wedding. See you then."

"Good-bye." Rich hung up the phone and shook his head, shocked by everything that had happened. Trying to put the events out of his mind, he looked in the mirror again to make sure his hair looked good, and then walked outside.

The archway in the Tylers' backyard had white roses and English ivy intertwined throughout. Wooden chairs were set up in many rows in front of it, with a white walkway rolled down the center aisle. White rose petals and green leaves were heavily strewn down each side of the aisle. The rows were packed with guests and Arlene was the last person seated, taking her place in the front row. She looked almost regal in her pale green dress with matching wide-brimmed hat. Jimmy, Steve, and the groomsmen—Sid, Clive, and Neil—were very handsome in their black tuxedos as they walked out from the tent where they had been waiting and stood in front of the wooden archway.

"Bright and fine day," said Jimmy, rubbing his hands together as he looked at Steve.

"Yes," Steve said, looking up at the sky. He glanced back at Jimmy. "So just how nervous are you, anyway?"

"Tremendously nervous and tired."

Steve smiled.

"I didn't sleep half the night. I had to keep kicking you," said Jimmy. "You kept trying to touch my bum and my chest."

"Sorry. That's explains why my leg hurts today."

Sid laughed. "Steve figured it was his last effort to stop you from getting married, Jimmy. He decided he wanted you after all."

"I could have had him years ago if I'd wanted him," said Steve, rubbing his chin and looking at Jimmy. "He is quite cute, though, isn't he?"

Jimmy grinned. "You can't fool me, mate. I know it was Erin you wanted."

"I've been rather enthusiastic about her, haven't I?"

"I must say that I've been quite surprised at what a good lad you've been," said Jimmy. "I've not heard any more tales of appalling behavior since the boat incident."

Steve pulled on his collar. "It's been agony for me to behave. I don't think I've been more respectful in my entire life."

Jimmy laughed. "Perhaps you're turning over a new leaf. These Tyler sisters are amazing."

Steve nodded. "So what do you think of my choice then?"

"Bloody marvelous," smiled Jimmy as he slapped Steve on the back.

The sound of "Pachelbel: Canon in D" started playing in the yard as the boys looked toward the house. Charlotte started her walk down the aisle with Carrie, Angela, and Erin following behind, each carrying a bouquet of purple orchids. Erin's blonde hair was piled on her head in twists and curls. The lavender dress she wore flattered every curve, as Steve noticed right away when he saw her. Their eyes locked and they beamed at each other as she took her place over by the other bridesmaids, to the left of the boys.

As Lisa and Rich emerged from the house, the guests stood to face the bride and her father. Lisa was stunning in the bridal gown of her own creation; she carried a bouquet of white roses as she walked down the aisle. Jimmy gasped when he saw her. Steve had to push up against him because he was afraid Jimmy was becoming weak in the knees. Rich kissed Lisa on the forehead as he left her at the archway with Jimmy.

Lisa and Jimmy were married under the archway, with Erin and Steve at their sides. They turned and faced the crowd after the ceremony to a thunderous applause as they were introduced as James and Lisa Emerson. Grinning from ear to ear, they started their walk back up the aisle.

As Steve put his arm out for Erin to take, he turned to her. "You are gorgeous." She viewed him for a moment and smiled. "So are you."

Erin and Steve looked up as a number of cameras began to take their pictures. "You know you've got it coming tonight," he said as they walked up the aisle.

"Then we'll both get what we want," she replied as she squeezed his arm.

Michelle spent her first evening in Paris visiting some of the many nightclubs and cabarets. Unquestionably expensive, she needn't worry, since her bank account was overflowing. Charlie's money was now hers, and she didn't feel the slightest bit of guilt over what she had done. She was thrilled to be in Paris again and had no regrets about anything.

Sitting in a dance club near the end of the night, she sipped a glass of Cristal. A tall, attractive gentleman walked by and made it a point to smile at her. She tilted her head and nodded, thinking that it would be nice to have some company. He came over to her table and she felt an immediate attraction to him as he bent down to speak with her.

"Unescorted tonight?" he asked with a French accent.

"Yes," she said, smiling, as she stared at him with her big brown eyes.

He looked her over slowly. "What's a beautiful girl like you doing sitting all alone on this Saturday night in Paris? It's just not right."

"I'm new in town," she said, picking up her glass and rolling the champagne around in it.

He nodded. "May I ask your name?"

"It's Gabrielle." She held out a well-manicured hand for him.

"Gabrielle, I am very happy to meet you," he said as he kissed it. "I'm Louis."

Michelle surveyed the handsome fellow for a moment, then rested her chin on her hand as she gazed intently into his eyes. "Have a seat, Louis. I'm in need of entertainment."

The reception was going strong. The tent was illuminated inside with the white lights on the ficus trees. Lavender candles were lit on every table. Dinner was over and the dancing and partying had begun. The DJ spun dance music as Lisa and

Jimmy walked around, mingling with their guests and thoroughly enjoying themselves. Sid and Clive seemed to be getting on well with Carrie and Angela, laughing and dancing at a table all their own. In an unoccupied corner of the tent, Erin was straddling Steve's legs as they sat in a chair. Her dress was open on one side, showing a major portion of leg. Large strands of hair were falling down from her upswept hairstyle, and one of her arms was in Steve's halfway unbuttoned shirt, with the other one around his head. Her mouth was glued to his and she looked very unprofessional.

Rich saw them in the corner, but couldn't make out who it was. He grabbed Lisa and Jimmy, who were walking by.

"Who's that?" asked Rich, straining his eyes to see which members of the wedding party they were.

Lisa looked over to the corner of the tent that Rich was staring at. "Erin and Steve."

"What? Have I been clueless?" asked Rich, looking at the couple more closely. "When did that start?"

"Maybe in London," said Lisa. "I'm really not sure."

"Steve's been trying to get her attention ever since she arrived in Michigan," said Jimmy, looking at Rich. "I guess he finally made an impression on her."

Rich cleared his throat. "I can see that," he said. "Good thing I didn't check on Erin last night when I got home. Lisa, can we get one of those room divider screens or something to put around them? They look almost indecent. I'm sure we still have one of those folding screens in one of the bedrooms upstairs," he said, thinking of where he'd seen it last.

"Dad, it's okay," said Lisa, trying to pacify him. "They're not that noticeable."

Arlene walked over to them. "What's everybody staring at?" She looked over to the corner and smiled. "Oh, Erin and Steve. Aren't they adorable?"

"So you knew about this?" asked Rich, turning to Arlene.

"Why yes, dear. Didn't you?"

"No. Why am I always the last to know everything?"

"Dad's are always the last to know," said Lisa matter-of-factly.

Rich shook his head. "Arlene, do we still have that folding room divider screen? You know the one I'm talking about?"

"A screen? Nonsense," she said.

Arlene walked over near Erin and Steve and turned off the lights on the ficus trees around them. The entire area got darker, but they didn't seem to notice that anything had changed, and they continued kissing.

"Now they can have some privacy," she said as she came back to the group and looked around the tent. "Oh, I haven't talked to Gwen Cornell yet and I see her over there. Excuse me." She smiled as she stepped away from them.

Rich looked back at Erin and Steve and shuddered as he saw Steve's hand sliding up Erin's thigh. He looked around the tent quickly, then turned to Lisa. "I don't care what your mother says. Get rid of them," he said, motioning his head toward Erin and Steve.

"All right, Dad," said Lisa, rolling her eyes.

"Jimmy, I want my new son-in-law to meet the CEO of the company I work for," said Rich to Jimmy, patting him on the back.

"Direct me to him, then," said Jimmy as he followed Rich away from there.

Erin touched her lips; they felt swollen and wet. Moving her fingers down to her chin, it was wet too. Thinking that she should wipe them off, she started to move her hand to do that. She then saw him set the champagne bottle back down on the floor and his face came towards her again. Smiling, she put her arms around his head and went to him.

"Well, well. What do we have here?" said a voice.

Erin and Steve stopped kissing and looked up.

Lisa stood there for a moment with arms folded, watching them. "Look, it's the maid-of-honor and the best man, thinking that they're hiding in a corner from everyone so they can suck face." She grinned. "You two are kind of cute."

Erin and Steve glanced back at each other and smiled.

Lisa continued talking as she tapped her platform shoe against the floor. "You're both a mess, though."

"She won't leave me alone," said Steve, explaining. "I don't believe she can keep her hands off of me."

Erin's mouth dropped open at this remark.

"Right. I'm sure your hands have been idle," said Lisa. "Steve you have makeup on your face and your shirt is open. Erin, your hair is coming undone, your wrap-around dress is almost completely unwrapped, and one of your shoes is over there." Lisa motioned her head to the left.

Steve reached down to the floor again, picking up a champagne bottle they had sitting next to their chair. Handing it to Erin, she took a drink first and returned it to him. He took a long gulp from it before setting it back down. They both returned their attention to Lisa.

"Dad was just here and saw you two," Lisa said very seriously.

"He did? What did he say?" asked Erin as she put her hands up to her hair, trying to fix it.

"He said to get a room," said Lisa, giggling at her play of wit as she walked away from them.

Erin and Steve smiled as they turned their attention to each other again.

"I see you have your bracelet on," he said as he glanced at her wrist.

"I haven't taken it off." She leaned forward to hug him. "Sounds like my dad wants us to leave."

"No wonder. Just look at you. You're nearly undressed." Steve paused as he stared at her for a moment. "I did tell you that I'm going to have you all night, didn't I?"

"No," she grinned as she rubbed her nose against his.

"Well, I am."

"Then we'd better leave," she said to him as she got up from the chair, "because I've made some plans, too."

She adjusted her dress, which truly was quite askew. He bent down and picked up the champagne bottle before he stood up.

"Where are we going?" he asked her.

"We're starting out at the hot tub. I have the temperature turned down so it's just like bath water. Then it's on to my bed for the rest of the night." She smiled at him.

"Oh?" he said, raising his eyebrows and thinking about the possibilities.

She saw one of her shoes over where Lisa had pointed, but didn't see the other. Being barefoot would be fine. Walking over to the side of the tent, she unzipped an exit that was the size of a door, and grabbing Steve's hand, they slipped out.

Rich took Jimmy over where Bruce was standing at the dessert table. He was taking his last bite of wedding cake and set down his empty plate as they approached.

"Bruce, I would like for you to meet my son-in-law, James Emerson. Jimmy, this is the CEO for Triangle Health Plan, Bruce Washington."

Jimmy extended his hand for Bruce to shake.

"Nice meeting you, Jimmy," said Bruce, nodding his head as he shook Jimmy's hand. "I'm glad that both of you have joined me. I have had numerous work-related phone conversations today and frankly, I'm ready to have a few drinks and relax."

"I think we all need to have some fun," said Rich, smiling. "You'll find the bar is well stocked."

"Before I head over there, I wanted to speak with Erin," said Bruce. "She showed unyielding persistence in finding the abuse and violations that have been committed, and she deserves congratulations. I know she spent a lot of time on this and gave this matter her full attention."

Rich looked ill-at-ease.

"Where is she?" asked Bruce, scanning the room. "I haven't seen her since the wedding."

Rich was at a loss for words and looked to Jimmy for support.

Jimmy spoke up. "I believe she is giving someone her full attention at this very moment." He turned toward Rich and grinned.

"That's our Erin," Rich said and laughed nervously.

Jimmy changed the subject to help things out. "Bruce, isn't it fantastic that Rich has made such a quick recovery?"

"His determination is amazing. Rich has made a mark in a number of ways recently. The speech he gave to our Board of Directors was quite potent. He is well liked and highly respected at Triangle, as well as in the community."

"I believe that Triangle needs to become more dynamic," said Rich. "Our members are demanding better quality from us. As we increase our enrollment, this will become even more meaningful."

"I agree with you," said Bruce, smiling.

Rich appeared to be thinking for a moment. "You know, Bruce, technology is becoming so important that we have to do everything we can to update ours. Wanting our physicians and hospitals to be compliant with safety standards and quality isn't enough. We have to do it, too."

"It's a shame that Southeast, with its progressive atmosphere and high safety standards, wasn't able to see the flaw in their system," said Bruce.

"Promoting a culture of patient safety doesn't necessarily guarantee superior performance all of the time," said Rich raising his eyebrows. "We are still human. What Southeast has done is to show how important safety and quality are. The coronary bypass fiasco was quite an unexpected blow to them, but they will come back from this. Their commitment to safety and quality is obviously very strong and is something everyone needs to strive for."

Bruce nodded. "Not every hospital will be able to spend as much money as Southeast does. Mercury Memorial Hospital is a great example of this. Where is the money going to come from? Medical costs are staggering; we know that. However, you did say that the care you received at Mercury was exemplary, from the emergency room to the intensive care unit."

"Yes, it was," Rich remarked. "Arlene and Erin were quite impressed. Unfortunately, their paper charting made it possible for Dr. Campbell to effortlessly throw away physician orders and test results. Mercury can't afford to do what Southeast does. So what's the answer?"

"We just have to keep trying," Bruce responded. "One thing that will happen is computers will play an even bigger part in patient care in the not-so-distant future. That might be part of the answer for some of the smaller hospitals with staffing problems and money issues."

Rich nodded.

Bruce continued, "There are no easy answers and we know changes aren't going to happen overnight. That's why it's called 'continuous quality improvement.'"

Jimmy had been looking back and forth between Rich and Bruce for the last few minutes and finally spoke. "I only know how to play guitar, write songs, and sing. You lost me a long time ago with your conversation, but it's easy to see that Rich has an enviable reputation from what he says and does. He must be a real asset to your company."

"Jimmy, you're exactly right," said Bruce, putting a finger up. "This brings me to another matter. I have some good news for you, Rich."

"I'm always happy to hear good news."

"With my recommendation and the approval of the Board of Directors, we would like to invite you to be the next chief medical officer for Triangle Health Plan."

Rich didn't say a word for a moment. "This is a surprise," he stammered. "I'm speechless."

"Congratulations," said Jimmy as he grinned at Rich.

Bruce held out his hand to Rich.

"Thank you, Bruce," said Rich, shaking his hand vigorously. "I'm honored, and I'll do my best to restore confidence in the company."

"We knew you would be the right man for the job," said Bruce, smiling. "Now let's go get that drink."

Going into the house through the garage, Erin and Steve had easy access to the hot tub room without anyone noticing. Erin had been there earlier in the day and had put the "do not disturb" sign on the outside door. As they went into the room, she closed the door and locked it. She rolled the light dimmer switch to low and went over to the hot tub, turning it on. Putting her hand in the water, it was at a perfect temperature. The vertical blinds on all of the windows had been closed earlier and she had moved the tall, wrought iron candle stands to the four corners of the hot tub. Everything was ready.

She went back over to the door where Steve was standing and took the champagne bottle away from him, taking it with her to the side of the hot tub. Taking a long drink of it, she sat it down on the ledge. *It is time,* she thought. *Don't think. Just do it.* Staring intently at Steve, she untied her dress at her waist and let it ceremoniously slide off her shoulder and fall to the floor.

"Is that all you had on under your dress?" he asked, shaking his head in disbelief when he saw only her strapless lavender bra and matching thong.

She nodded. Erin could tell by Steve's gaze that Lisa was right; the thong rules. She pulled the pins from her hair and shook it out. It looked wild and disheveled. Putting her left hand behind her back, she unhooked her bra and let it drop to the floor. Steve's eyes were fixed on her breasts. She picked up the long wooden fireplace matches she had left on the ledge and struck one, then walked around the hot tub, lighting the candles. The diamond bracelet she had on glittered as the fire from the candles shone on the stones.

Steve was gaping at her and he couldn't look away.

She finished what she was doing and turned to Steve, giving him her best smile. "I didn't ask you if you wanted to get in the hot tub with me. Do you?"

He tried to speak but was unable to, so he just nodded his head *yes*.

She looked at him and slowly blew out the match. Walking back to the entrance to the hot tub, she climbed in and continued to hold his eyes in her gaze as the candles illuminated her. Sitting down, she put her hands under the water and removed her thong. She lifted her left arm out of the water, stretched it out straight and dangled her thong on her index finger. Slowly, she let it slide down her finger to her fingernail, where it hung for a moment. Staring at him, she panted, "I'm burning for you," as she let the thong fall to the floor.

Steve had been unable to breathe; he thought his heart had stopped beating. When her thong hit the floor, the trance he was in seemed to be broken and he was able to take a few quick breaths and he felt his heart beating again. Starting to scramble to get his clothes off, he didn't know why he hadn't already taken them off. Then he looked at Erin and knew why. He had been unable to think when he had seen her that way. Having trouble unbuttoning the rest of his shirt that Erin hadn't already unbuttoned, he took his hands and ripped it open as the buttons popped off and hit the floor. His hands were shaking as he tried to undo his trousers—and couldn't.

He looked up at her and laughed. "I've been wanting this to happen ever since the first day I met you. Now that the time is finally here, I can't even get my trousers off."

Erin couldn't believe what was happening. She laid her head back against the hot tub and giggled.

Focusing himself, he found the hooks on his pants and undid them. Erin watched as his pants dropped to the floor. He hurried over and climbed into the hot tub and they put their arms around each other and grinned. The action was just beginning.

THE END

Printed in the United States
29553LVS00001B/12

9 781589 613416